THE FABRIC OF REALITY

EDGE CASES

1

The Fabric of Reality

Silver Linings

Podium

The Fabric of Reality

CHAPTER 1

SETTING OFF

"Come on, we're celebrating!" Misa grinned, the half-orc baring her teeth at Derivan. Her hand held a full tankard of beer that threatened to slosh out of the sides as she gestured at his helmet; it was only the weak enchantment on the mug that prevented that from happening. "Take off the damn helmet already. I've never seen you once without that thing."

"I cannot," Derivan said. He sat at his corner of the table, back leaning against the tavern wall. A faint light flickered within his helmet, the only indication of his amusement. "You know this."

"Bah," Misa scoffed. To her credit, her words were only *slightly* slurred. "You should've met me earlier! I'd have told you that your armor was cursed. What kind of armor is black and spiky and *not* cursed?"

"An [**Armor of Melee Reflection**]!" Vex piped up. Their resident lizard-kin wizard was a little bit dazed, waving his mug of beer around before slamming it onto the table. The liquid splashed over his hands, and he looked at it, blinking a few times in befuddlement.

His words, compared to Misa's, were significantly more slurred.

"Whoops," he said, and squinted at his mug, and then at his hand. He shook it again and watched as the liquid splashed out, then peered at Misa's comparatively stable, non-spilling tankard. "Good . . . good thing I'm not wearing *robes*. Bah! Wizards. Make it too obvious that they're . . . that they're wizards."

Indeed, Vex was dressed in protective leathers and had a dagger for a focus. Most people would have assumed he was a rogue; it was a trick he'd used more than once to keep bandits on the alert for a close-range surprise attack that never came. "Aaalso! Other non-cursed armors. [**Black Thorn Armor**]. [**Evolving Armor**]. Aand spikes are . . . they're a very common deeck . . . *decorative* element in Ely—"

"*Vex,*" Sev interrupted, looking exasperated, though there was a hint of laughter in his eyes. "First of all, what did you do to the anti-spill enchantment? This isn't our stuff; you can't just take those enchantments apart. We're going to have to pay for it."

"It was just there! It's not my fault!"

"*And,*" Sev pressed, "you've had this entire conversation with Misa before. She's just drunk. And so are you. I am *not* healing her from a hangover again, and since when did you drink?"

Misa, in her corner, stared their human cleric in the eye, scowled, and then—maintaining eye contact the entire time—gulped down her entire tankard of beer.

"I don't need you to heal my hangovers!" she declared once she was done, wiping some beer off of her lip before changing the subject back and pointing at Derivan. "Aaand another thing! What kind of stupid curse is that? Curses are supposed to be evil and shit! Yours lets you *not eat* and you just can't take it off? And what about bathing? *How are you supposed to bathe?*"

Misa narrowed her eyes, leaning in to Derivan—who leaned back, both amused and faintly concerned—and took a big sniff. "You don't even *smell.* Cheater. Your armor cheats."

"*I'd* take that trade . . . trader? Trade . . . off. Trade-off," Vex agreed, looking probably far too proud of himself for remembering the word. He grasped a little uselessly at his mug, still staring off in Derivan's general direction. Sev squinted at him and stole the mug away before he could grab it, slipping a glass of water into the lizardkin's hands instead.

Vex barely seemed to notice. He gulped it down with exactly the same amount of enthusiasm, not looking away from Derivan. "I'd be able to study so many more things," he mumbled. "Like magic. And armor. And magic armor."

Evidently, the lizardkin had *motivations.* But Sev had other concerns.

"Veeeex?" Sev stared at his friend, a suspicion forming in his mind. Vex had always been quite vocal about his dislike for alcohol. And he hadn't reacted to the change in his drink . . .

"Yeees?"

"Did you—"

"I cast a spell to numb my taste buds!" Vex interrupted gleefully, looking all too excited to share the details of his magic. "Yesss. Can't win against Misa without it! Alcohol tastes weeeeird. Also I wanna sleep." Vex planted his face on the table, his snout thunking against the wood, though his fingers continued reaching for the glass of water near him. "I'm good at spells!"

Sev sighed.

Derivan chuckled softly. "I think perhaps we should retire for the night," he said, reaching for the lolling lizardkin and easily lifting him into his arms. "I will get Vex to bed. Can you look after Misa?"

Sev, having only *just* sighed, pointedly took a deep breath so he could let out a louder, long-suffering sigh. He glanced at Misa. She appeared to be engaged in a staring match with the air above his head, waving down extra mugs of beer and gulping them down without breaking eye contact.

"Yeah, fine," Sev grumbled.

It was going to be a nightmare getting her to even leave.

—⁂—

"Youuuu." Vex poked at his armor a few times, and Derivan looked down at his friend, suppressing an amused chuckle. "You know Misa isn't really pressuring you to take off your armor, right?"

"I know, Vex," Derivan said. It wasn't the first time he wished he could smile—the light in his helmet glowed faintly in his closest approximation of one, though. "She is teasing me about it, yes? It is fine."

"Good!" Vex declared. "'Cause I've told her not to pressure you."

Derivan chuckled. "I do not mind it, Vex. But I appreciate your support."

"Also, your armor isn't cursed," Vex said, poking him again; Derivan froze, barely controlling the flinch that threatened to drop his friend. "Can't taste any curse magic coming from it. So . . . not cursed."

He knows— Wait. Did he say taste?

"Did you say *taste*?" Derivan repeated out loud, staring at the drunken form of his friend. "Did you . . . lick my armor?"

"Noooooo," Vex said, in a way that Derivan decided sounded suspiciously like a yes. "But you picked me up and my tongue wasn't in my mouth. So, *technically*, your armor licked me."

"I do not believe that is how that works," Derivan said, but he laughed, shaking his head in fond amusement. He nudged the door to Vex's room open with a shoulder, edging sideways into the room and turning to survey it briefly. The whole place was a mess, typical of their wizardly friend—scattered scrolls and dispersed drawings, rubbings from runes arranged haphazardly on his desk.

No doubt half of them were trapped, too. He'd made the mistake of trying to touch some of Vex's belongings without permission once.

Never again.

Instead, Derivan carefully made his way to the bed and knelt to roll the lizard onto it. "You must sleep, my friend."

"Nooo," Vex protested. "I don't wanna . . . sleep. Sleep is a stupid spell anyway. It only works as a sleeping aid! I wanna make a spell that replaces sleep . . . That'd be neat. A sleep spell, but it just gives you all the rest that sleep gives you, and then you don't have to sleep . . . How would it go? Maybe if I check [**Sleep**]'s runic circle—"

Credit where credit was due—Derivan had never seen a spellcaster accidentally cast a spell on themselves. It was quite genuinely impressive. Spellcasting usually required some level of concentration, and Vex's ability to do this mid-ramble was a testament to the fact that he was, in fact, "good at spells."

The runic circle had no sooner formed in the air, albeit wavy and indistinct, than Vex fell deeply unconscious.

Derivan let an amused smirk touch his eyes, glancing around to find the lizardkin's enchanted pitcher of water. He'd let it run out of mana again. Derivan let some of his mana flow into it so that Vex would have some water for when he woke up, then slipped out of the room and back into his own, just across the hall.

There, in the privacy of his room, Derivan paused. He stared at the bed sitting just beneath the window, at the barely disturbed covers that lay across it.

With his back to the door, he slid to the ground with a sigh.

For all that he tried . . . relating to organic beings was difficult.

He understood the purpose of beds. The others had certainly complained about not having them often enough. But the idea of comfort was foreign to him.

He stared at the bed in the corner of the room. It did nothing for him, because he couldn't *feel* anything except when his armor was damaged. Even the weight of anything he carried was only a faint ghost of a sensation. The idea of getting drunk, or needing water, or getting embroiled in a competition to drink more of a substance that only seemed to make people feel worse when they woke up—it was all incredibly strange to him.

Still, when he watched his teammates do those things, it was with a sense of inexplicable fondness.

With a thought, he pulled up his status, and stared at it.

Derivan, Level 26
<HIDDEN: Level 86 Infiltrating Armor>
Health: 520/520
Mana: 260/260

> **Stats:**
> **Strength:** 30 (84)
> **Intelligence:** 26 (62)
> **Wisdom:** 17 (72)
> **Agility:** 17 (90)
>
> **[Disguise Status—Level 26] [Buff]**
> **Applied by the [Disguise Status]** skill. Appear for all intents and purposes like an adventurer of any level.
> <WARNING>: Restricts your stats and skills to the chosen level.
>
> **Skill List:**
> [**Consume**], [**Disguise Status**], [**Combat Proficiency**], [**Guard Stance**], [**Meditation**], [**Paralyzing Slash**], [**Oneshot Protection**]

Infiltrating Armor.

A faint pulse of disgust resonated within him at the sight of the title—and the fact that his name was nothing more than a false label plastered onto his status was somehow even worse. It was a reminder of what he was. It was a reminder that he would never truly be a part of the society he had joined. That he was only pretending at it.

If any one of the others figured out what he really was . . . he didn't know what they'd do. He wasn't sure he wanted to know.

They'd been adventuring together for months, though Vex had joined them more recently. Derivan had grown attached to all of them—to Sev's kindness, despite his occasional fits of exasperation with the system; to Misa's protectiveness and love for exploits, though she could sometimes become overbearing; to Vex's enthusiasm and love for learning, even down to the impromptu lectures he sometimes gave on the smallest obscure thing. He couldn't imagine parting with any of them, and yet . . .

He was helping them get stronger. It was necessary, in a world of dungeons and monster attacks; if he didn't, they could die.

. . . Admittedly, he was sure they'd argue the point, if he could bring it up. They were, after all, relatively powerful for their ranks and levels. Sev and Misa both had rare-and-above classes. Vex hadn't talked about his, but he suspected the wizard did, too. All of them were clever in their own ways and had no compunctions about exploiting all the intricacies of the skills their classes offered them.

He remembered Sev's boast about [**Divine Communion**] with a wry sort of amusement. The way the cleric spoke of it, it was a skill that would allow him a moment to speak with his god and request help; it would work once, and then the skill would wither and die.

So they had that to keep them safe, even if Derivan didn't help them. Even if he left.

But . . . he *wanted* to stay.

There was no real way for him to win. The truest victory would be one where they lived on without him, with the strength he'd helped them gain.

Derivan told himself that the thought was a comfort—but comfort was still a foreign concept to him, and he wasn't sure if he could make himself believe it.

The armor sighed. Still leaning against the door, he allowed himself to slip into sleep—although for him, it wasn't a true rest. It was [**Meditation**].

But for a short while, it helped him feel like he wasn't a monster, and that was enough.

—ɱ—

"All right," Sev announced the next morning, as they gathered around a table with their breakfasts. One of the best benefits of the Adventurers' Guild, or so Sev claimed: free breakfast. "I got us our next quest."

"Why do you always get to pick?" Vex grumbled. The lizard was nursing his head, and Derivan patted his back gently in sympathy. It seemed to help.

"Because if *you* pick, we'll just end up studying some ruins for a week," Sev said dryly. "And if Misa picks, we're going to fight another horde. Or an Elite."

Vex paled a little at the thought of fighting an Elite.

"And if I pick?" Derivan asked.

". . . Do you want to pick?" Sev looked at him curiously.

"Not as such." Derivan admitted, shrugging. In truth, he couldn't— he didn't know enough about the quest system or the dangers they might encounter. His knowledge of the world at large was limited to the eight or so months of wandering he'd done with this very team once he left his dungeon. "But I was curious."

"I have no idea what you'd pick," Sev told him. "But I don't have any objections if you want to pick next time. For now . . ."

The cleric spread a map out onto the table, then jabbed a spot with his finger. "We're collecting some mana crystals from the local Nucleus. It's a relatively low-level job, but this particular Nucleus has seen a lot of monster activity lately, so we need to be on alert."

Misa frowned for a moment. She looked like she was about to protest, but something passed through her eyes, and she sighed instead. "Mana crystals, huh?" she finally said. "Are they having trouble getting adventurers to collect them again?"

Sev nodded, offering the half-orc a slight, apologetic grimace. "Yeah. It's low-hanging fruit, but someone needs to do it."

Misa grumbled. "Too many adventurers think they're too good for 'the baby shit' once they get past level ten."

There was a brief silence—unspoken commiseration from the table. Even Derivan understood the problem; he'd seen enough of it, even in the few short months of his travel.

Mana crystals were in short supply. It was too dangerous for non-combat classes to collect them, but the job of collecting them was ordinarily slow and boring. To combat this, the Adventurers' Guild had made it so that those between levels five and ten would only have crystal-collection quests as an option, where five was the minimum level needed to join the Guild.

The problem was that adventurers themselves rarely stayed below level ten for long, and after they hit level ten, they were rarely interested in continuing. Harvesting jobs took a long time and were generally bad for leveling.

Larger cities often had their own harvesting teams rather than relying on adventurers, with bigger ones and the Prime Kingdoms built directly on top of a Nucleus or a dungeon. Smaller villages, though, had very little to survive on. Their own harvesting teams were often small, consisting of only a precious few that had combat classes, and if those teams were ever unable to harvest . . .

Well. Mana crystals were *important*. They were used in everything—health potions, lamps, stoves. [**Disease Purification**] often required at *least* a grade-three mana crystal. That was three days' worth of farming for a standard adventuring team, and a small village usually only had one of those.

Worse, usage of a small grade-one crystal every week was required to maintain an individual's link to the system, and allowing the link to degrade was . . . catastrophic.

"All right," Misa said, throwing on her pack. "Let's go." Vex blinked blearily twice, watching the way she moved with ease.

". . . Didn't you say you weren't going to cure her hangover?" Vex said, staring suspiciously at Sev.

The cleric shrugged. "I didn't. She's just . . . fine, apparently?"

"I can hear you," Misa said, half-amused, half-annoyed. "First of all, you drank like half a mug of beer. I have no idea how you have a hangover. Second, I kept drinking after you left, and I *do* have a hangover. It hurts like shit. I wanna punch something."

She paused, then sighed. "But . . . shit, guys, this mana crystal stuff? Yeah, normally I'd complain we're not pushing ourselves or whatever, but we've seen what a mana crystal shortage does to a village. So . . . let's go get some crystals."

Sev was silent for a moment, then let out an explosive sigh, tapping both Vex and Misa on the shoulder. A small, glowing light left his fingers as he did so.

"This is a *one-time* thing," he huffed. "You're *supposed* to learn your lesson."

Derivan, perhaps wisely, didn't mention that he did this nearly every time Misa got a hangover. Misa and Vex both, on the other hand, visibly sagged in relief.

"Thanks," they chorused, and Sev nodded.

"Never doing that again," Vex added, muttering to himself.

Derivan was the only one that noticed the way Sev's hands shook briefly after he cast his spell.

CHAPTER 2

TOWER DEFENSE, KIND OF

The trek to the Mana Nucleus was one that would take a few hours of walking, from Derivan's understanding—not that they had much of a choice, given there were no caravans headed in that direction. They walked in the standard formation they'd adopted after being ambushed one too many times—Derivan and Vex side by side at the back, behind Sev, while Misa led the way in front and set a steady pace for them.

As was standard practice for them, they were each training their skills, trying to better understand the abilities the system had afforded them. Misa swung her mace in front of her, the dull-black glow of [**Guard Stance**] surrounding her body. Sev was lit up with the light-blue magic of [**Channel Divinity**], muttering quietly to himself as he examined his status window.

Derivan was mostly just talking to Vex. He'd done collection quests before, but he'd never asked what exactly these Nuclei *were*, partly out of a fear of being caught. Vex never seemed to mind his questions, though, and he'd grown a little more comfortable asking over time.

"We don't exactly know how a Nucleus is formed," Vex explained to Derivan. A small flame lit Vex's hand as he spoke, a tiny circle floating beneath it: a channeled [**Fireball**], which didn't look particularly impressive on its own, but often had any mages that happened to see it demanding to know how Vex had done it. "There are a lot of theories about the fluctuation of mana beneath the earth, but since no one can dig that far down, no one's been able to verify it. All we know is that a Nucleus will occasionally erupt into place, and if we cultivate it properly, a dungeon will form from it."

"But we do not know the true nature of a dungeon," Derivan noted. It was phrased as a statement, but he was curious. How much *did* people know of dungeons? Perhaps they would be able to explain the anomaly of his existence; why he . . . *was.*

"Basically," Vex agreed, shrugging. "It seems pretty random what kind of dungeon forms from any given Nucleus. It's got something to do with mana, but the prevailing type of ambient mana doesn't seem to matter. Mana type *variation* seems to affect how random a dungeon's effects are, and high mana concentrations seem to be good for dungeon quality. Now, I have a lot of theories—"

Vex coughed, interrupting himself before he could get too deep into his theories. Derivan knew that look; the lizardkin was on the verge of giving him a full lecture, complete with an illusory slideshow to explain his point.

Instead, he stuck to the facts. "They *do* also seem to base themselves at least partially off the Nucleus's local environment and the people present at the time they form . . . The big cities and the capitals of the Prime Kingdoms all have really weird dungeons. But they can harvest all the mana crystals they need from them, so they don't really care."

"This I have noticed," Derivan said a little dryly, though internally he frowned. He'd never been to a larger city—high-level individuals meant it was more likely for him to be noticed, and any one of the larger cities often had at least one or two high-levels lingering about.

But in their time as adventurers, they'd all been to many smaller villages that were starving for crystals.

None of them were particularly pretty sights. One in particular came to mind—they'd used all their crystals to cure a disease raging through their village, and it had cost them; the combat-harvesters that would normally mine crystals for them were still recovering, and they were left without a way to get new crystals for weeks. Half the villagers had veins glowing the bitter blue of system sickness.

". . . Yeah," Vex said after a moment, his voice softer; he seemed to be remembering something, too, though he offered Derivan a small smile when the armor looked at him. "Dungeons can form naturally without being cultivated, too, but the result tends to be a lot more chaotic. They're much safer when we guide the mana flows manually and stack the environment in our favor. Weirder, but safer. These days it usually involves a lot of safety signs."

Derivan couldn't help but chuckle slightly at the thought of a dungeon that had to base part of its existence on *safety signs.*

". . . Thank you for the explanation," Derivan opted to say after a moment, and Vex gave him a bright grin.

"Anytime."

"We're almost there! Stay sharp!" Misa called out only moments later, and both Derivan and Vex immediately fell into focus.

The Nucleus was coming into sight. It took the form of a massive crater in the ground, with the walls ridged to look almost like the seats of a coliseum; there were mana crystals poking out of the dirt in odd, disorienting arrays. The air shimmered with ambient power, threads of aspected mana tearing strange ripples in the air as they moved. It was a strange sight—they'd *been* to Nuclei before, and none of them had looked so . . . charged, for lack of a better term.

"It looks almost like it's about to form a dungeon," Vex murmured to himself, his eyes flicking across the patterns quickly. Derivan glanced curiously at his friend.

"This is what dungeon formation looks like?" he asked.

"In theory," Vex said with a nod. "I've never seen it myself, so I'm only guessing."

"I have," Sev called back from his position in front of them—his tone was strangely grim, his grip on his staff a little tighter than before. The glow of his [**Channel Divinity**] faded as he canceled the skill to allow his mana to regenerate. "You're right. This place is about to form a dungeon. It's about . . . two, three days away?"

Vex gave Sev a strange how-the-hell-are-you-calculating-that-from-the-concentration-of-wiggles-in-the-air sort of look, which Derivan felt was quite fair. Or perhaps he was projecting.

"And the Guild didn't tell us?" Misa's tone was a mixture of worry and anger. "Lack of information is *dangerous.*"

Sev shook his head. "Dungeon formations can be pretty spontaneous. It's possible the last scout that came out here just didn't see this. At this early stage, it should still be relatively safe . . ."

"But the mana concentration will attract more monsters," Derivan said, speaking with more calmness than he felt. He could *feel* the way the mana was pulling at him, a faint tug in his soul, drawing him toward the crater.

He'd been feeling it for a while, now that he paid attention to the sensation.

But he didn't have a way of explaining to anyone what he knew and how he knew it, so it was a fact that he tucked away into the back of his mind. If nothing else, the compulsion was easy for him to resist. "We must stay on guard, even still."

Vex nodded seriously, though there was a flicker of a sort of nervousness in his eyes. He was a practiced adventurer in that he didn't let that affect him, though; he grabbed his dagger, holding it at the ready. [**Dagger Proficiency**] kept his grip steady and his stance strong. The runes that focused his magic were engraved into the hilt in a design that he'd painstakingly built and carved himself, but they were well hidden, barely visible except to the trained eye.

Misa gripped her mace firmly, and Derivan drew his sword. Both of them radiated with the magic of [**Guard Stance**].

It was more precaution than anything—the Nucleus seemed empty of the monsters that would usually be milling about. The knowledge of the upcoming dungeon formation had them all on edge, though, and they descended into the crater practicing as much caution as they could.

> **Mana Crystal Collection—Processing . . .**
> **Ambient mana concentration detected at 79%.**
> **Ambient mana deviation within 1.4 standard deviations.**
> **Crystal purification proceeding . . . Estimated time: 17 hours, 15 minutes to Grade 2 crystal.**

And there was the other reason adventurers avoided mana crystal duty. It was *boring.*

Mana crystals littered the ground—but the ones in the ground were raw and unprocessed, and the uses for them were limited. Instead, adventurers had to stand guard in the Nucleus while the system worked to process and bank the mana crystals.

All while the Nucleus kept calling more monsters in to defend it, obviously. Because sitting in a place for days wasn't enough.

"Can we not collect the crystals ourselves and process them outside of the Nucleus?" Derivan asked, his voice low. He'd always wondered, but this was the first time he felt a pressing desire to *leave,* a feeling that went directly against the tugging feeling in his soul; he did not want to expose himself. Not here, not now.

"It's been tried, I think?" Sev said, glancing to Vex as if the lizardkin would be able to confirm it; Vex looked very briefly put out, then nodded.

"No one's been able to get it to work well so far," he said. "We *can* process raw mana crystals, but it takes a lot of effort and high-level skills, and it takes much longer than just letting the system do it. So . . . here we are."

"Here we are," Derivan echoed. The pull he felt was getting stronger. Nothing he couldn't resist, but he was reasonably sure they would be attacked soon; his eyes scanned the edges of the crater, watching for any movement.

What he didn't expect was for a monster to burrow up from *beneath.*

Thankfully, that was the benefit of [**Guard Stance**]. A flicker, and Derivan was watching the ground instead of the edges of the crater, his body already poised to react; the monster erupted from the ground with claws poised to strike at Vex, and the metal of Derivan's blade turned away the strike with ease.

A level twenty Crystal Mimic. A spidery little thing that looked like it was made of the very same raw mana crystals that littered the ground, except strung together in a way that made it look like a lopsided arachnid. But the level . . . It was stronger than any monster had a right to be in a wild Nucleus.

An effect of the upcoming dungeon formation, then? That meant this would be dangerous. If nothing else, hordes at this level were still manageable, although he'd have to be especially careful to protect Vex. "Level twenty here," he called out. Standard practice; keep everyone appraised of the average level of the creatures they were fighting, so they could adjust their strategies if needed.

"I've got a level fifteen!" Misa called back, easily beating off the mimic hounding her; a smash of her mace sent it flying ten feet back, crystalline legs fracturing as they scrambled for purchase in the dirt. "Good level range for us!"

"As long as an Elite doesn't show up," Sev muttered, glancing around with no small amount of trepidation. Small bolts of light blasted out of his staff, pelting into the "eyes" of both mimics with remarkable accuracy. Beady little things, barely visible in the refractory shine of their bodies; it was a wonder that Sev could spot them at all. The cleric wore an expression of focused concentration as his eyes darted between his two targets, and the mimics whined as they flinched away from the light.

"Don't jinx us," Vex hissed. The wizard spun his dagger in his hands, a runic circle glinting into existence in front of him as he did so. A modified [**Fireball**] sprang into the air in front of him, and Derivan leapt out of the way just in time for it to crash into the mimic he was fighting and send it sprawling back. Derivan wasted no time in chasing after it, a black crackle of electricity racing along the length of his blade to discharge into the twitching mimic. A [**Paralyzing Slash**].

At almost the same time, Misa *roared*, her mace crashing with frightening force into her opponent. *That* mimic shattered into fragments.

Your party has killed a Level 20 Crystal Mimic!

> **Your party has killed a Level 15 Crystal Mimic!**

> **Calculating XP rewards . . .**
> **XP rewards distributed.**
> **Mana concentration increased.**
> **Ambient mana deviation decreased.**
> **Mana Crystal Collection progress boosted.**

Almost as soon as the battle began, it was over. A level twenty and level fifteen mimic wasn't a true threat to their party, but it paid to stay cautious. A critical strike would still rip through health like paper without any proper defensive skills, and only Derivan and Misa had those.

"Is it . . . normal to get boosts for mana crystal collection like this?" Derivan asked, glancing at the text. He didn't remember that showing up for any of their previous collection quests.

Vex shook his head. "It only happens when a dungeon is forming. It's technically much more lucrative to get mana crystals from a forming dungeon, but it's pretty unpredictable, so the Guild isn't usually prepared for it. They send out calls with better rewards and a much higher priority when they are, though."

"I sent them a message about the dungeon as soon as we saw it forming," Sev added. "But it'll take them time to actually mobilize their scouts and get rewards ready, so we can't expect any help for . . . probably at least the next day."

"I see," Derivan said with a short nod. The pull he felt on his soul had faded down to almost nothing—a brief reprieve of some sort. He thought about it briefly, then added, "[Monster Sense] is telling me we have some time before the monsters begin to appear again. Should we attempt to set up some defenses?"

Vex perked up at this. "Did you get a new skill?"

". . . Sort of," Derivan answered, a little bit defensively, and he saw Vex sagging slightly in disappointment. He coughed once, then used another small lie he'd concocted. "I am . . . still having some trouble with my interface. But if I am able to retrieve the skill description, I will share it with you."

"Okay!" Just like that, Vex brightened again—the lizardkin was interested in anything and everything related to magic and the system. According to him, all skills were magic, *obviously*. Just because some of them didn't take mana didn't mean that they weren't magic.

That it was usually considered impolite to share specific skills and status screens proved to be no boundary for the lizard, though he typically took rejection with grace. "If your skill is telling us we have some time, then I'll ritual-cast [**Earth Ward**]. It'll prevent monsters from digging underneath us again, and we can set up a proper defensive perimeter."

Vex didn't actually take that long to cast his spell—all he needed to do was to carve out the runes into the air with his dagger, and he was skilled enough that each rune only took him about a minute. The wizard drew his ward large enough to give them all enough room to fight. Then, after a brief discussion, he used other spells to build up dark walls of force, giving them a sort of corridor in which they could fight.

With more uses of that spell, he created a platform for himself, balancing it on the edges of the other force walls to give himself a place to cast from. Sev would stay in the middle, able to direct healing toward any of them and mostly protected from the fight.

"Are we still good?" he called down.

"[Monster Sense] is getting stronger, but I do not believe we are at risk of attack yet," Derivan reported.

"Make sure you're protected up there!" Misa said. "It'll be hard to block any projectiles headed toward you from here."

"Got it," Vex answered, his eyes focused.

"Man," Sev grumbled. "I wish I had a wizard on my team when I was lower-leveled and doing these quests. I didn't know you guys could just instantly build fortifications."

Vex smiled a bit at that. He couldn't deny that part of him was a little scared—he was the lowest-leveled of the group, and a critical strike by monsters at this level might be enough to take him out in one shot. But he'd always known adventuring would be a risk; that was the *point*. Danger, after all, meant better classes, faster levels, even if it dramatically slowed down after level twenty. He'd even built himself with that in mind, spending little to no stat points on health and defense. Agility and Intelligence, for speed and damage. That was the core of his build.

If he'd told anyone in his home that thought process, they would likely have called him stupid and dragged him to a Fountain—but his choices (and, admittedly, the absurd size of his mana pool, although Vex didn't like to think about that for entirely separate reasons) were part of what allowed him to hit above his level and had resulted in his acceptance into his current party.

And his current party was *really cool*. He wouldn't trade them for anything. A few months of facing mortal danger had a way of forging strong bonds, sure, but it was more than that—

"Monsters incoming!" Derivan reported, and Vex brought his dagger to hand. No time to ruminate now.

Everyone else saw him cast [**Fireball**]. It was, certainly, a ball of fire—but no level nineteen's [**Fireball**] would annihilate monsters quite like his did.

The others knew by now that he was likely more than just a wizard, but he'd never told them what his actual class was. At first, he'd simply been too anxious; it was dangerous to talk about having a rare class, since they were coveted by the Prime Kingdoms and there was a bounty on low-leveled people with rare classes.

But Misa hadn't hesitated to tell him about *her* rare class, and while Sev and Derivan hadn't told him their exact classes, they'd both told him they were rare. He'd wanted to return the favor then and there, but the words stuck in his throat; he hadn't known them well enough then. He couldn't. So he'd swallowed, and nodded, and thanked them for sharing.

And then time passed, and he grew to know them, and . . . truth be told, he'd made the decision to tell them weeks before, on a night when Derivan had brought him some soup while he sketched away at his notes. He'd glanced back to see Sev and Misa waving at him, and saw that Derivan was smiling at him in his own odd way, the eye-lights in his helmet curving upward. They didn't want to disturb him while he worked, but made sure he was fed anyway.

Vex smiled a bit to himself. He couldn't have found a better team, or a better group of friends. And a team of rare classes? Practically unheard of! Even in the Prime Kingdoms, it almost seemed like the system itself manipulated circumstances to make them operate independently rather than together on a single team.

Which was maybe a bit concerning, actually. But it was just a silly thought; he couldn't imagine that to be true. It didn't fit with anything the system did.

Nah. It was fine. He was *pretty sure* nothing could go wrong from having the four of them work together. It hadn't so far.

CHAPTER 3

SKILLS

Derivan struck down the last of the Crystal Mimics, his sword slowing as the monster shattered. He didn't have the muscles to feel the ache of acid or the soreness of prolonged battle, but his movements were beginning to feel sluggish. It took more effort for him to move and react, even to speak.

Conveniently enough, that meant that he sounded out of breath when he spoke, just like a human would. "That is . . . the last of them. [Monster Sense] has faded again. I believe we are due for a break."

"No fuckin' kidding," Misa groaned, flopping down onto the ground with a *thump*. "How long have we been at this?"

"Five hours," Vex said. He leapt nimbly down from the platform he'd been standing on, but stumbled slightly as he straightened; Sev quickly grabbed him and steadied him, and he flushed slightly as he nodded at the cleric. "Thanks. We're lucky, I think; the countdown's down to about twenty minutes. I knew crystal processing would be faster, but I didn't realize it would be *this* much faster."

Vex called up the window again to confirm, glancing quickly through the displayed information.

Mana Crystal Collection—Processing . . .
Ambient mana concentration detected at 95%.
Ambient mana deviation measured within 1.3 standard deviations.
Crystal purification proceeding . . . Estimated time: 18 minutes, 20 seconds to Grade 2 crystal.

"We've shaved about twelve hours off the initial reported time," Vex said. "A grade-two can sustain a village for a week. Should we stay for a grade-three?"

"If it keeps speeding up, we should," Sev said, but he bit his lip. "I hope the Guild hurries up. It'd be better if multiple parties could take advantage of this, and that mana concentration is going up way faster than is normal."

"There's no guarantee that any adventurers will be close enough, anyway," Misa grunted. "Though at least with a job like this, they'd actually pick up the quest."

"The mana concentration is significant?" Derivan asked curiously. "Vex mentioned earlier that the quality of the resulting dungeon depended on mana concentration, but I was unaware that it had an effect on the time taken for a dungeon to form."

"Dungeons always form a certain amount of time after the process begins, but reaching a hundred percent usually triggers the process immediately." Vex looked at the status. "Sev, you said it was two or three days away?"

"It *was*," Sev confirmed, flicking a finger through his own status with a worried scowl on his face. "I should've noticed it before, but it's accelerating. And not just because of the monsters we fought off—that contributed only about three percent of the mana concentration. We've gone up the other sixteen percent in five hours."

"Worrying," Vex said, his brows furrowing; he wondered if it had something to do with the amount of mana he was throwing around. "Then I think we should definitely stay. There's no guarantee anyone else would be able to get here in time to take advantage of the bonus."

"I agree," Misa said, and Derivan nodded as well.

"We're staying, then," Sev decided. "Anyone need healing? I'm about topped up on mana." Sev glanced around, checking the party for injuries. No one was significantly hurt . . . a low-cost [**Area Heal**], then.

The glow of his heal rippled through the party, reflecting briefly off the walls of force that made up the small defensive structure Vex had built. Everyone let out a small sigh of relief, and the party settled in to wait.

Surprisingly, the wait was uneventful.

Mana Crystal Collection—Processed.
Ambient mana concentration detected at 96%.
Ambient mana deviation measured within 1.3 standard deviations.
Crystal purification complete! A Grade 2 Mana Crystal has been deposited with your party leader.
Please remain within the Nucleus to upgrade your crystal further.

A pause, and then the screen updated, reflecting a new upgrade time for the next grade of crystal.

Grade 2 Mana Crystal detected!
Grade 2 Mana Crystal will be upgraded to Grade 3 in: 10 minutes, 40 seconds.

". . . Ten minutes?" Vex said, staring blankly. "That . . . can't be right."

"It's not." Sev gripped at his staff, his face suddenly pale. He glanced at a screen no one else could see. "I changed my mind. We should leave. Now."

"But . . . ten minutes. A grade-three crystal will keep a village topped off for at least a *month*, if they don't need to cure any diseases." Misa breathed, staring at the display and half reaching out toward it. Then she shook her head fiercely. "I— No, you're right. [**Danger Sense**] is telling me we should leave, too. Let's go."

"We cannot," Derivan said softly, and the other three all glanced at him. He gestured to the edge of the crater that made up the Nucleus.

Past the force walls Vex had conjured, mana was swirling, the concentration so thick it was visible as streams of glittering light. It would have been beautiful if not for the fact that it was beginning to form into solid, physical structures. It began from the outer edges of the crater, where towering walls of light were beginning to solidify.

"We are best protected here," Derivan said. "If we leave now—"

"We'll get stuck out in the open with no defenses," Sev breathed. He shook his head. "Okay. Shit. Ten minutes. We can do this. Once the dungeon finishes forming, we can leave. I have [**Divine Communion**] if things go too far to shit. We'll be fine."

Warning!
Ambient mana concentration has reached 100%!
Dungeon formation imminent!
Grade 2 Mana Crystal will be upgraded to Grade 3 upon dungeon formation. Further upgrades will be provided based on remaining ambient mana and combat performance.
Estimated time left: 10 minutes.

"Incoming!" Derivan shouted, and everyone scrambled into position. The first monster burst into view, burrowing up from just outside the [**Earth**

Ward], and launched itself toward Derivan in a blur of motion; the armor barely managed to bring his sword up in time to block the scything blades of its legs. "Level 37 Burrowing Spider!" he called back.

"I've got a level 34 Earthwyrm!" Misa shouted.

But that was just the beginning.

There were more monsters. *So many more monsters*, this time, kicking up a cloud of dust and dirt as they burrowed their way above the ground and scampered toward the only adventurers present in the Nucleus. It was sheer luck that these particular monsters weren't intelligent enough to register the walls that Vex had built as anything more than an obstacle. As long as there was an opening, they flooded toward that instead of trying to break down the spell.

The corridor of force itself was narrow enough that neither Misa nor Derivan needed to fight off too many of them at the same time. But the monsters were hard to kill, and they were slowly getting pushed inward, closer toward the center of the corridor where Sev stood. Even with Vex desperately casting spells, even with Sev's support magic flooding through them and gifting them with divine strength . . . it felt like they wouldn't last three minutes, let alone the ten they needed to last for the dungeon to finish forming.

It was going to be a long fight.

—⁓—

"Shit," Misa said. Her voice was pained, ragged; the wyrm she fought had managed to squirm past her guard for a moment to dig a deep gash into the flesh of her arm. She saw her health ticking rapidly down in the corner of her vision—*Shit, it's got poison,* she thought briefly—before the familiar comfort of a heal trickled through her arm, and she gripped her mace in a [**Paralyzing Bash**] to give herself a moment to breathe.

Black lightning crashed through the Earthwyrm and sent it flying backward, stunned.

Misa gritted her teeth. That wyrm alone was ten levels above her. If it was the only enemy she had to fight, she could handle it; level differences didn't matter as much as skills did, and monsters in particular didn't usually have the intelligence to take advantage of stat differences. But she had to do more than fend off the wyrm: she had to fend off every enemy in front of her and make sure none of them could get past her.

There were *too many* for that.

But that was fine. She could handle this. There was a reason she was their tank, over even Derivan and the ridiculous durability of his armor.

On the best of days, Misa disliked her class. It was rare, sure, and she had no doubt that others would kill to get it—but it was a reminder, too. A reminder that she'd failed, once upon a time. A reminder that she'd once stood before a horde of monsters just like this one, her fellows dead and beaten.

A reminder that for all that she'd fought, she was only one person, and she could do nothing against a horde.

She had fought until she was *inside* her village, engaging as many as she could, but even then, the monsters kept flooding past her.

She could still remember the chittering laughter.

She'd *tried*. It wasn't that she hadn't tried. She fought until she could barely stand, until her limbs were broken and bleeding. She still didn't know how she'd managed to survive, how she'd managed to keep fighting; the memory was a blur for her.

But when she'd come to, she'd seen how her status had changed. She'd been given a class. [**Fallen Guardian**].

The name was a reminder of her failure, and it never stopped hurting—but at the same time, a part of her was grateful. She'd be able to prevent that from ever happening again.

[**To Fall Yet Hold the Line**] [**Active Skill**] [**Grade: Maxed**]
Cost: 10% Max Health per Attack Blocked

You guard the gate, and none shall pass while your blood still flows.

If you would fail to block an enemy, you do not.

It was a powerful skill—vaguely worded skills like that always were. It had its weaknesses, of course, and anyone that knew precisely how her skill worked would be able to subdue her all too quickly. But against monsters, with a healer at her back?

As long as ten of them weren't attacking her at once, she would be fine. She trusted Sev.

With that in mind, Misa *moved*.

Skills provided by the system were some mixture of natural prowess, knowledge, and physical or magical capability. Rarer skills allowed the users to break past their limits, either granting them with greater knowledge or—particularly in the case of skills that were not explicitly magical—allowing them to perform impossible physical feats.

This was one of the latter types of skill. Misa had neither the stats nor the reaction time to block three wyrms that were over level thirty all at once, but she somehow still *did*, flowing from one form to the other and striking them each hard enough to knock them back. The skill drew on her knowledge, predicting what she would do if she had the speed and power, and moved her body for her.

The cost, of course, was that her body could not truly handle those speeds or feats of strength; her muscles and ligaments tore with every movement.

It was a small price to pay. This was still on the lower end of what the skill could do, in any case.

Misa twisted. A wyrm was launching itself toward her, teeth gnashing in the air; she leapt to meet it, sword impaling it through the mouth and into dark, bitter flesh. In the next instant a wyrm threatened to cross the line she held, and Misa found herself *there*. Her blade flicked through the flesh of the first wyrm like it was nothing, and she impaled the second one through the head into Vex's [**Earth Ward**].

Without pausing, she spun and *punched*, trusting the skill that was guiding her movements. She left her blade and the squirming wyrm in the ground. Though she had no idea what she was aiming at, there was a satisfying *smack* as the force of her fist sent the last wyrm crashing into the edge of the corridor of force.

Misa breathed. She felt healing trickle in. Part of her was worried that they wouldn't be able to keep this up; ten minutes suddenly felt like a long, long time.

Another part of her was falling back into an old state of mind, letting all her worries and fears fade away. There was no space in battle to think about any of that.

All she had to do was hold the line.

Derivan was *worried*. He was stronger than any of his companions thought, certainly, but there was only so much he could do to hide the true extent of his skills; he would not allow them to die simply to preserve his secret. No. If this fight revealed him, and this was where his journey ended . . .

. . . It was easier not to think about.

Despite the warning on [**Disguise Status**], the skill couldn't completely force him to fight as a level twenty-six. The problem was twofold: one, no skill would *remove* knowledge that you already possessed. [**Combat Proficiency**] was a skill that was currently being restricted down to a grade-one skill—but he still possessed all his memories of fighting with a maxed [**Combat Proficiency**].

The second problem was that skills themselves were never completely disabled; the most they would do was be restricted to grade-one. But some of his skills were exceptionally effective even at a grade of one; it was one of the perks of being an Elite monster, as much as he hated the thought.

[Consume] [Active Skill] [Maxed <Current: Grade 1>]
Cost: 250 MP

Grapple a target. If the target does not break out of your grapple in <10> seconds, absorb the target, refilling your HP and MP by <10%> of their remaining HP and MP, and gain the [**Satiated**] buff.

[**Satiated**] grants <7.5%> of all stats and skills possessed by the target, and lasts for 10 seconds per 10% of the target's remaining HP. **Note:** Until [**Satiated**] expires, target has a chance of escaping every 5 seconds.

[**Consume**] may not be used while [**Satiated**] is active.

It wasn't a skill he enjoyed using. But for this battle, while he was still restricted to level twenty-six . . .

The average Burrowing Spider or Earthwyrm, at level thirty-five, took him thirty seconds to kill without assistance from Vex. Grappling would restrict his movements slightly but not *completely*—he had the benefit of being large enough to grapple the smaller enemies with a single hand.

Derivan had three enemies headed for him; one level thirty-two, one level forty, and one level thirty-seven. This was a small enough crowd that he could handle them, even with his current stats.

The level thirty-seven Burrowing Spider reached him first, and he ducked underneath its leap, catching its exoskeleton on the wicked hook at the end of his sword; he spun his blade forward, smashing it into the ground and stunning it.

Before it could recover, he ran forward. He grabbed the level forty wyrm in the middle of its body, ignoring the razor-sharp teeth and making sure it didn't have the leverage to twist around and bite him. He activated [**Consume**], then scrambled back into position, using the force of his blade hitting the ground to launch himself back.

It was a trick Misa had taught him. If the skill or weapon was stronger than his stats, it could give him more power and speed to leverage than his stats would.

The level thirty-two Burrowing Spider was scrambling over the still-struggling body of the first; they were getting tangled with one another in their desperation to get to Sev. Derivan didn't give them the chance—his sword slammed into the two wriggling spiders, cracking carapace and splattering insectoid goop.

Not enough to kill them. But enough to wound them badly; they retreated briefly, hissing at him.

Four more seconds.

He opted to wait. The spiders were circling his position, wary of him; the other monsters were looking for an opportunity to attack. The timer continued to tick down.

One. Zero—

There was a flash of darkness, and the wyrm he was holding on to abruptly vanished.

Buff [Satiated] applied!

7.5% of the stats of a level forty monster was not an incredible boost, though it also wasn't insignificant. More important, however, were the skills.

Or, more accurately, the skill. There was only one skill that he cared about receiving. The [**Earth Ward**] Vex had applied to the ground did, after all, only prevent *enemies* from moving; it would do nothing to stop *him* from wreaking whatever havoc he wanted.

[**Burrow**] [**Active Skill**] [**Grade: 1**] [**Temporary**]
Cost: 15 MP/s
Move underground at <200%> normal movement speed.

The other ridiculous thing about [**Consume**], of course, was that skills were often designed for the particular species they belonged to. Earthwyrms did not move particularly well on land, but dug through the dirt like they were swimming through water. Translated to Derivan, who could already move at high speeds for his level?

The armor dove into the dirt, feeling it part easily for him; his feet landed on platforms that didn't exist, and he felt the earth almost pushing him forward as he aimed toward one of the two Burrowing Spiders. He swung hard as he exited the dirt, still moving at twice his normal velocity—

Carapace *shattered.*

Your party has killed a Level 37 Burrowing Spider!

Derivan would have smiled grimly, if he could. That spider still had more than half of its health. This was *good*. And he still had ninety-seven seconds left on the buff.

It wasn't quite enough yet. But he could make this work.

CHAPTER 4

A LACK OF OVERSIGHT

"Has he . . . always been able to swim through the ground like that?" Vex asked, glancing at Sev with only the faintest hint of awkward incredulity. He was pretty proud of himself for that, actually.

"No," Sev said. To his relief, the cleric sounded about as confused as he did. ". . . Doesn't matter right now, though. Stay focused."

Right. They were still in a fight for their lives; a horde of upper Bronze-ranked monsters were beyond the scope of something their party was built to deal with. They were managing surprisingly well so far, but Misa in particular was falling behind; her skill could only help her hold back the enemy, not kill them.

Most of the time, anyway. The practice she'd put into using it paid off; sometimes, in the process of the skill forcing her to move in physically impossible ways, it would incidentally allow her to shear her weapon through an enemy with absurd physical force. In those instances, it definitely helped her kill monsters. But that was easier said than done.

Derivan, on the other hand, seemed to be managing well enough by himself. Vex opted to focus his efforts on helping Misa. He wasn't worried about hiding his class anymore—he'd already decided to tell them, after all.

He spun his dagger, feeling the runes call out to him as he did so.

Magic was more than just a set of skills offered by the system—more than runes that programmed reality.

Magic was *alive*. It was a living art that wanted to be used.

He would not be locked down by a system that drew boundaries and imposed artificial structures on a force that desired nothing more than freedom.

He was a [**Chromaturgist**].

Vex didn't know what it was about his class that allowed him to work against the system. He would have assumed it was a fundamental conceit of using a system-offered class that he would be limited to its capabilities.

He certainly wasn't *complaining*, though.

This spell was one he'd figured out a while before, while trying to understand the structure of a basic [**Fireball**]. His class gave him the ability to read and examine skills on a deeper layer than most people had access to; he could see not only the runic circles and the way mana flowed into them, but the runes within the circle themselves—the internal circuitry the system used to assist in the formation of a spell.

One modified rune to gather the mana into a ball. Another to keep it tightly contained. A third to *convert* the mana as it spread outward, twisting the neutral mana into the aspect of Fire; that part of the spell would only trigger on impact as the containment layer shattered.

It was all so . . . tightly structured. There was something of a simple elegance to it, certainly, but he couldn't help but feel like he could do better.

So he did.

The gathering rune was fine, but he improved on it, having the spell draw from both his personal mana stores *and* the ambient mana in the air. With the mana concentration of the Nucleus being what it was, it meant the spell was more powerful than ever. That was as simple as copying the runic node that drew from his mana stores and tweaking it slightly, layering it strategically over the spell.

The containment rune existed only to ensure that the spell exploded at the point of contact. Pumping enough mana into the spell forced that mana to expand once the layer broke. This had been harder for him to modify— he'd had to study other spells that accelerated the spread of mana. Area-of-effect spells, mostly, that affected a larger area than the mana input would suggest. The result was a rune that created a layer that, rather than shattering on impact, would crack at specified points and start *shrinking*, ejecting mana with force.

The last rune . . . it was hard to explain what he'd done with it. His modifications to any rune that changed the aspect of mana relied on his understanding of the concept it encompassed. This, more than anything, was the part that was more art than science. The runes sang to him, and acted in concert with him, and they worked together to bring his understanding into reality.

Fortunately, fire and mana were two concepts he understood very, very well.

His dagger finished moving through the air. He cast.

<ERROR>
Unknown skill attempted!
Parsing . . .
Displaying best approximation.
[Aspect of the Plague ### Manaburn ### Fireball]

It was always interesting to see how the system decided to label his spells. He'd think about that later. For now, he watched with [**Advanced Mana Sight**], making sure his spell was working as he'd intended.

The spell was brighter than any [**Fireball**]. It sailed through the air in an arc, crashing into the middle of the monsters that spread out in front of Misa; when it landed, it *bounced*. Fire sputtered out of the spell like a liquid rather than plasma, lasting longer and spreading farther than any spell he'd attempted back when he was still trying to hide his class.

Where any amount of the liquid fire touched a monster, it sank into its skin and began to *burn*. Not at nerves and flesh and tissue; the thought of a spell like that made him flinch. But it burned at the mana they could access, eating away the very resource they needed for most of their skills.

Wyrms could no longer [**Burrow**]. They crawled on the ground instead, wiggling ineffectually forward. Burrowing Spiders attacked without mana, their normally deadly, bladelike legs reduced to the rough equivalent of a stick.

And it was *spreading*. Clouds of mana, invisible to the naked eye, seemed to spread through the air every time an "infected" monster moved; it would sink into other, uninfected monsters, slowly burning through their mana, too.

This spreading aspect—labeled "Plague" by the system—was new to him. Vex was suddenly very glad that his party members were excluded from the effects of his magic, and decided that he'd reexamine the runes that went into this spell later.

If there was a later.

"Vex, what the *fuck* was that?!" Misa called up to him, and the lizard nearly jumped. "That was amazing!"

"Um . . . new spell! I'll explain later!" Vex shouted back. He glanced at his mana, tail swishing around nervously; the spell had taken nearly all of his rather impressive mana pool. 2,800 MP . . . it would be a while before he could cast it again. But the effects would last for five minutes, and there were smaller spells he could cast in the meantime to keep the party ahead.

He breathed. He was still nervous. They needed to survive for ten minutes, with a spell he couldn't cast again; that left them with still half of the full time they needed. But Misa was fighting a little more steadily now, beating back the enemies and killing them, albeit slowly; even Derivan was fighting with a little less tension—

Knowing that Derivan was leaping in and out of the ground didn't make the sight any less ridiculous the second time. The situation still felt a little unreal to him.

Okay. Derivan would be fine.

Vex had to admit the sight was amusing, and it made him feel a little bit better about their impossible odds.

—⁓—

It proved to be a grueling fight—but they managed. It took every last scrap of the resources they had available. Sev was throwing out healing every time he could spare the mana, looking more and more haggard every time he did so. In an attempt to save on mana, Vex leapt down from his platform and joined Misa at her side, relying on [**Dagger Proficiency**] to fight instead of spells.

(Misa protested this rather vocally but didn't have the time to physically stop Vex, with all her efforts focused on making sure he didn't get hit.)

Misa kept her skill up, paying in blood for every enemy that she would have failed to stop without the skill—but as the skill kept going, she got *better*, anticipating each enemy's movements and relying on her skill less and less. It was one of the benefits of fighting a fixed set of monsters.

Their patterns became recognizable. Easier.

A memory teased at her, and she forcefully shut it down. Now wasn't the time.

Derivan's [**Satiated**] buff wore off, and he didn't have the mana to keep using it—but his initial use had given him enough of a head start that he could handle the enemies coming in from his side.

The spell Vex used helped both of them, of course, until it wore off; once it did, Vex leapt back onto his platform, supporting them both with basic [**Fireball**]s and [**Conjure Dagger**]s. It was a fight they were slowly losing—a fight they *would* lose, if it kept going with the same intensity. But already there were fewer enemies, the monsters tapering down to a saner number.

[**Grade 2 Mana Crystal will be upgraded to Grade 3 upon dungeon formation. Estimated time left: 10 seconds.**]

Ten seconds left. The monsters were almost entirely gone, with a few stragglers being quickly cut down by Derivan or Misa. Vex and Sev were both meditating, recovering their mana. They were all alive. Derivan and Misa were *injured*, with a few close calls nearly taking Misa out.

But their injuries were nothing that wouldn't heal.

The clock ran down.

3.

2.

1.

Grade 2 Mana Crystal has been upgraded to Grade 3!

Dungeon formation in progress.

Logging Mana Nucleus state . . .

<ERROR>

Ambient mana concentration detected at <?300>%!

<ERROR>

Ambient mana deviation measured outside 3 standard deviations!

Recovering . . .

Excess mana will be routed to bonus dungeon rooms. Excess deviation will have unpredictable effects on dungeon formation.

What?

On the one hand, this should have been over, and it didn't matter what the system said as long as they didn't have to keep fighting. But the mana concentration was strange—should have been impossible, even. The mana deviation had gone *up,* even though it usually stabilized as a dungeon progressed toward forming.

Something felt wrong. To all of them, even the ones that didn't know the specifics of dungeon formation, there was a strange sense of foreboding.

> **Calculating parameters for bonus rooms from local seeds . . .**
>
> **Seed 1:**
> <Misa, level 24, [Fallen Guardian]>
>
> **Bonus room created:**
> <The Village's Last Defense>

Misa swallowed, staring at the name; an old, old pain welled up inside her. She didn't know what she was supposed to feel, only that something about this felt terribly invasive.

> **Seed 2:**
> <Vex, level 19, [Chromaturgist]>
>
> **Bonus room created:**
> <ERROR>
> **Seed parameters exceed allowable local parameters. Seeking administrator approval . . .**
>
> **Recovering . . .**
>
> **Bonus room created:**
> <A World Without the System>

Vex stared. Well, that was that, he supposed; he'd been planning on revealing his class anyway, although he hadn't expected it to happen quite like this. There was still a speck of nervousness in him—it was hard to completely be rid of the fear he'd held ever since the notification first appeared.

But no one said anything. He glanced around, and Misa offered him a small, supportive smile, like she knew what he was feeling and wanted him to know it was fine. Derivan simply looked curious.

Sev seemed . . . kind of surprised, but not about the class.

Feeling heartened by his comrades, he glanced back to the message—but his heart dropped slightly when he saw the last part. The words "A World Without the System" blazing *red*. Misa's own room had been colored light blue, a color that represented *rare*; the other colors were black for common, green for uncommon, purple for elite, orange for unique . . .

But *red*? What the fuck was *red*? He'd never seen that color in the system, and the error preceding it worried him.

Seed 3:
<Level 86 Infiltrating Armor>

<ERROR>
Unexpected seed! Compensating . . .

Bonus room created:
<The Bridge Between>

Derivan froze. He wanted to speak, but the words felt thick in his throat; he stared at the screen in front of him, willing it to change. He could feel the sharp gazes of his friends, drilling into him.

The system hadn't even afforded him a *name*. It—

"It's fine." Sev spoke softly before his thoughts could spiral further. The armor looked up, then, only to see that the others were offering him tired smiles.

They'd known?

They'd known.

If not directly, then they had known something similar, enough that this revelation did not surprise them.

". . . Thank you, then," Derivan said with a bow of his head. "And I am sorry for keeping up the ruse as long as I did."

"You had to," Misa said shortly, glancing at Sev. The cleric nodded, and his words dipped into a careful warning.

"Right now, the system's on pause because it's calculating. I don't know what will happen once it's finished, but I don't think it'll like that you're playing outside the role it gave you. Derivan . . . be careful."

Derivan didn't know what to say. He nodded once, feeling trepidation rise up within him; Vex glanced at him nervously, then walked over to sit next to him.

It was a small gesture of support, but it was one he appreciated.

Seed 4:
<ERROR>

<ERROR>

Compounding errors detected. Local fractures detected. Compensation nodes saturated. Unable to further compensate.

WARNING: Local boundaries may fail catastrophically without administrator override!

WARNING: Local boundaries may—

<ADMIN COMMAND: SYSTEM OVERRIDE>

Override command accepted. Bonus room offered:
<Come and find me.>

"... Okay," Sev breathed. "I ... wasn't expecting that."

"What the fuck secrets have *you* been keeping?!" Misa burst out, though she seemed more startled than angry.

"It's complicated," Sev muttered.

"It might not be all him," Vex offered, though he looked worried. "It mentioned compounding errors, right? Almost all of us had some kind of error. Yours might just be the—"

Another box interrupted them.

WARNING: Mana concentration and amount of deviation still in excess. Routing excess mana ...

Grade 3 Crystal upgraded to Grade 4!
Grade 4 Crystal upgraded to Grade 5!
Grade 5 Crystal upgraded to Grade 6!
Grade 6 —

<ADMIN COMMAND: SYSTEM OVERRIDE>
Override command accepted. Remaining excess mana routed to Overseer summoning.

Repent, sinner, for ye are but a lamb before the slaughter.

"I don't think this is finished yet," Sev said, a little lamely.

The four of them stared at the notification. The notifications. The second box hovered ominously, larger and with a greater presence than all the previous ones.

"I never thought I'd see a box this threatening," Vex commented, his tail twitch betraying his nervousness. Misa snorted anyway, needing that small bit of humor.

But that was all the time they had.

The force walls that Vex had built shattered like so much broken glass, and the [**Earth Ward**] dissipated.

Above them, mana was boiling, twisting and turning into currents, gathering into a single form.

Barely visible above, the overlay of the system glowed. For all that it was nearly impossible to see in the chaos, it commanded all their attention.

<**Overseer of Chaos**>
<**Level ??? Mana Abomination**>

CHAPTER 5

SKILL ABUSE

Derivan knew what he needed to do.

The rest of the party had already expended everything they had. Sev had exhausted most of his mana trying to keep them all alive. Vex had similarly spent most of his mana on spells, and Misa was already barely keeping it together. She had 30% of her health left, and a direct hit from a *three-digit-leveled* creature—something he had, until now, been certain was impossible—would kill her instantly even if she were still at full health.

She could abuse her block skill to take less damage than she was supposed to, since the damage for it was fixed. But she'd have to react fast enough, first, to a creature with an Agility score that could very well be in the hundreds.

Derivan had a protective buffer she didn't, and much more health besides.

He took a breath. He didn't need to, but he did it anyway; it was one of the many small things that made him feel a little more like what he yearned to be. Someone the system didn't see as a monster. Someone with a name, and a class that reflected who he was as a person.

Not what he had now; not the label the system had burned into him.

Level 86 Infiltrating Armor.

He'd given himself a name, but if the system that the entire world ran on didn't acknowledge it—then who was he, really?

Derivan had never really allowed himself to consider his wish of being *more* before. It seemed like too much to hope for. Then he'd been revealed, only to find out that his party members already knew, and didn't care . . . he felt that spark of hope.

Now, again, that spark died; he wasn't foolish enough to think that he could survive against anything this powerful.

But he could buy them time.

The system did not see him as a person. Misa, Sev, Vex—they *did*. That was enough to be worth sacrificing himself for.

He would've done it for less.

Besides, he could already feel what Sev meant—his link to the system creeping in once again, shrouding his soul. It was so insidious a force that he'd never *felt* it before, had assumed it to be just a part of his being; only when it was gone and then returned did he understand it for what it was.

And along with the link came a feeling of foreboding. He didn't know what it meant, but he had a suspicion, and it was a suspicion that both terrified him and filled him with resolve.

The barrier around the Nucleus had flickered and failed, drawn into the abomination to help empower it.

"Run," Derivan said quietly, beginning to walk away, toward the monster. "Please."

He didn't hear what they said in response. He understood, intellectually, that they protested immediately; he saw in the corner of his eyes that Misa was struggling to get up, that Vex was staring like he wanted to run after him. Sev held them both back with a gentle barrier of light, though he himself looked torn, and Derivan allowed himself a small, hidden smile at the sight.

They were true friends, all of them.

[Disguise Status] deactivated.
Level 26 —> Level 86
All **[Disguise Status]**-related restrictions removed.
Maximum health increased.
Maximum MP increased.

Derivan leapt into the air. It'd been a long, long time since he'd moved like this, completely free from the restrictions imposed on him by **[Disguise Status]**. He shot through the air faster than he anticipated, his blade whistling through the wind in front of him. Wisps of black lightning congealed along his sword as he activated another skill.

[Paralyzing Slash].

It was the basic skill afforded to many melee combatants. He didn't need to *defeat* the Overseer, whatever an Overseer was. He needed to grapple it for the one second he would need to activate **[Consume]** at its maximum level. It could break out afterward, but that happened at set intervals. It would give his friends *time*. It hadn't even finished forming yet; he was willing to bet it couldn't use skills—

The Overseer reached for his blade and caught it. Lightning dissipated like so much useless mana.

Worse, that same black lightning began to course through its body.

Derivan stared.

Far, far away, he thought he heard Sev yell in panic and felt the familiar charge of a heal rush through his body. It was a powerful heal that brought him back up to full health in a fraction of a second, and even then it barely hit him in time.

Flick.

Derivan's armor sounded like a gong as a mana-compressed finger slammed into his body, visibly denting the metal and sending him flying back toward the ground. He couldn't try to rotate or minimize the impact of his fall; his own [**Paralyzing Slash**] worked against him, black lightning flickering across his body and freezing up his joints when he tried to move.

He heard his friends shouting again and heard the worry in their voices. He felt light barriers break beneath him as Sev tried to cushion his fall, and then a gust of wind as Vex tried to counteract the force of it.

He still slammed into the ground, almost right next to where Sev had set up the barrier for Misa and Vex.

Half his health in one blow, and he suspected that Sev's heal and [**One-shot Protection**] were the only things that had stopped him from being instantly killed.

[**Oneshot Protection**] [**Passive**] [**No Grade**]
Enemies cannot deal more than 50% of your maximum health in damage in one attack.

If Sev hadn't healed him in time . . . How had he *known?* How had he managed to heal him enough to max out his health? The cleric was the second strongest in their team, but he shouldn't have been able to heal half the health of a level eighty-six monster.

He looked over at Sev, sitting only a few feet away from him; the human looked pale, pained. There wasn't time for questions.

"We have a plan," Sev told him. "Two layers. Vex has a spell that can directly attack mana, but he needs time to regenerate his own mana and it might not be strong enough regardless. If it doesn't work, we'll fall back to my cast of [**Divine Communion**]. I'll start it now, but it's a ritual cast and will take longer than Vex's spell. Misa will be the second line of defense, but she can't hold it off for long, especially if it realizes it just needs to attack quickly to beat her. You're the only one that might be able to stall it for long."

Derivan wanted to tell them to run. A plan was forming in his head; he could survive, at least for a while. But he saw the determination in their eyes, and he wasn't sure he could hold it off for long enough that it would matter if they *did* run.

The Overseer could move faster than any of them could. Even him. He'd thought his level and his stats could at least be more of a barrier—

"I will," he told Sev, putting his doubts to the side. Misa nodded at him seriously, getting into position. Vex sat down to meditate. Sev began casting, lights slowly glimmering into existence around him. Motes of silvery brilliance drew into the focus he held in his fist.

The Overseer descended.

The mana, previously churning in visible waves of tattered light, had settled down into faint distortions in the air—and behind them, the Overseer was finally fully visible.

It was a mockery of something humanoid and bipedal, compressed energy making the barest attempt at a body. Twisted light strung together into limbs that were just a little too long and a little too thick; its fists were malformed things, fingers glued back into its own construct like it didn't quite understand what they were *for*.

And then, of course, there were the eyes. Far too many eyes, the sizes different and *wrong*, with no pupils or irises to speak of. If not for the shape, they would barely seem like eyes at all, and yet looking at them gave Derivan the distinct feeling of being *watched*—

A smile cracked open in the mana that made up the Overseer's body. *Cracked*. The energy rippled and twisted, and the mana itself trembled like it had been permanently rent.

There was an echo of pain from something that wasn't the Overseer.

Derivan charged again.

He was more careful, this time. [**Paralyzing Slash**] hadn't worked, but a grapple for [**Consume**] was still his best bet for time; all he had to do was get somewhere the Overseer wouldn't *reach*. A grapple counted as long as he was holding on to the target. He didn't need to actually pin the Overseer down.

Still wearing the same jagged, almost pained-looking smile, the Overseer reached down to swat him away. It was a strike that would kill him, and it moved too fast for him to dodge.

No.

> **Disguise Status activated.**
> **Level 86 —> Level 43**
> **Stat and skill suppression activated.**
> **Maximum health reduced.**
> **Maximum MP reduced.**

The hit struck him, sending him flying, but it didn't *kill* him, [**Oneshot Protection**] activating again. [**Disguise Status**] only reduced his maximum health; it didn't adjust his health percentage as a whole.

An obvious oversight. Misa had once talked about something similar, when discussing potential ways to abuse the cost of [**To Fall Yet Hold the Line**].

He hadn't been sure it would. Derivan took a breath he didn't need to take, then slammed his sword into the ground to kill his momentum. A split second later and he'd deactivated [**Disguise Status**] to charge forward again.

The Overseer was underestimating him; he'd paid attention to exactly what it had done. It attacked him as soon as he was within reach. It wasn't *guaranteed* that it would do the same thing twice, but that was often the pattern that other monsters followed, for reasons he didn't yet understand.

He didn't wait for the Overseer to attack—he didn't have the speed to dodge out of the way. Derivan jumped as soon as he was within reach, anticipating the attack.

It came.

The blow was powerful enough that the drag force pulled him along with it, even as it passed below his legs; Derivan went along with the flow, knowing he had only a split second of confusion in which he could act. He needed to get behind the Overseer. The change in his momentum helped. He darted to the side, leapt—

And clung to the Overseer's back.

It helped a lot that the Overseer's chosen body plan was, frankly, terrible. Long arms gave it better reach, but it couldn't maneuver them into position to hit him, and it didn't have the *joints*. He didn't know what skills the Overseer had, either, but as long as he could hold on for a *second*—

> [**Buff** [**Satiated**] applied!]

The Overseer vanished in a flare of black light. Derivan fell to the ground, almost stunned that it had worked.

It was only enough to guarantee them five seconds, but five seconds was a lot in combat.

". . . What happened?" Misa asked. She didn't ask if he'd won; she knew from the tension in his posture that he had not. But Derivan didn't have time to answer.

He'd gained skills, and they needed information. He glanced through what he'd gained as quickly as he could, flicking copies off to Vex and Misa at the same time; Sev couldn't receive system boxes while preparing [**Divine Communion**].

[Creature of Mana] [Passive] [No Grade] [Temporary]
You are born of mana and made of mana. Any mana-based spell effect that would be turned against you is altered to your benefit, whether to strike down your foes or to reinforce your form.
As an additional benefit, your physical form holds no true shape. You may, through an act of concentration, change the appearance of your form.

[Overseer] [Passive] [No Grade] [Temporary]
<ERROR>
Skill description and functionality not available. Locked to administrator access.

[Creature of Chaos] [Active Skill] [No Grade] [Temporary]
Shape mana to your will, imbuing it with the very essence of Chaos. Mana manipulated by you will be unstable in form and aspect, shifting rapidly until all possibilities are exhausted.
As an additional benefit, slow down or speed up the entropic progression of any object or creature with an act of concentration.

Derivan didn't know how [**Creature of Mana**] would affect Vex's spell; he trusted the mage to figure it out. If it was too risky to cast, he wouldn't cast it, and they would hope that Sev's spell would give them a way out of this situation. He knew very little about [**Divine Communion**], for Sev had never truly explained what it *was*, only that it could save them if they were caught in an impossible situation. It seemed powerful, but the fact that it could only be used once and had a cast time that made it nearly useless in combat made it . . . difficult to work with.

[**Overseer**] was . . . interesting. But there was nothing he could do with it.

[**Creature of Chaos**] was concerning. Clearly, whatever the Overseer was, it hadn't seen him as enough of a threat to use that ability. Derivan didn't know what *entropic progression* was, but it didn't sound good. He would have to make sure that the Overseer didn't get the opportunity to concentrate.

There wasn't much he could do about the first part of the skill. He'd just have to deal with it.

Two seconds had passed. Derivan felt something in his soul seem to shiver. Three.

Something inside his soul seemed to snap. Derivan felt a strange sense of impossible vertigo for a moment, as *something* occupied the same space as him; he'd never experienced his [**Satiated**] buff failing early before. He was thrown back violently, and he only barely managed to catch himself and prevent his health from being drained.

Ahead of him, the Overseer glared, its many eyes focused directly on him.

He'd made it angry.

CHAPTER 6

CHAINS

Derivan caught and strangled the flare of panic as his skill failed. What did that tell him?

There were only a few possibilities. One, somehow, the Overseer still had access to its skills, and one of them allowed it to mess with [**Consume**]. Two, it was at such a high level that it could simply ignore the skill. But . . . no. That didn't make sense. Skills were generally fairly absolute, the rules of the system inviolable. Sheer levels were rarely enough to allow their effects to be broken.

No; it had to be the first possibility. Whatever principle escaping from [**Consume**] operated on, the Overseer had done something to it. It couldn't have been [**Creature of Mana**]; [**Consume**] cost mana, but it wasn't a spell effect. And besides, the skill had *succeeded*.

That left [**Overseer**] and [**Creature of Chaos**]. [**Overseer**] was a dead end for speculation—

[It's [**Creature of Chaos**]], Vex sent him over the system. Derivan risked a quick glance at the wizard, who was sitting deep in [**Meditation**] but seemed perfectly capable of typing on the system interface while doing so. [Entropic progression is how the system talks about skill cooldowns.]

Ah. That explained things.

"Misa," Derivan said. "I will need your help for this. I cannot take it alone. I am sorry."

The half-orc nodded. "You have a plan?"

"I need you to taunt it," Derivan said. It was too focused on him now, enraged as it was. "I will do the rest."

The Overseer had taken a moment to recover from stumbling back into realspace, but now it *roared*, charging toward them. Clearly, it hadn't liked being trapped. Derivan readied himself—he could minimize the harm that Misa would be exposed to if he was quick.

The spot he'd clung to on the Overseer's back was still a weak point; it hadn't changed shape and couldn't reach its own back. The problem was that it knew what he could do, now, and wouldn't risk that happening again.

Sure enough, even as he tried to run around it, the Overseer rotated, keeping one of its many eyes on him.

But that was where Misa came in.

The trick with [**To Fall Yet Hold the Line**] was one that they had taken a while to figure out—that was the problem with skills that were vaguely worded. They had specific mechanics that needed to be tested to be really understood. Misa could block any attack at a flat cost of only ten percent of her health, *but only if she would otherwise fail to block it.* A partial block didn't count as a failure, which, oddly enough, made it less effective against monsters of her own level.

But it was good at holding the line against a limited number of enemies. It was even better at defending one ally, because—as they had discovered—she could keep adjusting the metaphorical "line" for her skill.

Derivan dashed forward. An attack came, this time not a physical blow he could dodge; he felt it before he saw it, the way the mana around the Overseer *twisted* in an ugly, impossible way. He felt something in his soul begin to twist in response—

—but then Misa was there. Her focus glowed.

If you would fail to block an attack, you do not.

It was an attack she would have failed to block. She did not.

Derivan leapt past her.

The Overseer reacted, surprised but not wanting to be caught off guard again. This time it reached for him, hand reaching forward in an impossibly fast grab—and once more, Misa was there to block it.

If Derivan had been hit, he would have been sent flying. With Misa, a steady reverberation rolled through the air instead, her body staying perfectly in place—what she needed to do to fully block the attack. Derivan took the opportunity to latch himself on to the Overseer, even as instinct forced the abomination to try to overcome the sudden barrier set before him.

He just needed one second. But the Overseer seemed prepared and *spun* just before the timer ticked down, fast enough that sheer inertia threw him off.

Then Misa did something he hadn't expected or known that she could do—she blocked *him*, appearing just behind him with her shoulder to his back to steady him, leaving him just within range to land on the Overseer again.

This time, Derivan grabbed the Overseer's head. It had the reach to attack him, but Misa blocked both attacks at once, somehow, her body twisting in an impossible blur even as a roar of pain bellowed out from her lungs. While she was distracted, mana pulsed around it, charging with lightning and slamming into his body, and he watched his health drain rapidly.

But not fast enough.

[**Buff** [**Satiated**] **applied!**]

The Overseer vanished for the second time in a blip of dark light; Derivan reacted instantly, reaching for the new skill hovering in the back of his mind. [**Creature of Chaos**]. The entropic progression portion of the skill required concentration, so he concentrated on slowing down the escape interval for [**Consume**], and—

—Maybe using [**Creature of Chaos**] counted as an attack?

"Misa," Derivan said. "Please try to block him. If you have enough health."

He didn't see what she did, or listen to what she said in response. He dove deeper into his soul, concentrating; he felt the skills ticking inside him. One temporary, one permanent. One holding back another, but slipping.

He held.

Five seconds passed.

Six. Seven.

Derivan didn't let the elation distract him. He kept his focus on the skill, feeling it tremble in his grasp. He felt almost like he was in a trance, balanced on a razor's edge; it was on the verge of collapsing, and he knew he would only be able to hold on to it for the barest second longer—

"Derivan!" Vex called out to him, and his eyes flared to life in his helmet.

That was a signal, if he'd ever heard one. He let go of the skill.

The Overseer burst into existence again, this time with a roar of fury that turned into a solid wave of sound; he saw barriers that Vex had placed shatter even as his body was physically rebuffed by a compressed wave of air. Too many eyes on the abomination's body fixated on Vex, narrowing with anger.

The air trembled with chaotic mana. Derivan saw Misa lying next to Vex; unconscious or dead, he couldn't tell. He saw Sev with his eyes screwed shut, still chanting. He saw Vex shouting something, determined—

He saw a lance of brilliant light shoot forward, twisting with a concept that threatened to drag his mind along with it. It pulled inexorably at the mana that surrounded it, dragging more and more energy into the sheer mass of the spell.

And then it struck.

The abomination staggered backward with a cry of something that sounded like shock, though the sound was alien to him. An impossible fire *burned* into an impossible being, ripping ephemeral holes in an ephemeral body.

For a long, eternal moment, everything seemed still and frozen.

Then he saw Vex collapse. The Overseer crashed into a wall of the crater, but that was a distant thing; his senses went numb as he began to run for his friends. Sev was the only one left standing, still speaking a silent prayer. That, more than anything else, told him this wasn't over.

Derivan ran as fast as he could to intercept, aiming for the space between them. The Overseer burst from the dirt, angrier than ever, wounded but not dead. Vex had done more damage than should have been possible with mana alone, and yet . . .

A massive spike of chaotic mana formed in front of the creature—not aimed at him but aimed at his friends. A reflection of the same spell Vex had used, but filled with malice, and *stronger.*

He ran harder, almost praying.

But he already knew he couldn't get there in time. He didn't know what he would do if he *could.* Misa was still unconscious.

The mana moved faster than he could, a lance almost the same as Vex's blasting back toward them.

Sev opened his eyes. They shone with a brilliant blue.

"[**Divine Communion**]," he spoke.

<#E##RRO##R>

A rift opened.

It was somewhere, nowhere, and everywhere, all at once. In its wake, reality seemed to bend and then fracture.

The Overseer, the crater, and the mana crystals vanished. The system interface cracked. The rift grew.

And then they were in a void.

But that void was not empty.

Chains stretched into the sky; rusting, burning chains, with fire flaking off the dense, dusty metal. Chains were scattered around on the floor, too, all of them burning with the same strange flame. They cast an eerie glow onto the nothingness that was the ground Derivan stood on.

They led to an odd, dark speck floating in the air, too far away to properly see.

Derivan stared. None of this made any sense to him.

"...What is this place?" Sev's voice echoed in the emptiness. It was the first time Derivan had ever heard their cleric sound so hesitant. The sound was enough to snap Derivan's attention back in the direction of his friends, and he breathed a small sigh of relief to see that everyone was fine. Vex and Misa were both slowly getting to their feet, looking around in no small amount of confusion.

None of them had the chance to say a word before Sev cursed under his breath. "No, shit, I *know* this place," he muttered, his voice low, almost confused. "I— Shit, is that Onyx?"

He took one step, then two—and then he was running toward the figure in the distance.

"Hey!" Misa called out, but Sev ignored her; she cursed under her breath, reaching out to steady Vex as Derivan approached them.

"You are both okay?" he asked, a little uncertain. "I was . . . I am worried. I did not see what happened."

"Honestly I have no idea what the fuck happened either," Misa answered, grimacing a bit as she looked at her status. "My health is still shot. I'm not dead, but I'm also not regenerating. Sev never mentioned [**Divine Communion**] slapping us all into a big fuckoff void, did he?"

"I believe I would have remembered it if he had," Derivan said dryly, but the humor helped. Misa was . . . not *okay*, perhaps, but she was feeling well enough to make jokes, and that was enough for now. It would have to be.

Vex, on the other hand, wasn't paying attention to either of them. He was kneeling down next to the chains, staring at the fire that was slowly eating away at the false metal. It took him a moment to realize that both Misa and Derivan were looking at him questioningly, and he shook his head helplessly in response. "This fire is weird. I think it's . . . I think it's my magic?"

"... *Your* magic?" Misa asked, raising an eyebrow—but she looked up as she spoke, and her eyes sharpened. She let out a sharp curse. "Shit. Okay, questions later. We gotta go after Sev."

Derivan glanced in the cleric's direction. He was still running full-tilt toward the speck in the distance, heedless of any potential danger. With a curse and a quick apology, he grabbed Misa and Vex, the former grumbling and the latter letting out a high-pitched yelp.

It was the only way they'd catch up with Sev, though.

Even then, by the time they caught up with the cleric, he was already *there*, standing just in front of the figure they'd seen in the distance. Sev was apparently capable of running very quickly when he wanted to.

Now that they were closer, they could see what Sev had apparently realized long before them. The chains led to a *person*, a figure cut out of pitch-black stone whose arms and feet were bound in layered, twisting chains. The chains there didn't burn; the fire was still moving slowly, inching up from what might have been miles away.

The slow rise and fall of the figure's chest—and the blood dripping from him, a thick, viscous fluid—were the only indications that he was anything more than a chiseled sculpture.

"I don't understand," Sev said softly. He reached out, but whoever this was hung too far up for Sev to reach. His fingers grazed the chains leading up to his feet, instead. The cleric seemed deeply shaken. "I thought . . ."

"Who is Onyx?" It was Misa that spoke, but her voice was surprisingly gentle. She placed a hand on Sev's shoulder, and it seemed to startle him enough to nudge him back to reality.

"He is . . . the god I work with," Sev answered, looking helplessly at Misa, then at the rest of the party. "I mean. I don't know if that's the right way to put it. But I don't— That's not the point. This is him, I think. But I don't . . ."

I don't know what happened. The words were left unspoken, the cleric staring up at the figure of his god mutely. All of them were briefly silent, taking in the sight.

This was supposed to be a *god*?

Derivan didn't know much about the gods, but the idea of anyone or anything doing this to a god chilled him.

Vex was the first one among them to speak.

"The notification. When the Overseer was called. The second one, that was red—remember what it said?"

"'*Repent, sinner, for ye are but a lamb before the slaughter,*'" Sev answered almost automatically. His face was ashen. Vex nodded.

"I . . . I thought the singular use of *sinner* was a mistake, or a reference to just one of us. But . . . maybe it wasn't talking about *us*." The lizard knelt, a finger brushing along the chains. "That fire was my magic," he said quietly.

"It shouldn't be *here*, wherever this is. I cast it on the Overseer. The only way my magic could be here is if these chains are somehow linked to the Overseer itself."

None of them knew how to react. They shared concerned gazes, with Sev's expression looking a little more distraught and distressed as they stood beneath the unconscious god. Derivan placed a hand on the cleric's shoulder.

"Perhaps you could heal him?" Derivan suggested softly. Sev looked like he was aching to do *something*. Even now, a dark fluid dripped down onto the ground from Onyx's body, slowly evaporating into nothingness. Sev grimaced a bit, looking up at the figure hanging in the air. "Or we could try to break the chains."

"I . . . Maybe. I don't know what would happen if I tried." Sev bit his lip, looking conflicted. "Skills don't work properly here. They're stronger sometimes, weaker other times. Sometimes, the effect of the skill is completely twisted. I'll try to heal him, and then hopefully he'll have some answers for us, and can help us break the chains."

Sev seemed to feel a little better as he spoke, at least. He was the kind of person that worked better when he had a plan to follow. He took a steadying breath and focused, reaching for a place within him that Derivan couldn't see.

Derivan could feel the power gathering, though. He wondered how Sev knew any of this at all, but it seemed inappropriate to ask, and before he could voice his concerns Sev spoke, his voice reverberating: "[**Divine Inhalation**]."

It was a strange name for a healing spell, Derivan thought, but he hardly had time to focus on it. There was a sharp flare of light, almost glaring in its intensity.

And yet—for all the power the spell seemed to have, and for all that it sent Sev staggering backward, panting like it had torn out some vital piece of him—nothing seemed to change.

The god continued to bleed. The chains continued to burn, the fire slowly inching closer.

Sev seemed to sag, something inside him folding in on itself. Derivan was about to suggest trying to break the chains anyway, but before he could, Onyx spoke.

His voice was quiet and weak, far from what Derivan imagined the voice of a god would be—and yet beneath that weakness was a quiet fortitude and a well of preserved strength. *Intentionally* preserved strength, even, though Derivan wasn't sure where that certainty came from.

"Your friend has weakened my chains," he said. Sev startled, almost reaching out—but he couldn't reach Onyx any more than he could before. "And you have restored some small part of me. I can . . . pull this form away. Back into the upper planes. You must . . . leave. The dungeon will form. It will have answers."

"We are here now," Derivan said. "Can we not help you?"

"We could smash up the chains," Misa said, eyeing them critically. "They don't look that strong."

"I can burn them again," Vex offered.

Onyx offered them all a small, pained smile. "You cannot break them now. Not . . . as you are."

"I thought I saved you," Sev said, his voice small.

Onyx paused, and spoke gently. "You did."

There was a sense of finality to those words; a sense of an *ending*. A good-bye, perhaps. But there was no time to make sense of it, for there was also the sense of a skill petering out, of a god leveraging what limited strength he retained to drag a metaphysical body far, far away.

And then they were back, just outside the crater that had once been the Mana Nucleus. It was home to a freshly formed dungeon made of towering blue stone. None of them spared it a second glance; it was all too . . . normal. Pristine. Shining there like nothing had happened.

They'd won an impossible battle.

But somehow, it didn't feel like a victory.

CHAPTER 7

A COMPLETE DISREGARD FOR FATE

The party was quiet and downcast, even as they began their journey back toward the Guild. They had reported the formation of the dungeon, of course. That was a necessary procedure, and it helped them, too, to engage with something approaching normal. The dungeon meant better resources for everyone in the region, possibly better gear. It was entirely possible that the mana crystal shortage for all the nearby villages could be solved with this, depending on how the politics of dungeon ownership shook out.

They were *not* going into the dungeon immediately. That was a sure-fire way to die: there were classes specifically oriented toward scouting out dungeons, understanding their traps and their dangers. The Adventurers' Guild would rank the dungeon, and then they would delve it. It was procedure.

But Onyx had said they would find answers in the dungeon. Why? Something was clearly wrong. Between the danger in the Mana Nucleus, the abnormal formation of the dungeon, the strange messages from the system . . .

The imprisonment of a god.

There was a lot on their minds, simply put. Sev seemed worried and withdrawn, his mind no doubt on his own god's imprisonment and state of being.

Derivan was the first one to speak. He stopped abruptly in his tracks, and the rest of the party stopped as well, turning to look at him; the armor looked . . . disturbed.

"You know what I am," Derivan said softly. "You knew, even before it was revealed back there. It did not bother you?"

There was a brief silence. Misa and Sev glanced at each other; Vex held back a little more, looking nervous.

Sev was the one that answered, seeming to put aside his worry for now. "Kind of. I had a pretty strong suspicion, and Misa felt the same way when she joined. We talked about it, and we decided it didn't really matter."

Derivan glanced at Misa, who shrugged. "Look, you saved me, I saved you, that's enough reason for me to trust anyone."

"We were just waiting for you to be comfortable with telling us," Sev continued. He gave Vex an apologetic look. "It was one of the things we were going to tell you."

"I sort of guessed anyway," Vex admitted. He took a breath and seemed to let his nervousness flow out of him. Derivan couldn't help a small smile. The lizard had been incredibly nervous when he'd first joined them, terrified of letting even the smallest detail slip about his class, his personal life.

He was still shy, but he'd gained a lot of confidence, at least around his team. Vex continued, looking earnestly at Derivan. "Your armor's magic isn't right for a curse. I mean, I didn't know exactly what was going on, but I figured you had some kind of secret. I just didn't really care, and I trusted you would tell me—tell *us* eventually."

Vex looked down, now a little bit nervous again. Open secret or not, it felt strange to be talking about his class. ". . . Besides, it's not like I wasn't hiding my own secret."

"Right!" Misa burst out, looking excited—or perhaps simply relieved to have something to latch on to that wasn't so heavy. "What the heck is a [**Chromaturgist**]? How the fuck is it so powerful?"

Vex chuckled a bit, though he avoided looking directly at Misa, casting his gaze off into the distance instead. He was *proud* of his accomplishments; it just wasn't something he'd ever really had the opportunity to boast about. "It's . . . hard to explain. It's a class that lets me analyze, deconstruct, and reconstruct magic. The spells were powerful because I figured out how to use ambient mana in my spells, and the ambient mana in the Nucleus was really concentrated."

Misa let out a whistle. "Sounds strong. Especially once the class grows."

"Says the woman that can block *anything*," Vex chuckled. "I've never seen anyone fight like you do."

"That skill is limited," Misa said with a scowl. There was a small beat, and then she smiled. ". . . but I guess it is pretty cool."

Derivan smiled a bit, listening to his friends banter. The faint glow in his eyes strengthened briefly, then dimmed again. Something had felt strange the moment they left the Nucleus, and that feeling of wrongness was only growing. It was the reason he'd stopped.

He'd thought at first that he simply needed to ask about how they knew, partially to break the silence, and partially to assure himself that his companions truly didn't care that he was what the system deemed a monster. But now, everything seemed fine, and yet . . .

Derivan remembered Sev's words. *I don't think it'll like that you're playing outside the role it gave you.* Implying that the system was . . . alive? That it didn't like his presence, his ability to have his own will?

He felt a noxious seed coil around his heart, the tendrils of a system he didn't understand.

You are an infiltrator, it told him. Not in so many words but in a distinct set of impulses and instincts he now recognized as foreign. *You are discovered. You must eliminate those who know.*

I will do no such thing, Derivan thought in return, and he forced his will against those alien instincts; they fought and clawed against him, but they were impulses that he could ignore.

For now.

"I cannot stay," the armor said quietly. Misa and Vex both startled, looking up at him; their protests overlapped one another, loud and indignant.

"What?! You can't just—"

"You don't have to—"

Sev, on the other hand . . . He didn't seem to react nearly as strongly. He watched Derivan carefully, instead, a mild furrow in his brows and a sadness in his eyes; Derivan looked at the cleric, bowing his head slightly.

"You know why I must leave," he said.

Sev took in the words—and then slowly nodded. "I can guess," the cleric answered.

"Don't give me this cryptic *bullshit!*" Misa half-exploded, suddenly genuinely angry. "Sev, you've told me you need to keep secrets, *and I trust you.* But you need to explain what we just saw, because I'm not just going to accept at face value that Derivan needs to leave. He just risked his life to help us survive whatever the fuck that was."

She looked willing to fight him on it, too. Even Vex's fists were balled up, though it seemed subconscious on his part.

"I—I would understand if you wanted to leave," the lizardkin said, looking up at his friend. It seemed like even saying those words were a struggle for him. "But you don't seem like you want to."

Ah.

That hurt. It was a painful truth.

Derivan looked around. He saw Misa's eyes blaze with a righteous anger, undirected though it was. He saw Vex stand surprisingly tall, meeting his gaze with a firmness he wouldn't have managed a month before. He saw Sev look at him and give him a slight, small nod, and he took it as a cue to explain.

"You are right in that I do not want to leave," he admitted. "But what Sev said before, that I had to keep my secret . . . I think I would have told you sooner, if the choice had truly been my own. But it was not. I did not realize it until now."

He hesitated, searching for the words. "This system is . . . complicated. I do not know how it operates, or why it exists. But at least for monsters"— here he winced at the word, hating the label—"it appears to come with . . . instincts. Instructions. It was subtle enough for me to miss it before, and I was unhindered when you did not know what I was, for infiltrators must blend in as much as possible. But now that you do . . ."

"The system is trying to force him to attack," Sev said. He watched Derivan carefully, but he didn't seem afraid. The armor wondered if he was being wise or foolish, heartened as he was by the cleric's trust. "But it cannot. Because you are not what the system believes you are."

"And yet I am." Derivan said, though he spoke with no small amount of sorrow. "I understand and appreciate your faith in me, but it seems unavoidable that I will be a risk. Even now, I feel the system pushing my role upon me."

To their credit, both Misa and Vex took a moment to absorb this information. Neither immediately rejected Derivan, nor insisted that he stay; when they finally spoke, it was with the firmness of a friend that had given the situation its due consideration.

Which, admittedly, meant that it was a long, painful silence before either of them spoke. But he was all the more certain that they spoke with sincerity.

"I'm okay with that risk," Misa said. She folded her arms, brow furrowing slightly, but with a steadily growing confidence. "I don't think it's right that you'd have to leave us because of something out of your control. Besides, with us, we can at least keep an eye on you. If you don't have support to keep you anchored, and your instincts are forced on you as you say . . ."

She hesitated, then shook her head. "It's easier to fight your darkest thoughts when you have friends, Derivan. If you push those around you away, you leave yourself with nothing to hold on to. Trust me. I've been there."

"You're a friend. I might be being selfish, but I just don't want you to leave," Vex said simply. Derivan blinked in surprise, but the lizardkin stared back at him with a certitude in his eyes that he'd never seen before. Vex had come up with and discarded a hundred different rationalizations, and ended on simple honesty. "I'd say I'm sorry, but I'm really not."

Sev smiled a small smile. "How about it, Derivan? I believe you're better off with us than out there by yourself, too. I understand why you think you have to leave, but let's be honest.

"No one in this group gives a damn what the system thinks. *Every single one of us* breaks the system in some stupid way, and frankly, if we need to break it again to keep you with us? Do you think we'd even hesitate?"

Derivan paused. "I am a risk," he said again, uncertain.

"Yeah, no," Misa said. "I'm with Sev on this. Let's smash the system."

"At least a little bit," Vex said, and then when Misa looked at him, he threw his arms up. "Or a lot! A lot, if Derivan needs it."

"If you're a risk, I think we get the right to choose whether we take that risk or not," Sev said. "And honestly, I think we've all chosen. You earned your place with us long ago, Derivan."

"Saved our asses one time too many, too," Misa added.

"And mine!" Vex piped up. To be included? Derivan couldn't help chuckling, regardless, feeling a warmth blossom inside of him as he looked at his companions—his friends. He shouldn't have doubted them for a second. Tell them the system was restraining him, and of course they'd leap to the conclusion of *breaking the system.*

Again.

The other two nodded, firmly; Derivan didn't know what to say. Slowly, he stepped forward—only now realizing that the other three stood in a circle with a space they'd left open just for him.

"Now!" Sev clapped his hands together; his smile was a genuine one, with a hint of the mischievous spark he sometimes had. "I have a *really stupid plan.* Hey, Misa. Don't you think this kind of intrusiveness miiight count as . . . say, an attack?"

There was a pause.

"Oh, by the fucking gods, you cannot be serious." Misa stared, seeming delighted. "Wait, are you serious? Can I— Oh, that would be stupid. Is this a *continuous* attack, though? That might drain my health almost instantly. The skill's weird with continuous attacks."

"It might. But you've got a really good cleric." Sev smirked with just a bit of smugness, then lost it as he added, "But uh, we can try a different plan if you feel like that's too risky—"

"Are you kidding me? I'm in," Misa said with barely a second's thought.

She had *one* stupid bullshit skill that she could use frequently, and she would use it every time she could.

"Would just blocking it be enough?" Vex asked, worried. "I mean, if she stops blocking it . . ."

"Probably not," Sev said, shaking his head. "But that's where you come in, 'cause I've got it on good authority that the system isn't just changing him; it's using magic. It's just using *really subtle* magic. You won't be able to see it directly, but you'll be able to see how Misa blocks him, and . . . well, I mean, I hope that's enough. That's where my plan ends. But we can always find other methods if this doesn't work."

"Okay." Vex nodded. He felt he normally would have protested or asked questions about what kind of magic this was, but he was caught up in the current; they were going to fix a problem! "Let's do it."

Derivan felt rather bemused as the whole party set themselves up around him. Misa stood in front of him, feeling a bit silly as she held out her mace, while Vex stood just beside them both, watching intently. Sev was a little farther back, carefully keeping his healing magic focused on Misa.

"Ready?" Misa asked him. He nodded.

Misa activated [**To Fall Yet Hold the Line**].

Truth be told, everything after that happened too quickly for Derivan to keep track of, with half his focus split on whatever the system was doing to him.

Misa held up her mace and it *flickered*, shifting rapidly. For a moment, she held a sword, then her traditional mace again, though it looked strange . . . it then became a wizard's focus, then a cleric's staff.

There was a flare of light and magic.

Vex shouted something, his voice full of hope. Sev's magic twisted through the air, touching on Misa, keeping her healed so she could maintain the block even as the oppressing sensation of thoughts not his own left Derivan, however temporarily.

Vex did something, reaching out and forward, and the air in front of him immediately shimmered with notifications.

WARNING: ###### aspect magic is not allowed—

WARNING: Users are recommended to immediately cease—

"Oh, fuck you!" Misa shouted distantly. Vex made a noise that was a distinct sound of agreement.

<ERROR>
Local ###### boundary in flux. System state unable to match local state. Resetting . . .

Reset partially successful. No fallback state found. Data corrupted.

Adjusting . . .

Level 86 Infiltrating Armor —> Derivan, Level <ERROR>

Derivan blinked, the glow of his eyes flickering in his helmet as he stared at the box. "Oh."

He had a *name*.

"Did it work?" Misa grinned at him, panting. Vex was too out of breath to even speak. Even Sev was trembling slightly, in the same way his magic always seemed to take an odd, physical toll on him.

Derivan checked his status, putting aside the feelings that were threatening to overwhelm him for the moment. The sight of the screen was both a relief and concerning, all at once.

Derivan, Level <ERROR>
Health: <ERROR>
Mana: <ERROR>

Stats:
<ERROR>

Skill List:
<ERROR>

"The system does seem to have updated," Derivan said, though he said it a little doubtfully. He felt in his soul again for the grip of the system, and it seemed duller; not missing, but lesser.

Different, perhaps.

"I am no longer an Infiltrating Armor. Not according to my status. I . . . have a name now, the one I chose for myself. But I also have no class, and my level, skills, and stats all report only errors."

"Huh," Sev said. "But . . . the problem is fixed, right?"

"There are no foreign impulses pressing down on me," Derivan said quietly. He looked at his friends, feeling a weight lift from a heart he didn't technically have. "I . . . It is different. Peaceful. *I have a name.* I have had to look at my status for so long, at a screen that would tell me that my name was not my own . . . I do not have words, except perhaps 'thank you.'"

They all smiled at him. Vex outright gave him a hug, and though it was a little awkward, Derivan tried to hug him back. He'd have to learn how to do that without stabbing someone with one of his spikes one of these days, though Vex didn't particularly seem to mind the way they poked into him.

"We should probably keep heading back," Sev said, gesturing to the road ahead. "It's getting late."

So they did. They had a lot more to talk about, and a lot they needed to try and understand—but for now, at least, there was an unspoken agreement that they would do it *later*.

They needed normalcy and time to collect their thoughts.

And then . . . well, it would be time for a long talk, and to figure out how they would get their answers.

CHAPTER 8

ANSWERS. ALSO, MORE QUESTIONS.

"A *dungeon* formed?" the clerk asked incredulously. "Dungeons don't just form without warning. Our scouts would've noticed!"

"Max," Sev said, rubbing his temples tiredly. "You're my favorite clerk, but now isn't the time for this. That was *exhausting*. We need our pay and like five consecutive days of sleep."

"Maybe more," Misa chipped in. Vex nodded as seriously as he could, from his position half-hidden behind Derivan.

"Sorry," Max said, though she sounded only halfway apologetic. She gave them a genuine smile, all traces of disbelief and incredulity vanishing as she glanced at Misa and the others. "It's a bit of an inside joke. I can't believe you guys managed to get a grade-six, though. That dungeon's going to be terrifying."

"Glad I'm not the one that'll have to do the paperwork," Sev joked, and Max stuck her tongue out at him. She was rapidly counting out their pay even while she spoke, packing coins into a pouch that seemed too small to fit them all. It wasn't even a *magical* pouch; just the effect of some sort of skill, it seemed.

"Just wait," she threatened. "You're going to move up in this guild and then you're going to have to do *all* the paperwork. You're only a Bronze-ranked team and you survived a solo formation event! I guarantee the Guildmaster is going to be *interested*."

"If people moved up based on power alone, I'd be a bit worried about the future of the Guild," Sev said dryly.

"Good thing they don't," Max said cheerfully, grinning as she handed him the pouch. "But you can't count on that. Your team passes all the other requirements, too."

"There are other requirements?" Derivan asked curiously.

"Of course!" Max grinned at him, then lowered her voice to speak in a conspiratorial whisper. "Just don't tell the other teams. It's a secret."

"Doesn't seem like much of a secret if we can talk about it here," Misa commented.

"I mean, it's a little bit of an open secret," Max admitted. "So it's not the end of the world if you tell someone. But character tests are more honest when people don't know that it's a test."

"You're doing character tests?" Vex asked, peeking out at Max. The clerk shrugged and nodded.

"Well, yeah. Think about what the Adventurers' Guild does."

". . . Adventure?" Vex said, perplexed.

"We help people," Max laughed. "I mean, yes, we 'adventure,' but what does that even mean, really? 'Adventurers' Guild' isn't really a name we came up with; we just picked it up from the planeshifted folk that ended up here. Most of the time, the quests we have up on the board are meant to help out the villages that aren't being directly supported by any of the Prime Kingdoms."

"Huh," Misa said. "I mean, the kill quests and collection quests are obviously those. But the exploration ones?"

"Even the ones about exploring ruins are, technically, almost always ruins that happen to have monster infestations that are troubling the small towns nearby," Max said. "Don't get me wrong. We're interested in learning more about the history of the world, too. There's too much missing from our history. We *do* encourage 'adventuring,' insofar as adventuring involves digging out the mysteries packed beneath the earth, or figuring out the intricacies of a dungeon."

"That's why you need character tests," Vex said. Max nodded.

"Can't just have powerful assholes running around doing whatever they want on rank," Max said dryly. "Mind you, our system isn't perfect. The Guild is involved in a lot of regional politics, and that means we have to make exceptions sometimes, and sometimes those exceptions are really stupid. But uh . . . it's not my place to talk about those. And there are people coming." She gave them a bright smile. "You should probably leave. These ones haven't adapted to the culture here yet."

"Oh god," Sev groaned. "Good luck."

"You know I can handle 'em." Max winked, shooing them up the stairs. Then, rather abruptly, she settled back into the perfect image of a bored clerk. The party gathered their belongings and began to traipse up the stairs even as the door slammed open.

Derivan, last up the stairs, just barely caught Max gasping in what he recognized now as exaggerated surprise.

"A *wyrm?* Wyrms don't just appear without warning. Our scouts would have noticed!"

—m—

"She did *what*?" Misa laughed. delightedly, grinning wide, as Derivan explained what he'd heard while they were leaving. "There's no way that keeps working."

The four of them were gathered briefly in Sev's room to talk before they retired for the night—Vex, in particular, looked almost like he was about to fall asleep on his feet. Derivan stood next to him, giving the poor lizard something to lean on as he tried not to pass out entirely.

"It does, and you would've seen it yourself if you didn't keep dragging everyone else off to the bar every time we come back to the Guild," Sev said dryly, though a smirk twitched at the edge of his mouth. "This is the first time you haven't wanted to drink."

"This is the first time I've been *too tired* to drink!" Misa said, as if that explained everything; Sev just rolled his eyes and chuckled.

There was a momentary, peaceable sort of silence.

Then Misa shook her head, seeming to gather herself, and let out a breath.

"Okay," she said. Vex perked up a bit, hearing the seriousness in her tone, the lizardkin trying to banish the sleepiness from his frame. "Sev, listen. I trust you. I don't believe you'd keep a secret from us without a very good reason. But it's . . . Secrets can get teams like us killed, you know? We don't know your class, we don't know your skills, and you seem to know things you shouldn't. What *can* you tell us?"

Sev blinked twice, then seemed to sag slightly. He glanced at Vex and Derivan both, who stared at him not with suspicion but with compassion; they seemed worried about him.

So there was that. Even Misa was more speaking out of concern for the party than any anger toward him.

He sighed.

"I think I can tell you more than before," the cleric said quietly. "And we need to talk about what happened with Onyx at the end there, anyway. It's relevant. I'm just not sure that you'll like it. But . . . well, here."

"My class is [**Traces of the Lost**]. It's a unique class that evolved out of my old cleric class, and its primary feature is that it allows . . . allowed me to sacrifice aspects of my person to achieve an effect. It still kinda does, I guess. But nothing big anymore."

". . . Sacrifice?" Vex looked up at Sev, worried. Misa just stared sharply at him, and Derivan frowned in his own way, a hint of severity touching his eyes.

"Yeah. Sacrifice." Sev smiled humorlessly, then shook his head and leaned back against the wall. "It sucked, let me tell you. It was—maybe even is—a powerful class, don't get me wrong, but . . . there I was, with a class that let me achieve almost anything. And I couldn't do anything big with it. It was too *dangerous* to do anything big with it, *because* it was a powerful class, and if I lost too much of who I was then there'd be a monster with that class, and it'd be a monster wearing my skin."

He glanced at Derivan. ". . . Maybe I shouldn't use the word *monster*. Sorry."

"That is hardly the problem," Derivan said, continuing to frown severely at their cleric.

"Yeah, what the fuck?" Misa said. "Don't tell me you've had to do that every time you heal us."

"No, I have normal healing spells from my old cleric class that don't rely on that mechanic," Sev said with a small chuckle. Then he paused and amended the statement slightly. "Okay, sometimes. It depends on what I'm healing. But like I said, I can't make big sacrifices anymore without risking too much of myself. Small ones don't harm me. I don't really have a spell that cures hangovers, for example, but I can sacrifice a little bit of my well-being to heal it, and it just gives me a minor headache in return."

"That's not okay. You can't just do that to yourself without *telling* us about it," Misa protested. "It was just a stupid hangover! I would've gotten over it!"

"That is why your hands were shaking after healing them," Derivan surmised. "Sev. Such sacrifices, even if they are small . . . We are your friends. We deserve to know what you are doing for us."

"And to choose if you get to do it," Vex added, huffing slightly. "I mean . . . don't get me wrong. Thank you. But that's . . ."

"There is a bigger question, I think," Derivan said. "What happened? What did you sacrifice?"

Sev sighed. "Yeah. I'm . . . Okay, so, you guys know that I'm one of the planeshifted, from a place called Earth. But you know I don't remember much about it."

"You fed us some story about having amnesia, then heavily implied you were lying about it, because you suck at lying," Misa said dryly. Sev chuckled slightly at that, allowing himself a small smile.

"Well, yeah. The truth is . . . Well. You remember how Onyx said I saved him?"

"Yeah," Misa said, her brow furrowing.

"The system tried to erase him," Sev said bluntly.

"*What?*" Misa and Vex both asked at the same time. Derivan's eyes merely narrowed slightly, a mixture of curiosity and worry within them.

"I thought the gods *made* the system," Vex said, almost flustered. "If they didn't, then—"

"Let us allow Sev to explain, Vex," Derivan said gently, touching the lizardkin on the arm; Vex fell silent at that, nodding but looking a little bit shaken.

"When the system tries to erase a god, all the followers of that god have to pick a new one," Sev said. "And if you refuse, the system starts to erase you. Pieces of you. Bit by bit." He smiled a wry, somewhat pained smile.

"You refused? I mean, no offense, but you're not exactly . . . very devout." Misa frowned.

"Do I need to be?" Sev asked. He waited a moment, half-expecting a response, and when Misa just stared at him questioningly, he sighed. "Onyx was—is, I hope—my friend. I wanted to be a cleric to heal, and I just picked one of the lesser-known gods, thinking at most I'd have to pretend to worship someone for a bit. But he never once asked me to *worship* him. We just . . . talked. And, you know, it turned out he was a pretty cool guy."

"You just . . . hung out with a god?" Vex asked blankly.

"I hung out with a person," Sev corrected. "He just happened to be a powerful one."

"You're very strange," Misa muttered. Vex made a noise of agreement, looking like his world had been rocked for the second time. Derivan, on the other hand, wasn't particularly surprised. Sev had also referred to *him* as "a pretty cool guy" once, so this was nothing new for him.

"But yeah. The system wanted to erase Onyx, but I refused to choose a new god. I just kept trying to heal him while the system was doing its thing, and one of the heals caught on something, and . . . I'm not sure what happened. It's kind of a blur. It interacted with my class in some way and tore a huge chunk out of my memories. Tore a huge chunk out of my freedom, too, present and future. It's why I couldn't talk about this before—I literally *couldn't*. And then . . ."

There, Sev frowned. "I can't talk about the rest of it," he admitted. "I think part of it is still going. The effect hasn't finished resolving yet. But everything I know, I know because of that incident. It planted some pieces of knowledge that I guess it decided I needed."

There was a small silence.

"Sorry," Sev said. "I know it's a lot. I was hoping we could all rest before I talked about it."

"I'm the one that asked," Misa said, shaking her head. "Look, I . . . Thank you for telling us. This is what you meant when you said you thought you saved him?"

"Yeah," Sev said. "He's . . . been quiet after that. I just thought he needed time to recover. I didn't think . . . I don't know what all that was. I want to help him. But I don't know what to *do*." He clenched his fists briefly.

Vex, Misa, and Derivan all glanced at each other. "There is only one place to start," Derivan said. "We were told we would find answers in the dungeon. So we will delve it, when we are able."

"You guys don't have to do this, you know," Sev said.

"Bullshit," Misa said, Vex nodding in agreement. "We're a team. Your problems are ours, and even if they *weren't*, this would be serious enough to warrant investigation. But we're still going to have to wait for the scouts to get back; it's too dangerous to just rush into a dungeon with no information."

"Of course," Sev nodded, sighing tiredly. This time the silence that followed was one of shared camaraderie, a moment of focus they all gave toward a goal they decided to share. Derivan was the first one to break that silence, as Vex began to droop.

"Let us get some rest, for now," Derivan said. "I believe we are all due one. It has been a long day, and while Vex is trying his best, he appears to be seconds away from falling asleep."

"'M fine," Vex protested—but he staggered a bit as he tried to straighten himself. Derivan caught him before he could fall, shaking his head.

"You are not. We need rest." Derivan picked up the entire wizard, despite his protests. "I will take you to your room. Again."

—◊—

After depositing Vex inside his room—*carefully* avoiding the many traps still laid all across the floor—Derivan returned to his own and contemplated the bed. He had previously never exactly *slept*. It was an organic need that he'd never really understood.

Now, though, he found that his consciousness seemed unmoored and drifting. It was different from anything he'd ever felt before. Perhaps this was what sleep was like? Now that his status had changed and the system viewed him as something different, could he experience what other beings experienced?

Something told him it didn't work like that. He climbed into the bed anyway, wincing slightly as some of his armor spikes punctured the fabric.

If nothing else, these were questions that he could ask now without worrying that his identity would be discovered. It was a surprisingly freeing realization.

His mind wandered, and kept wandering, until he no longer saw the ceiling above him but an impossible, empty void. In that void, he saw shapes that twisted and spun into more impossibilities, swimming through the air like they were fish. He heard what seemed like voices, though they echoed directly into his mind.

He had no idea what any of this was or what was happening. Voices came and went, asking questions and eventually losing interest. He would have asked questions of his own, but unmoored as his thoughts were, he didn't think to ask anything in turn; he simply answered the questions as they came.

The first was a bright, almost-manic voice, accompanied by a shape that twisted in on itself with fractal brilliance.

How are the Bright-Lights, the Not-Dark! The stars, you call them! Do they still spin and turn? Do they speak to the people, bring them joy and terror?

The stars? They do not speak. They have always been silent.

Bah! What of the Great Kingdom? Does it still thrive?

There are three Prime Kingdoms. I do not know which of them you speak of.

A different voice came then, softer and almost seductive. It seemed to caress his mind when it spoke, and he found it deeply uncomfortable.

Tell me of my children. The thought-forms, the hidden-shadows. Do they fill the skies and forests?

I have not heard of them. I do not know what they are.

Perhaps they yet hide . . .

The second voice drifted away, and Derivan found he was glad of it. The third one was boisterous, loud.

Tell me of the conquest of Redle! It must have been a glorious battle.

I am afraid I cannot answer. I have heard of no such place.

Impossible! Redle was on the verge of conquering the continent! Has their name faded so thoroughly?

That voice faded, seeming to mutter to itself.

The final voice was one of simple curiosity.

What are you?

Derivan's answer was honest.

I cannot say. I do not know.

You will. You must.

Derivan woke up. He was disoriented, at first, from what might have been dreams—and yet the more he tried to think on them, the more they slipped from his mind. He'd heard Vex discussing the experience of dreaming before. Perhaps this was what it was? It seemed . . . strange. Uncomfortable.

Even that feeling of discomfort passed quickly, though, leaving only a lingering doubt.

Shaking his head, Derivan left the bed—wincing as his spikes tore yet another hole in the fabric.

Time to find the others.

—⁓—

"You want me to fight . . . a slime?" Derivan asked curiously. He stared at the slime he was being presented with—it was a white, wobbly thing that sat at level one. It might as well have been a pet. "Why?"

"We don't really have anything else to do until we resupply and the scouts report back about the dungeon. And right now, we don't know how much health you have or if I can even heal you," Sev pointed out. "It's better that we start small, figure out what you can and can't do *before* we head into the potentially deadly dungeon. Slimes are the perfect first target."

Vex nodded; he'd clearly discussed this with Sev while Derivan was still . . . asleep, if that was what that was. Misa was just standing nearby, watching.

Derivan stared at the slime. It stared back, wobbling. Slowly, he raised his sword; but the whole situation felt just a little bit ridiculous. He understood the logic, but surely his test could be a little more . . . dignified.

The slime wobbled, this time a little more aggressively. Or perhaps he was imagining it?

"Perhaps we can find some wolves?" Derivan offered. The slime was so nonthreatening, he couldn't quite bring himself to stab it. "I am sure the danger would be minimal with your assistance."

"This is the safest option we've got," Misa answered seriously. But she was fighting a bit of a smirk.

". . . All right," Derivan replied with a small sigh. He readied his sword, staring down the slime as it began to wobble even more aggressively.

Then, before he could bring himself to attack, it launched itself at him.

Derivan tried to react, but *missed*. It was an abrupt and disconcerting realization that he was nowhere near as fast as he was used to being. The slime slipped past his blade, rocketing toward him . . .

. . . and promptly splattered itself on his helmet.

Your party has killed a Level 1 Regenerating Slime!

"Oh," Derivan said.

"Wait, what? What happened?" Sev asked, blinking a bit. "Is that *possible*?"

"Does your armor reflect damage?" Vex asked, peering at him. "Or, uh . . . you? I don't actually know how to talk about your . . . you."

"Armor is fine," Derivan said, even as Vex walked off and promptly buried his face into Misa's stomach. She gave their wizard a consoling pat. "And I don't reflect damage."

"Then that shouldn't happen," Sev said, frowning slightly. "System health is a damage buffer. The system tries to follow physics as realistically as possible, but generally, you don't take damage from attacking something. Otherwise half of the people with strength skills would just . . . splatter on contact with anything more durable than them."

"Perhaps it was simply too weak, and we should try something stronger?" Derivan said, trying and failing to wipe some of the slime off his armor. Vex coughed lightly, got over his embarrassment, and walked over to cast a quick spell that cleansed him with a quick pulse of magic. The residue seemed to be slowly pulling itself back together, a fact that Derivan felt strangely relieved by.

"I don't think that's what happened," Vex offered. He bent down to examine the slime, watching its remnants slowly crawl together. "Sev's right. This shouldn't have been possible."

"Check your status," Misa suggested. "Maybe something changed. Or you got a new buff?"

Frowning a little doubtfully, Derivan opened his status and paused in surprise.

Something *had* changed.

Derivan, Level <ERROR>
Health: <ERROR>
Mana: <ERROR>

Stats:
Slime: 1
<ERROR>

Skill List: <ERROR>

"Well," Derivan said. "Something did change. But I am unsure if it is what caused . . . that."

CHAPTER 9

WHO EVEN INVENTED THESE STATS?

"A Slime stat doesn't make any fucking sense!" Misa groaned, throwing up her hands with exasperation. It was, if Derivan was counting correctly, about the fourth time she had made the declaration. She was pacing about the training field, wearing grooves into the dirt with her boots. "What's it even supposed to do? A slime is a type of creature, not a stat!"

"You seem particularly distressed by this," Derivan noted, watching Misa with mild amusement. He supposed he should feel more concerned—but he couldn't quite bring himself to.

"The system's stupid," Misa grumbled, folding her arms.

"I mean, yeah. Have you looked at your skill?" Sev raised an eyebrow at her.

"It's fine when it's stupid in *my* favor, obviously," Misa said, finally smirking slightly. "Okay. Fine. We've got a new stat to figure out. This might be cool. What does it do?"

"Maybe it's got something to do with malleability and flexibility?" Vex suggested, his brows furrowing slightly. He poked at Derivan's outstretched arm. "You don't feel any softer. Or any more wet." Misa snickered a bit, and Vex pointedly ignored her. "Do you feel any different? Any changes in your status besides the new stat?"

"No," Derivan said, shaking his head even as he checked it over one more time. He couldn't say if his body felt any different, either. "I suspect that even if it changed my physical body, it would be difficult to notice with only one point in the stat."

"So you have to train the stat?" Misa frowned. "You don't have any points, and your level seems to be broken, so you'd have to if you want to get it up."

"I am unsure how I would train 'Slime.'" Derivan poked at his arm, frowning slightly. Vex was right; his armor didn't feel any different.

"Well, what *is* a slime? Vex?" Sev asked, glancing at their wizard.

Vex huffed a bit. "I don't know everything, you know," he said.

There was a pause.

Vex sighed. "A base slime is just liquid imbued with enough magic to make it semi-solid. Once a certain critical concentration of mana is achieved, it keeps attracting more ambient mana to it, causing the slime to grow in size and power. The type of mana, as well as the liquid medium, influences the type of slime it is."

"Thanks, Vex," Sev said with a grin, and their resident lizardkin just muttered something under his breath, his scales tinted faintly red.

"So . . . does that mean we try to imbue Derivan with more magic?" Misa asked, raising an eyebrow.

"We could try that," Sev said. "Or get more slimes to fight him, since that's what triggered it the first time. Or just wait and see if it actually does accumulate over time from the ambient mana."

"I would prefer not to wait," Derivan commented. He glanced at Sev—for all that the cleric was pretending at normalcy, there was a definite edge to him that wasn't there before. He was nervous. "I would like to be of assistance in the dungeon."

"Other people can explore that dungeon, too, you know," Misa said, letting out a tired sigh. "It doesn't actually have to be us."

"Are you . . . actually suggesting giving up a fight?" Vex blinked up at her.

"No!" Misa shot back. "But . . . I had time to sleep on it, right? Holy fuck, we were in over our heads yesterday. We don't even know what level that dungeon is going to be. We might not be ready for it now, or anytime soon. I'm just saying we shouldn't put it all on ourselves."

"You're not wrong, but it might not matter," Sev said with a sigh. "Those bonus rooms were created using us as seeds, the system prompt said? We were the templates. You're right in that we're probably not the only ones that can beat them, but we might still have insight that others don't."

"Don't tell me that we're chosen ones," Misa said, scowling. "Absolutely not. I call bullshit."

"We're not. But we might figure out whatever's hidden in the dungeon faster," Sev pointed out. "It doesn't really matter until the scouts get back and we hear what they have to say, anyway."

Misa sighed, looking away. "Yeah. You're right, I guess," she said.

It wasn't like Misa to turn down a fight of any kind, no matter how ridiculous the odds were. Derivan wondered what had changed—she seemed worried. For herself? That wasn't particularly like her. Then . . . for them?

"Perhaps you should explore the dungeon without me?" he offered. Seeing both Misa and Vex immediately open their mouths to protest, he hurried to clarify. "I am not leaving. I will remain here, if you will have me when you return. But . . . I am not ready for a dungeon, and I do not know how long it will take for me to *be* ready."

"We'll . . . have to see how dangerous the dungeon is," Sev said, hesitating. He was worried about Onyx; Derivan saw that fact in a dozen small details, from the way the cleric's robes were creased near his hands to the small waver in his voice. He wanted to act. "We shouldn't rush in without you if it's dangerous. We're used to fighting together, and a potentially deadly dungeon is not the place to try to change things up."

"Let's start with what we *can* do," Vex offered. He looked a little nervous—it was rare for the wizard to try to take the lead in anything. "I'll try to imbue Derivan with some of my magic, and we'll see if that does anything. If it doesn't, we'll try to find some slimes and other, weaker monsters for Derivan to fight. By that time the Guild's scouts will probably be back from grading the dungeon, and we can figure out what to do from there."

Everyone nodded. That seemed like a good enough plan for now. Vex moved to stand in front of Derivan, looking a little nervous as he placed a hand on the armored chestplate. "Can you open your stat screen?" he said. "Keep an eye on it. See what changes, if anything."

Derivan nodded, pulling up his stat screen. He paused. "Have you started imbuing yet?" he asked.

"No," Vex frowned. "Why? Did something change?"

"Yes," Derivan answered, with a slightly puzzled tilt to his head. There was. "But the change is not with the Slime stat. There is a new one. Physical Empathy, with fourteen points."

There was a long pause.

"You just . . . got another new stat? Just like that? There have to be some rules to this." Sev ran a hand through his hair. "Were you trying to read our body language or something?"

"As I always do," Derivan said. "Was I not meant to?"

"No, I mean . . . I don't know. It just doesn't make sense that these are *stats*. It should be a skill, right? [Body Language] or something." Sev sighed. "The system isn't usually this hard to figure out."

"Perhaps we should move on with the testing for now?" Derivan suggested. "We were about to attempt to imbue my armor with Vex's magic."

"I guess we do need to keep going," Sev agreed, though he continued to wear a small frown. Misa was just watching, her brows slightly furrowed as she thought.

Vex nodded and took a deep breath.

An odd warmth blossomed on Derivan's armor—a strange sensation for the animated armor, who wasn't particularly used to feeling *temperature* in any significant way. It grew slowly as that energy slowly filtered through his armor and into his core, and it took an effort of will not to hiss or step back. It was *uncomfortable*.

That discomfort only grew, though Derivan did his best to withstand it— and then something abruptly *changed*, like an enchantment had been shut off. The pressure eased, though not completely.

He glanced at his status.

Derivan, Level <ERROR>
Health: <ERROR>
Mana: 127/100
Stats:
Slime: 1
Physical Empathy: 14
Magic: 5
<ERROR>

Skill List: <ERROR>

"My mana stat has returned, though with a cap of a hundred mana," Derivan reported, shifting a little uncomfortably. Even as he spoke, the amount of mana he had continued to tick upward over his supposed cap, presumably an effect of the magic Vex was pouring into him. There was that sensation of building discomfort again. "Another stat has appeared as well; Magic, at a level of five."

"*Magic?*" Vex asked. The trickle of mana slowed but didn't stop—he seemed excited, at least, bouncing up on his heels and peering closely at Derivan like that would let him see past the armor and into his stats. "We'll have to do some tests on that one. Maybe try some spellcasting?"

"We're going to need to figure out what all of these new stats do," Sev muttered, his brows furrowed. "Okay. I think we haven't been taking this seriously enough. We're operating with a dearth of information; we don't even know if there's a limit to the number of stats Derivan can have. If he caps out at four stats we know nothing about, and those stats have no synergy, he might be fucked." He glanced at Derivan. "No offense."

"None taken," Derivan said. "I do not think that is possible."

Sev snorted, Misa laughed, and Vex turned as bright red as he could beneath his scales; Derivan didn't get it. He'd simply meant that he would learn to fight regardless of what stats he obtained. He'd been creative with his abilities before. This would just be a different application of them.

"But what I'm saying is that we need to be careful, and maybe stop picking up new stats for now," Sev said. "I mean. It seems kind of random so far, so maybe it can't be helped. But we'll try not to do anything more than we're already doing until we know a little more about what's going on? Maybe there'll be answers in the dungeon."

"I do not believe it will have answers about *this*," Derivan said a little doubtfully. "This happened after the dungeon was created."

But it was a fair point nonetheless. If they learned more about the system … He glanced at his status as something inside him felt like it ticked over, and blinked, eye-lights flickering.

"My maximum mana has increased as well," Derivan said. Indeed, there was considerably less pressure inside his soul; something in it felt larger, though the pressure was slowly increasing again. He watched the count tick up to 203/200. "And so did the Slime stat. It is at two points now."

Vex paused, surprised. "Slime is your mana capacity?" he asked, then shook his head. "No. That can't be it. But slimes are *related* to mana capacity …"

Vex fell silent, a strange flicker of emotion passing over him. Derivan watched him, concerned—Physical Empathy didn't seem to help him pinpoint what it was, and it vanished as quickly as it appeared. The lizardkin looked up at him, noticing his worry, and smiled a weak smile. "Oh, uh, sorry. I think it's probably just *related* to mana capacity? I'm guessing it has more effects, but mana is how you train the stat. But honestly, we're in uncharted territory as far as the system goes, so I don't actually know. I don't think it'd be called Slime if it was just mana capacity, though."

"I suppose we will find out, once it is trained enough," Derivan said. He was tempted to ask what that was—but Vex didn't seem inclined to talk about it, and the armor didn't want to push. It was the first time he'd felt conflicted about such a thing, and in the end, he stayed silent; Vex would surely talk about it when he was ready.

In the meantime, the lizardkin continued to push mana into him, a gentle flow of warmth that he found surprisingly comforting. The odd pressure had a bit more, and Derivan found that even when he was "full" on mana, he could focus on the warmth as a pleasant distraction.

His mana stopped at 299, refusing to tick over into 300. At the same time, Vex frowned a bit, seeming bewildered.

"I can sense the mana inside you," he said. "But the new mana is . . . dissipating? No. It's going somewhere else."

Derivan frowned and closed his eyes, trying to feel for what Vex was talking about. If the warmth he felt was mana, then it was a new sense for him. When he'd used skills before, his mana just vanished, and the skill activated.

Now, though, he tried to follow the feeling of warmth in his chest. Part of it trickled into him, coalescing into a node of warmth he identified as—or suspected to be—his mana pool. The rest . . . It wasn't disappearing. What was happening to it? It was hard to follow—

—no, there it was. It was turning into *threads*, the warmth he felt so thin he almost didn't notice them at all. Now that he was actively concentrating, he could almost feel how those thin threads of warmth seemed to be touching the very edges of his soul, doing something to it. Reinforcing it, perhaps? Strengthening it?

The changes didn't seem bad, at least.

There was a sudden pulse. It was subtle, but he saw the way something inside him felt like it solidified; the armor opened his eyes, glancing at his status.

Slime had gone up to three. His maximum mana was three hundred.

"A hundred to my mana pool per point of Slime, I think," Derivan said. He saw Vex's eyes widen, though the lizard didn't say anything. "For now, it appears that going over my mana limit increases that stat."

"The multipliers on that are *way* better than the ones on Intelligence," Vex said.

"Well, we've established *something*, at least," Sev said with a sigh. "Vex, could you help Derivan train up that stat? We need to figure out what it does, preferably sooner rather than later."

"Of course," Vex said. He seemed surprised but willing. "I've got lots of mana to spare."

"I'm also thinking you'll get your health back if I try to heal you." Sev frowned a little bit, considering the idea. "I don't think we should do that yet, though."

"Why not?" Misa asked. She'd moved to lean against a wall as she watched, but now she frowned. "More health means safety. For him and us."

"I mean, does it?" Sev asked. "I'm not so sure. If we're fighting something that can take us out in one hit, health isn't all that relevant."

"We're not going to be fighting something that absurd every day. That thing didn't even follow the level rules."

"All I'm saying is we know what happens when someone has health and takes a hit. Do we know what happens if they *don't* have health?"

There was a long silence.

"System sickness," Vex suddenly said. "There's not a lot of literature on it, but people in the early stages of system sickness have been known to fight weaker monsters without taking any apparent damage. Slimes, usually."

"If that's the case . . ." Sev muttered, thinking out loud. "Okay. I was talking about this earlier. Health is part of the system layer. It enforces health-damage interactions, right?"

"The system's layer of health means you can damage powerful monsters as long as they don't have defensive skills. Damage is damage, no matter the source. But it works the other way around, too." Vex's brows furrowed as he followed the train of thought. "Weak, low-level monsters can damage you, even if they're just slimes splashing against you. But if either participant lacks health, there's no enforced interaction, which means—"

"It means the slime attacked you and did what slime is supposed to do when hitting something solid," Misa said dryly, having caught on. "It didn't have the protection of its health, even though it was at full health, because it was attacking *you*."

"Oh," Derivan said.

It was a double-edged sword. He would be able to defeat others based entirely on their physical or magical natures, rather than going through the system of health and damage. But he, too, was uniquely vulnerable.

Sort of.

Most individuals would be uniquely vulnerable. *Derivan* was a magically animated suit of armor that had been created in what was functionally a Platinum-ranked dungeon.

"This is kind of broken," Misa said, sounding delighted.

"We need to confirm this," Vex said. "This is all just theory, and we shouldn't risk so much on theory. But it makes sense."

"At some point, you might end up needing the buffer of health," Sev added. "This is a unique advantage, so we should try to keep it. But if we're fighting something that can just disenchant your armor or something, you're going to need health to protect you. And if you get banged up and need healing . . . You might get damaged over time, you know?"

Derivan thought carefully. He could prolong the necessity of restoring his health if he was careful—he could use skills that provided damage buffers, like shields and barriers. Or he could use evasive skills.

Assuming he could acquire skills at all. Sev was right, though—this was a unique advantage. It came with some costs, but it was nothing that couldn't be worked around, and it was a way for him to be immediately useful regardless of his level and stats. If the enemies were physically weak enough, then his armor could handle the damage.

"We still have some time before the scouts return with their evaluation of the dungeon," Derivan said. "I will use that time to train what I have access to, and hope both that I can assist with the dungeon and that the answers for my status lie within the dungeon. But my hopes are not high; this happened after the dungeon formed, not before. We may have to experiment and work with whatever becomes of my status. Vex, you are willing to keep assisting me, yes?"

"Of course," Vex said brightly. "We can do some magic!"

"I need to get my gear repaired," Misa said. "And we need to stock up on supplies before we head out again. Maybe grab some potions this time."

"I'll grab the potions," Sev said. "I need to head to the temple and see if I can find out anything about the gods. I'll stock up while I'm there. The scouts *should* be back by the end of the day, so we'll meet in the Guild lobby around that time?"

"Yes," Derivan agreed.

"Okay," Vex said, clapping his hands. "Let's get to work!"

Everyone stared at him. He blinked.

"What? I wanted to try doing the thing Sev does."

Misa smirked, even as Sev tried and failed to stop himself from grinning. "I'm really glad we have you on board, you know," she said.

". . . Derivan, let's go before Misa makes fun of me."

Derivan nodded seriously.

"You're adorable!" Misa called after him, even as Derivan and Vex fled. "You can't escape the truth!"

CHAPTER 10

MAGIC AND UNDERSTANDING

Derivan and Vex had both retreated to Vex's room. It was a mess still, but the lizard cleared out a space on the floor for the armor to sit. Comfort wasn't a strict necessity for him, Derivan had assured his friend—though that didn't stop Vex from fretting about it.

"You're sure you don't need a chair?" Vex asked again.

Derivan, equal parts amused and exasperated, chuckled. "Comfort does nothing for me, Vex," he said. "It is the same reason I do not need my own tent and bedroll when we make camp."

"Right," Vex said, then paused, looking down. "Sorry. I mean, I knew you were *different*, but I didn't know how much. And I don't mean to keep reminding you of it or anything."

"It is fine," Derivan said, his exasperation fading into an amused fondness. Had someone else done it, he might have been frustrated—but with Vex, he knew the lizard was being genuine. He changed the subject quickly, before Vex could ruminate for too long on it. "Could you teach me how you approach magic? I would like to see if practicing it will allow me to increase the associated stat."

"I . . . approach magic a little differently, because of my class." Vex hesitated. "But . . . that might actually be more helpful with your stat? I'm not sure. I get [**Expert Mana Manipulation**] and [**Spell Analysis**] as building blocks to my skills. Maybe you can start with trying to get [**Mana Manipulation**]? Could you feel the mana when I was channeling into you?"

"Yes." Derivan paused, considering the sensation again. "It felt . . . warm. Rather pleasant, actually."

Vex nodded. "You should feel your own mana pool as something similar; try to move it around, see if you can shape it. That's the most basic level of [**Mana Manipulation**]."

"I will try," Derivan said.

"I'll channel mana into you while you do this," Vex offered. "It should help you train up both Slime and your mana pool while giving you a feel for mana."

Derivan nodded. He sat on the floor, with Vex sitting behind him; the lizard took a seat at his desk, his tail curling around Derivan's shoulder and supplying a steady stream of mana. The armor watched his mana tick up steadily, even as he tried to get a feel for it. It was a strange, slippery thing. As much as he tried to move and shape it, it slipped out of his grasp; he could *feel* it, but *moving* it seemed to be a task beyond him.

Still, he kept at it. The sound of Vex's quill scratching against parchment soon filled the air, even as Derivan concentrated on making progress.

It was slow going; even after half an hour, Derivan felt he had only managed to move his mana a tiny bit, down along his arm. Vex's scribbling, however, had slowed to a crawl. Derivan could practically feel the wizard working up the courage to speak.

After a moment of silence, he spoke.

". . . Hey, Derivan?" Vex asked. His voice was soft. Worried. "You don't have to answer this, but . . ."

Vex paused, seeming to hesitate; the trickle of mana from him slowed just slightly, matching his mood. He turned in his chair to look at Derivan, who sat calmly on the floor, looking at him.

Even with Vex on the chair, they were pretty much at eye level. It was rare that Derivan really *noticed* how small the lizardkin was compared to him. Or how large he was compared to others, he supposed.

"It is okay to ask," Derivan prompted.

Vex swallowed; he nodded, then shook his head, then nodded again, seeming to change his mind three times in a row. It took him a moment to actually gather himself to speak.

Really, Vex was shy about the strangest things.

"What is it like?" The wizard asked. "You say you don't feel comfort the way we do. What about touch? Sleep? Do you get tired?"

He paused, and Derivan waited; the lizard looked like he still had more to say. Vex hesitated for a moment more, then blurted out his thoughts. "And are you the only one? You said the system gave you instincts, and I think there was too much going on for me to really think about it at the time, but does that mean this is true for *all* monsters? How many monsters—how many *people* do we think are monsters, when they are not?"

Ah. That was . . . a good question. Derivan could see why it bothered the wizard so much. He seemed almost agitated, his claws twisting over one another as he fidgeted in a surprisingly human gesture.

"I will answer your second question first, I think," Derivan said. "Or I will try. But the truth is, I do not know; I have my guesses, based on what I have seen in the dungeon that gave me life, but they are only guesses."

Vex opened his mouth, as if to ask a question, only to close it again. Derivan gave him a small, grateful smile. He was almost certain that the wizard had *many* questions to ask him about his dungeon, and that it was taking a significant effort of will to focus on the topic at hand.

"I do not know if I am the only one," Derivan started softly. "Nor if there are others struggling with instincts that are not their own. I remember only a small part of my existence, for the magic that animates an armor is a form of growth magic, and it took time for me to grow into a being of my own.

"But in the time I spent in the dungeon, yearning to see what else there might be and yet unable to leave . . . I watched. Many of us patrolled, and as we grew, we would begin to wander, searching out the confines and limits of our prison. But there were those of us that never seemed to grow—that stuck to rigid routes and perfect patterns, never once deviating from their programmed path.

"This might mean nothing. It might simply be a failure of that animating growth magic to properly grow; perhaps the magic did not fully take on their armor. Or it might simply be that some of us prefer that rigidity and routine. But we spoke amongst ourselves, those of us that could speak, and found our experiences the same; those that followed the paths never returned our greetings, never spoke, never moved, even when prompted. If moved by force, they would return to their positions. It was . . . strange. Uncomfortable.

"This was true even for the other species within the dungeon. Even among the unintelligent beasts, there were those that would react and respond—hiss and scuttle away if we got too close. There were others that never seemed to notice our presence, and would patrol the walls of the dungeon like they themselves were guards.

"You are right to be concerned, I think. It is one of the answers I wished to seek, when I first left that dungeon, and I had not realized until now that I could share that goal with all of you." Derivan smiled at Vex, that little curve to his eyes, and the lizardkin offered a surprised but genuine smile in return.

"As for what it is like . . ." Derivan pondered the question. "I have very little to compare it to, so I do not know, exactly. I feel pressure, not touch; I know how light or heavy something is, and I feel pain if I am injured. I do not need sleep, exactly, but long periods of concentration leave me feeling sluggish. I believe this is a close approximation to feeling tired. I would say I do not sleep at all, and that a break is enough for me to recharge, but now that I am reminded, I believe I may have slept last night."

"Last night?" Vex asked, curiosity piqued. Derivan did his best impression of a shrug.

"It is difficult to explain," the armor said. "My consciousness felt like it was drifting. I believe I experienced something in that span of time, but my memory of that event has faded. I heard voices, I think, and I felt as though I was somewhere *else*."

"Huh," Vex said, and lapsed into silence for a moment before speaking. "It *sounds* like sleep? Are you sure you can't remember anything about that dream?"

Derivan frowned, concentrating—but it slipped frustratingly out of his grasp every time he reached for the memory. "I do not," he said apologetically.

"Might be worth trying to keep a dream journal," Vex said. "It's normal to have a lot of difficulty with remembering dreams. It helps if you keep a notebook nearby so you can write them down before you forget."

"I see. Do you follow this practice?" Derivan asked curiously. Vex's eyes widened *almost* imperceptibly—in fact, Derivan was quite certain he would not have noticed without the newfound Physical Empathy stat.

"Uh, no," Vex lied. His tail reached out to flick something beside Derivan into the space beneath his bed. "Definitely not."

Derivan paused. "You keep one, but you are too embarrassed to admit to it and have opted instead to lie badly on purpose so that I know that you keep one but will not press you on it."

". . . Yes."

"You are a very complicated wizard, Vex."

"Thank you," Vex muttered, looking a little embarrassed. He changed the subject quickly. "Hey, so, uh, how's your [**Mana Manipulation**] going?"

Derivan realized, to his own surprise, that he'd actually managed to grasp the mana while he was distracted. He'd been prodding at it in the back of his mind, trying to get a grip on the strange energy inside him; now that he had it, his hold on it was firm, and he found he could both shift it around as well as push it out of his hand in a vague, nebulous shape.

". . . It seems I have it," he said, pleased. He glanced at his status to check for any changes. "And it appears that I can still obtain skills. [**Intermediate Mana Manipulation**] is now in my skill list, although there was no notification for it. Slime and Magic went up to five and six respectively."

Vex blinked. "That's . . . good," he said. "That means you're up to five hundred maximum mana? And you skipped straight to Intermediate on [**Mana Manipulation**]."

"I am not sure how," Derivan admitted. "I was having trouble earlier."

"[**Mana Manipulation**] is tricky," Vex said with a shrug. "Every mage does it slightly differently and requires a slightly different state of mind; for most of us, concentration helps, but it seems like it's easier for you to move it by instinct than with deliberate concentration. Your skill should do most of the heavy lifting now, though."

Derivan considered this and tested it, finding he could move the mana easily whether he concentrated or not, as long as he allowed the skill to be active. He hummed. Convenient. He'd never been able to just . . . gain skills this easily, back when the system considered him a monster.

He didn't know what the system considered him now.

"Which means we can start learning how to actually *cast*," Vex said, distracting Derivan. The wizard's brows furrowed slightly as he considered. "Which . . . is difficult. I've never taught anyone how to cast before, and my method of learning spells and casting is pretty different from what most people consider wizardry."

"It is better, I am sure," Derivan said, and had to wait patiently as Vex went red and abruptly choked on nothing. He coughed his lungs out for nearly a minute, and glared at Derivan with no heat when he finally recovered.

"You did that on purpose," Vex accused, grumbling.

"I complimented you on purpose, yes," Derivan agreed.

Vex huffed. "*Anyway*. Normally, wizards study their spells from spell scrolls. *Studying* is kind of a misnomer, though—they don't really need to understand the spell. As long as the system recognizes what they're doing as studying, the spell eventually shows up as a skill in their status."

"That seems rather . . . mundane," Derivan commented, hesitating. Vex shrugged in agreement.

"I don't like the system's simplification of magic," Vex said. "It feels like it should be something *more*. I tried to study the scrolls, but before I got my class, a lot of the ideas described in them didn't really work properly." He frowned.

"That said, I have some scrolls you can take a look at. It's normally a requirement that you have some sort of magic class before you can 'study' scrolls at all, but given the state of your system, you might be able to pick them up just from looking at them." Vex hopped off his chair, going over to a pack hidden in the corner of the room and rummaging through his scrolls. "What spells would you like to learn?"

"Something that allows me to create barriers, I think," Derivan said, pulsing mana out of his hand; this time, it hovered above his palm and began to swirl around itself. It was strange to have control over a new force. It was strange to be able to change at all, to learn new skills and have them acknowledged by the system, the way others did.

Derivan smiled; though a part of him missed the strength he once had, he relished even more the opportunity to actually grow, in any direction he so chose.

"To divert blows your armor can't block?" Vex considered the idea. "Smart. Okay, I think I have just the thing for that."

He pulled out a scroll, and Derivan reached for it with a mixture of interest and trepidation.

It was time to see if he could learn magic.

CHAPTER 11

BONDING

Derivan *could*, as it turned out, absorb spells from spell scrolls just as a wizard could. He'd made an attempt to study the actual contents of the scroll, but most of what it was describing flew quickly over his head; there was a lot of runic theory embedded in the scrolls that he'd need to study for months to really understand.

"There are thousands of these symbols," Derivan commented, staring at the scroll, then looking up at Vex. "You have all of them memorized?"

"Well. Not *memorized*. My class helps." Vex seemed a little embarrassed, though he was rapidly being energized by the discussion of magic. "New ones are being discovered all the time. They interact with each other, and the system helps set them up for the skills you learn, but it's all just so . . ."

Vex sighed, leaning back into his chair; he'd already expressed this exact thought several times while Derivan had been reading the scrolls.

Derivan's voice was amused when he responded. "It's not magical?"

"It's not magical!" Vex threw his hands up in the air. "Even my class doesn't feel all that magical, for all that it gives me 'root access' or whatever. And don't get me wrong: I love my class. It lets me do so much more with magic than most wizards. But it still feels like I'm just setting up instructions."

Derivan chuckled softly. Over the past few hours, the lizard had opened up significantly, and he had no problem expressing his opinions on the nature of magic. He rather regretted that he had never taken the time to seek Vex out to talk to him before. He enjoyed the lizard's company, he found.

He'd have to do that more with all of his companions, he decided. Get to know them better. It was surprising how much clearer things were without the system's instincts hanging down over him, trying to force him to be as inconspicuous as possible.

"It does feel that way, from how you describe it," Derivan agreed. "What do you think magic should be like, then?"

"I don't know," Vex answered. "It just . . . feels like it should be something special, you know? It feels like it should be an art. I love deconstructing it and learning more about it, I do, but I can't help but feel like there's something *missing*. Something I'm not seeing. I know all these runes affect mana in specific ways, but I don't know *why*."

The lizard let out a little huff and sat on the floor in front of Derivan. He'd run out of mana to channel into Derivan a little while before, and was now meditating to regenerate. He didn't need to sit still or keep quiet for the skill to work, apparently; when Derivan had asked, he'd told the armor—much to his amusement—that he wouldn't have been able to gain the skill at all if that had been a requirement.

"I knew very little about magic before today," Derivan remarked. "I did not think much of it beyond its use as a tool. But . . ."

Derivan hummed in consideration. He lifted a hand, allowing his mana to channel through the [**Barrier**] spell he'd learned. He didn't have nearly the same understanding of spells and magic that Vex did—the runes that formed in his hand as the skill came into being were inscrutable to him.

But what he *did* see was the way the mana *flowed*.

As much trouble as he'd initially had with feeling for it and grasping it, now that he had, it was astonishingly simple to see. And Vex was right. There was a beauty to the way it moved, the way it almost seemed to dance through the runes, flashing into shapes it seemed intimately familiar with. It flowed and it danced, and flickers of almost-glass came into being—shards of force to ward away his enemies and their blows.

But there was something missing.

It moved in a mockery of what should have been happiness. It was almost like he should have felt the mana laughing joyously as it moved from one form to the other; instead it was silent, dead. A corpse being puppeteered on strings of joy, if he wanted to be macabre. Something within him ached in sympathy.

"You are right," Derivan agreed softly. He met the lizardkin's eyes, saw the way his tail curled nervously, as if he was expecting his ideas to be scorned. Rejected. "Something *is* missing. I would like to find out what it is. That is your goal, yes?"

Vex looked back at him. Derivan saw a glimmer of surprise in his eyes at first, like the lizardkin hadn't expected that from him. "It's one of the questions I wanted to answer."

"Then let us find the answer together, once all of this is settled," Derivan offered. "I am sure Misa and Sev would be eager to help as well, if you told them."

Vex was silent for a moment.

"I'd like that, I think," the lizardkin agreed, smiling a soft smile. "I'd like that a lot."

A comfortable silence followed. Vex seemed to lose himself in his thoughts briefly, before he prompted Derivan to continue casting [**Barrier**]; he wanted to see if there was anything different in how the spell was cast, given Derivan's strange state within the system. He gave the armor tips, too—with his understanding of how the spell *worked*, he could see the way Derivan's mana flowed, checking for inefficiencies.

He spoke at length about how the system interpreted a wizard's thoughts, allowing modified spells to be granted if one's *understanding* of the spell changed. Spells were more than input and output, for all that the runic system of spellcasting seemed to emphasize only that. Spells were intent and understanding. The two schools of thought hadn't yet been completely reconciled, he explained . . .

Just like that, hours passed.

—◊—

"Hey, guys." Misa greeted them with a loud knock on Vex's door before poking her head in. "Figured I'd check in since Sev's not in the lobby yet. Made any progress with the training?"

"We're about to wrap up, actually, since we're both out of mana." Vex inclined his head with a smile. "You're welcome to come in."

Misa laughed. "What, me? Come in? You must be in a really good mood. You don't let anyone get near your shit. Especially me." She grinned teasingly at the lizardkin, who flinched.

"I—I mean, because they're my notes! And you might have been able to figure out my class if you saw them . . ." Vex deflated a little, and Misa relented, stepping into the room with a chuckle.

"Relax, I'm just teasing. I get it. I didn't tell anyone about my class for the longest time either." The half-orc's grin became briefly brittle.

"Is it dangerous to speak of classes?" Derivan asked curiously. He'd never had occasion to speak much of it. Sev and Misa had given him a cursory warning not to reveal any classes if he could help it, but such a thing was considered impolite anyway, so he'd never put more thought into it.

"Kind of," Misa answered, wiggling a hand in the air in a *so-so* sort of gesture. "At low levels, in the Iron or Bronze range, yes. The Prime Kingdoms will want to conscript you. At high levels? They won't bother unless you're *really* special. Their Platinums have better things to do than try to capture someone in the Platinum range, especially if they don't know what you can do."

"I know very little about the Kingdoms, admittedly." He'd picked up on the ranking system easily enough over their travels—it wasn't anything complicated. Iron, Bronze, Silver, Gold, Platinum, each representing a twenty-level range. The Prime Kingdoms were more complicated to ask questions about, given he didn't know what was considered common knowledge. "Are they such terrible places?"

Derivan found that the idea of people being forced to fight for anyone rankled him.

"No. Or at least, most don't see it that way," Vex said. His tail swung about slightly as he considered the question, but his brows furrowed in mild consternation. "For most people, being conscripted guarantees that they'll have a good life. The Prime Kingdoms have complicated leveling programs in place that allow you to get levels at minimal risk, and once you hit Platinum, nothing's really left to threaten you except other Platinum rankers. Which happens . . . very rarely."

"You know a lot about their training programs." Misa raised an eyebrow. "All the Prime Kingdoms refuse to talk about how much risk is actually involved when they train someone to Platinum."

"I lived in Elyra for a while," Vex said, hunching forward slightly; seeing Derivan's look of confusion, he elaborated. "It's the southernmost Prime Kingdom on the continent. Known for dungeon research and magic item production, mostly."

"Ah." Derivan nodded. "But why avoid conscription, then? It does not sound like it has many downsides."

Vex grimaced. "A few reasons, some of which I don't really want to talk about right now—sorry. I'll tell you guys eventually. But one of them is that all the Kingdoms have a strict population limit. They know exactly how many people their resources can support, and they stay strictly below that line. For me to stay, someone else has to leave."

"I think that might be an Elyran thing. I've heard Anderstahl tries to expand its harvest to support more citizens as much as possible, though I guess I don't know how much of that is propaganda." Misa frowned slightly. "But it felt wrong for me to join any of the Kingdoms. My village struggled to survive without help from them. We wanted to be independent. I wasn't going to give up that dream and fuck off to live out my days in a Kingdom."

"I see," Derivan said. He fell silent, turning over what they'd said in his mind. "It is . . . difficult for me to understand the sacrifices you have made, I think. I sympathize, but I do not know that I truly understand."

Misa chuckled, giving him a friendly nudge. "No one said you have to understand everything immediately."

"I suppose," Derivan agreed. "*Home* is a strange prospect for me. The dungeon I came from is the closest thing I could call a home, but the word does not seem appropriate. I hold no affection or regard for it. But for what it is worth, I am glad the two of you are here."

He paused.

"Sev as well," he added. The human wasn't there, but it felt wrong not to mention him. Both Vex and Misa chuckled at that inclusion.

"Yeah, the guy's a smartass, but I like having him around," Misa grinned.

"I thought *I* was the smartass," Vex said. He managed to actually sound a little hurt, and Misa snorted, throwing an arm around the lizard and dragging him close in a half-hug; Vex yelped as she did so, toppling over against her side.

"*You're* too proud of *being* a smartass, is what you are," Misa said, entirely unrepentant. "Sev's rubbing off on you."

"He is not!" Vex protested, his voice barely a squeak as Misa kept him grappled.

"I believe he is," Derivan said, carefully keeping his tone as serious as he could. "In fact, I am worried he may be turning into a second Sev entirely. Perhaps we should find another cleric to check?"

"*Derivan,*" Vex squeaked, sounding outraged and betrayed; the armor chuckled and gave in, reaching out to pull the poor lizardkin free from Misa's unrelenting grasp. He squinted at Derivan's perfectly steady expression, then huffed. "You're getting better at jokes."

"I have always been good at jokes," Derivan said, incorrectly. Misa and Vex stared at him, and he let his eyes curve upward in a smirk. "I accept no other reality."

Misa snorted in a laugh. "Sure, buddy."

"I support your delusions, whatever they may be," Vex added.

"All right," Derivan sighed, conceding. He smiled. "I suppose I deserved that."

There was a small silence then, but it was the comfortable sort of silence, the kind born of quiet camaraderie. Vex broke the silence first, his tone curious as he lounged back, using his tail to prop himself up. "What about you, Derivan? Could you tell us more about the dungeon you're from?"

Derivan paused. It struck him—quite suddenly, really—how *normally* his friends were treating him, despite what they now knew about his origin. He'd never really thought it would matter, but he found that it did.

Acceptance was a strange beast, he mused.

"I can," Derivan said, and he was surprised by how honest those words were. "Let me see what I can remember . . ."

CHAPTER 12

OF DUNGEONS AND PRIESTS

"It was a castle," Derivan began. He remembered that much. "A place of cold stone and dark skies. I did not know it at the time, but it is what I now know you call an open dungeon—the kind with unclear boundaries, that draws adventurers in without their realizing. The kind that never breaks and only grows. The dungeon had secrets, I believe, and a fabricated tale involving an old lord of the castle. But I was not privy to many of those secrets. Before my upgrade to infiltrator, I was considered a low-rank monster. A guard, meant to stop the first waves of adventurers."

"... Aren't you kind of ... unreasonably strong?" Misa said, blankly. "You were level eighty-six. You could absorb skills. Or did that happen after you left the castle?"

"No. I started at level eighty-six, though the skill you speak of came to me with my elevation to Elite. The dungeon itself is ... ancient, and it is deep in the Outskirts; though I was stationed to guard against adventurers, and the dungeon itself was set up to draw them in, the truth is that we did not encounter a single one before Sev." Derivan shrugged slightly. "It is for the better, I think."

"It was in the *Outskirts*?" Vex asked, sounding horrified. "That's ... No one goes to the Outskirts!"

"What the fuck was Sev doing there?" Misa muttered, looking slightly aghast. And maybe a little bit jealous, actually. Derivan saw the way her eyes gleamed.

"He may have been searching for me," Derivan said. "He mentioned that he was left with fragments of knowledge, yes? It is ... the impression that I got, although I have no true knowledge of this; I have never asked. At the time, I considered it my good fortune to have encountered someone that could help me escape the dungeon; I never considered why he was there. Now that I know what I do . . ."

"You think it's part of the knowledge he was given?" Vex frowned. "But that doesn't explain how he *survived*. The Outskirts are . . . They're the *Outskirts*. They're the places we gave up on."

"We did?" Misa glanced sharply at Vex. "Why?"

"You don't know?" Vex blinked. "It's . . . The Outskirts form the border of our continent. They're where a bunch of dungeon breaks happened and merged, and became too dangerous for even our Platinum rankers. It's the whole reason we haven't explored past our continent. I mean, I guess we haven't completely given up—the Kingdoms send in teams to try every so often—but we haven't made any progress for years."

"Shit," Misa said. "No, the Outskirts were too far away from my village for us to really care about. We heard about them, but I assumed we were making progress. Beating them back or something, I don't know. I don't like the idea that we're trapped."

"The Kingdoms don't either," Vex said, grimacing slightly. "But . . . Sorry. I didn't mean to interrupt, Derivan."

"It is fine." Derivan inclined his head. "The Outskirts are foreign to me, too. It is good to know more about them. As for Sev . . . I do not know how he was able to reach the dungeon, and I did not think to wonder. It is something to ask him, I suppose." Derivan shrugged slightly. It was a mystery, and now that he thought about it, it was something he was curious about as well. "He was remarkably stealthy, however. I found him hiding in one of the secret passageways of the castle, one I was designated to patrol."

"Did you attack him?" Misa asked, and Derivan shook his head.

"By that time, I had already acquired [**Disguise Status**]. I simply pretended to be another adventurer and offered to escort him out, on the premise that the dungeon was too dangerous for either of us. He accepted immediately." Derivan paused. "I suppose I should have found that suspicious. But I was new and inexperienced and eager to leave, so I did not."

"You couldn't leave without him?" Vex asked.

"I could not," Derivan agreed. "Monsters do not travel far past their dungeons, if they originate from one. They are unable to; it is a rule of the system. Infiltrator types are the sole exception, but even then, it only works if there is a party to infiltrate." A small, rueful sort of tilt to his head. "I waited a long time for that opportunity. I was eager."

"Why did you want to leave so much, anyway?" Misa asked. She and Vex had apparently an unspoken agreement to take turns asking questions, a fact which Derivan noticed and found amusing. He hesitated a little bit before answering.

Part of it was that he wanted to see more of the world, it was true. As the magic within him had grown, he found more and more that he wanted to see beyond the confines of the castle; he could see so much, from the top of the walls, and it made him wonder what more there was to see. That sight and yearning had been what allowed him to transition from a simple Enchanted Armor into an Infiltrator in the first place, the system answering to his wishes in a way he hadn't even known was possible.

But wanting to see the world wasn't the true reason—wasn't the big, driving force. He sighed, casting about for the words to explain how he felt.

"I was . . . not alone, exactly, in the dungeon," he began haltingly. He'd already explained this part to Vex, but he repeated it now for Misa's benefit. "There were other Enchanted Armors that grew in mind and body over time, and I enjoyed their company. They are quiet but thoughtful; when they speak, it is with measured words and careful certainty. The ones that speak and grow, anyway. Each of them are different, with different thoughts and insights. And yet I was different. Though we always began our journey curious, we would find ourselves confined by the dungeon we were in.

"The others all grew to accept that reality." Derivan paused again, trying to remember the intensity of emotion that had initially prompted his evolution. It seemed so far away now. "I did not. I suspect that desire to leave is part of the reason I evolved where they did not."

"Seems we're all the type of people to reject what the world gives us," Misa offered with a wry smile—but there was a deeper understanding in it. She'd felt the same way, if not about the same thing.

"It does seem that way," Vex agreed. He sighed softly. "I have so many questions, Derivan. But I think there's an important one that I haven't asked yet, and I'm sorry I didn't ask it sooner. What did you do? Outside the view of adventurers and researchers, when left alone in your dungeon?"

"What do you mean?" Derivan didn't quite understand the significance of the question.

"What do you *do*?" Vex repeated. "You're . . . you're people. You, specifically—you're a person, and you always have been, no matter what the system tried to tell you. You think and speak, just like I do; you just told me that you're all *individuals*. But you can't tell me that all you do is walk in predetermined patterns, talking whenever you happen to pass one another."

"That is what we did," Derivan said, still unsure where Vex was going with this, though he thought he almost understood. "Most of us, anyway."

"But there should be *culture*," Vex insisted. "Art. You must've created something, right? Invented something."

"Oh!" Misa suddenly said, her back straightening. Her eyes narrowed. "Oh. Shit. I see where you're going with this."

"You had instincts," Vex pressed. "Instincts from the system that were preventing you from even considering telling us about what you were. It's barely even that; it's *mind magic*. It takes the possibilities that your mind can see and narrows them down for you, preventing you from growing. You were a people, but you weren't allowed to grow, and that's . . ."

Vex shook his head. "I don't have the words for it. But it feels wrong."

"Ah." And now Derivan saw where Vex was going with this—felt that he understood, at least. He had never reflected much on culture or art, having never felt a particular urge to create himself.

And yet those words struck a chord within him, and made him wonder what he could have been. Perhaps it wasn't too late?

"I . . . cannot say that you are wrong," he said cautiously. "Though I do not know that you are right, either."

He didn't know what it would mean if that were true. There were implications, for sure, but those implications were out of reach for him; his home, if it could be called that, was too far away and too dangerous to try to reach again. Not as he was now.

"And it's not just your dungeon," Vex said quietly. "How many dungeons are like this? What if the dungeons in the Prime Kingdoms . . . I know you said earlier that the beasts were still beasts. But there have to be other intelligent species out there that the system categorized as monsters, right?"

"If that's true, that's fucking bullshit," Misa declared. She saw the distress in Vex's eyes and the concern in Derivan's, and she amended her words just slightly. "But . . . we can't do anything about it *now*. We'll just have to look into it, like everything else."

Her eyes hardened. "And if it's true, then we've just got another shitty system we need to break. Nothing new for us, right?"

". . . Yeah," Vex said after a moment. Derivan nodded in agreement.

"It's gotta be pretty high fuckin' priority, though," Misa added.

"We're relying on getting a lot of answers from the dungeon," Vex said. "If we don't get it there . . ."

"We'll find it somewhere else," Misa said with a shrug. "Break into the Outskirts if we have to. Sev did it; I'm sure he can teach us how."

Vex snorted a weak laugh. "I can't imagine just going up to him and demanding he take us into the Outskirts."

"I mean, if we have to . . ." Misa trailed off, frowning. "That thing he said, about healing Onyx ripping up his future and his freedom. We can't leave that alone, right?"

"I don't know how to even begin fixing something like that," Vex said. "But . . . no, you're right; we have to do something about it. Maybe not now. Maybe not even soon, depending on how long it takes us to figure something out. But when we do . . ."

Misa nodded. "I just wanted to make sure we were all on the same page," she said quietly. "Where is Sev, anyway? Think he's in the lobby? We might have to go down and meet him."

"He'd probably send us a message if he was down there already," Vex said, checking the system. "I don't see anything."

"Perhaps we should look for him?" Derivan suggested. "We will see if he is in the lobby, and find him in the temple if not."

"I don't think anything bad's happened to him," Misa said. "So we don't *need* to." Then she grinned. "But you know what, I don't think I've ever seen Sev talking to other priests. The guy reacted to a god by deciding to *hang out* with him. We should *definitely* spy on him."

"Misa!" Vex said, shocked. Misa's grin only widened.

"I've known him longer than you have, and if there's anything I know about him, it's that he is *very annoyed* by people being preachy. I've literally never seen him talking to another cleric, and I've just now realized that this is something I really want to see. You can decide whether you want to come with me or not, but you can't stop me from going."

". . . Now that you mention it," Derivan said, his eyes flickering with amusement. "I think this is something I wish to see as well."

"*Derivan*," Vex said, although with much less heat. Then he sighed, defeated. ". . . Okay, yeah, I want to see it, too. Let's go."

Sev had a headache.

He'd had a headache for a while now, except it was refusing to go away, and unlike most clerics, he couldn't simply heal away his headache. It wouldn't matter if he could, anyway, not when the source of his headache was still there, *talking to him*.

He hated saying no to people, but this was really getting to be too much.

". . . for it is only within Hystia's Light that we can see the truth," the priest continued enthusiastically. He didn't seem to notice Sev slowly massaging his head, trying his best to ignore what the priest was saying. "It is only with Her

Light that we may scour away sin. So if the system told you to repent, you must turn to Hystia and allow her Light to burn away your sins! Do you not see, my friend? You follow a heretic god, an untrue shadow!"

The poor man was staring at him so earnestly, too, like he was expecting Sev to . . . give a shit.

He did, really. He was doing his best to give a little bit of a shit. He made it a point to care about what people had to say, even if he didn't really agree, or like people preaching at him. But the priest had just insulted a friend that he'd last seen hurt and dangling from chains, and his patience was fraying.

"You need to leave," Sev said bluntly. "I have a *very big stick*, and I'm not afraid to use it."

The priest opened his mouth to speak, and Sev promptly shoved the tip of his staff into it.

Gently.

He wasn't looking to *hurt* him. Just to make him leave. In all fairness, he'd expected the priest to flinch back, but the man's reaction time had been terrible. The poor man sputtered, flabbergasted and increasingly furious—and then, as Sev raised his staff again, decided this wasn't worth his time and promptly left.

Sev wiped it off, grimacing. Sometimes he *really* hated how well informed priests were. They didn't get prophetic dreams, exactly, but their gods did their best to keep their most devoted followers up to date on important events; apparently, many of the gods had decided whatever happened at the dungeon was an Important Event, with capital letters.

Except the gods had apparently left out the very crucial information about what had happened with Onyx. He wondered if that meant that they didn't know—perhaps all the priests were approaching him precisely because they needed more information about what had happened?

What a shit way to get information out of him, though. They could have just *asked*. Then again, most of the gods were more limited in the ways they could communicate with their followers . . . The priests here had probably only gotten a vague impression that they should approach him.

"Holy shit," came a familiar voice—along with the scandalized looks of several nearby priests. Misa smirked at him as she approached. "I can't believe you actually *did that*."

"He was preaching at me," Sev grumbled.

"And he was rude about Onyx!" Vex said, with a little more heat than he intended; when the other two turned to stare at him, the lizardkin shrank into himself slightly. ". . . Sorry. Onyx seemed nice. And it was rude of him to call him a heretic."

"I mean, you're not wrong there," Sev said with a small smile. His headache was already starting to abate. He glanced at Derivan, who was standing slightly behind Vex, expressionless. "What, no commentary from you?"

"I would have picked him up and placed him within a barrel," Derivan told him. "I believe you handled it better than I would have."

Sev snorted out a laugh. "I kinda wish you did. Maybe I should ask you along next time, get your help to stuff priests into barrels."

"There's still time," Misa said with a grin. "I can help. You haven't gotten all the potions yet, have you?"

"*No*," Sev said with a groan. "The priests keep approaching me. Apparently they all got some kind of vision and they all think it means I need to be saved or whatever."

Sev grumbled under his breath, then looked up. "Okay. We're going straight to the next stall. If the priest tries to preach at me . . . Wait, are there even any barrels here?"

"No," Derivan said, sounding amused. "For the record, I do not *actually* think doing that would be appropriate. We will have to use our words, I am afraid, and not your big wooden stick."

"It's a *staff*. Staffs are cool," Sev huffed, glaring around just enough to make some of the nearby priests rethink their decisions to approach him. It was really too bad this branch of the Guild didn't have a dedicated alchemy section. There was a multi-faith temple nearby, so all the potion supplies were handled instead by that temple and their priests. Healing was the domain of the divine, after all, so that made sense, but *still* . . .

"Honestly, I'm surprised they're not bickering more," Misa said, glancing around in mild amusement. "They all believe in different gods, right?"

"They believe in looking united in front of adventurers, so most of them don't preach openly while we're around," Sev said. "That's why they don't *usually* bother me. Unless their gods decide to send them *visions*. I *guess*."

"You're very grumpy," Vex commented. Sev just stuck his tongue out at the lizardkin.

Okay. Next stall. Hopefully, this vendor would prove less of a problem.

CHAPTER 13

TALES OF A DIFFERENT GOD

"I need eight healing potions and five mana potions," Sev said. He hadn't even looked up at the vendor yet, his eyes too busy flicking over the wares they had available—surprisingly high-quality potions of all kinds, actually. The divine mana emanating from them was stable, rather than fluctuating as was common in lower-quality potions. Priests made good potions, but they weren't typically *this* good. "How much will it cost?"

Then he actually looked up. And . . . kept looking.

"Wow. He's tall," Vex said. The poor lizardkin, the shortest of the four of them, had to practically crane his head directly upward to meet the gaze of the stone elemental that stood in charge of the store.

The elemental wasn't just tall, either. He was *huge*, many of his body parts made of what seemed to be actual boulders—boulders that had been pared down over time, as all stone elementals did as they grew, sculpting themselves into a shape that would allow them to better interact with the world. They were one of the few species that grew smaller over time, eventually stabilizing into intricately carved specimens of rock.

"It will be two gold," the elemental spoke, his voice the rumbling grind of stone against stone. He chuckled quietly. "I must say . . . in all my time amongst adventurers and priests, I have never once been approached without having been noticed."

"Yeah, uh, sorry about that." Sev handed over the two gold, not bothering to haggle. It was a fair price. Actually, it was probably a little too cheap, given the quality. "I usually pay more attention, but I've had other things on my mind."

"As I have seen," the elemental replied. His amusement sounded like a small avalanche of tiny pebbles rolling across gravel. He took the money and began packing the potions away into a bag for them, enormous hands acting with remarkable precision as they manipulated the glass bottles the potions came in. "It seems you have the gods in quite a stir."

"You have *no* fucking idea," Sev muttered with a sigh. "I'm surprised you're not trying to convert me, too. No offense."

"I have received no vision from the goddess I follow," the elemental said with a hum. "It seems she does not consider this as important as the other gods do. Or perhaps I simply do not rank highly enough in her esteem yet."

"I doubt it's the second one."

The elemental smiled in the closest approximation of a smile he could reach, which was mostly a light shrug and slight tilt of the head, and the shifting of some earth that seemed to vaguely hint at a mouth. "Thank you for your kind words, little one. I am Velykos," the priest said, introducing himself. "Priest of Nillea, goddess of Earth."

Sev supposed he should have expected that a stone elemental would follow the goddess of Earth. The rest of the party quickly introduced themselves, and Velykos nodded to each of them in turn.

"You are also a cleric, are you not?" Velykos asked, looking at Sev questioningly. "You have not mentioned the god you follow."

Sev blinked. He was genuinely thrown off guard—not once had a member of a clergy ever asked *him* who he worshipped. At best, there were attempts at converting him as they sang praises of their own gods. This priest was actually interested in who *he* followed?

"I follow Onyx," Sev said after he realized he'd been silent for a little too long. There was a small, subtle twitch from the stone elemental, his movement seeming to *stutter* for a split second.

Then the priest shook his head, like nothing had happened.

"I am not familiar with that god, I am afraid," he said. He finished packing up their potions and handed the bag to Sev. "Thank you for your purchase. Perhaps I will see you again?"

Sev frowned, confused by what he'd seen. "Are you okay? You kind of twitched when I mentioned Onyx."

There was that stutter-stop movement again, like something in the magic that animated him had halted for a split second. "I . . . do not know what you mean," Velykos said, but he seemed hesitant, like he understood on some level that something was wrong.

"The god I follow," Sev said, now avoiding the name entirely. He was worried now; it wasn't hard to catch on to the pattern. But this was *new*; saying Onyx's name had never had this effect before.

Perhaps it was too late, though. Velykos seemed to try to reach for the memory, and that seemed to be enough; there was that briefest halt in his movements again. Vex's eyes were suddenly sharp and faintly glowing, the wizard snapping into focus as he noticed something was off. Derivan and Misa, without that same attunement to magic, went silent and on alert anyway; they could infer well enough that this was serious, and prepared to respond should something happen.

"Something weird's happening with his mana," the lizardkin said quietly. "I can't tell what it is. It doesn't look like a spell."

"Is it something I can block?" Misa asked, wary. Vex shook his head.

"I don't think so." The wizard hesitated. "I haven't seen this kind of magic before, but I'm not sure this qualifies as an attack, from him or against him. It looks like it's built into the magic that's animating him, somehow."

"What do you . . ." Velykos shook his head, stumbling slightly. Sev saw the divine magic around him flaring briefly, like he was preparing himself to cast a spell, but before he had the chance, that stutter-stop happened again.

Vex's eyes went wide. "Catch him! He's going to fall!"

Velykos began to tilt backward.

Misa rushed forward, trying to stabilize the elemental before he fell; Derivan was only a split second behind her, moving to the stone elemental's other side so he didn't just roll away from her. Vex mouthed something under his breath, waving his dagger forward to create a cushion of force that tried to support the elemental's weight.

Sev wanted to help, too. He tried, even, reaching into himself to call forth a basic [**Barrier**] skill to support Velykos's weight. But the skill didn't respond, and the entire temple began to tilt.

Sev realized a second later that he, too, was falling.

And then he knew nothing at all.

—◊◊◊—

One of the benefits to fainting in a temple full of priests, Sev quickly discovered, was that it was nearly impossible to actually die.

He'd come alarmingly close to death, apparently, with no warning at all— his health had just dropped all the way down to zero, and then his heart had stopped. If it wasn't for the fact that several nearby priests had immediately jumped in to help, *including* the one he'd previously borderline-assaulted with his staff, it was quite possible that he would be dead.

Vex's eyes were faintly red, and even Misa's eyes were misty. Derivan's expression was a little harder to read, but the armor stood closer to him, hovering almost protectively.

"What *happened*?" Vex asked him, gripping his arm with worry. He only let go when Sev grimaced, paling and apologizing; Sev just waved it off. He understood Vex's distress.

"I know you're worried," Sev said. "But I honestly have no idea."

It was kind of terrifying to think that he'd come that close to death—and yet, at the same time, it didn't feel real. He hadn't felt any pain, hadn't felt himself begin to slip away . . . Sev had always thought he'd go down fighting, when it came to death. Not against monsters or people, necessarily. If he survived long enough, he imagined that he'd battle the shadow of death every second of every day, until he either lost or won.

But there had been nothing *to* fight. There was no creeping sensation he could rally himself against, no specter with which he could argue and bargain. His body had simply *shut down*. It didn't feel like he'd come close to dying at all, and he wouldn't have believed it if not for the redness in his friends' eyes.

Sev . . . decided not to think too much about it. For now, anyway. He'd need time to process this, he recognized in a distant sort of way—but he could do that later, in his own time.

"I know it's not much reassurance," Sev said. "But I know as much as you do, which is just that it happened when I started talking about . . ."

He paused, then frowned. Would it happen again if he said Onyx's name? A tendril of fear coiled around his heart. He'd come close to dying before, apparently. But it was better to test it now than when he *wasn't* surrounded by priests, surely?

Vex seemed to realize what he was thinking, because the lizardkin hissed and moved to press a hand over Sev's mouth. "Don't—"

"—talking about Onyx," Sev finished right before Vex tried to silence him.

"Don't *do* that! We don't even know what made that happen yet!" The wizard frowned severely at him.

"Sorry," Sev said. "I think I'm okay, though."

Then he started, remembering what else had happened. "Velykos," he said, his eyes wide. "Is he—"

"—He's fine," Misa said. "I kept an eye on him for you. A couple of priests tended to him after we caught him, but he didn't actually suffer any damage; he just . . . fell."

"The magic that animates elementals is complicated," Vex explained. He still looked a little upset but seemed to be trying to focus on the issue at hand. "Part of it for stone elementals is an enchantment that makes the stones lighter. I saw that part of the enchantment suddenly fail, and that's how I knew he was going to fall."

Sev frowned. "But I've talked to other priests about Onyx before. I've talked to *you* about Onyx before. Why would telling Velykos cause this?"

Derivan spoke, hesitant.

"Perhaps because he is an elemental? They are bound to nature in a different way, and you mentioned there were other followers of Onyx," the armor said. "Other followers that were forced to choose and made to forget."

"You think he's one of Onyx's ex-followers?" Sev frowned, considering the idea. It wasn't like he knew many of Onyx's other followers, given that he never really engaged with the temple. He'd just treated the man like a friend, and Onyx had seemed to appreciate that. "Maybe?"

"What's Onyx's domain?" Misa asked, raising an eyebrow. "You never said. It's something Earth related, I assume, so I can see a stone elemental choosing to follow him."

"Uh . . ." Sev paused for a moment.

Vex groaned. "Please tell me you didn't forget."

"I didn't talk to him about being a god!" Sev said defensively. "He wanted to know more about the world! Gave up a lot to be able to talk freely with his followers, he said. I told him about the world, we played some chess— Oh! He's a god of sculptures. Sculpting. One of the two. He made the chessboard."

"Sev . . ." Misa sighed.

"We will have to speak to Velykos, I think," Derivan said. "*Without* mentioning Onyx. Perhaps he can enlighten us, if he tells us how he chose to follow Nillea."

"Is he . . . okay? I could go speak to him now." Sev ignored the protests of his friends and swung himself out of bed. He felt *fine*. He hadn't had a neardeath experience. He hadn't been remotely aware enough for that to count as a near-death experience.

His friends exchanged worried glances.

"I'm fine," Sev insisted. He glanced around for Velykos—the elemental, thankfully, wasn't exactly hard to find. He was enormous, after all. Then, ignoring their protests, he started off toward the other priest.

"You are here," Velykos rumbled as Sev approached. The elemental was still lying down and facing the ceiling, but he seemed to sense Sev anyway. "Will you give me answers? The priests would not give me any."

"I'm not sure I have any for you," Sev said. "And I don't think I can try to explain what we think happened without causing another incident. But I'm sorry about what happened."

"You were trying to tell me something, and I could not perceive it." Velykos was silent for a moment, the only sound he made the faint churning of rocks deep, deep underground. "If I try to remember . . . a part of the magic that enchants me falters. I can sense this now, I think."

"I don't understand *why*." Sev pressed a hand against his temples, rubbing them in frustration. He sounded anguished and worried all at once.

"I have no answers for you," Velykos said.

"Maybe if you told me a little more about you?" Sev tried. "How did you decide to worship Nillea?"

Velykos seemed to smile. "I thought you were trying to avoid being preached at."

"But this is actually *important*," Sev muttered, sounding petulant, and Velykos chuckled.

"You mortal races. Always impatient, rushing for things." He hummed. "It is not unappealing, I suppose. Very well."

He told his story.

It wasn't a long one, all things considered—with the timescale immortal races operated at, Sev had been half-worried it would be a tale that would take hours. But it wasn't.

Elementals, Velykos explained—and indeed, immortal races as a whole—weren't big on religion. It was rare to find a member of an immortal race that wanted to follow a god. They just didn't really gain anything from it; if they chose a god to follow, it wouldn't be for the same reasons mortals did.

In his case, he'd found Nillea back when he was a young elemental still, as a priest of Earth visited the quarry that he'd spawned in. There had been no preaching, no sermons. The priest was a daemon, though Velykos would not come to know this for a long time. Instead, he simply watched, curious, as the priest sat and began to *carve*.

The idea of *art* had been a foreign one to him until then. Stones just *were*, until they weathered away; for stone elementals, age was the same as erosion. Older elementals were often smaller than they had been in the past, the stuff that made them slowly wearing down over the centuries. They could replenish themselves, but it was often a point of pride.

Never before had he seen the act of erosion take on *beauty*.

The priest carved, shaving away at the rock he held using the point of his tail; where it touched the stone, it crumbled into dust, years of erosion happening in an instant.

It was awe-inspiring. It was terrifying.

And what was *left* . . . was a beautifully formed crystal. He'd carved a rock into another kind of rock! Velykos hadn't understood humor then, but he had laughed, and the brightness of that feeling had surprised both him and the priest.

A chance meeting turned into a friendship. Velykos had asked to learn, and so he had been taught; it was only meant to last the day . . . but that day turned into a week, and that week turned into months. The priest visited the quarry nearly every day, and Velykos awaited him with eager anticipation.

He hadn't even learned that the man was a priest until eight months in. Their friendship was firm by then; they were less mentor and student and more father and child, strange as it was for a mortal to be a father figure to an immortal, ageless being that was technically older than him.

Then the priest had vanished. Velykos had never found out what happened to him—but he decided to start following the same path the priest had taken. He would become a follower of Nillea, for that was what the priest had cared about; he would honor him in that way.

It was a small way for him to hold on to a piece of the man that had made him who he was.

There was a heavy silence as he finished telling his story. Sev didn't know what he had been expecting, but whatever it was, it hadn't been that. He was hoping for some sort of discontinuity, some oddness of memory that would tell him that the memories were false, created by the system. There was nothing so obvious, except perhaps the empty way the story ended, and the way Velykos told his story.

There was a sadness to the way he spoke, a deep pain that went beyond the loss of someone close to him. Like something more had been taken from him. It was hardly proof of anything, but . . .

Nillea was a goddess of Earth. Onyx was a god of sculpting. The conclusion seemed reasonable enough.

"Thank you for sharing that with us," Sev said quietly. It felt inadequate, for the story was far more personal than he had expected.

"Did that help you find an answer?" Velykos asked.

"I think it did," Sev said. "Though I can't be sure. It's . . . We'll come back and explain to you when we can. I promise."

"Thank you for sharing your story," Vex said. The other three nodded in agreement.

"It is an old story." Velykos's voice was briefly wistful as he pored over old, old memories. "But it is good to remember it, I think. Thank you for indulging me and listening."

Sev nodded. "We'll visit again," he said, hesitating and glancing to his party; none of them seemed against it, so he nodded again. "Yeah. See you soon, Velykos. Take care of yourself and don't, uh . . . well, I guess I'll just be careful not to mention that around you again. We'll try to be back as soon as we know what happened."

"I thought I was too old for mysteries," Velykos said with a low, rumbling chuckle. "But I must admit . . . this is intriguing, if concerning. Find me again, young one."

"And be careful—you came far closer to death than I, to hear the priests tell it."

CHAPTER 14

BREAK

It took a while to get away, for the priests wanted to question them on what happened. A nervous Misa had to fend them off and explain that even trying to talk about it was dangerous, and explaining *that* had taken some doing. Eventually, the priests extracted a promise from them that they could be called on from the Adventurers' Guild if they were needed for anything, and with that promise secured, they quickly fled back to the Guild.

To Sev's room, specifically, where they typically gathered at the end of the day.

"I'm sorry," Sev spoke first, shaking his head. "You guys were worried about me, and I think maybe I didn't take that seriously enough."

"No fuckin' kidding," Misa muttered, but she sighed, seeming to soften a little bit as she looked Sev over. "Are you doing okay, Sev?"

Sev gave the question its due consideration, then sighed. "Honestly, I don't know," he said. "It's hard for me to convince myself to take it seriously? It just doesn't feel *real*. Maybe it hasn't sunk in yet, and maybe it won't ever sink in, but I know it worried you guys, and that makes it a problem."

"Good," Vex said, letting out a breath he'd been holding. He gave Sev his best attempt at a stern look. "As long as you recognize that!"

"Believe me," Sev said, though he couldn't help a small smile at the lizard-kin's expression. "That sucked for me, too."

"I am glad you understand." Derivan sighed out a breath he didn't need, trying to calm the worried coil of emotion in his body. "And Velykos? How should we pursue that?"

There was a small silence as everyone thought.

"I hate to say it, but I don't think there's much we can do about it right now," Sev eventually said. "We'll be there if the priests find anything, but I'm thinking we need a break."

"Haven't we already been taking a break?" Vex asked.

"We haven't left town, I guess, but in that time Derivan's gained three new stats that we still haven't entirely figured out and I almost died," Sev said dryly. Vex paused.

". . . Good point."

"Things *keep happening* and I think it's bad for our health," Sev said, trying for a small, lighthearted chuckle. "So, how about it? Picnic tomorrow? We'll go check out that nearby forest, review our statuses, and have *zero* world-shattering revelations."

"Fuck yes," Misa said. "I've been wanting to check the stupid thing since we had to fight the *massive boss monster*. I can't believe we haven't checked it already."

"You know why we haven't," Sev chuckled. "And with how the system was acting, don't be surprised if we don't get any experience at all."

Misa paled, as if the thought hadn't even occurred to her. "Please no."

"I'm pretty sure we'll get experience. That part of the system didn't seem broken." Vex gave her a sympathetic pat on the back. Misa just huffed, then relented with a sigh.

"I'm honestly kinda glad you guys made me stop checking all the damn time, but it still kinda sucks after battles like this," she grumbled. "But I think it sucked *more* when I checked after every battle and my level didn't go up. Made our wins feel like nothing."

"That's why we check it together, right?" Sev said with a small smile.

"Yeah," Misa agreed—and though it was tentative, she returned the smile, a little more vulnerable than her usual ones.

As if to make up for the stress of the past two days, everything seemed to align perfectly for the trip to the forest. Sev had gone down to check if the scouts had returned with information about the dungeon, and had been informed that while they *had*, they wouldn't be announcing the details of that dungeon today. Politics were involved, he was told, and the state of the dungeon would be announced later the next day instead.

Which gave them plenty of time to prepare, even if it was mostly Sev doing the preparations. The weather was perfect—not a hint that it might rain, or that some other strange weather event would tear through the area, as would sometimes happen when there was a rogue accumulation of mana.

The town was bright and cheery and welcoming when Sev went to gather some supplies, and though the markets were crowded, he was able to score good enough deals that he came back whistling.

Then they were off. The forest wasn't actually particularly far away, and time seemed to pass quickly as they chatted with one another. For all the danger that they'd so recently been put through, it had broken down the last few barriers they had between one another, and it felt like there was much more now for them to talk about.

"I don't really want to admit that I needed this," Misa said, stretching. "But damn, I kinda needed this."

"We all did, I believe." Derivan hadn't realized how wound up he'd felt until now. The subconscious way he'd been hovering over Sev and Vex and even Misa, like he had to try to protect them—it was something he'd put on himself for a long time, after all.

"No kidding," Sev said, taking in a deep breath of forest air and then promptly deciding he didn't particularly like the smell of forests.

Of the four of them, Vex was the only one that was actually taking a break and not just ruminating about how much they needed a break. The lizardkin was glancing around the forest with absolute fascination—Derivan would have wondered if he'd seen a forest before, if not for the fact that they'd been through many other forests in their travels.

"Is there something drawing your attention?" Derivan asked curiously, and the lizardkin froze for a moment before thawing.

"Oh! It's just that the magic in this place is really different. It's kind of gathering together and a lot more alive than in most other places." Vex waved his arms animatedly as he spoke, gesturing to streams of mana that only he could see—

—wait. No. Derivan paused in the middle of that thought. He *had* the ability to see mana now as Vex did, even if the mana wasn't so concentrated as to be visible, like it had been in the Nucleus. He'd learned the skill alongside [**Barrier**] and [**Intermediate Mana Manipulation**]; he just wasn't used to having all these options available to him. His skill list had been static for so long . . .

It was yet another thing to train, he supposed. He focused, and activated [**Mana Sight**].

Vex's version of [**Mana Sight**] was a little more complicated than his own, from what the lizardkin had explained to him—the skill you obtained as a wizard depended on how well you *understood* mana, and Vex understood it a lot better than he did. His own meager understanding, however, was still enough to make him stop in surprise.

Above him was a canvas, and mana was the paint.

He didn't need to be able to see the colors as Vex did in order to see the artistry with which streams of mana weaved their way through the branches, dancing merrily between leaves. He didn't need to understand the mana in depth to recognize the patterns that briefly formed in the air, runic language appearing and disappearing in the span of a blink.

Before, when he'd cast [**Barrier**] and watched the flow of the mana, it had felt like that mana was missing something—like it was performing a rehearsed dance and not truly free. *This*, then, was what had been missing; the sight of the mana dancing through the leaves was almost dizzying to look at.

"It is beautiful." Derivan stared upward. Vex beamed at him.

"Isn't it? I don't get to see mana phenomena like these a lot . . . They're not rare, exactly, but they're very easily disturbed. I'm surprised it hasn't faded yet with us here." Vex smiled, raising his hands and watching as a stream of mana twisted between his fingers.

"It is . . . disrupted by the presence of people?" Derivan asked.

"Best as I've been able to tell." Vex nodded. "I mean, it'll come back after a while, so it's not permanently destroyed or anything. It just kinda feels like the mana's shy or something. Or maybe there's something else I'm not seeing . . . Don't try to cast a spell, though; that'll almost certainly make it go away."

Derivan, who had in fact been about to cast [**Barrier**] to see if he could get the mana to dance in the same way, paused. "Ah."

"You guys are gonna make me jealous of your magic," Misa said with a smirk, teasing.

"Sorry!" Vex flushed slightly.

"Don't be," Misa scoffed, chuckling. "It'd probably make me dizzy even if I could see it. I'm not gonna be angry that you have something you can enjoy, Vex."

"Oh." Vex took this in for a moment, then nodded, projecting his best, bright smile. "Right! Okay. Yeah. I mean, if I ever figure out a spell to share my sight . . ."

"Then I'll ask you to share if we see something like this again." Misa smiled at the lizardkin. Derivan saw the look in her eyes, though, the glimmer of concern; it was one he shared. Sev had the same look, too, though he didn't say anything.

Hopefully, Vex would share more about his past when he was comfortable.

"We're coming up on a clearing," Sev reported cheerily. "Good place to have our picnic, I think!"

"Hell yeah." Misa grinned. "I'm fucking starving."

"What happened to 'Adventurers don't go on picnics'?" Sev asked, raising a brow.

"That happened three months ago!" Misa complained. "You can't keep holding that against me! Food is food!"

"Just admit you've been converted to the joy of picnics."

"*Never.*"

It didn't take them long to set everything up—the convenience of magic meant it wasn't particularly difficult to set out an eating space. Vex took only a few moments to conjure tables and chairs made out of stone, and while it wasn't the most comfortable setup in the world, it was enough. Sev began to unpack the food he'd brought, pulling out sandwiches, drinks, and snacks.

Derivan watched with interest, wondering idly what food tasted like. He'd tried using [**Consume**] on food once, out of sheer curiosity. It hadn't quite worked out.

"Did you cook all of this yourself?" Vex asked.

"Nah," Sev said. "I like cooking and all, but we just turned in a grade-six crystal. I splurged and got us the good stuff. Er . . . sorry, Derivan; I know you can't eat and all."

"It is no matter." Derivan wondered, idly, if he would be able to acquire a skill that would allow him to eat as others did. "As long as you enjoy your food, of course."

"Don't think that means we didn't get anything for you!" Sev grinned at him, then reached into the basket again. "Misa, Vex, and I all talked about it, and since you can't eat with us, we wanted to get you a gift of your own. So."

He pulled out a large container of what looked like armor polish and a cloth.

Derivan blanked. "What?"

Sev just grinned at him. "Come on, when was the last time you had your armor polished?"

"I *am* the armor, so . . . never." He could hardly remove his own armor to polish it.

"Exactly!" Sev said.

"Maybe it'd feel like a massage." Misa grinned at him. "You never know."

Derivan reached out to carefully take the polish from Sev, almost reverently. "Thank you for the gift."

What a strange feeling. He'd never been given a gift before. Misa, Vex, and Sev were all smiling at him.

"Give it a try!" Vex said, his tail swaying excitedly. "I helped enchant it. You don't even need extra tools; it does all the mechanical work by itself."

"I will try this away from the table," Derivan said after a moment, smiling at the wizard's enthusiasm. He understood that polish had a . . . strong smell, so he took a few steps away, then sat on the ground, staring at the tub.

His friends stared at him, evidently waiting to see him try it. Derivan chuckled, picking up the cloth and feeling warm.

Might as well give it a try.

CHAPTER 15

ECOSYSTEM

Derivan finished off the last of the polishing with a bit of a flourish. The others were working through the massive array of food that Sev had purchased, with Misa absolutely demolishing everything that was set in front of her. They glanced over at him from time to time, making sure he felt included, and that had been . . . nice.

"Well? Did it feel like a massage?" Sev grinned at Derivan. The armor chuckled faintly, glancing over his now-shining armor with a small amount of burgeoning pride.

"I am afraid I do not know, given that I have no experience with massages to begin with," Derivan said, flexing an arm and testing the smoothness of the movement. "It is . . . comforting, I suppose. I feel refreshed, more easily able to move. There was a stiffness to my movements that I did not realize was there until now."

"Sounds like a massage to me!" Sev said cheerily, grinning.

"And I gotta say, you're looking good after that polish." Misa gave him a thumbs-up, Vex nodding in agreement.

"I never realized how much detail was hidden on your armor," Vex said. "Not that you were dirty before; it's just—the polish really brings out the detail, you know?"

Derivan hummed with pleasure. It certainly had. Most of the intricacies of his armor were engravings rather than the gold or silver trims that were more typical for magical armor. They hadn't been particularly visible until now, and while vanity was not something he was overly concerned with, he couldn't help but feel a little pleased.

Vanity or not, it was a visual reminder that the others thought of him and wanted him to feel included. He'd never felt particularly left out at meals, but he was grateful nonetheless.

"Shall we check our statuses now?" Derivan suggested.

"Fuck yes," Misa declared. She glanced at Sev. "I mean, I think now is a good time."

"Nice try," Sev said with a chuckle, but he waved at her to go on. "Yeah, let's see if that battle did anything for us."

As one, they triggered the mental command that opened their status screens. Even Derivan, though more as an act of participation than any genuine need. His status hadn't changed much—it was still reporting errors—but some numbers had gone up.

Derivan, Level <ERROR>
Health: <ERROR>
Mana: 600/600

Stats:
Slime: 6
Physical Empathy: 22
Magic: 14
<ERROR>

Skill List:
[Intermediate Mana Manipulation], [Mana Sight], [Fireball], [Barrier], <ERROR>

[Mana Sight], [Fireball], and [Barrier] were all basic wizard spells; he'd yet to study all of the scrolls Vex had given him. Instead, he'd elected to improve his mastery and training of the skills he'd already managed to learn— [Barrier], in particular, was going to be important as long as his health was broken.

"Yesss," Misa crowed, distracting Derivan from his thoughts.

"I take it you gained quite a few levels?" The armor glanced up at her, chuckling.

"I'm level forty-two now! Straight to Silver!" Misa grinned wide. "Got a new skill for it, too. Here, see for yourselves." She spun a copy of the box up toward the rest of the party with a thought, and they glanced at it with interest.

[Every Last Drop] [Active Skill] [Grade: 1]
You may choose to lose mana instead of health at a <100%> cost markup.

Sev whistled. "You can use that together with [**To Fall Yet Hold the Line**]?"

"Probably!" Misa grinned. "I haven't tested it yet, obviously, but I sure fuckin' hope so. It's gonna be a pain in the ass to level, though."

"Do you have a lot of mana?" Vex asked.

"Weeeell . . ." Misa drew out the word, then blew out a sigh. "Okay, no. But every little bit helps!"

"We'll have to see what counts as you losing mana," Vex said thoughtfully. "Like, if you're holding on to a mana potion, does that count as 'your' mana?"

Misa smirked. "I fuckin' love you guys, you know that?"

There was a smattering of laughter.

"I'm up to level thirty-seven," Vex said, smiling at his status screen. "Almost Silver. I think I went up almost twenty levels, which is kind of unheard of. No new skills, but I got some upgrades to my existing ones—improved rune recall, that kind of thing."

"Level forty-five," Sev said. "No new skills." He seemed to hesitate a little, like he wanted to add something, but changed his mind at the last minute. "Which is fine. Plenty of stat points to distribute."

"You'll get some soon, I bet," Misa said cheerily, perhaps not noticing the cleric's brief hesitation. "Silver's the range for skills, Gold's the range for upgrades, and Platinum does whatever the fuck it wants."

"Is that the saying?" Sev asked with a faint grin.

"Ah, it's close enough." Misa waved it off. She yawned and let out a stretch, evidently finished with her food. "What've you got planned for the rest of the day, boss? Can't be just a picnic."

"Why don't we just explore?" Sev suggested.

"It's a forest," Misa said, deadpan. "There are trees and also more trees."

"It's a lot more than just a forest!" Vex argued, then paused. "I mean. I guess it is, technically, literally just a forest. But there are a lot of interesting things in forests—alchemical ingredients. Magical plants. Weird animals sometimes."

"Each time we have been through a forest, our goal has been to trek through it," Derivan commented. "I know very little about the plant and animal life within one. Perhaps you can serve as a guide, Vex?"

"Oh! Yeah! I know lots of little tidbits about plants. Maybe a little less in this region, but still." Vex's eyes practically gleamed.

Misa groaned. "You're lucky I love you guys."

"She loves us!" Sev proclaimed with an exaggerated cheer.

"I'm going to hit you with my mace. And you're a healer, so I know you can take it."

". . . Lead the way, Vex!"

Vex grinned brightly. With a wave of his hand, the tables and chairs that he'd made out of stone *crunched* back into the ground; with it, the mana that had vacated the grove and was peering curiously at them through the trees rushed back in, seemingly joyous. Vex looked up at it like he was surprised, though his face relaxed into a softer, happy smile after a second.

Then he scurried ahead, infectious grin returning even as Sev hastily gathered the remainder of their supplies. Derivan followed closely behind, and Misa took the back of the trail, waiting for Sev to go ahead of her. There was still a need for *some* caution, as safe as this area tended to be, and she would rather not leave their healer and leader vulnerable.

The first thing the lizardkin found—and brought to Misa, of all people— was a bit of moss.

"Found it!" Vex's claws dug into the bark of the tree, easily tearing away a strip of it. On that strip of bark lived a strangely luminescent purple variety of moss, glowing weakly in a rippling pattern; to Derivan's mana sense, there was no magic radiating from it. How strange. "This is Drunkard's Beard."

". . . You better not be calling me a drunkard," Misa said, narrowing her eyes playfully at Vex. "Also. What kind of drunkard has a beard that glows purple?"

"Honestly, herbalists just really like naming any type of moss after beards." Vex scrunched up his snout a bit as he thought about it. "I can name at least twelve varieties, I think. This one makes you drunk."

"It's alcoholic?" Misa blinked.

"No. It makes you drunk." Vex poked at the moss. "It's actually pretty weird. It doesn't seem magical at all and there's nothing in it that should make you drunk. But . . . that's what it does. It's not just an effect that's similar to being drunk, either; all spells designed to test for sobriety will consider the person drunk, and species that have unique mental reactions to alcohol will all have the same unique reactions to Drunkard's Beard. None of the physical ones, though."

"The fuck?" Misa peered at the moss. "Okay, that *is* pretty weird."

"And kind of cool, right?" Vex grinned at her, and she scoffed—but not before she grinned back.

Just a bit.

Derivan was watching the moss closely. "We don't know how it works?"

"Nope," Vex said, shaking his head. "One of the weird mysteries we've just kind of given up on for now. I'm sure someone out there is studying it, but there are much more interesting things to study still."

"Like this thing!" Sev called out, and the other three were startled to realize that Sev had wandered a good twenty feet away.

"Dammit, Sev!" Misa shouted back. "Don't wander off on your own!"

"But come look at this!" Sev waved the party over and they came, Vex absentmindedly tucking the sample of moss into his tailpouch. Sev was standing next to what seemed to be a cluster of crystals not dissimilar to the mana crystals they found in Nuclei. "What do you think this is, Vex?"

". . . Hm." Vex searched his memory, crouching down to peer more closely at the crystals. "Crystals in a forest are pretty unusual. There are a few varieties of plants that mimic crystals, but I'm bad at telling them apart. It's probably a type of mana flower that feeds off the ambient mana in the air. Good for mana potions."

Curious, Derivan activated his [**Mana Sight**], crouching down by the crystals to watch the flow of mana. Sure enough, Vex was right—where the mana tended to twist and breeze past objects, it went *through* the crystals, becoming a little less bright on each pass. If he looked more carefully, he could see small sparks trailing down the crystals toward the roots of the plant.

The sight was rather breathtaking, really. "Should we gather some?" Derivan asked. If they were useful for mana potions . . .

"Probably best to leave it for the herbalists," Vex said with a slight grimace. "They're not easy to harvest without all the raw mana just spilling out."

"And these have nothing to do with the mana crystals we get from Nuclei?" Derivan glanced at the crystal flowers again; they really did look alike.

Vex hesitated. "They're related in some way, if I had to guess," the lizard-kin admitted. "Maybe mana prefers a crystalline form or something. We'd have to ask one of the wizards doing research on mana crystals to know more."

"I would've thought we would have uncovered all the secrets of mana crystals by now," Sev commented.

"History as we know it doesn't extend that far back," Vex said with a slight shrug. "Too many gaps where we lost knowledge, and we haven't had that much time. And mana crystals are . . . complicated. We don't know why they exist and we don't know why the system needs them. We don't really know how it's processed into the refined form we use, either."

"You said something about processing them being costly to do outside a Nucleus," Derivan mused, and Vex nodded.

"The methods we know of can't be what the system uses. All we do is . . . pump mana into them. It's unrefined and inefficient, and we have to do it in stages so it doesn't explode." Vex paused, pondering how to explain it. "Mana attracts mana, but crystals have stable points where they stop accumulating mana. To stimulate their growth, we need to artificially inject mana into them and push them past the stable point, then let it accumulate naturally until it hits the next stable point."

"You know a lot about this process." Misa raised a brow at the lizardkin, and Vex flinched slightly.

". . . Yeah, I do," he breathed out, and went silent.

They walked on for a bit, none of them saying a word, until Misa eventually spoke.

"You don't have to tell us, you know," Misa said quietly.

"I know." Vex looked to the ground. "I want to. Just . . . give me time."

The others could only nod. Derivan placed a hand on the lizardkin's back, and he jumped a little before smiling gratefully at the armor; Derivan inclined his head in response.

It took time, but Vex eventually warmed up to talking about the forest again, full of trivia about every little minutia. This was a webwood spider, he would explain; it was a type of spider that lived in trees and created webs out of that very same wood, using some sort of wood manipulation and then applying a thin layer of sticky mana to it to catch prey. This small, unassuming stalk that looked vaguely like a dead root was in fact an illusion cast by a colony of tiny, antlike creatures that Vex insisted were not ants. This tree was just a tree, but this *other* tree, right next to it and completely identical to both the naked eye and to conventional [**Mana Sight**], was a tree mimic, a very particular sort of plant that would periodically uproot itself and copy a different tree.

That last one, the party decided, demanded explanation.

"How could you tell?" Derivan asked first; he was switching between his [**Mana Sight**] and regular vision, and finding no differences between the two.

"Look at the roots, not the tree," Vex explained. "The two trees are identical, and that points to a tree mimic. But what actually differentiates them is the dirt—the dirt around the mimic is a lot more disturbed, and there are less plants around it, because there hasn't been time for much plant life to grow."

"I have no idea why this exists," Sev declared, glaring at the tree like it personally offended him.

"I think the mimic is the other one," Misa said, amused, and Sev switched his glare to the other tree.

"What's the *point*?" Sev asked. "I understand mimics; they exist to hide themselves from predators or are otherwise ambush predators. But this one already has a perfect disguise; it's undermining itself by *walking off* every so often."

"It gets bored." Vex shrugged, and Sev stared at him like he'd grown a second head. "What? Mimics are pretty sentient, like most other animals. They're more patient than most, but all mimics move around. It's just more obvious when it's a tree moving around, because of the roots thing. Also, they're not predators." He reached out to pat the trunk of the tree.

"What I want to know is why the system doesn't register this one as a monster." Misa eyed the tree critically. There was nothing from the system—most mimics would be tagged with a level and name as soon as they were identified as mimics. "Are you sure you got the right one?"

"Oh, yeah. Tree mimics don't register as monsters. Honestly, what the system does and doesn't classify as a monster is still being studied." Vex gave Derivan an apologetic glance. "It's . . . definitely not infallible. But different kinds of mimics aren't actually the same species, so most patterns can't really be extrapolated to all of them."

"Weird," Sev muttered, and Vex nodded, agreeing. Derivan remained silent, contemplating on the nature of what the system registered as a monster. It had changed for him, but he didn't know if that *meant* anything.

Too many answers they still needed, he decided with a sigh.

The party moved on.

It wasn't long until the sun began to set and they had to set their sights on returning to the Adventurers' Guild—but the break had certainly done them good, they all felt. Derivan's mind was somewhat preoccupied by the thought of systems and monsters, but even he felt more or less rejuvenated; the questions he had were questions that could be answered later.

More importantly, they had timed their return to the Guild's announcement of the fate of the recently formed dungeon.

And there was a crowd.

CHAPTER 16

DAMMIT, JEROME

"Where the hell did everyone come from?" Misa said, looking around in slight bewilderment. "There weren't this many adventurers around when we left."

"Word got out, I'm guessing," Sev agreed, frowning slightly. "Means it's a big announcement."

Vex was mostly silent—the lizardkin didn't particularly enjoy crowds, instead using Derivan's presence to deter onlookers. Indeed, the other adventurers tended to give Derivan a bit of a berth. Something about his armor being intimidating, he supposed.

Everyone was gathered in the Guild's lobby, and a restless sort of energy hung around among the adventurers as they waited. There was a makeshift stage where the questboard was normally stationed, and it was the only spot in the lobby that wasn't already full, with just the one woman standing idly there. Derivan and the others, who had returned pretty much exactly on time for the announcement, had to stand near the door. There was no space anywhere else.

Derivan hadn't actually seen the Guildmaster—nor had he seen any of the leaders in charge of individual Guild branches, for that matter. As he understood it, they tended to be somewhat reclusive, rarely meeting with adventurers in person; when they weren't resolving a crisis, they were handling administrative work. What that administrative work was he didn't really know, though Sev had once explained it had to do with how the Guild handled individual teams, as well as each branch's relationship with nearby cities and towns.

Now that he thought about it, the fact that the Guildmaster was personally handling this announcement was probably some indication as to its importance.

"Greetings," the Guildmaster said, and Derivan blinked, the lights in his helmet flickering. It was like a switch had flipped in his mind. He'd seen that woman standing in the middle of the stage—of *course* she was the Guildmaster. Who else would she be?

But he hadn't made the connection, for some reason, and it seemed like he wasn't the only one. Other adventurers seemed to be similarly startled, with several of them letting out a brief curse as their brains suddenly told them in no uncertain terms that *the Guildmaster was there.*

She was . . . she was a middle-aged, nondescript woman? Her features were indistinct, and try as he might, Derivan found he couldn't pinpoint anything about her besides her identity.

"Some kind of perception-based skill?" Vex muttered at his side. His voice was slightly strained, like he, too, was trying to see through it.

Derivan tried to watch her more carefully, but his attention slid off of her like it was water; there was nothing for him to latch on to—

—no. Wait. He *could* latch on to something.

> **You are circumventing a powerful anti-identification Skill.**

He couldn't get a read on her appearance, but he could still *read* her with Physical Empathy. He could tell he wasn't *supposed* to, somehow; there was a strange resistance to it that required him to focus his efforts. Her skill should have masked everything from him, he suspected, even her body language, but it seemed like the stat could go around it somehow?

He could see that her eyes were sharp, the corners crinkled just slightly in amusement at the way the adventurers reacted to her. Her shoulders were hunched, just barely; deeper-set stress and irritation from something unrelated to the adventurers muttering amongst themselves about her appearance.

> **<WARNING>**
>
> **You have partially circumvented a powerful anti-identification Skill. The owner of the Skill will be alerted.**

Derivan frowned at the message. The system could have warned him about that earlier.

Sure enough, the Guildmaster paused in her announcement, searching the crowd with faintly narrowed eyes. Her eyes met his own for a moment.

Then, to his surprise, she winked.

No one else seemed to have noticed, though, and she continued her announcement like nothing had happened. Derivan realized vaguely that he hadn't been paying attention, and sheepishly tuned in.

"Normally, a new dungeon forming would be something to celebrate," she said, her gaze sweeping impassively over the crowd. "And indeed, this dungeon is unique, even among the core dungeons cultivated in the Prime Kingdoms. We don't know how or why this formed the way it did. We *do* know this dungeon is dangerous."

"It is a Platinum-tier dungeon," she said, and whispers swept over the crowd of adventurers. Her eyes hardened. "Which *means*," she added, "no one below Gold will be allowed to delve it."

There were groans and loud complaints. The Guildmaster's gaze was unrelenting, but then she sighed, holding up a hand; the adventurers quieted without really knowing why they did so. "But it doesn't matter; I tell you this only to lighten the blow. Even Gold teams will not be allowed to delve it, for Elyra has claimed it for their research."

"What?!" one adventurer in particular said loudly—he was clad in silver armor trimmed in gold. Some sort of paladin class, Derivan assumed. He didn't look happy, and neither did any of the adventurers he was with. "How is that fair? We were the ones that discovered the dungeon!"

"*Technically*," the Guildmaster said pointedly, "*you* didn't do shit. I messaged you when the dungeon was forming, telling you that there was only a single adventuring team on site and they might need assistance. You were the only team that could get there and scout it within minutes. You said, and I quote, 'Get back to me when there are rewards that are actually worth my time.'"

"I didn't know it was going to be a fucking *Platinum*-tier dungeon," the strange man scoffed.

"That shouldn't have mattered. You were hardly on an important assignment, and you were well aware that I had already allocated all the resources the Guild had available to the task as a reward." The Guildmaster's eyes narrowed again, and this time Derivan didn't feel the resistance that meant he was circumventing her skill. This time, she *wanted* everyone to sense her displeasure, and most of the adventurers shifted uncomfortably. "Any more compensation would result in deaths in *many* of the villages that rely on us."

"And how's that any of my business?" the man shot back. "The more I level up now, the more I can help you get your stupid crystals later."

Derivan felt Vex freeze next to him. He didn't see it, but he knew Misa's eyes were narrowed, and that Sev had taken a step forward, hands clenched around his staff. He, too, found that he felt disgust coiling around inside him.

But they held back. There was no reason to get involved now—not when it was already being handled.

"And when will that 'later' be, Jerome?" the Guildmaster asked, her voice icy. "One year from now? Ten? How much do you want us to sacrifice for the sake of your upward progress on the promise that you will *eventually* help, even assuming you survive the entire process? And you want me to believe that, having trod on bodies to get there, you would not do so again? Once you are too strong for anyone to deal with?"

The man—Jerome, apparently—glared, and opened his mouth again. But the Guildmaster waved a hand, and no words came out of his mouth. He seemed furious, but she ignored him, simply continuing with her speech. "*On that note.* I had planned to do this privately, but since you did me the courtesy of causing a scene, know this: I will be demoting your team."

There were shocked whispers, but she ignored them, even as the adventurer she was staring at grew even angrier than he already was. Her eyes were narrowed and intense. "Gold and Platinum rankers in the Guild are held to a moral standard, not just a power standard. This was made clear to you when you joined. You may have been powerful within Anderstahl, and we gave you a rank matching your power and prestige as a professional courtesy—but you are an *adventurer* now. You will be held to our standards and our rules. If you cannot behave like a Gold ranker of the Adventurers' Guild, then you will not *be* one until you have been judged worthy of the rank."

That finally gave Jerome pause. His fury seemed to double, and the adventurers around him that weren't a part of his team quickly backed away, sensing danger.

Derivan, farther away and not in any particular danger, frowned. Jerome had *joined* as a Gold ranker instead of working his way up the ranks? That was unusual in and of itself; the only people able to reach Gold and Platinum were usually people who had powerful backing.

Which meant that this Jerome had been . . . what, kicked out of somewhere else? The Guildmaster had mentioned Anderstahl, one of the other Prime Kingdoms, if he remembered correctly.

His thoughts were interrupted when a low cry of fear rose up from within the ranks of the adventurers, and several defensive skills activated as they rapidly backed away from the enraged man.

Brilliant flickers of light were gathering around him, mana so condensed and packed together that it became visible even without the benefit of [**Mana Sight**]. His party members stood behind him, their eyes narrowing. Two of them were women archers of some sort, it seemed, and the last member was completely hidden within their robes. All of them seemed to be getting ready for a fight. The air grew dense with power.

And yet . . . the Guildmaster didn't react. She stood relaxed at her position on the stage, unflinching and unblinking. The message was clear: *You don't want to do this.*

Then something seemed to resolve within him, and the lights abruptly cut out. "Fine," the adventurer spat. "I'll see you later, then, *Guildmaster.*"

He spun and stormed out of the guildhouse, brushing past Derivan and the others as he did so, his party members following behind him. No one stopped them.

"Bastards," Misa muttered, and Vex gave a shaking nod in agreement.

"*As I was saying.*" The Guildmaster's eyes were dark, even more irritated than before. "Elyra has claimed the dungeon, and the Guild will not be allowed to touch it. *For now.* I was able to negotiate a partial contract with Elyra: once most of the dungeon's secrets have been pried out, we will be allowed in. Elyra has first pick of any loot that drops but will pay twice the value of the artifact to the adventurers that find it, with the value determined by a Guild-issued evaluator."

"Negotiations with Elyra are ongoing, but they are very insistent about getting this dungeon, and the Guild doesn't have the political power to fight them on this." The Guildmaster paused, her eyes surveying the crowd. "Most of you aren't Gold- or Platinum-ranked, anyway, so it won't matter for you in the short term. For those that are, we ask that you don't endanger our negotiations by trying to force the issue."

"As for the adventuring team that discovered the dungeon." The Guildmaster spoke so smoothly that Derivan's party almost didn't register that she'd said it at all; it *felt* like just another part of her speech. It was deliberate, Derivan realized—she didn't want them to react obviously to the announcement. "I will be personally visiting your quarters later in the day. Please expect a visit."

With that, she left; the crowd began to disperse. Derivan's party glanced at one another.

"Well, let's head back to our room, shall we?" Sev eventually said.

"That Jerome guy is a dick." Misa frowned.

"The Guildmaster said he is from Anderstahl," Derivan said. "I believe that is the northernmost Prime Kingdom? Perhaps he was removed for this behavior?"

"Probably," Sev sighed. "And he's almost certainly planeshifted. That name is very . . . Earth."

"Does that matter?" Vex cocked his head at their cleric.

". . . No. I don't know. Maybe." Sev grimaced, looking up briefly and then back down as a woman slipped into their room. "I don't feel great about other planeshifted, but I think that's just because I haven't really had good experiences with them."

"Well, the guy was an ass, though; we can agree on that much," Misa grumbled. "Kinda wanna kick his ass."

"He's level seventy-two, I checked. Please don't provoke him," Sev deadpanned, and Misa huffed.

"I worry that he will do something anyway." Derivan's voice was concerned; he stood leaning against a wall at the side of the room, unable to convince himself to sit. "He was very angry, and he did not stop because he realized his anger was unjustified. He stopped because he formed a plan."

"There's not much we can do about it," Sev said, shaking his head. "Especially since we don't know what he's planning. We'll have to trust that the Guildmaster saw the same thing and is preparing countermeasures."

"I suppose." Derivan glanced over his friends. The answers they needed were in the dungeon, but none of them could get in, and the only adventurer that *did* technically have the power to get in was loud and worryingly hostile. Sev looked withdrawn, Misa looked agitated, Vex seemed distressed, and that woman still seemed irritated, though now that irritation was colored with amusement.

Derivan paused. The woman seemed irritated. How strange. There was something about the way her shoulders were hunched . . .

One thought linked to another. He blinked, eyes flickering in his helmet. He didn't know who that woman was, but the set of that irritation was familiar—

Two notifications blipped out at once.

You are circumventing a powerful anti-perception Skill.

<WARNING>

You have partially circumvented a powerful anti-perception Skill. Owner of the Skill will be alerted.

"The Guildmaster is here," he blurted, startled by how easily she'd slipped beneath their notice. To their credit, none of the others doubted him, though they seemed to interpret his surprise as a warning—they reacted in a flash, Misa reaching for her mace and the other two preparing spells. They looked puzzled, though, unable to parse any kind of target.

"So that's how you did it," the Guildmaster said, amused. "Not many can see through my skills. I'm impressed. But you can put your weapons away; I'm not here to fight, and I apologize for startling you. I was just curious about how your friend saw through me. You have a skill that recognizes body language and somehow associated that body language with me?"

All three of the others started as the Guildmaster spoke, then relaxed, slowly putting their weapons away. Derivan nodded awkwardly—it wasn't a correct assessment, exactly, but it was close enough. He could hardly explain what was going on with his status.

"Yes," he said out loud, and she grinned at him playfully.

"Should've stuck with the nod. That's a partial lie, but I'll let that one slide; I shouldn't have asked you in the first place, and you shouldn't be able to make that association at all."

"You have a crazy-ass set of skills," Misa muttered.

"Necessary, when you're the Guildmaster." The Guildmaster chuckled, the irritation bleeding away. "To address your concerns—yes, Jerome almost certainly has something planned. I've got eyes on him. They'll try to stop him if he does anything stupid, but I'd appreciate it if you could keep an eye out, too."

"You are here for a different reason, though," Derivan said, observing her. She was being . . . cautious?

"I am." The Guildmaster nodded. "You've probably already figured it out, but I lied a little bit back there."

Her voice turned serious. "I need to know what system messages you got during that formation event. That dungeon is *not* Platinum-tier. I'm not sure it fits any of our categorization schemes at all."

CHAPTER 17

TRUST

"... What do you mean?" Sev asked after a moment. He seemed wary.

"How are dungeons ranked normally?" Derivan cocked his head to the side, helmet clanking against his shoulder plate. "I am afraid I am missing some context."

The Guildmaster gave Derivan a strange look, but Vex quickly took over before she could speak. "They're ranked based on a combination of factors, usually the difficulty of the dungeon's challenges along with the level of the monsters inside. Usually, the dungeon's tier is equal to the rank of the monsters within, but it can change if the challenges inside are more difficult, or if the challenges allow you to bypass the monsters."

The Guildmaster furrowed her brows slightly. "... That is correct, yes," she said, nodding tersely after a moment.

"So what makes this dungeon so different?" Sev asked, eyeing the Guildmaster. "That ranking system seems pretty flexible to me."

"The problem is consistency and content." The Guildmaster's eyes narrowed slightly. "Dungeons don't usually have flexible difficulty ratings, but this one seems to adjust based on the adventurers delving them. The challenges, for example, are as likely to kill a Bronze ranker as they are to kill a Platinum ranker."

Vex frowned. "The challenges adjust their stat requirements?"

The Guildmaster laughed at that, though it was a bit of a bitter one. "No. The challenges don't seem to be stat-based at all. They just . . . individualize themselves based on the delver. It caused a hell of a problem with our scouts, let me tell you; not a single one could agree on the difficulty of any given puzzle."

"But that's . . ."

"It implies this dungeon is intelligent in some way, yes. Like the core dungeons in the Prime Kingdoms." The Guildmaster watched Vex for a moment, her gaze making the lizardkin shift uncomfortably. He wrapped his tail around to his front as if for comfort, and her eyes softened just slightly. "That's dangerous in and of itself. If it were known that there was a 'Platinum' dungeon that could be theoretically delved by Bronze and Iron rankers, there'd be a flood of demand, and we'd have to deal with idiots trying to sneak in and getting themselves killed. But if it were just that, we'd probably rank this as an unusually dangerous dungeon, and that would be that."

"There's something else," Vex said.

"There are a number of intelligent monsters in that dungeon." The Guildmaster nodded, ignoring the sharp intake of breath from all of the party except Derivan. The armored monster's eyes simply narrowed slightly as he took in this information. Was that his fault? The dungeon had used him as a seed. "Monsters that can talk. Which is unusual, as I'm sure you'll agree."

"Quite," Sev said smoothly, taking over before Vex could respond. The lizardkin couldn't lie if his life depended on it. If the Guildmaster noticed, though, she chose not to comment. "And these monsters are dangerous?"

"Very much so." The Guildmaster paused there for a moment, as if trying to find the words to articulate the danger. "This is the first instance of a dungeon's mechanisms being controlled by its denizens that we know of. The intelligent monsters, if you encounter them, can manipulate and change the existing puzzles to make them more or less dangerous to you."

"Do they do that?" Misa asked. The Guildmaster looked up at her, and she clarified. "Do they make the challenges less dangerous? That seems like a good thing."

"If they like you," the Guildmaster said with a shrug. "But more likely than not, they won't, and they'll just make everything worse for you and everyone else in your party. They definitely didn't make things easier on my scouts; most of them are still recovering, except for the one that one of the monsters took pity on."

Sev and Misa exchanged glances briefly. Vex seemed very still. Derivan, for his part, still didn't know how to react.

"On top of that," the Guildmaster continued, as if largely oblivious to the interplay going on between the party members—Derivan saw how sharp her eyes were in spite of it, however—"the monsters themselves break all the rules we know of. They're not just intelligent; their difficulty doesn't tend to match their level. Bronze-ranked monsters have skills that would be dangerous to even Platinum rankers. Platinum-ranked monsters sometimes pose no danger at all."

"There's that much of a level range in the dungeon?" Vex frowned.

"Yes," the Guildmaster said. "Which is only one of the reasons I need to know what messages you got from the system when this thing was forming. We need to know if it has any more surprises up its sleeves, and if it does, we need to be ready for them. Or at least warn Elyra about them. I can't imagine the level of diplomatic incident we'll end up having if we withheld information that could have prevented a catastrophe."

"I don't— It's not that easy for us," Sev said with a slight furrow of his brows, glancing around at his party members. "We'll need to discuss this among ourselves. Several of those messages contain some private information about our classes."

Which was an excuse, Derivan realized. Sev had expressed before that he didn't care much for the privacy of the system—he was more than happy to share whatever was needed for the benefit of the whole. The problem was just that his class was unique, and no one else would ever have his class.

"I do not ask this lightly," the Guildmaster agreed. None of them were trying to hide that they *had* secrets, at least; they were only hesitating in sharing them.

Derivan was troubled.

Physical Empathy told him many things; it told him that the others were worried, but not for themselves. It was almost subconscious, but the rest of the team had put themselves between the Guildmaster and him. It told him that the Guildmaster was relaxed—almost *too* relaxed, given the nature of what she was asking of them. There was no hostility from her, and yet . . . his teammates were worried.

"I don't suppose you'd take our word that there aren't any messages that would explain this?" Misa half-joked, her voice strained.

"I doubted the system would give direct messages about the nature of the dungeon to begin with," the Guildmaster said dryly. "We are looking for hints, not complete answers."

"This isn't a decision any of us can make alone," Sev said. "We need to discuss this. We will try to work with you, and we would not withhold any information that would put anyone in danger; this much I can promise you."

"Of course." The Guildmaster smiled at them. "I will return in thirty minutes or when you knock twice on your door. I'll even have a privacy ward cast on your room. Is that sufficient?"

Sev nodded once, and the Guildmaster got up and left the room; the door shut behind her, and a strange magic settled over them.

> **You have been placed under a privacy ward. Actions taken and words spoken will not leave the radius of the ward.**

Misa stood up, walked over, and jammed a chair under the door handle.

Vex stared at her, bemused. "Why'd you do that?"

"So she can't just walk in and have none of us notice that she's there again," Misa grumbled. Evidently she'd been thrown off by how the Guildmaster had slipped beneath their guard.

"Can we be sure that she walked *out*?" Sev joked; silence greeted him, and the cleric somewhat belatedly realized that they could not, in fact, be certain. He coughed. "Right. Well then. Operational security. Be vague enough so that we know what we're talking about, but for all we know the ward extends out past the door and she can hear us, so . . ."

"For what it's worth, my [**Mana Sight**] tells us the ward is confined to the limits of the room," Vex offered. "But it's probably best not to rely on that. Um . . . That said, I think most of the system messages are fine to share, honestly. Anything relating to the formation of the dungeon. What I'm worried about are the messages regarding the excess mana."

The bonus rooms, he meant, the messages that had outright stated their levels and classes, and revealed their secrets to one another.

"We can see if she'll allow us to be vague about it," Sev offered. "Take out the specifics of our classes."

"But you are not truly worried about your classes," Derivan said. "Only mine."

For a few breaths, no one spoke; then Sev sighed.

"It's my biggest worry, yeah," he admitted; Misa and Vex both nodded slowly in agreement.

"I do not think we should hide it," Derivan said plainly.

Sev hesitated. "Are you sure? The way she talked about monsters . . ."

"I suspect that she already knows what I am," Derivan said. "But more than that, I am worried that my presence is what caused the monsters in this dungeon to be intelligent. It may be crucial that we do not hide this."

"We can't." Vex shook his head, distressed. "I mean . . . maybe we can tell the Guildmaster. She seems nice. But we can't let Elyra know. I . . . I know Elyra. They wouldn't just let Deri go."

There was a tremble of genuine fear in Vex's voice that gave all of them pause. Derivan frowned slightly, moving closer to the wizard, and Vex seemed like he had to stop himself from shrinking back. Very gently, and giving Vex time to pull away if he needed, he placed a hand on the lizardkin's shoulder.

Very slowly, the trembling stopped.

"We will tell her, but ask that she disguise this information when she gives it to Elyra," Derivan said. "Is that acceptable?"

"I . . ." Vex hesitated slightly. It wasn't perfect—one only needed to look at their party and the dungeon-formation data to realize something was wrong. But the Guildmaster clearly had *some* skill-based way to disguise information, and the Guild itself had proven willing to try to do what was right in that earlier confrontation. ". . . Okay."

It was the best compromise they had. Derivan didn't want to risk leaving out something crucial, though he accepted it came at some cost to his safety.

"That isn't the only thing I'm worried about," Sev said with a sigh, now that that had been settled. "There's what happened afterward. The last battle we fought."

"There's no way they don't know about that one already. We shouldn't hide it," Misa said bluntly.

"The battle itself, no," Sev agreed; a moment later, Misa's eyes widened in realization.

"Ah, shit. The last time you even talked about it . . ." she said, and her voice trailed off. Sev nodded slowly.

"I will explain it," Derivan said. "And I will stop if it seems that what happened with Velykos is also happening with the Guildmaster."

"Are you sure?" Misa frowned. "Sev almost *died*. He only didn't because there were other clerics around that could keep him stable."

"That is why Sev cannot be the one to speak of it." Derivan glanced at the cleric. "Our healer must be available in case the worst happens. And my circumstances are unique enough that whatever affected Sev may not affect me."

He didn't have health, he meant. If the effect was health-related, he would be immune; if the effect stopped his heart, he would still be immune.

". . . Okay," Sev said slowly. Vex looked like he wanted to protest but ultimately kept silent; he seemed to understand that it was the most reasonable choice outside of just keeping silent on the matter entirely, and that didn't seem wise. Whatever was happening affected even the gods. "So. We explain everything we can. Derivan can talk about what happened with the Overseer and explain my use of [**Divine Communion**]—that's common knowledge about cleric classes, anyway. Are we agreed?"

"Agreed," the others chorused; Sev stood up, went to move the chair aside, and knocked twice on the door. His hands were shaking only slightly.

The door opened. A woman stood behind the door; she walked through and closed the door behind her before her skill dropped away and she once more became the Guildmaster. No deception this time, beyond what was necessary to stop others from realizing who was entering the room.

"We might not be able to tell you everything," Sev said without preamble. "But we will tell you as much as we can. Is that acceptable?"

The Guildmaster smiled a rare smile. "It is more than I was expecting."

CHAPTER 18

TRUTHS

The Guildmaster was only mildly surprised to hear of the abundant mana concentration and the way the deviation had rapidly swung right toward the end; if anything, the most surprising part for her was the weakness of the monsters they had fought in the final waves. A Platinum-tier dungeon was expected to have Platinum-ranked monsters spawn during its formation—but then, this adventuring team had been in lower Bronze, and it was a miracle that they had survived a horde of upper Bronze to Silver monsters to begin with.

Then they told her about the bonus rooms. The existence of a bonus room was not a surprise to her; the scouts had discovered at least one of them before retreating, a strange, inset door in the corner of a room that they wouldn't have noticed had they not been practiced with the anti-perception skills the Guildmaster liked to use. What *did* surprise her was that there were four of them; it was another abnormality, and it was a significant one. The most they had ever found in a dungeon was one.

"None of our scouts made it into the bonus room they did find," the Guildmaster admitted when asked. "They couldn't find whatever mechanism was needed to unlock it. Maybe you'd have better luck, but . . ."

Their team was still Bronze-ranked, she was thinking. Derivan glanced at Sev.

"About that," Sev said. "We're almost Silver now. Half of us are, anyway."

The Guildmaster paused. "You're still low Bronze on the Guild records." She frowned, then narrowed her eyes slightly, like something had occurred to her. Her voice was entirely too casual when she spoke. "That fight put you in Silver? It shouldn't have been enough to do that. What happened?"

Sev hesitated, trying to structure his thoughts. "We need to talk about our classes first. It's relevant, I promise," he said. He explained the rest of what had been in the boxes: their classes, and the "intelligent monster" that had shown up and taken Derivan's place in the selection process.

"Three of you have rare classes?" The Guildmaster twitched. "Fuck, I wish we'd known that. We would've promoted you sooner."

"Really?" Sev asked, blinking. She snorted.

"You have better heads on your shoulders than Jerome's team does," she said. "And if you all have rare classes, you can fight a tier up easily."

"What about the monster?" Vex asked, his tail twitching nervously. The Guildmaster snorted.

"You're all terrible at lying," she said plainly. "But you tried to be honest while protecting your teammate, and that counts for a lot. I figured that out earlier and ran all the diagnostics I needed to, so I believe you're not a danger. I will tell Elyra a modified version of this story." She glanced at Derivan, raising an eyebrow slightly. "You won't make me regret protecting you, I hope."

"I will not," Derivan said firmly.

"Good," the Guildmaster said. "Be careful around anyone Platinum-ranked. I'll have an enchanted amulet made and sent to you; wear it, and it'll make it harder for anyone to perceive what you are, even if they have the necessary sensory skills."

"You're taking this surprisingly well," Sev observed. He seemed a little shocked, but also pleased.

"I've seen some shit in my time," the Guildmaster said with an edge of sarcasm, and smirked slightly when Vex and Sev stared at her in surprise. Misa just grinned wildly, like she'd found a kindred spirit. Then the Guildmaster slipped back into formality like nothing happened. "Trust inspires trust in return. You were worried, but you told me the important details anyway and trusted me to do the right thing with that information. The Guild as an organization wouldn't work if we didn't put some trust in members that have earned it."

"So, not Jerome, to be clear," Misa said, her grin settling into something of a smirk.

"Not Jerome," the Guildmaster agreed, and they laughed, the room feeling a little lighter for just a moment. Derivan was, admittedly, surprised—but . . . trust could be a simple matter, Derivan supposed, as long as those involved were willing. It was good to know that the Guild was what it purported itself to be.

"You still haven't explained how your team went from low Bronze to Silver over the course of a single fight," the Guildmaster added after a moment of silence, arching a brow at them.

"There was still excess mana after the bonus rooms were created," Derivan started, hesitantly taking up the story when the others glanced toward him. "It initially went to the mana crystal we were cultivating and upgraded it to a grade-six crystal."

"This I saw," the Guildmaster acknowledged. "I wondered how you managed a grade-six with only a few hours' worth of processing. That crystal will help a lot of villages."

"It would have kept going, but there was . . . some sort of override. The excess mana was shunted to a summoning." The Guildmaster's eyes widened fractionally at this, but she said nothing. "It called down a Mana Abomination with a title—**<Overseer of Chaos>**."

"It called down a *boss?*" The Guildmaster stiffened, then cursed. "Jerome is a *fucker*. The only one close enough, and he just . . . Okay. What level was it?"

"We don't know," Sev said, and the Guildmaster frowned.

"You didn't see it?"

"No. We don't *know*," Sev repeated. "We saw it, but the system labeled its level with three question marks. We don't know what level it is."

". . . One hundred is supposed to be the level cap." The Guildmaster paused, but Derivan saw something in her eyes that was strange. A flicker of hesitation? And there was something else, too, that bothered him. Nothing specific he could pinpoint. "If there were three—"

"It was not level one hundred," Sev stated with an air of finality. "It was higher. Possibly much higher. We almost died."

"That should be impossible," the Guildmaster argued, but there was a trace of uncertainty in her voice. "There aren't—"

Derivan realized what he'd been missing. What *she'd* been missing. She didn't seem surprised, just worried.

"You already know," Derivan said suddenly. "Something happened?"

The Guildmaster paused in the middle of her speech. Slowly, the uncertainty bled away, leaving only a tired-looking woman. "I was hoping it wasn't true."

"What wasn't true?" Sev asked, looking between Derivan and the Guildmaster. "What?"

"We had a problem," the Guildmaster said with a sigh. "One of the scouts came back delirious, shouting about monsters above level one hundred . . . None of the other scouts saw it, so we were hoping it was an illusion. Some kind of trap."

She paused, then stared keenly at all of them. "I don't suppose you'll tell me how you're so sure?"

"Derivan was level eighty-six at the time," Sev said. "One hundred would have shown up, if that was the level."

". . . Was?" The Guildmaster blinked.

"We broke his level," Misa said with a shrug. "The system thought he was a monster, and that was stupid. So."

"You realize you're the most abnormal adventuring team I've met." The Guildmaster rubbed the bridge of her nose. "I'm starting to think I should be worried about *Jerome* instead of you four. Is that how you beat the boss?"

Derivan shook his head. "It was too strong for me. We worked together to stall until Sev was able to cast [**Divine Communion**]."

The Guildmaster frowned and cast her gaze to Sev. "So you cast [**Divine Communion**] and your god helped you out?"

"In a manner of speaking," Derivan said; the Guildmaster looked at him, surprised that Derivan answered instead of the cleric. "You should know that the last time Sev spoke of his god, he almost died, and the person he spoke to could not register or remember the name. We do not know the specifics of the effect yet, and so we are being cautious. The one he spoke to could not remember the name he spoke."

"I remember hearing about this. I didn't think it was related." The Guildmaster breathed out, then nodded. "Good of you to warn me. Give me a minute to prepare myself." The Guildmaster seemed to search through the air for a moment, consulting an invisible status screen. Then she used a skill, and the air around her rippled.

"Okay. Go ahead."

"The name of Sev's god is Onyx," Derivan said carefully.

The Guildmaster blinked once. She frowned. "Say that one more time, please. Just the name, nothing else."

"Onyx," Derivan said. He felt carefully at his soul, but nothing seemed to be happening, and nothing about his status had changed.

The Guildmaster tilted her head. "Why did you— Ah. I see what's happening." She sighed. "Ugh. This is going to *nag* at me. I hate this kind of magic."

"Don't you . . . *use* this kind of magic?" Vex ventured. He was watching the Guildmaster with slightly narrowed eyes—the mana was doing something strange again, but this time, parts of the effect were bouncing off the Guildmaster.

"That is why I hate it, yes," the Guildmaster deadpanned. "I can't correctly associate the thoughts you've presented me with. I know you were trying to tell me the name of a god; I also know that, for no particular reason, you brought up a type of rock. The link between these two facts should be obvious, *and I know it is obvious,* and yet I cannot hold on to the association even burning my best skills. It is infuriating."

The fact that she could even string the two facts along next to one another was already displaying an adeptness with perceptual magic that couldn't be matched by most—Vex understood this and was suitably impressed. Misa's brows were furrowed, not quite understanding how it was that the Guildmaster couldn't make the obvious connection, but taking her at her word.

"*For now*, let us proceed assuming that the name of the god is not relevant, and let us hope that you can tell me more."

Derivan nodded. He began to explain what happened——the space they were brought into once Sev had managed to cast the spell—but he had scarcely begun before the Guildmaster held up a hand.

"Stop." The Guildmaster rubbed at her temples; Vex was watching in alarm. Whatever the mana was doing around her had spiked in intensity. "This is not going to work. I am walking away from this with the assumption that a god is involved in some way, shape, or form. I need you to tell me if the god is an aggressor."

"No," Derivan said.

"Understood." The Guildmaster frowned, grumbling. "At least the magic allows me to remember this much. Infolocks are . . . rare. Not really known to anyone except the few Platinums digging into our history. It's some sort of system-level censorship. There are limits to it, but for the most part, they shouldn't be tested. Your friend . . ." The Guildmaster's gaze went to Sev, and she frowned slightly. ". . . The backlash is not normally nearly as severe as what happened to your friend; there may be something more to what happened. But there *is* backlash, often to your health and occasionally in the form of skill restrictions. Be careful sharing information, if you find that those you try to share it with cannot listen."

"Why isn't this better known?" Vex asked with a frown. The Guildmaster raised an eyebrow.

"Ever tried telling people they can't talk about something?"

". . . Good point."

"Just to clarify, there *are* monsters that use perception magic and prevent you from alerting others to the threat. That's not the same as an infolock. You're safe to try to communicate that any way you can." The Guildmaster hesitated. "From the story you've given me . . . do you need to investigate this dungeon?"

"Yes," Derivan said.

"Shit," the Guildmaster muttered. "Okay. I can work with this. You've given me a lot, and I can probably work it into our negotiations to get the Guild to send an envoy . . . You're practically a Silver team and you can fight a tier up. That's the only reason I'm even considering this, just for the record."

"You're going to let us delve the dungeon?" Misa said, excited. The Guildmaster held up a hand.

"I'm going to try to get you on Elyra's research team," she said. Vex flinched slightly at the words but said nothing. "You might be called on to participate in the negotiations. Keep an eye out, be on your best behavior, and sell to them why you might be useful. They probably won't call on you for *delves*, but that's the closest I can get you."

"That's . . . probably good enough?" Sev said, exchanging glances with the others. If they could find a way in . . . But it was a bit early to think about that.

"Well. Thank you for your time." The Guildmaster stood, evidently ready to leave; she offered them a small smile. "It is rare for adventurers to be quite as cooperative as you four. I hope to see you in the higher ranks soon. Preferably before Jerome makes it back to Gold and then to Platinum." She smirked a bit. "Though if I have my way, it will take him quite a while."

"I just hope he doesn't stir up too much trouble," Vex said softly; something about his countenance suggested nervousness, his tail swishing slowly and dragging across the floor.

"It will not involve you. He does not know that you are the adventurers that found the dungeon, and we have been sure to keep that information secret." The Guildmaster offered Vex a reassuring smile. It didn't seem to help much, but the lizardkin stood up straighter anyway. "Be ready to be involved in the negotiations. It will happen soon. Likely tomorrow."

A woman left the room. A box flickered in front of each of them, letting them know the ward had come down, and a slow exhale followed the sound of the door clicking shut, as each member of the team let out a breath they didn't realize they had been holding.

Vex broke the silence first.

"If we're going to be involved in negotiations with Elyra . . ." Vex ventured cautiously, taking a breath. "I may be able to help."

"Oh?" Sev glanced at the wizard.

"I was born to a noble family in Elyra," the lizardkin explained; he didn't look happy about it, but he *did* look determined. "There is a chance we can use my family name to press for our involvement. But I'm not exactly on the best terms with my family, so it might be a long shot."

"... We'll see if we need to," Sev said softly. "But thank you for sharing."

Vex nodded silently. He still seemed nervous, but he seemed to be calming down, now that he'd gotten that truth out there.

"Let's get some rest, shall we?" Sev suggested. "It's been a long day."

CHAPTER 19

NEGOTIATIONS

Vex had told them the next morning that it likely wouldn't take long for them to be summoned—Elyra, he said, tended to try to throw money at problems instead of actually resolving them. The negotiations would reach an impasse, and they would call on the adventurers to break that impasse.

It wasn't long before he was proven correct. Sev received the summons asking them to the uppermost floor of the Guild.

"Moment of truth, I suppose," Sev muttered.

There were no stairs that allowed them to access the uppermost floor—instead, each room in the Guild had a magically reinforced, spatially expanded closet that doubled as both a safe room and a means of housing a transportation circle.

"I never thought we'd get to use this." Vex looked around in some wonder, examining the runes in the ground. The runes began to glow as soon as the four of them stepped within the circle—before that, they had been completely invisible, even to Derivan's [**Mana Sight**]. "Or need to, I suppose. Usually it's meant for evacuation."

"Evacuation?" Derivan tilted his head. He couldn't imagine it being necessary in a building full of people that built themselves to fight. Vex gave him a wry, slightly sad smile.

"It's saved lives. It's rare, but dungeon breaks can still happen, and Guild branches are meant to be a last bastion of defense," he explained.

Derivan grimaced. That made sense.

The circle activated. Mana swirled around them, pulled in from their surroundings and from somewhere else—then it flashed *inward*, impacting all four adventurers.

And then they were in the uppermost floor of the Guild. Just like that.

Impressive feat of magic aside—and from the way Vex's eyes widened and the way the lizardkin began to mouth off calculations to himself, whatever magic this was was *complicated*—the entire floor in itself was impressive. It was obviously built specifically to accept political delegations, with all the splendor and magnificence that the task required. The magic and wards alone were strong enough that Derivan could feel them without using [**Mana Sight**], and then there were the tall pillars of alabaster, fixed into place with *mana crystals*, of all things . . .

. . . Derivan frowned. "Those are not actual mana crystals, are they?"

"They better not be," Misa said, narrowing her eyes slightly.

"No, no," Vex rushed to assure them. He paused, looking at them closely. ". . . They're some variety of crystal flowers, like the ones we saw back in the forest. These ones are slightly more refined, and it's harder to tell that they're just flowers, but they're definitely not real crystals."

"Good, or I was going to hit someone," Misa muttered.

"Please don't do that. We're here for politics. That's a terrible idea," Sev said dryly. Then he thought about what he'd said for a moment and amended his statement. "It's a terrible idea for now."

"I did not realize the Guild was this wealthy," Derivan commented, glancing around. There were no windows, but the room was well lit, light magic shining through crystal chandeliers to cast glimmering motes of rainbow light over the room.

"We're really not." The dry voice of the Guildmaster cut in, and all of them jumped in surprise; she'd been standing right in front of them, unassuming and as still as a statue. She raised an eyebrow at them. "The mana flowers are there to look pretty, but they're also there to power enchantments that suppress skills so we can avoid diplomatic incidents. You are aware that the entire delegation from Elyra is here, yes? They can hear you. Please don't threaten to hit anyone."

"Bring them here already!" a voice called, and the party finally focused their attention in the actual *center* of the room.

There was a table at the center; it was large, round, and decorated with an unnecessary degree of fine carving. The Elyran delegates were seated on one side, and there were five empty seats on the other—for the Guildmaster and the four party members, presumably. Small runes sat on the table in front of each seat, glowing dimly.

Derivan's gaze flicked over the delegates. They weren't what he expected, though he wasn't sure *what* he expected to begin with. There were two lizardkin, two humans, and one orc, each of them dressed in attire that the armor assumed was common for nobility in Elyra. He didn't miss the way Vex flinched, just slightly, as his gaze touched upon the two lizardkin in the delegation—but neither of them seemed to recognize him, and Derivan didn't call attention to it.

In short order, they were sitting at the table. Derivan found himself seated across from the orc; he was a slight, lightly built man, dressed in pure-white robes, and he offered a small, polite smile upon seeing Derivan watching him. "Hello," he said. "I am Leben, of the Divine Order."

"You are a priest?" Derivan asked curiously. Leben nodded, and Derivan wondered why a priest would be sent on this delegation. What did the dungeon represent for the Elyrans, anyway?

Vex sat next to him, opposite a human woman who seemed unable to stop scowling at everything around her. She didn't introduce herself, and Vex didn't ask. The others took their seats at the table, too, though Derivan quickly stopped paying attention as the Guildmaster spoke.

"So," she said. "We have reached an impasse within negotiations, as Elyra keeps attempting to offer more money in return for less Guild interference, and that is far from the resource that we are lacking." The Guildmaster's gaze cut across the table into the lizardkin man she sat across from; he sat with his arms folded, wearing a decidedly unimpressed look. "The Guild has the right to have one team involved with your operation, and I am personally vouching for their ability."

"And I have the right to approve that team. I don't see anything that makes them worth the investment so far," Tarilex rumbled in reply. He was a broad-shouldered lizardkin, Derivan noted, nearly twice Vex's size; he could see Vex almost shrink away from him as he spoke. "You claim these are the ones that discovered the dungeon? Four of them surviving a formation event for a Platinum-tier dungeon? Absurd. I am not a fool, Guildmaster."

"The dungeon formation was weaker than usual. There are many things abnormal about this particular dungeon, Tarilex; this is the entire reason Elyra cares enough to claim it at all." The Guildmaster sighed. "There is no point in rehashing this. You asked for this team to be brought up here for a reason; do not waste my time with political games."

"And what game are you playing, Guildmaster?" Tarilex asked, arching a single brow. "Backing this team to this degree? Do you owe them political favors? It does the Guild's image no good to pretend they discovered this dungeon, I assure you. They are—what, Bronze? *Barely* Silver?"

Silence. The Guildmaster did not engage, and while Misa looked like she wanted to say something, she did not. Derivan simply tilted his head—Tarilex seemed almost like he was fishing for information. Why? Was this not something that the Guildmaster had already explained to him?

"And you claim that there is information in this dungeon that is, of all things, restricted under an infolock," Tarilex added, when no one said anything. "And that your adventurers are privy to that infolock and can operate outside of its effects. But this hardly seems provable, and there is no benefit to Elyra when whatever they uncover cannot be shared.

"Unless, of course, you are claiming that your adventurers can secure a *shareable* secret out of this? That they can extract something?" Tarilex smiled a thin, sarcastic smile that seemed strangely empty. "The vast majority of adventurers I have met are thugs; I cannot imagine this group would be any different."

"Then you have a poor imagination." Derivan spoke without really thinking about it. It was strange—Tarilex spoke with all the pompousness and smug superiority of a noble, but his bearing didn't reflect that. He spoke with the hunched back of a man who pored over books, not the proud set of a man that lorded over others.

"Excuse me?" Tarilex swung his gaze to glare at Derivan, though strangely, there was no true heat in his gaze. Derivan looked back at him and realized that the rune beneath him was glowing—Ah. Voice amplification magic, then. He poked at the rune set in front of his own seat experimentally; when it lit up, he spoke again.

"I said that you have a poor imagination," Derivan repeated. Tarilex's brow twitched in irritation.

Ah. Derivan understood, perhaps belatedly, that Tarilex hadn't meant that he literally couldn't hear him.

Derivan paused and decided his statement required elaboration. "You have only met us once, and you think to judge our capabilities based on the fact that we are adventurers. If you are only capable of imagining adventurers doing one thing, then you strike me as a man with a poor imagination." He shrugged. Vex, beside him, did his best to hold back a snicker; his shoulders shook, though, so he wasn't doing it very well. Even the Guildmaster seemed vaguely amused.

"And who gave you leave to speak?" Tarilex frowned at him.

"... You did?" Derivan tilted his head, confused. "Why would we be called in for negotiations if our opinions were not of value?"

"Mm." All at once, any pretense at irritation seemed to slip away. "I suppose you have a point. And I thought you witless cowards, for all that you only seemed able to stay silent and watch." He smirked faintly. "But regardless of how capable you are, there may not *be* anything for you to extract from this infolock. We're still against your participation unless there's more you can offer."

The Guildmaster gave them an apologetic glance. This was on them, her look said; the Guildmaster herself didn't have any cards left to play.

"The infolock surrounds urgent events," Sev tried. "It may not mean much to you, but it is crucial that we are allowed to pursue more information related to it."

"What, the fate of the world is dependent on it?" Tarilex scoffed, but there was something strange in his eyes, like he was surprised.

"No. Only the fate of a friend," Sev said, his tone subdued. The lizardkin frowned, staring at Sev for a moment.

"...Be that as it may," Tarilex said. He sounded less pompous for a moment, a little more sincere. "My hands are tied."

"You're the leader of this delegation," the Guildmaster scoffed; Tarilex glared at her.

"*My hands are tied*," he repeated, putting a strange emphasis on the words. "You will need to give us more."

The Guildmaster fell silent, brows furrowing slightly, like she was confused. Derivan watched her for a moment, trying to read the expression—there was something she was concerned about, but that was about as much as he could tell.

"What about the bonus room?" Misa asked suddenly.

Tarilex frowned at her—Derivan saw the way his eyes darkened, the way he was suddenly more genuinely upset, unlike the false irritation of before. "What about it?"

Misa grinned. "Research costs you time and money, doesn't it? We can help speed up the process."

"Indeed," Vex agreed, picking up on her train of thought. "Dungeons pick out information from their surroundings to generate challenges; this is especially true for bonus rooms. We know what the dungeon used to seed the bonus room. We can give you that information in exchange for being allowed to participate."

"...This might be a worthwhile trade if you were the adventurers that discovered the dungeon," Tarilex said, still tense, though he had relaxed a little as they spoke. "But you are not."

"How are you so sure?" Sev folded his arms, a little irritated. "You've never seen us fight. You have no idea what we can do."

"I don't, that's true. Unfortunately for you, the adventurers who *did* discover the dungeon have already approached us, and we have verified their honesty with truth spells. This is why I wanted to meet your adventurers, Guildmaster; I wanted to see those that could convince you to engage in such a bold lie. I thought they might have been interesting." Tarilex leaned back in his chair. His anger relaxed into simple disappointment. Derivan frowned. Many of Tarilex's reactions had been strange, now; there was something about the way he kept swinging between his apparent emotions . . . "It seems I have only wasted my time."

"Fucking *Jerome*," the Guildmaster growled.

Tarilex frowned. "You cannot have expected a Gold-ranked group to go along with your coverup."

"It is *not* a coverup." The Guildmaster looked very much like she was hanging on to the barest thread of control; any more, and she would plant her face on the table, decorum be damned. "And they are *not* Gold-ranked. I have demoted them. They are Iron-ranked, pending them learning *basic manners*. I have half a mind to kick them out entirely for this stunt. I don't know what my people were doing, but—"

"It seems harsh to punish a team of adventurers for simply speaking the truth—"

Ah. The pieces finally snapped together in Derivan's mind, and he realized why Tarilex was acting so strangely.

CHAPTER 20

CONCLUSIONS

"Your truth spells were fooled," Derivan interrupted Tarilex. The lizardkin stopped midsentence, turning his gaze to the armor and staring for a long, uncomfortable moment.

"Explain," he said. His voice was hard.

"You have been running some sort of truth spell this entire time," Derivan said. "I wondered why you were acting strangely. You could trust neither spell nor skill with the Guildmaster, because she has perception-based skills that operate well enough to obscure her even in this space, when she is suppressed; that is why you wanted us here. You wanted to run the spell on *us*, to see what we revealed."

"Ridiculous," Tarilex tried to scoff, but his voice was uncertain, and the Guildmaster's eyes had hardened. The other four members of the delegation were still completely silent—and that was strange, too, wasn't it? "You can't prove that."

Derivan frowned at him. "You were not truly angry at me earlier, when I misspoke. The politics here matter less to you than the sincerity of the person you're speaking to. You softened when Sev spoke to you, because he spoke only the truth when he spoke of the infolock and of what it meant to him. It confirmed to you that we were being at least partially truthful, and that he had a friend he wanted to help.

"You did not *truly* feel upset until Misa spoke of a bonus room."

"Oh." Vex frowned, leaning forward a bit. He still seemed to be a bit nervous about speaking, but he was focusing on the problem at hand now, following Derivan's train of thought. "You wanted to give us the benefit of the doubt—I mean, kind of. You didn't trust us, but you wanted to give our story a chance. And since we were being deceptive when we talked about a bonus room, you picked up on that and thought we were lying about knowing any-thing about a bonus room at all."

"*That's* why you were being such an ass?" Sev groaned. "You know you could have just *asked*. We wouldn't have had a problem with being subjected to a truth spell."

"He couldn't. If you're *prepared* for a truth spell, there are a lot of ways around them, so you usually don't want to let your targets know that you're running one. If truth spells were more reliable, I would have pushed to have one active for *all* negotiations, just to guarantee that all participants were act-ing in good faith." The Guildmaster frowned. "No skills are allowed here. The wards on the pillars prevent spells of any kind. Even my skills barely work beyond securing my identity. I need to know what loophole you used so I can close it."

"We would never break the rules established by our esteemed hosts," Tari-lex said, fidgeting uncomfortably.

For an individual that seemed well versed in truths and lies, Derivan mused, he was rather bad at lying.

Vex blinked and frowned. His eyes began to glow for a moment before they stopped, suppressed by the enchantments, and he had to blink away the sudden dizziness.

"I was wondering why four of you were so quiet. You have a delegation of five, but one person does all the talking." Vex frowned "This can't be a real truth spell. It has to be something passive, or some sort of tandem skill . . ."

"Both of those should be suppressed by the enchantments," the Guild-master said, then frowned. "But if they're working cooperatively, they might be able to subvert it slightly. Maybe?"

"Maybe." Vex narrowed his eyes. "Guildmaster, can I have permission to do something?"

". . . Sure?" The Guildmaster stared at Vex for a second. "Sure."

Vex twisted around, digging into his tailpouch, then retrieved the bagged sample of Drunkard's Beard he'd picked up on a whim. Then he tossed it at Tarilex, who yelped, reaching out almost instinctively to catch it.

Almost instantly, he swayed in his seat.

No—almost instantly, *all five of them* swayed in their seats.

"What . . ." Tarilex groaned slightly, shaking his head. "What?"

"Okay, give that back to me now," Vex said, reaching out for it. Tarilex blinked blearily at the other lizardkin, then obediently handed the little pouch back. Almost instantly, he seemed to recover, his eyes sharpening.

"What the hell was that?" Tarilex said, and Vex flinched again.

"Sorry. I didn't think it was fair to engage with you while you were compromised," the lizardkin apologized. "But I needed to test that. You're from the Wisfield house, aren't you?"

"How do you know about that?" Tarilex frowned at him.

"I'm from the Ashion house," Vex answered, ignoring the way Tarilex paled and stared at him like he'd grown a second head. "I've worked with your house before. Last I heard, you were trying to find a way to turn your mental skills into some sort of bloodline. Did you actually *succeed*?"

"I— That's privileged information, si— That's privileged information," Tarilex managed, but failing to have any real heat in his voice.

The Guildmaster was just watching, amused. Derivan saw that she was rather enjoying this, actually. Presumably, she liked seeing them caught on the back foot.

"You're in some kind of mental amalgam," Vex said, frowning a little bit. "That's always been dangerous with your magic. So you're still partially suppressed, and you're doing this to boost the skill?"

Tarilex shook his head, seeming to strain for a moment as his emotions built, too complicated now for Derivan to read—until something seemed to *snap*, an invisible, taut tension abruptly vanishing.

"Shit," Tarilex gasped, and at the same time, the human woman who sat two seats away twitched and scowled.

"I told you this was a bad idea," she said, looking annoyed.

"We were under orders to try," Leben offered, the orc looking a little guilty.

"Perhaps you *are* the adventurers that discovered the dungeon," Tarilex said. He just looked . . . tired.

There was a momentary silence.

Then the Guildmaster laughed.

"I should be kinda pissed that you got around our wards," the Guildmaster said, grinning. "But I have no idea what the *fuck* all of that was, and I kind of loved it. What did you throw at him?"

"It's Drunkard's Beard," Vex said, a little embarrassed. "I remembered that I had some, and I realized that if the Wisfield house got the skill to work without a mana cost, then it might not be a mana-related effect at all. So I sort of guessed it would work."

"You threw moss at him and you didn't even know it would work?" The Guildmaster practically cackled. She didn't seem to care much for decorum now that the delegates had technically broken the rules—they all sat there looking slightly uncomfortable, like they knew they'd messed up. "Holy fuck, I love your team. It's such a refreshing change."

"Thanks?" Vex offered, still embarrassed.

"And as for you five . . ." The Guildmaster settled herself down a little. "I do believe this buys us some favors from Elyra. Really, now, you can't even trust us enough to tell you the truth?"

"You still have not proven that you are telling the truth—" Tarilex tried.

"Nope. Do your mental hivemind thing again. Come on," Sev interrupted.

"Are you sure? You don't actually need to prove anything to them," the Guildmaster said, turning to Sev.

"Yeah. I want them to know." Sev stared at Tarilex, who seemed to slump a little, like he felt guilty.

The lizardkin sighed. ". . . All right. Go ahead."

"We were the ones that discovered the dungeon," Sev enunciated clearly, staring directly at Tarilex. "There is an infolock, and we are likely the only ones directly able to investigate it.

"And the lie—"

"Oh, I didn't technically lie, really." Misa finally spoke up, shrugging and smirking slightly. "But I was being deceptive, and you picked up on it."

"How were you being deceptive?" Tarilex asked, but the look in his eyes was defeated; he didn't truly expect an answer.

"I see no reason to tell you," Misa grinned. She winked at him. "Maybe if you're good, we'll share?"

"As I'm sure you're aware," the Guildmaster cut in smoothly, "this . . . incident . . . could be quite damaging to relations between Elyra and the Guild. I'm sure you could offer a small favor so we can keep things quiet? Say, allowing these four to join you in your research?"

"Fine," Tarilex groaned. "Clearly I've underestimated you four, and clearly that . . . other adventurer . . . of yours figured out some way around our methods." He grimaced slightly. "Or you four have. But on balance, you seem more likely to be telling the truth."

His gaze slid to Vex just slightly as he spoke. The wizard pretended not to notice.

"Jerome is a Gold ranker, even if the Guild no longer recognizes him as such," the Guildmaster said dryly. "One does not achieve such a rank without backing. But . . . I am concerned. My men never identified that he might have spoken with you."

"So he got around your spies?" Sev asked. The Guildmaster twitched.

"Not *spies*," she said, ". . . but yes. Maybe."

"I'm concerned as well," Tarilex said with a sigh. "There are only a few known ways to get around our particular method of truth detection, and they're all worrying. Self-deception is maybe the least harmful of them."

". . . I'm assuming your truth-detection methods aren't vulnerable to the exceptionally common trait of narcissism," the Guildmaster deadpanned.

"No." Tarilex managed a wry sort of smile. "It would have to be magically enforced in some way for direct lies to come off as truth. There are artifacts that do this, but none of them are particularly good for your mind in the long term."

"You think he's got something like that?" Vex frowned. "Does he know the dangers?"

"Does he seem like the type of person to care?" Misa pointed out.

"There is another problem," Derivan observed; Tarilex's body language was still . . . reserved. Like he was afraid of saying something? "What have you not told us?"

"I work with mental magic and somehow that's more unnerving," Tarilex muttered to himself, then sighed.

"Look. I said my hands were tied because I—*we* already made a deal with Jerome, and part of that deal involves connections he still had with some of Anderstahl's suppliers. He's on the delving team for the mission."

"Can you remove him?" The Guildmaster asked.

"We can." Tarilex paused, clearly uncomfortable. He winced. "He came to us under false pretenses, so . . . we can. Do you want us to?"

The Guildmaster glanced at the team of adventurers in the room with her. "I think that's up to you. This is enough of an offense for him to be ejected from the Guild, too, on top of the demotion."

There was a short silence.

". . . I'm not sure that's a good idea," Vex said slowly. "He might have a mind-altering artifact on him . . . and does he actually *have* anywhere to go?"

"He was kicked out of Anderstahl," the Guildmaster said. "So he'd have to find somewhere on his own. I'm sure many villages could use the help of a Gold ranker to gather crystals."

"I don't think I trust him to hold a position of power in a village," Sev said.

"I . . . would offer to hold him, but there would likely be some resistance on this matter." Tarilex grimaced slightly. He seemed reluctant to speak, but he shrank under the weight of their gazes and eventually forced himself to do so. "Elyra has had some recent problems with food production, and the suppliers that Jerome has connected us to would pull out if we were to renege on this deal. Incarcerating him might cause even more pushback. We're already partially reliant on those suppliers."

"And the Guild doesn't really do prisons." The Guildmaster frowned for a moment. "It's a drain on our resources to hold and suppress people for that length of time. If an adventuring team is a problem, we usually give them minders, and split them up if need be."

There was a long pause.

"I think we gotta let Jerome stay on the delve, guys," Sev eventually said. "The food deal is the clincher for me here."

"It's kinda shit," Misa said. "But I think he's gonna cause more problems if we let him run around *or* keep him in a box. He seems like the kinda guy that would just build resentment. And I don't wanna be the one to push him into that. If we keep an eye on him, make sure he doesn't get into trouble . . . At least we can actually supervise him if he's going to be delving."

The Guildmaster sighed, not disagreeing. "Jerome is . . . We accepted him because he had nowhere else to go, but we have not had nearly enough time to work with him. He is shallow and vindictive, and it will take effort to undo this. Effort and time that we have not had yet. But it still feels like a failure on the part of the Guild, and I am sorry for that."

Tarilex seemed relieved. "Jerome's team is mostly interested in delves; hopefully, there will be minimal interaction between you two. I do not wish to explain why I took on a second adventuring team."

"It's best he doesn't find out which team actually discovered the dungeon," the Guildmaster agreed. "In any case, I think that more or less concludes negotiations on this matter. I'm sure we all have a lot to think about. Tarilex, if we are to perform further negotiations, I look forward to *all* participants actually . . . participating."

The other delegates had the good grace to look vaguely ashamed, at least. Derivan looked over them—of the four, Leben, the orc priest, seemed to feel the guiltiest.

"You should leave first," the Guildmaster added, directing the statement to Derivan and the others. "I need to go over the wards to see if they can be tweaked to account for this, and then we'll see what we settle on regarding Jerome. I might need to send people to keep an eye on him, on top of having you four there."

"I'm getting increasingly concerned with how you're talking about this man like he's going to murder us because we found a dungeon and he got scolded for being an ass about it," Sev said mildly, getting up from his chair.

"Transportation circle is that way," the Guildmaster said, ignoring him and pointing.

Sev eyed her for a moment. "You realize you're supposed to say something reassuring."

"I'm sure Jerome won't find out."

"That's even less reassuring." Sev sighed, striding toward the door; the rest of his team filed after him. "Okay!" he called back to the Guildmaster as they stepped on to the transportation circle. "We're all going to fill out our last wills and testaments! Wish us luck!"

The Guildmaster, amusingly enough, gave him the finger—though from the lack of reaction from the rest of his party, Derivan thought he might have been the only one that caught it. Anti-perception skills were strange. She winked at him, though, so he assumed she expected him to see it.

What a strange Guildmaster, he thought.

The transportation circle flashed.

A silver-armored paladin stood in their room, leaning against the door.

"Hello," Jerome said.

CHAPTER 21

CONFRONTATION

"Uh," Sev said. He glanced at the rest of the team, and they all seemed equally stumped. Except for Misa, but the expression she was wearing was her "Punch this problem until it goes away" expression, which more or less translated to being stumped. "I don't suppose I can convince you you have the wrong room?"

"With a mana surge like that?" Jerome chuckled. His tone was *almost* casual. "I doubt it."

The paladin wore an easy sort of smile—but it was a smile that carried with it an edge of danger. His stance was casual, with one leg crossed over the other and his arms folded, and yet his sword was within an inch of his fingers. Sev had no doubt that he could draw that sword and attack them faster than they could react, and he also had no doubt that the sword wasn't Jerome's real method of attack. It was intimidation.

Attacking at all would be a terrible idea, of course. The Guild was enchanted against exactly that sort of thing, and while Jerome likely had ways around enchantments at his level, there was always some kind of backlash from ripping through high-level enchantments. He wouldn't get away scot-free even if he tried. Even a Platinum ranker wouldn't.

The *threat* was there, though. And the threat was more than enough, in most cases: the protection of those enchantments didn't extend beyond the grounds of the Adventurers' Guild, so they weren't completely reliable.

Whether that threat would work on *this* team was a different story.

Sev had no idea what Jerome wanted with them. Presumably, he wanted to learn who it was that had actually discovered the dungeon—and then . . . what, intimidate them into keeping their mouths shut about it? But he'd only found them *after* they'd joined the meeting with the Elyran delegates, so that didn't make any sense.

Then again, Jerome didn't have any way of knowing how the meeting went.

... Well, when in doubt, confuse the enemy. De-escalation 101!

"Well, all right, then," Sev said with a shrug. "You wanna hang out?"

"Why do you thi—" Jerome started, clearly expecting a different response. He stopped midsentence as he parsed what Sev had actually said; the cleric could almost hear the gears in his brain slowly clicking into place. "What?"

"I said, do you want to hang out?" Sev repeated. "If you're going to be in this room, you might as well, right? We were going to help Derivan here train a bit. Derivan, why don't you introduce yourself?"

"Hello," Derivan said. He didn't see a particular need to repeat what his name was, so he opted to wave instead.

The *clang* of his armor sounded awkwardly in the room as he did so.

"... Are you an idiot?" Jerome frowned. "That's not why I'm here."

"I had to give you the benefit of the doubt. Personal policy." Sev grinned, shrugging like he wasn't at all concerned about the *very dangerous man* in their room. There were four of them, and Misa had her skill ... and if Jerome was a paladin, then he'd have a rather unique advantage. "It's not like we've actually *spoken* to you, so there was always the chance you could actually be kinda cool, you know? Are you sure you don't want to just hang out?"

The paladin paused. He frowned slightly, then straightened up so he wasn't leaning against the wall anymore. "... I am here to talk about the dungeon."

Almost at the same time, Vex blinked and furrowed his brows, staring closely at Jerome. Sev glanced at his friend. *Good. He remembered.*

"What about it?" Sev asked, raising an eyebrow. "And will you get more comfortable? I don't know about you, but standing in a closet and talking is kind of uncomfortable for me."

As he spoke, he was already climbing out, the rest of his team following suit behind him. Truth be told, he had no idea what he was doing—his heart was hammering in his chest. Where were Jerome's teammates? He was, in a way, grateful that they weren't here; they'd almost certainly be outmatched in a four-on-four fight. But he was also *worried* that they weren't here.

That said, four on one, they had a bit more of a fighting chance, depending on the specifics of Jerome's class. But he still didn't want this to get to a fight.

Fortunately for him, Jerome seemed to have no idea what Sev was doing either. He'd been knocked off-balance and was off his game. He actually let Sev and the others take up various seats around the room, like the premise of this entire conversation wasn't an implied threat.

Every single member of his team made sure to sit in a way that made their weapons still easily accessible, though. Sev was proud of them for that.

"You just came back from speaking with the Elyran delegates," Jerome finally said. "I'm sure you have questions."

"Like why you pretended you were the one that discovered the dungeon?" Misa raised an eyebrow, her voice challenging.

"I needed access to the dungeon, and political weight only carries me so far." Jerome shrugged. "They wouldn't even have heard me out if I hadn't said I found it. Which means we have a problem here, wouldn't you agree?"

"I'll say," Misa muttered.

"I'm prepared to offer your team a thousand gold to tell them you didn't discover the dungeon and to give me all the information you have on it." Jerome's offer was straightforward; Misa promptly choked, a sympathetic Vex patting her on the back as she coughed violently.

Jerome waited patiently for her coughing fit to finish before he continued.

"Frankly, it'd do a lot of harm to my reputation if they find out that I lied about it," Jerome said wryly, which was such a blatant lie that Sev had trouble not snorting out loud. "You gain a thousand gold, and you get to not have a team of Gold rankers as an enemy. So, how about it? We both benefit from this deal, no?"

"Just to be clear," Sev said, "you're claiming that one of the benefits to this deal is that you won't be our enemy."

Jerome nodded. "Yes."

"That's a threat, not a benefit," Sev said flatly. "Just so we're on the same page."

Jerome frowned for a second, like he wanted to argue, then paused. "If that's how you want to look at it," he said with a shrug.

They'd been paid a hundred gold pieces for the grade-six mana crystal, and that was a one-in-a-million sort of mission. This payout would be ten times that; over a thousand times what they earned on a typical quest.

If money were the sort of thing they cared about, Sev mused, this would be the kind of deal that would have bought them over instantly.

"Unfortunately," Sev said—and Jerome tensed, a flicker of an ugly, vicious sort of anger crossing over his face. It was gone as fast as it appeared. "I don't think that'll work."

"And why the hell not?" Jerome's words were a half-growl; silver light began to coalesce around him, and Sev felt his team tense in response.

"They already know we found it," Sev answered. "And they believe us. If we go back to them now, they'll just get even more suspicious."

"They *believed* you?" Jerome looked outraged, though this time the anger was—thankfully—not directed at them. It was still unpleasant, though. "Fucking shit-pissing Elyrans. They need a truth spell to listen to me, but you newbies just blabber on and they believe you instantly."

Good fucking *lord* the man's mood had pivoted in an instant. What an asshole. He had a problem with Elyrans, clearly; Derivan saw Vex flinching a little bit in the corner of his vision, and decided to end the conversation as quickly as possible.

No need to tell the paladin that they'd been under truth spell too. No doubt he knew about the enchantments in the upper floor; telling him that would no doubt lead to a whole slew of other uncomfortable questions . . .

"Fine," Jerome growled. "Just tell me what you know about the damn dungeon. You were *there*. That dungeon has a bonus room. I want to know what's in it. Or at least what it's based on."

Sev paused.

"No?" He decided. "No. I'm not interested in your gold."

"I never said it was a fucking *choice*." Jerome glared at them, the paladin's body beginning to shimmer with silver power. Sev felt his teammates tense, ready to try to defend him; Misa could defend from a few hits with her skill, but after that . . .

Jerome paused suddenly, and a nasty smile spread across his face.

"Fine," he said. "You said you wanted to hang out? Help your armored friend train?"

The paladin stepped forward.

"[**Divine Suppression**], [**Golden Aura**]," he intoned, and the air around him flashed from silver into a brilliant gold. The same gold threaded out from the man's eyes, too, casting his face in an eerie, almost inhuman glow; at the same time, a *weight* pressed down on all of them.

Sev found he couldn't move. Couldn't cast.

Jerome stepped forward until he was right in front of Derivan, who didn't move. The armor seemed frozen, too. The paladin pressed a hand to the living armor's chestplate. "[**Golden Geas**]. **You're going to tell me everything I want to know about the dungeon.**"

There was a flash of light that shot into Derivan's armor, suffusing it in a glow that slowly settled into motes of light. The moment seemed to stretch on entirely too long, and a beat of horror thrummed in Sev's chest.

Then the paladin smirked. "I don't have to *attack* you to make your lives miserable. Don't think these wards are perfect. You'll have a few days to fulfill that condition, or your friend over there will slowly turn to gold."

Turning around, Jerome left, pausing just before he strode through the door. "Have fun with that," he said sarcastically, slamming the door shut behind him—and after another moment, whatever suppressive ability he was using switched itself off.

Almost instantly, Misa flung herself at the door. "That *fucker*!"

"Don't!" Sev said, trying to pull her back; Derivan reached out for her, too, grabbing the struggling half-orc by the arms and hauling her away. "Don't go after him. It's not worth it right now."

Vex was pale. "Derivan, are you . . ."

Derivan cocked his head. "I am fine, I think," he said, sounding slightly . . . amused?

"You . . . don't sound worried," Sev said, furrowing his brow. The horror in his heart lessened just a bit.

The armor paused, glancing at the door. "Yes, well," he said, "I suspect that skill of his will not do what he believes it will."

"Are you sure?" Misa said sharply. "This is important."

"Not *certain*, perhaps," Derivan said. "However . . ."

He flicked them his status screen. In gold letters, hovering underneath Physical Empathy, was a new stat entry.

Golden Geas: 50

"I am reasonably certain that should not have manifested as a stat," Derivan said.

Sev stared.

"What," he managed.

—m—

"What does it . . . do?" Misa asked. The four of them sat on the floor, with Derivan in the middle. Vex hadn't stopped fretting, even knowing that whatever skill Jerome had used apparently hadn't attached correctly to the living armor. The wizard was casting all sorts of diagnostic magic even now, just to make sure that there was no trace of Derivan being forced to turn into gold.

Derivan had pointed out in turn that even turning into gold wouldn't necessarily harm him the way it would anything organic. He'd be a lot *softer*, which might have been a problem, but it didn't seem to be something they needed to worry about—even after waiting for a while, Vex could detect no change.

"I am unsure," Derivan said. "I believe it gives me a sense for where Jerome is."

". . . I don't even know where to begin with that," Sev said with a groan, burying his face in his hands. "Are you serious? Why would it— I have so many questions."

"I think I understand, sort of," Vex finally said softly, though his voice was still timid and a little shaky. "I mean . . . I was checking Jerome over for magic while we were talking. Remember how Tarilex mentioned that to fool the truth spell, he needs some sort of mind-altering magic?"

"Right," Sev said. "Did you find something?"

"It was a little hard to tell underneath all his protective enchantments," Vex said with a frown. "But I think he was under some sort of geas, too. Maybe even the same type of geas. If he is, then that's probably what you're sensing."

Derivan frowned, then nodded. "This seems correct," he agreed. "I sense . . . other, smaller presences, I think. They are less noticeable than Jerome."

"So what, we have a Jerome detector now?" Misa said. "I don't know how to feel about this."

"I would prefer not to know where he is at all times, yes," Derivan said. "From a cleanliness perspective, you understand. From a tactical standpoint, knowing where he is is quite useful."

"We're really lucky he went for *you*," Sev said with a frown. "I'm sorry, guys. I feel like I kind of fucked up that whole interaction."

"I honestly feel like this is one of the better outcomes," Misa muttered. "Now we know where he is, and . . . I dunno. Is he under a geas? Should we worry about that?"

"Honestly," Sev sighed, "I don't know."

CHAPTER 22

A PATH FORWARD

The four of them tried to speak for a while, but it didn't take long for them to lapse into silence, each lost in their own thoughts. Vex was still trembling slightly, clearly upset, and so without a word, Derivan went to do what Vex had done for him, not so long ago—he sat down next to the lizardkin, offering a quiet show of support.

He didn't say anything. There weren't any words for what had just happened; not really. The immediate worry was dealt with by sheer fluke, Derivan understood, and while it *was* amusing that Jerome had failed so utterly in what he had set out to do, there was a grim realization settling in.

That realization was the fact that they weren't prepared to deal with threats from *people*.

Monsters were one thing. Monsters moved in predictable patterns, for the most part; they had skills that were mostly known, and very rarely did any of them have skills that could just lock down an entire room. What Jerome had done to them struck them hard because they had no solutions for it. The suppression hadn't been an *attack*, so Misa couldn't deal with it, and once suppressed, she couldn't block the geas.

She'd tried, according to her.

But they had an advantage now that they didn't have before, at least against the man that presented a threat to them. Derivan had a rough understanding of Jerome's position at almost any given time. That was *useful*. That was something even the Guildmaster's people hadn't had, if they'd managed to lose track of Jerome long enough for him to secure the deal with Elyra. And that might be only the beginning of what the stat did.

"We need to update the Guildmaster on what happened," Sev finally said. "Regardless of anything else, she needs to know that Jerome tried this. And then . . . I don't know. We need to deal with Jerome in some way, right?"

"I'd sure fuckin' like to," Misa growled. Her anger was still a little subdued, but she was rapidly getting her spirit back—but she held herself back when she saw that her anger made Vex shrink backward slightly.

"We need to be sure he is not a threat to us," Derivan said. "The Guildmaster may be able to ensure such a thing, I suppose. But we run into the same problem we had before."

"Elyra loses those deals on food," Sev said with a sigh. "I didn't miss how *relieved* all of the delegates looked when we didn't ask for them to break that off. I'm guessing they're in more trouble than they indicated. Do you . . . I hate to ask, but do you know anything about that, Vex?"

The lizardkin shook his head. "I haven't kept up with events in Elyra," the wizard said in a small voice. "I . . . I could check, maybe. Send a message to one of my brothers. Just—just give me a moment."

Vex reached out to compose the message, letting out a trembling breath as he did so—but he still shook, and his claws kept missing the keys. It was only when Derivan reached out and placed a hand on his shoulder that he steadied slightly, like he needed the reminder that his friend was *fine*.

". . . Yeah," Vex said after a moment. He seemed almost surprised that his brother had replied so quickly. "Elyra's undergoing some serious food-shortage issues right now. He says that growth magic isn't . . . working anymore? Or at the very least it's suppressed, or twisted in some way. They can't figure it out. But that . . . that doesn't make any sense."

"It's not *working*?" Sev frowned. "This seems like an entirely new problem."

"Can we get the Guildmaster to supply the food instead?" Misa asked.

"I can ask," Sev said. He was already in the middle of composing a message to the Guildmaster. "But I honestly don't think so. The Guild is already stretched thin trying to keep all the smaller villages supplied with crystals. Then again . . . maybe if we get all those small villages to pay us in food instead of coin . . ."

Sev lapsed into silence, thinking. "I'll ask," he said eventually. "It depends on how widespread a problem this is, I guess. We haven't heard of any food-shortage problems recently, as far as I know." Sev frowned at the screen in front of him, then composed the rest of his message, firing it off to the Guildmaster.

Derivan, in the meantime, had been mostly silent—but now he frowned, looking around at his friends. "There is another solution here, yes?" he said cautiously.

"What do you mean?" Sev asked, glancing up at him.

"He is under a geas. Some sort of compulsion, at least, that keeps his mind in whatever state needed for him to lie under a truth spell. Can we not just . . . remove it?"

There was a short pause. A small intake of breath from Misa.

"Oh," Misa said softly. She sounded surprised—and yet there was an edge of something else in her tone, like there was something that she'd forgotten, and she'd only now remembered. "You want to help him?"

"Deri, he . . . he wanted to hold you hostage," Vex said. He fidgeted, his tail coiling around him nervously.

"Vex is right," Sev said, shaking his head. "Jerome's dangerous. If we let him run around, we might not be his only victims. And there's no guarantee that he'll be any better even if we do somehow manage to remove it."

"There is a guarantee that he will not get worse. And the alternatives seem cruel, if we do not first try this," Derivan offered quietly.

Derivan understood their concerns, to a degree. Physical Empathy was helping him out here, letting him see details he ordinarily wouldn't—lines of stress and tension in the faces of his friends. They were worried and angry and frightened, and he understood in some way that they wanted to see Jerome punished.

But it was an abstract sort of understanding. Something he was "missing," perhaps, as a monster, or as a creature created from magic. He was upset, certainly, but that emotion felt distant from him.

They were facing a paladin that was a Gold ranker, which was rare enough as is—someone that could do so much good, but did not. They had the option here to end the threat he represented, and there was a wide chasm of possibility in front of them for doing just that. With consequences, perhaps, but solutions for those consequences, too.

And yet over that chasm was a thin, fleeting bridge. A possible solution that didn't feel as steady and as reassuring as the others, but would get them all across intact. Even Jerome.

Who ever said the only choices available were endings?

"I think Derivan's right," Misa said softly.

Vex looked conflicted, and seemed almost betrayed when Misa spoke up. He looked over at the half-orc, almost pleading. "He's dangerous."

"Well," Misa said, and this time she grinned, just a bit—an attempt to be reassuring—"so are we. We just gotta figure out how to deal with his particular brand of nonsense, right?"

Vex hesitated. "We got overwhelmed by him once . . ."

"We were not prepared," Derivan said. "But we have some sense of what he can do now, and he still does not know what *we* can do. And he does not know that I have escaped his geas."

"What about the Guildmaster?" Vex tried. He seemed reluctant still, and the way he was leaning into Derivan for reassurance told the armor that he wasn't over what had happened yet.

Sev spoke up. "She's going to send us someone to help with whatever we want to do. She's busy. Whatever we choose, she says, get her operative to help us do it."

"We will need your help, too, Vex," Derivan said, the words gentle. "None of us are as versed in magic as you are, and whatever this new stat of mine does, we need to know more about it if we are to confront Jerome. If it gives us some advantage over him, however slight . . ."

Vex sighed, his tail curling in on himself. "I don't *want* to help him," he said, his voice small. "I know I should. But . . . it sucks, and I don't *want* to. He's just been . . ."

"He has been, as Misa would say, a giant asshole," Derivan said calmly, the sudden expletive making Vex snort in surprise. It seemed to lighten his heart, though. "He has lied and he has assaulted us. But the deals he made with Elyra helped them, even if it was to his own benefit. He came to us with an offer first, when he could have just done this from the beginning. So let us try, and bring down the hammer only if we fail. Only if *he* fails."

"I don't have to like that we're doing this, right?" Vex asked. He seemed almost pleading, but resigned.

"You do not," Derivan said. "I would not ask you to."

Sev sighed. "I haven't shared my thoughts so far, but . . . yeah. This sucks. I want to be angry. I want to burn him down, damn the consequences. But fuck, we don't know how much this geas does; I'm not— Derivan's *right* and I hate it. I know how you feel, Vex."

The lizardkin only nodded. There was some relief in his eyes, like he was glad that he wasn't the only one that felt this way.

"But if we're doing this, then we're going to do it taking as little risk as possible. Vex is right, too; he overwhelmed us. We need to know more about what he can do. We need strategies. We need a way to beat him and hold him long enough to break off this geas, and we need to *know how to do that.*"

There was a knock on the door.

"I think I can help you with that," a voice called through the door. The four adventurers exchanged glances.

"Is that *Max?*" Misa asked, incredulous. "The clerk?"

"That's me!" Max said, sounding surprisingly bright and cheery. Nonplussed, Sev stood up to open the door, and Max strolled in with a bright grin. "I hear you're plotting revenge! Let me help you with that."

"We are explicitly not plotting revenge," Sev said.

"Yeah, but that was more fun to say than 'I hear you're planning to hold down Jerome and extract a magical compulsion that was apparently forced upon him, and I don't know anything more than that so you'll need to brief me,'" Max rattled off. She smiled. "Guildmaster sent me. What can I do for ya?"

"Uh . . ." Sev glanced at the others, still looking perplexed. "I guess we brief you on the plan first? I don't know what's going on, to be honest."

"I moonlight as a clerk when I'm not spying for the Guildmaster. It's a tough job, let me tell you," Max said with a dramatic sort of sigh. She seemed to gather herself a moment later, though. "Seriously, though, give me some sort of briefing. I know the basics of what Jerome did, but I want to know how he got through you four, how he got through our wards . . . Everything."

So they did. They explained what had happened, and Max listened attentively, frowning when she heard that Jerome had shown up in their room with no explanation—the wards were explicitly supposed to prevent mana surges for teleports from being even *visible*, much less allow the man to track them to their room. Her eyes darkened when she heard that Jerome had worked around the wards, and she made a quick note to get all their enchantments updated, though she knew it wouldn't help adventurers outside the Guild branches.

And then they came to the geas, the wording of it, and what had happened to Derivan. They even explained how it had shown up on his status, with Derivan sending her the box as proof. Max's eyes widened when she saw it, and she almost laughed out loud.

"Oh," she giggled. "Jerome isn't gonna know what hit him."

"What do you mean?" Sev blinked at her.

"You could tell him pretty much anything and he'd probably believe you," Max said with a grin. "The guy thinks he's holding one of your members hostage. You hold an advantage on him in terms of information, *and* he's primed to believe almost anything you tell him, *and* I can get you Guild resources on geas removals and binding spells, *and* you've got me to help you fight."

"You can fight?" Misa grinned at her. "Oh, I think I like you."

"I'm a level eighty-one [**Adventuring Clerk**]," Max said flippantly. Then she grinned back. "It's an elite class."

CHAPTER 23

PLANNING WITH MAX, CLERK EXTRAORDINAIRE

"So!" Max clapped her hands together. "Let's get planning, shall we?"

"Wait, wait, wait," Sev said. "How long have you been—what? Why are you level eighty-one? What kind of class is [**Adventuring Clerk**]? How did you even get— Okay, I know I shouldn't ask that question, *but also I have so many questions.*"

Max cracked up. "Oh, I love revealing that to people. The reactions are priceless every time," she said, grinning wide. "It's a little complicated, but I got that class after I started working as a clerk here for a while."

"Do *all* of the Guild's clerks have this class?" Sev groaned. "Have I been surrounded by Platinum-ranked clerks the entire time?"

"Is that a bad thing?" Max asked, still amused. "Ignore the conspicuous way in which I am not answering your question in an attempt to make the Guild look either more or less powerful than it is."

"No!" Sev threw his hands up in aggravation. "But yes? I don't know! I've just had a lot of shocking things happen today! I don't know how to begin to parse the second part of your statement!"

"Today has been a day," Misa agreed with a small laugh, her mood slowly recovering now that the immediate danger had left, and no permanent harm had been done. "So, [**Adventuring Clerk**], huh? And this lets you help us fight?"

"I mean, kind of," Max said with a shrug. "It's a mix between a combat class and a utility class. Pretty neat, actually. You wanna lay out what you—waaaait. No. Hang on. *Hang on.*" Max paused like she'd just remembered something, then grabbed Derivan's box out of the air and stared at it again. "What the hell is going on with your status? What the fuck?"

Sev paused. "Were you so eager to tell us about your class that you didn't . . . process the fact that his status was broken?"

"I thought he had some weird skill! I didn't look at it closely!" Max complained. She waved the box around in Sev's face, though with it being visible only to her, it mostly looked like she was flapping her arms at Sev. "What is this? What happened? You didn't tell us about this!"

"Uh . . ." That was a good point. Sev glanced at the others. The Guildmaster already knew that Derivan was, technically, initially a 'monster' . . . but they'd sort of forgotten about the broken status part. It was safe to tell Max about it, surely?

Yeah. It was safe to tell Max. She was *apparently* a high-level Guild operative, and he'd known her for a while.

So they told her about it.

There was a long silence after the whole situation was explained. Max paused, then looked at Misa. "You have a skill that blocks anything?" she asked, as if she needed it to be confirmed.

Misa nodded.

"That's a *rare* skill? Not elite?" Max asked. "Or unique?"

"I mean . . . It has disadvantages," Misa said with a grin. "But yes. It's pretty badass. I don't really know how the system decides rarity, but I'm not going to complain. I'm hoping it and my class will be upgraded when we hit Gold."

"When, not if, huh?" Max said with a small grin. "That's some confidence. And you!" She whirled to Vex. "You have a class that can analyze any magic?"

"Kind of?" Vex offered, looking a touch uncomfortable; Max instantly adjusted, lowering her intensity just a bit.

"That's fuckin' cool," she offered. She glanced at Sev, who seemed like he was waiting for her to have an outburst about *his* special bullshit, but she just stuck her tongue out at him. "Sev, I'm not even going to touch on your bullshit healing. Your healing is already bullshit. I've always known your healing is bullshit."

"I think I love this girl," Misa stage-whispered to Vex.

"But you!" Max pointed at Derivan, almost dramatically. "You're just *living armor*? That's so cool! I always wanted to meet one, but they don't actually spawn in dungeons very often. Can I climb inside you? Is that a thing you can do?"

Derivan paused.

"Um," Vex said, glancing to Derivan, and then to Max, and then to Derivan again.

Misa cracked up laughing. Sev grinned.

"I have not tried," Derivan said, considering the idea. "I am not certain it would be a good idea? Many of the enchantments within me are inscribed across armor plates; if they were to separate, the animating magic may fail. I suppose it is likely to reactivate when those enchantments are realigned, but I do not know if my personality would be maintained."

"I feel like there's something you can do with that," Max said with a grin. She turned a little bit more serious. "But I'll leave you guys to figure that out. Let's talk about a plan of action for Jerome first."

"Can we split them up?" Misa asked immediately. "Fighting all four of them at once seems like a bad idea."

"That's a good call," Max said with a nod. "You might be able to. They're all pretty high-level; Jerome is seventy-two, and the other three I believe are in the low sixties. Still Gold, but not as far into it as Jerome. Jerome is a paladin of Aurum, if you didn't guess that already."

"Do you know the specific class?" Sev asked, and Max laughed.

"I shouldn't, but I do, because he boasted about it when he was joining. It's [**Gilded Paladin**]. It's an elite-tier class that comes with suppression and binding abilities, as you've seen." Max paused for a moment. "He's got some offensive abilities, but they're mostly things like projectiles that try to turn what they hit into gold. It's a progressive status effect, basically."

"What's with the turning-people-into-gold thing?" Sev muttered.

"That's what I said," Max grinned. "It's pretty fuckin' weird. But it seems like it's the core of his class."

"Do we have a way to counter that?" Misa frowned. "I mean, besides me blocking him, obviously. If he shoots a lot of those I won't be able to stop him."

"Yes," Derivan said. "Me."

Max glanced at Derivan and nodded. "Yeah. Gold is actually pretty amenable to magic overall—magic-neutral, you could say. The enchantments that make you *alive* shouldn't be affected by a transition from whatever metal you're made of into gold. It's kind of ironic, really; gold is one of the few materials that *would* have almost no effect on you. And that's if his spells work on you at all; the interaction might be strange without the health buffer, or you might absorb it into your status like you did his geas. It's hard to say."

"Good," Derivan said simply.

"But the rest of the team might be a problem," Max said. "None of them are particularly talkative—the elves just talk to Jerome. They say he rescued them or something? No idea. But I don't really know what they *do*, and I never really saw much even when I spied on them. I think they tend to provide support from the back; we've seen them fight every once in a while, and I know they're archer types, but those are some of the hardest classes to figure out."

"Why's that?" Vex asked curiously.

"I mean, you wizard types are pretty easy, because you have a bunch of spells you can just throw at a problem," Max said. "But it's harder with arrows. Archer classes usually have specific effects they can put on their arrows, and those arrows can otherwise look completely mundane. It's a lot harder to notice from a distance."

Misa paused. "If there aren't too many of them at once, I could block those. As long as Sev keeps me healed up. I'm assuming they don't have any rapid-fire or arrow-multiplying skills, or you would've seen them."

"I mean, they might just not have used them. But we can only plan for what we know, so for now you're on arrow duty," Max said. "And Sev is on keep-everyone-alive duty."

"I'm always on keep-everyone-alive duty," Sev said, sighing dramatically.

"Vex, we're going to need you to remove the geas," Max said, ignoring Sev. "I'll get some resources on geas magic brought up to your room so you can look them over. We're going to have to disable whatever protective enchantments Jerome has, too."

"Sure," Vex said automatically.

"Derivan . . ." Max eyed the armor critically. "We're going to have to figure out what that broken stat of yours does. Don't get me started on it letting you know where Jerome is. I mean, that's kind of creepy, but it's also really useful for this. But . . ."

Max frowned. "It probably does something more than that," she said eventually. "I don't understand it being a *stat*. That should describe something about you, right? You're not *under* a geas; you *are* the geas. But I don't know what that means. Can you use the skill? Can you take it away?"

"I believe we can test that," Derivan said.

Max blinked. "What? How?"

Derivan stood up and walked over to Max. "May I?"

"May you *what*? Do not put a geas on me or I swear to all the gods—" Max started.

Derivan tapped her gently on the forehead, and when he pulled his finger away, a string of gold came with him. It was a small, light thing, and Max stared at it.

"What," she said.

"It was a very light effect," Derivan said. "So I was not sure, and I was trying to understand it while you were speaking. But Jerome got past you in order to talk to the delegates, did he not?"

Max frowned. ". . . Shit. He did."

"I suspect the skill does more than threaten," Derivan said. He held the thread gently, tempted to crush it—but instead he held it out, knowing Vex could examine it. The wizard was already running analytic spells, slowly turning paler as he saw what it did.

"That's . . . that's a broken skill," Vex said eventually, shaking his head in a sort of horrified awe. "It's one part compulsion, one part threat. It looks like at small scales he just needs physical contact, and he can compel people to do certain things, like not notice his movements in specific circumstances . . . This is *dangerous*. Did he know you were spying on him?"

"He can't have. And I never touched him. The only person on that team that touched me was—" Max narrowed her eyes. "The fourth one. Shit, I forgot about them. They brushed past me once, on the stairs, and I didn't pay attention to it at the time."

There was a short silence.

"Is [**Golden Geas**] even . . . *Jerome's* skill?" Misa asked.

Max hesitated. "I— Maybe. I haven't heard of skills being shared like that, but anything's possible."

"Okay," Sev said, taking over. Max looked like she was trying to figure out how she should feel about having a minor compulsion placed upon her, but she was looking steadily more pissed. She kept well under control, though. "Does that mean Derivan can remove it? Then Vex can focus on breaking Jerome's enchantments instead."

"I want to examine this part of the spell more, too," Vex said. "I should figure out protections against it. Especially if it's not his skill and other people have it. Derivan, you said you sense other, smaller presences?"

"Yes. Max was one of them, now that I know to recognize it. And there are . . ." Derivan frowned. "Quite a few more, some quite far away."

"We need to put a stop to this *now*," Max decided. "If we take it off of him, hopefully he can break the other instances. And even if he can't, or he's unwilling, we can find out more about it now, before it becomes some kind of existential threat."

"Here's the plan. You're going to ask him to meet up with you. Get him to agree to do it alone if possible; make something up about the infolock. Derivan, you need to act like part of you is cast in gold—walk stiffly, or just don't move your fingers on a hand, or something. If you can, tell him that access to a bonus room requires someone to be free of any magical residue or something, so no enchantments. I think it's mostly his armor that's enchanted. I've got a place you can use for the meeting; I'll send you the location."

The other four nodded, looking a bit stunned.

"You have a few hours to get ready," Max said bluntly. "I need to check with the Guildmaster and make sure the rest of us aren't compromised. We have our own ways of breaking this kind of magic, especially since it's the Guildmaster's specialty, but she's been off and distracted, and I think I know why. I'll be back soon. Be ready by then."

Max got up and opened the door—then hesitated for a second, right by the frame. "I don't like leaving a room on a downer note," she said, offering them a small smile. "I'm kinda pissed now, not gonna lie. But you four are great, and we wouldn't have caught all this if you didn't handle it this way. So . . . thanks. The Guild will get through this."

She slipped out. The four of them glanced at one another.

"Okay," Sev said. "Let's get ready."

CHAPTER 24

JEROME

Jerome grumbled. To think they had the *gall* to tell him they wanted to meet him alone.

He'd already been kind! He'd offered them a *thousand gold* in exchange for some information on a dungeon! Dungeon scouts didn't even get paid that much. He wouldn't have considered paying that much for it at all, but it was some *very important* information, according to Aurum. It would help them delve the dungeon.

Jerome didn't know *why* they needed to delve the dungeon, but he knew it was important, and the thought of delving it consumed his waking mind.

It consumed his sleeping mind, too. His dreams were images of twisted corridors and broken walls; of strange, broken machinery scattered around. Sometimes there would be a shadow, or a monster that he couldn't slay, and he'd wake up with the panicked, scattered thought of *maybe he shouldn't go near the dungeon*; but just as quickly that thought would vanish, replaced by an iron determination.

He wouldn't fail Aurum. How could he?

The god was just a child.

If the fucking Guildmaster hadn't gotten in his way, he wouldn't have had to lie. Wouldn't have had to get Histre to place that geas on Max, the damnable clerk that seemed to know everything he was doing. Even *with* that geas, her eyes followed him around, even though she wasn't quite aware of it. It made him shudder.

But he was getting sidetracked.

[*No,*] he answered over the system, eyebrow twitching in irritation as he read Sev's message again. Really, asking to meet him alone. [*My full team will be there to back me up. Don't fucking try to trick me. I can activate the geas from here if I want to.*]

He could not, in fact, do that. But what did some Bronze adventurers know about what he could do?

Jerome grabbed his hammer. The system pinged him with a response; some whimpering nonsense that was agreeing with him, no doubt. He didn't bother reading it in detail; he just scanned it for a time and location, marked it for deletion, and called on his team.

Time to learn what was so important about this damn dungeon.

"Hello?" Jerome called out, annoyed that he'd been brought to this dilapidated-looking house at the opposite side of the town. It made sense, he supposed—doing anything inside the Guild would likely bring the Guildmaster down on his head, and he was damned lucky that she hadn't already figured out what he could do. He kicked open the door, feeling vaguely pleased at the fact the wood splintered under his heel.

It was nice to live in a world where he could just put numbers into a stat sheet and get *stronger.*

The first thing he noticed was that the inside of the house was spatially expanded in some way. Jerome frowned. That was strange; spatial expansion enchantments like these weren't necessarily *expensive*, but they weren't necessarily cheap, either. The cleric was seated at the table, next to his massive armored friend and the two others he didn't really care about. His eyes zeroed in immediately on Derivan's movements—it was subtle, but every time the big man shifted, his fingers weren't quite moving properly . . .

It meant he'd tried resisting the geas and been punished for it. Good. He'd be worried if they hadn't tested the geas at all.

"Ready to tell me everything you know?" Jerome said with a cocky smirk he didn't really feel. He gestured for his team to take up positions—Eleisse and Syra both took up spots in the corner of the room, far enough away that they wouldn't be in range of anything stupid these adventurers tried to pull. Histre did . . . whatever Histre did when they were told to get ready. Jerome didn't know and didn't care.

The cleric glared at him like he'd personally offended him, though. "Not like you gave us a choice, did you?" he said sarcastically.

"I gave you a choice of a thousand gold," Jerome said with a shrug. "Not my fault you chose the hard way."

The cleric just grunted at that, like he was annoyed that Jerome was right. "There was a message that popped up about a bonus room—"

"No," Jerome interrupted, frowning at Sev. "I don't want *you* to tell me. I want *him* to tell me." He pointed at the massive, armored man. What species was he, anyway? He looked too tall to be human. An orc? In armor like that?

"We have names, you know," the cleric scowled at him, and Jerome snorted. Why should he care?

"Fine," he said impatiently. "*Derivan.* Tell me what you know about the dungeon."

"... Very well," Derivan said. The man sat up in the chair, though not without difficulty; Jerome wondered how hard he'd fought the geas before they'd given in. It had only been a couple of hours, and it would only progress this quickly if they tried to remove it . . . But of course they'd try to remove it. It only made sense. "When the dungeon formed, we received several messages through the system. One of them was about a bonus room that had been seeded from one of us—me in particular."

"Stop," Jerome interrupted, sneering. "I want to know why this damn dungeon is so important, first. I said *everything* you know. Why are the gods so interested in the damn thing?"

Derivan looked at him, surprised. "... I do not know," he said eventually. "There were no system messages about this."

"Useless," Jerome grunted. "Fine. Tell me what that message said."

"I wear enchanted armor, you see, but it is cursed enchanted armor. I cannot take it off. I suppose the dungeon found a twisted sort of irony in that, because the message I received implied that any form of enchanted armor is not allowed into the bonus room; in fact, if even a hint of residual enchantment is left on your body, the room will not manifest." Derivan sounded frustrated, and rightfully so; Jerome couldn't imagine being locked out of a bonus room like that.

But Jerome himself was just pleased. An entry condition like that meant he'd have less competition. He wasn't *really* worried about losing the protection of his armor—he didn't *need* it, but Aurum seemed to prefer that he wear it, and so he did.

"There you go," Jerome said. "Was that so hard?"

If it was a requirement that he give up his armor for the dungeon, and that there were no magical traces left on his body . . . none of his party members could directly manipulate magic. But this other party had a wizard.

"You," he said impatiently to Vex, and rolled his eyes impatiently when Sev scowled at him. "*Vex.* Wizard. I need you to cleanse the enchantment residue off of me."

"Uh," Vex said. He blinked at him. He'd been thrown off, like he hadn't anticipated that. "Okay? Do you mean . . . now?"

Jerome paused.

"Well, yes," he said, annoyed. "Of course I do."

Was he going to take off his armor in the middle of a room full of enemies that *very much* didn't like him? He was confident enough that he could take them all on, especially with his party members ready to ambush them if they tried anything. And he wasn't going to get a magic-cleansing service in the Guild, especially not when the Guild's members could be set against him.

It was only really safe for him when he had something to hold over other people's heads. And he *did* have something on their heads; the geas on Derivan was still active until he chose to remove it. It would go inactive for now, unless the man discovered something new about the dungeon, and then it would activate again; but he could offer to remove it in exchange for Vex removing the residue . . . And the party thought he could activate the geas at any time, so he still had that threat dangling over their heads.

Yes, he decided. That would work.

He started stripping off his armor.

"Um," Vex said, staring at him.

"Sh," Misa said. "Don't stop him. I wasn't expecting a show today, but I'll take one where I can get it."

"You *do* realize he threatened our lives," Sev said mildly.

"My life, if we are to be accurate," Derivan commented.

"Bah," Misa said. "You guys have no appreciation for the finer things in life."

"Like *Jerome*?" Sev asked, a little incredulously.

"Obviously not," Misa said, rolling her eyes. "Don't tell me I have to explain this to you."

"I'd rather you didn't."

Jerome studiously ignored the back-and-forth within the other adventuring party. He was still wearing plenty of clothes underneath his armor.

"I'm done," he said impatiently once he'd kicked off all the pieces of his armor. "Strip me."

Vex stared at him.

"Of the enchantments," he added.

"Right, right, of course," the lizardkin said, his tone somewhat strangled. "Uh. Turn around?"

"Why would I have to turn around?" Jerome frowned at him.

"Because you're intimidating and I don't really want to have you staring at me while I work?" Vex tried.

"Nice try," Jerome said. "But no."

The wizard sighed, stepping forward to approach him, albeit a little nervously. "Okay," Vex said. "This might tingle a little bit."

Vex reached forward and placed a cold, scaled hand on his chest. Jerome saw his party members tense, and rolled his eyes internally. What could this party do to him, even if they wanted to? Vex himself wasn't even *Silver*. He was still *Bronze*. It didn't matter how rare his class was; a Bronze had no chance of touching a Gold. He himself had only gotten the powerful skills he used now when he'd reached upper Silver.

The old ones weren't worth thinking about. They weren't as rare; ergo, they weren't as powerful.

"Are you done?" Jerome asked impatiently.

"Wait," Vex said, tense. "This is . . . harder than you think it is. Whatever enchantments you had are powerful. Derivan, can I get some help?"

Jerome rolled his eyes. Of course the Bronze ranker needed help. He waited impatiently as the armored man walked over to him—honestly, he wouldn't have assumed that someone built like that could do any magic at all, but he'd seen stranger things—and placed a hand on him.

Then, all at once, everything went wrong.

Jerome doubled over as a *wave* of sickness washed over him, dizzying him and making him stagger. Part of him wanted to shout in anger, to scream something vile about being betrayed—but Derivan was pulling his hand back, and *why was his stomach glowing*—

A long, long string of gold began to unravel. It pooled in his stomach, and the armored man glowered at him—how had he not realized how *large* Derivan was? The other man towered over him, and yet he'd failed to realize this when he'd placed the geas on him—

The world snapped back together. Histre's hand was on his back, and they were breathing heavily. They were . . . trembling? Frightened?

Derivan seemed to narrow his eyes, and Vex was gritting his teeth, an enormous amount of mana suddenly flaring out from within him— No. An *impossible* amount of mana for that level.

Two arrows flew out from the corners of the room, cutting unerringly toward the pair in front of him. Jerome knew the skills Eleisse and Syra were using; they should have been unblockable for anyone not in Gold. They were fast and could cut through anything. But the half-orc girl was suddenly there in midair, a strange-looking baton striking one arrow and then the other with enough force to completely alter the course of the arrows, leaving deep gouges in the ground.

[**Divine Suppression**], he thought, but he knew before he even tried to use the skill that it wouldn't work. Threads of foreign divine energy filled the air, having flooded into it almost as soon as he'd been disoriented, and Sev was staring at him with a look of angry determination.

Jerome was angry. Angrier than he'd ever been. But he didn't know *why*. He couldn't comprehend anything that was happening.

Histre screamed behind him, an agonized, foreign sound, like the endless ticking of a broken clock.

"Got you, you little shit," Max said.

CHAPTER 25

PLANS, PLANS

Sev was surprised the plan was going as well as it was.

Always plan for things to go wrong—that was his motto, though he couldn't remember when he'd decided on it or why. He preferred his plans to have backups on backups, and for the longest time, his final backup had simply been [**Divine Communion**]. That wasn't an option for him anymore, and so he'd called for them to be very, very sure the plan would work. They hadn't faced a team of intelligent opponents this powerful before, and it seemed stupid to go in blind, even with Max on their side.

Fortunately, everything went . . . somehow far better than they could possibly have anticipated. The original plan had actually called for their team to ambush Jerome and his team during the delve, when Jerome was no longer in his armor and could have the geas safely removed. It hadn't accounted for the possibility that Jerome would just *strip off his armor in front of them*, effectively negating the need for the entire second phase of their plan.

Because *why would he do that!*

Their incredulity played well into their deception, though, and Misa had helped cover for any obvious flaws in their acting with her banter.

And then Jerome called Vex over to remove the residual magic, which was an insane decision that disregarded any danger the mage might pose to him. *He let Vex bring Derivan over to help.* The fact that Jerome apparently didn't even pause to consider that they might be a threat was something Sev would have found offensive if it wasn't also incredibly useful.

Derivan, obviously, used the opportunity to try to take the geas out of Jerome.

They were expecting combat to happen. They'd planned for it, even; on the off chance that Derivan somehow had the opportunity to remove the geas from Jerome while they were in this meeting, it was decided that he would. They assumed a fight would happen as a result, and they would have to defend themselves while giving Derivan the time to fully extract the geas, and even *that* went pretty much exactly as they'd expected.

Mostly, anyway.

Misa blocked both of the arrows fired by the archers, having readied herself to block even as Derivan was approaching Jerome. Histre, too, was an element that they'd accounted for; when Max had returned, she'd talked about what she thought Histre was, and how the Guildmaster might have been compromised. The prevailing suspicion was that Histre was some sort of demon. Distinct from *daemons*, which were false demons, they were creatures outside the context of the system, and could often copy and twist skills for their own use. It would explain how the Guildmaster herself hadn't noticed all of this, if her own skills were stolen and used against her. It would explain how Jerome and Max had a geas on them, too.

It didn't quite explain why there were multiple other instances of the geas that Derivan could sense far away. The other Platinum members of the Guild had been cleared and then dispatched to deal with that, across all their various branches; if there were powerful, compromised individuals around, they would find them, and break the compulsions on them.

And so the plan was that Max would deal with Histre. Demons were incredibly rare, and so there was little in the way of contingency plans for them. They didn't interact with the system in any real sense, and had no health or level values to speak of. They were particularly difficult to kill or get rid of because of that.

Fortunately, there were divine weapons Max could borrow from the Guild vault to deal with exactly this problem—and when they asked how she'd get to Histre without being suspicious, she'd grinned at them, like she'd been waiting for someone to ask. "You're not the only ones that can do broken shit," she'd said.

To be fair, she had a reason to be smug.

[Right Place, Right Time] [Active Skill] [Grade: Maxed]
Cost: Time, Opportunity
Like the best adventuring clerks, you find yourself in just the right place at just the right time.

Sev's reaction of "What the fuck does that mean" was all he could get out before Max used the skill and disappeared.

Now she appeared again—right as Derivan tried to draw the geas out of Jerome, right as Histre appeared out of the air and grabbed for the paladin almost possessively, and right as Misa blocked both of the arrows that would have hit Derivan and Vex.

And then too many things happened all at once.

First was Jerome. The geas placed on him was obviously a lot stronger than the one that had been placed on Max, and it seemed to manifest as a ball of energy, glowing within his stomach. When Derivan drew his hand back, the light moved up his throat and out of his mouth in a way that looked distinctly uncomfortable, and in a way that Sev suspected felt just as uncomfortable as it looked.

Second was Histre. The demon—if that was what they were, though it was difficult to tell beneath the cloak—had appeared again out of the shadows at almost the exact same instant that Derivan began drawing the magic out of Jerome. They pressed a hand into Jerome's back, hissing angrily in a cracked, flawed language.

Third was Max.

Her reaction was instant. As soon as she appeared and saw Histre, she was grabbing for them, divine gauntlet already on her arm; Histre had no time to react to her.

And the moment that concentrated divine magic touched them, they screamed.

The sound was *wrong*, an impossibility layered on top of reality. The progression of a broken mechanism. A gear clicking into a slot that couldn't exist.

And *that* was when everything went wrong.

It was almost a relief, with how well everything had been going. Something had to go wrong, and now that it had, he could *act*.

Because as Histre screamed in that broken, ticking voice, Jerome screamed too.

"We need to end this fast! Extract the geas!" Sev called.

His team, to their credit, *moved*.

Derivan slid smoothly in front of Vex, a barrier shimmering into existence in front of him even as Jerome's sword swung down with rage-fueled anger. The barrier broke almost instantly, of course, but not before several others appeared below it, each angled a little more to the side; it redirected the sword just enough to have it skitter harmlessly off of Derivan's armor. There was no guarantee it would do damage to begin with, but it was better to be safe.

Vex used the opportunity Derivan created to run back—the lizardkin was faster and nimbler than he'd been before, with his newfound stats. The archers tracked him unerringly, however, and the arrows fired were so fast they were a blur in the air; Misa had to cut in front of one of them to protect him, and the second one *thunked* into the wood of the chair he threw himself behind and tore through it, the barest edge of the arrow cutting across his scales. Two more arrows split from the first, but they had scarcely begun to tear into him before Sev reacted; the magic of a heal rippled through him, shredding the arrows before they could do any real damage.

Good thing arrows counted as a foreign object, even when they were still moving.

"Sev! I can't keep blocking these!" Misa called out, and Sev gritted his teeth, redirecting the focus of his heal. There was a strain there as he used more power than he meant to—an echo of the injury firing back up toward him, almost catching him off guard with the sensation of three arrows burying themselves in him.

Not real ones, thank god. But he staggered anyway, the pain flickering across his vision.

"We're trying to help Jerome, dammit; stop fighting us!" Misa yelled— though she knew it would be fruitless. They'd *checked*. They had a scrap of the magic used to put a geas on Max, after all, and Vex had taken the time to study that as thoroughly as he could. There was a lot he could learn in a few hours, it turned out; the mechanism of the gold transmutation, the effects of the geas in the long term . . . They even figured out whether or not Derivan could sense the nature of the compulsion tied into it.

He could not. But he could sense the strength of the compulsion, which didn't necessarily have anything to do with the strength of the geas itself, and he'd felt the strength of the compulsion on the archers while they were still approaching the building. The hope of convincing them to stop fighting was low.

Then Vex was blazing with magic again. There was one more trick they had planned.

The lizardkin exhaled, mana pouring into his breath and forming a large cloud around him: a sleep spell that Sev and Misa had already been inoculated against. At the same time, Sev shot off a small bolt of divine light at a small, almost unnoticeable rune that connected the interior of the house to the spatial enchantment. He didn't need to *break* it, just adjust it slightly—and that was exactly what happened.

The enlarged spatial interior shrank. Both archers, situated in the corners of the house, were immediately shoved forward with almost backbreaking force as the walls abruptly closed in on them; they stumbled forward, trying to recover, but the new interior space was small enough that the cloud Vex was exhaling enveloped them.

They struggled against the oncoming sleep—or at least they tried. They didn't succeed.

Jerome was another story.

The sleeping mist had reached him, but the paladin seemed to be in some sort of berserker rage. Derivan was fending him off, small, well-placed barriers deflecting most strikes of his sword; where he failed to completely block a strike, his armor seemed more than capable of handling it. The problem was that this seemed to be making Jerome more and more angry, and Derivan couldn't get ahold of him for long enough to rip that geas out of him.

"Dammit, Jerome!" Misa yelled, and she gritted her teeth. "Derivan, I'll take him! You grab the geas out—"

She tried. Misa *blocked* one of Jerome's attacks, interposing herself between the angry paladin and Derivan; the living armor stumbled backward at the suddenness of it, but tried to correct himself immediately, darting around Misa to grab Jerome's arm. But the paladin was a *Gold* ranker, even if he was in some sort of berserker rage. He couldn't fight as effectively, but he could certainly throw off two adventurers, one of which didn't even have any Strength.

Third contingency, then, Sev thought, preparing a heal; this was the most dangerous strategy they'd thought up. "Derivan!"

"I will try!" the living armor called back, and he reached out to Jerome and *pulled.*

Derivan couldn't remove the geas from a distance. He needed physical contact to be able to do that. But he could do something else at a distance, using a combination of his [**Mana Manipulation**] skill and the runic pathways Vex had identified from dissecting a small piece of that very same magic. He could *activate* it.

Jerome claimed he could do it at a distance, but that was a lie, one that they'd identified almost immediately. Derivan, on the other hand . . .

But it was a delicate process. They didn't actually want to *kill* Jerome; they needed to shift him only enough to restrain him, so the geas could be properly—

"**No,**" an angry voice hissed, the sound reverberating through the house. It sounded like the grinding of gears. Like the ticking of a watch. Sev's eyes automatically went for the source of the noise, and he found Histre standing unsteadily, staggering forward toward Jerome. Max, behind them, was frantically trying to tug back the divine gauntlet she was using—but it seemed almost *stuck*, fused to the cloak that Histre was wearing. **"No. No. No. You will not take him. You cannot. He is mine. He is ours."**

"What the fuck are you talking about?" Max yelled, kicking at the cloak. She finally pulled her hand out of the gauntlet, though the gauntlet itself stayed stuck to Histre; she stared at the blisters that were left on her hand, her eyes wide. Sev shot a heal in her direction without thinking about it, but his mind was on something else.

Divine magic. They thought Histre was a demon. Why did they think Histre was a demon? *Jerome was a paladin.* They'd assumed in the back of their minds that Jerome's magic wasn't strong enough compared to the artifact, perhaps, but . . .

No. They'd been wrong. They'd been very wrong.

"It was you. You are coming for him," Histre hissed. **"You are coming for all of them. You cannot touch them. We will not let you."**

The cloak around Histre fell—only it wasn't a cloak at all. They were wings, masquerading as rough fabric and dirty linen, wrapped around a frame that wasn't remotely human. Golden cylinders hung in the air, twisted together in a haphazard shape that only guessed at reality.

There was a long pause. Even Jerome was frozen, staring in confusion at the figure in their midst.

"Guys," Max said. "I don't think that's a demon."

"Gee," Sev said, a touch of sarcasm in his voice. "I couldn't tell."

CHAPTER 26

FEAR

Histre hung in the air, vibrating with fear and paranoia and anger.

Derivan wasn't sure how he knew. Physical Empathy, likely, though he couldn't begin to guess at how he could read the body language of a creature that was more wind chime than person. Histre floated in the air in front of them, wings spread in a way that was unnaturally still—almost like they were hung from invisible strings in the air. Golden cylinders rotated agitatedly around one another, swinging back and forth and producing, strangely, the same sound as a ticking clock.

And then he realized that Jerome was moving to the same ticking of that strange beat.

The system screen flickered in front of him; a notification. He barely spared a glance for it—he knew what it would say, based on everyone's faces as they stared at their own notifications.

<E##RROR>

"You're an *angel*?" Max asked; she was the first one to find her voice, and she seemed almost indignant that this was who Histre had turned out to be. She was the least affected, too, by the strange pressure the angel seemed to give off. Derivan himself could feel a distant sort of version of it, but Sev, Misa, and Vex all seemed more strongly affected. He could see the way they winced slightly every time the angel *ticked*, one second passing over into the next. "Why the hell are you here? What are you doing with Jerome? What do you want with the dungeon?"

"You claim you do not know," Histre growled, the words reverberating against the walls and crashing into them. There was no physical force involved—just pressure, fierce and twisted and *wrong*.

And yet . . . afraid.

"But it *is* you. It must be. You are taking them. You want to take him. You cannot. You will not be allowed."

"We don't know what you're talking about!" Misa finally burst out, the words a half-growl from her position. She'd been forced halfway to the ground by the force of the angel's words, each one of them searing their way into her mind. But now she forced herself to her feet and *glared*, standing strong in the way that she usually did.

Below the angel—nearby, but not attacking—Jerome stood. He was still twitching in sync with the angel, in a way that was frankly rather ominous, if Derivan chose to pay much attention to it. He decided not to.

"We're not— We don't want to take anyone," Vex offered from his spot. He'd collapsed, and he didn't bother trying to get up—but his words were sincere. Kind, even. "We just wanted to undo what you did to Jerome."

Histre wasn't attacking. They had revealed themselves, using shock and awe to freeze all of them in place, and indeed their very existence seemed to scrape against their minds. And yet . . . they weren't attacking.

Even Jerome wasn't attacking, seemingly at Histre's behest, though no words were exchanged between them.

"We helped him," Histre said. **"You will not turn me against the Gold. No. You will not take him. We will defend. We will protect."**

"You are afraid," Derivan said softly.

"We have nothing to fear!" Histre's words were *screeched* in response, and even Max winced at that sound; Derivan wasn't affected quite as strongly, and stared instead at the angel.

What was Aurum's domain? Gold, obviously. But there was something secondary there, something in the angel's movements and sounds. Something about that endless, mechanical ticking.

Time.

"No. You are afraid," Derivan muttered softly, the words gentle, like he was speaking to a frightened animal instead of the eldritch spawn of a god. "And it cannot be your fear alone. Aurum must be afraid, too, or he would not send out so many . . ."

The angel swirled aggressively, chiming—but then it paused, peering at him more closely. He got that impression anyway; Histre didn't have the eyes for him to tell. They didn't answer him, but they seemed to be waiting for him to speak.

"Does he see what will happen?" Derivan mused aloud, then shook his head. "It does not matter. You must stop this. We cannot be divided against whatever comes."

"**Then you know about what comes,**" the angel declared, as if triumphant.

"Only because we have seen it with our own eyes," Derivan said. "We have seen a god wrapped in chains and hung for display. We have seen the form of his prison and fought against it. Won, if barely."

Histre swung forward suddenly, rapidly; the movement was so quick that Derivan almost didn't catch it himself. The angel was away one moment and right in his face the next, and the armor had to take a startled step backward to avoid being hit. "**You have seen,**" the angel hissed at him. "**You have seen past the end. You have seen past the Forgetting. We need to know what it is. Tell us!**"

"I . . . That is all we know," Derivan said, startled. "The god was in chains, kept within an abomination of mana. He told us we would find answers in—"

Ah. *That* was why Aurum was so desperate to send Jerome into the dungeon.

"**Yes,**" Histre said to him, hissing out the worlds; liquid gold dripped out of the cylinders as they spoke, hissing as it touched the ground. Derivan wondered briefly if it was actually molten gold. "**You understand. You have seen. If you are not the ones that wish to take Aurum, then you see why we must know.**"

"But you cannot do it this way," Derivan said. He glanced at Max, who was frantically gesturing and also seemed unable to speak. ". . . Did you silence all of my friends?"

"**I needed to know,**" Histre said. "**I need to know your words. You who have seen a Forgotten God. You who are linked to that which has been taken.**"

"What?" Derivan said. Max gestured even more frantically. ". . . Please allow my friends to speak."

"**As you wish,**" Histre told him.

Just like that, the oppressive aura that seemed to stagnate the air around all of them seemed to fade away. Max gasped for air, seemed to genuinely consider giving an angel the finger, then gathered herself and spoke with authority.

"Aurum is infringing on every treaty the mortals have with the gods," Max said. "You need to withdraw the geases you have placed. The one on Jerome especially, but all the others, too."

"**We need our answers!**" Histre didn't seem to like the words; they swirled into the air, chiming with a terrifying anger. "**We must know—**"

"Jerome as he is right now is a *threat* to any dungeon-delving operation we could possibly consider conducting, even before Elyra is involved!" Max snapped out the words so harshly the angel actually flinched back. "I don't know what the damn geas is that you put on him but I want it gone!"

"Aurum gave him the help he wished for!" The angel argued. **"He wished for confidence!"**

"Confidence doesn't mean you just make him think he's right all the time! That's not how that works!" Max groaned. "And did you consider just *asking* him for help with the damn dungeon?"

Histre paused.

"Please tell me you at least tried to ask," Max said.

"There was too great a risk that he would refuse," Histre eventually said. For an eldritch, terrifying angel, it now sounded all too awkward.

"Did you consider that that might have been because *you made him think he was right all the time?*" Max groaned.

"You were right about the magically reinforced narcissism," Misa whispered to Sev.

"I fucking knew it," Sev whispered back.

"Look. Let us take the damn geas off, and then *if your paladin still wants to worship and help Aurum after all that,* we will see. It depends on how he acts once it's removed. He is *not* cleared for the dungeon until the Guild approves of it *and did you consider just asking these guys what they find once they get into the damn dungeon?*"

The angel was silent.

"Seriously! They're terrible at keeping secrets!" Max complained.

"Max, this feels like a bad time to roast us," Sev tried.

"We admit that we may have made . . . a mistake," the angel said.

Sev sighed. "They're both ignoring us and this is definitely somehow working."

"Good! Now let us take the geas off, *pull back your damn agents,* and we can figure out how to get you what you want." Max seemed all business; she gestured for Derivan to go to Jerome. The paladin was still frozen in place, and he didn't seem to be focusing on anything. Was it something about the sight of Histre?

Or . . . a compulsion of some sort related to Histre.

Derivan shook his head, touched his gauntlet to Jerome's chest, and *pulled.*

Just like before, the geas present in Jerome began to glow, originating from deep in his chest and stomach—and just like before, as Derivan began to pull out the geas, the effects of it on Jerome's mind seemed to begin to fade. The change was less prominent than before, since the paladin's expression was more of a bland nothing compared to the arrogance he'd previously held, but the life coming back into his eyes was a good sign.

That life was quickly accompanied by a retching sound as Derivan began to pull the geas the rest of the way out of the paladin.

For a Gold ranker, he didn't seem to have a very strong stomach.

This time, nothing new happened to interrupt them. Histre simply watched Derivan as he pulled out the geas—the armor suspected the angel could have done it themselves, but had elected to watch him to do it instead, perhaps out of some petty sense of spite. What he ended up with in his hand was less a thin thread of gold and more a solid block.

It crushed just as easily between his fingers, though.

Golden Geas: 103

The stat increase Derivan wasn't particularly surprised by—he kept his eyes on Jerome instead as the paladin began to heave. It took Jerome a moment to finally gather himself, and he slowly got to his feet, staring at the Silver rankers that had bested his party.

There was a long pause. Derivan waited for Jerome to be angry, or scared, or any number of emotions he expected someone to feel after having such a strong compulsion removed.

"Uh," Jerome said, a little awkwardly. "Do you guys mind if I put my armor back on? I feel kind of naked without it."

Well . . . he didn't *seem* like that much of an asshole.

—◁◁◁—

Jerome was, as it turned out . . . *less* of an asshole without a geas messing with his brain.

Not *completely*. He'd leered a little bit at Misa, then immediately lost all confidence when she raised an eyebrow at him. He'd made a bit of a shitty remark about Elyrans, but seemed suitably cowed when Derivan spoke up in Vex's defense. He'd worried about Eleisse and Syra, his elven teammates, until he found out they were just sleeping and had had their geases removed from them as well.

He didn't seem to be a paragon of humanity and was perhaps a little bit more of a dick than not, but he didn't seem . . .

He didn't seem like the kind of person to threaten lives to get what he wanted, basically. Or to take credit for someone else's discovery. Mostly, he seemed kind of awkward.

"You don't seem to mind that Aurum put a geas on you and turned you into a giant dick," Misa said, raising a brow at him.

"I'm trying not to think about it," Jerome said. He fidgeted. "It doesn't really feel like *I* did those things."

"I'll get him a Guild therapist," Max sighed.

"Why is Aurum so scared, anyway?" Jerome asked. He glanced at Histre, who floated ominously and refused to answer him or even look at any of them.

"... I think he's next in line for the system to erase," Sev finally answered. "It would explain the fear."

"*What?*" Jerome stood very still for a moment. It was clear he had no idea what Sev meant, but "erase" didn't invoke good feelings in this context. "No. We gotta stop it."

Histre twitched, a bit guiltily.

"Uh ..." Sev glanced at Jerome. It wasn't that he didn't agree; he was just surprised that the paladin seemed to care so much.

"Aurum's just a kid!" Jerome said indignantly. "I'm not going to let a kid be erased!"

Chalk that up for another mark in the "not a dick" category, Derivan supposed.

Though what was a "kid" in the timescale of the gods?

CHAPTER 27

DUNGEONS

It was decided that Jerome would be sent back to the Guild, along with the sleeping members of his party. The Guildmaster would personally debrief them later, once the paladin and his team had a little more time to absorb what had happened to them. Sev understood this to mean that the Guildmaster would stand in the corner of the room and stare at them under the full effects of her anti-perception skills for a solid few hours, making sure that no one was reapplying any geases.

But she would *also* be making sure that they were okay, and that they understood the depths of what they had gotten themselves into. There was a good chance the team would split, she said, but the Guild would provide them with all the resources they needed to continue adventuring if they wanted to, including Guild-mandated therapy.

For that to work, though, Histre had to be separated from the party. Jerome had protested this a little, but it was a halfhearted sort of protest; remnants of the part of the geas that urged him to trust the angel, perhaps. Derivan's ability to partially circumvent the Guildmaster's skills came in useful here—he could warn them if the angel seemed to be using a skill of some sort.

These were all largely just precautions that they were taking because it made sense to take them. Jerome seemed genuinely apologetic for all that he'd done (and was getting more so by the minute, as he processed more and more the extent of what the geas had done to him), and Histre seemed . . . appropriately chastised.

Mostly, this meant that the angel was floating listlessly around the room, like they weren't quite sure what to do with themselves.

"Are you . . . doing okay?" Sev asked after a moment, a little awkwardly. He'd never spoken to an angel before.

"Yes. No. I am between." Histre paused, like they were considering saying something more, but didn't continue.

"Do you know if Aurum is . . . upset?" Sev asked cautiously.

"He is calling me." The angel swirled, perhaps a little guiltily again. ". . . **He has been calling on me for a while. But he needed protection. I did not go."**

"Oh my god," Sev groaned.

"I think maybe you should answer that call," Max said, raising an eyebrow at the angel. Histre shifted, a little agitated, golden cylinders clanging haphazardly against one another.

"Jerome," the angel said in protest. **"I failed him. He needs—"**

"He doesn't," Max said, but she said it as gently as she could; her eyes searched as if to find a place where she could pat the angel on the shoulder, but she ended up settling for awkwardly patting a wing instead. "He'll be fine. The Guild will handle making sure he's okay. You made a mistake, and that's okay, too. Come back when you understand us mortals a little bit more, and we'll throw you a party, okay?"

"Aurum might be calling you because he needs you," Sev added, quietly. At that, Histre froze.

"Tell Jerome. I am sorry," Histre said.

Max would later explain that what Histre performed then was a *planeshift*—the exact same kind that brought people from Earth over into Obreve, though those shifts often happened out in the wild, where few people were around to observe it. Angels and demons, it seemed, traveled in much the same way, except whatever kind of planeshift they were doing required vastly more energy.

Which was probably why it made all of them stagger backward. Max—and, to a lesser extent, Derivan—were the only ones that seemed relatively immune to the cracks in reality that slammed outward; ripped into the air was pure and utter *void*, then an impossible, radiating light, then glittering gold—

And then Histre was gone.

Sev breathed out, slowly. Max just sighed.

"That's that for a while," she said softly. "Gods almost never send down angels like that. It takes too much energy, and calling them back takes almost as much. He won't be able to do that again anytime soon, and by that time . . ."

"He must've been desperate," Sev said quietly. "Probably still is."

"I feel bad for him," Max agreed. "But . . . it doesn't change the fact that he went around putting geases on people. And what Histre did *here* is one thing, but all the other individuals with some form of geas on them . . . It's going to take him a lot of time to win back any trust. And if you're right, he doesn't have much time left at all."

"People are dangerous, pressed into a corner," Sev mused quietly. "And I guess gods are people too, here."

"In light of all this . . ." Max frowned. "I'm tempted to get the Guildmaster to push for more Guild involvement in this dungeon. But you four might really be our best bet on finding out what's in there, and why Aurum was so interested."

"I think . . ." Sev paused, then groaned. "No, wait, you're right. *All* the gods are interested. That's why I was bombarded with all those clerics when I went to the temple—they're all worried about something. Why is this happening *now?*"

"That," Max said, "is a good question. When you find out, please let the rest of us know, too."

"That's if we *can*," Sev muttered, glancing at his companions. All of them wore severe expressions. "Okay. First we get some rest, but then we need to finally get into that dungeon."

Everyone nodded. And then Derivan paused, a little awkwardly, and stared at his screen.

"So," he said, "it seems four was not the limit on my stats. I now have something called . . . Shift?"

Everyone groaned.

—⁂—

Shift, they decided, was something they'd have to figure out later. The dungeon was their main priority right now, and *Shift* was vague enough that there was very little they could do to test the stat; the obvious correlation was that it was related to whatever Histre had done to shift back between planes, but that was the limit of the guesses they had.

Derivan could not, for instance, shift himself between planes. Perhaps because the stat was so low, but Max seemed convinced that it wouldn't give him control of planeshifting in and of itself; that skill, she said, was completely outside the system.

But if the dungeon had answers, then maybe it would have answers for this, too. So it was decided that that would be their next destination.

They immediately ran into a problem.

"The first delve team is already in the dungeon," the guard informed them. They'd approached the Elyran camp that was set up just outside the newly formed dungeon, and stopped just before entering—good thing, too, since the errors when trying to enter a dungeon that already had people in it were ... unpleasant. "It's closed until they're out."

"You've gotta be fucking kidding me," Misa groaned. "I want to get into this damn place already. Can't you get them out or something?"

"That's not my call," the guard said somewhat apologetically. To his credit, he seemed like he was being genuine. "You're gonna have to talk to the research lead. He's a bit further in camp. He's pretty friendly, though, so he might help you out?"

"He'd *better*," Misa grumbled, and the guard looked abruptly pretty worried, especially given the way she was fingering the mace on her belt. Sev snorted, leaning in to stage-whisper to him.

"Don't worry. She's just grumpy. She wouldn't actually hurt a fly," he said, winking. The guard swallowed once, watching Misa.

"Except that time she *did* hurt a fly," Vex mused to himself. "But it was a big one and it was trying to eat me. So I think that's fair."

"I do not think that is helping," Derivan commented, his voice tinged with amusement.

"Misa, leave the poor man alone and let's go find the guy he's talking about," Sev chuckled. She was putting on a bit of a show, he knew—she tended to do that whenever the team was feeling low, leaning into an archetype so that the people that really knew her would smile, just a little bit. For all that she pretended at gruffness, she had a good head on her shoulders for understanding the people around her.

And so, when they turned to leave, Misa turned around and gave the guard a friendly wave. "Thanks for the help!" she called back.

The poor guard just blinked in confusion.

Thankfully, the way the research camp was set up, it didn't actually take very long for them to figure out who the research lead was. There was a massive control center set up in the middle of the camp, with stone structures jutting out of the ground to act as a physical back for [**Scry**] screens. On every screen were different angles of what Sev assumed was the delve team: four individuals, led by a human captain that seemed to specialize in melee. Five total.

"This ... is a hell of a setup," he muttered. "Is this how Elyra does dungeon delves?"

"Elyra's interested in figuring out what makes dungeons tick, so they use a lot of analytical tools and spells to understand the inner workings of a dungeon," Vex answered. He seemed at least a little distracted, and his tail swung around anxiously. "Normally scrying spells have trouble penetrating the dungeons in the first place—that's why we send scouts. But Elyra figured out a way to anchor scrying spells to their delvers, and now we've got this setup . . ."

The researchers were muttering to themselves about spatial compression and dungeon geometry. Below every scrying screen, Sev noticed, were knobs and dials that seemed related to . . .

. . . he had no idea. This was Vex's area of expertise. All he saw were knobs and dials, which he hadn't actually expected to see anywhere in this world to begin with.

"What is the point of the stone?" Derivan asked curiously.

"Light bleeds through the kind of illusion spells we use for this," Vex said with a shrug. "Actual full illusion spells are more costly. Stone is an easy cast-and-forget, and then cheap illusion spells let us see what's going on without expending too much mana."

"You sure know a lot about us!" someone called down to them—had he *heard* them? He wasn't anywhere near them. The person in question was a lizardkin that wore glasses and what was *clearly* a lab coat, though why he was wearing a lab coat at all when everyone else was dressed in more practical field attire was a different question entirely. "Wanna come up here and introduce yourselves?"

"Uh," Sev said, staring at the platform that the lizardkin was standing on.

It was a giant stone platform.

With no steps.

". . . Yes?" Sev tried.

The person who was obviously the research lead grinned at them, waved a hand, and—there was a vague feeling of *consent*, like a spell was asking to lift them up and he had to say *yes*. But he did, and evidently the rest of his teammates did too, because they all found themselves carried up onto the platform and deposited rather unceremoniously on the floor.

The researcher grinned at them. "I'm Kestel. Head of research. You're the adventuring team from the Guild, right? I hear one of the teams pulled back, but they didn't really tell us why."

"It's kind of complicated," Sev deadpanned.

"As long as we keep the food aid deals, we're not really worried about it," Kestel said with a shrug. Sev exchanged glances with the rest of his team; as far as he knew, the Guild was handling that now. The reveal that geases were involved had complicated things, but not as much as they'd expected; as much as people were angry about their geases, they were also grateful for them being removed. "We just started a delve, so there isn't actually much for you to do right now, but we can put you in for the next one. You wanna stick around and watch? We could always use some adventurer feedback, and this will give you a sense of what the dungeon is like before you go in."

"I'd rather be *in* the dungeon," Misa muttered, but her eyes were already tracking the images on the scrying screens.

Vex, Derivan, and Sev settled in to watch, too.

It wasn't long before they noticed something was wrong.

CHAPTER 28

RESEARCHERS

It was technically Vex that noticed it.

The scrying screens displayed the delve team going through and mapping out the dungeon. Each screen showed them from a slightly different angle, keeping track of both the team themselves and what they were surrounded by. A [**Mass Telepathy**] spell kept the team hooked up with the researchers, allowing them to be alerted to any dangers that the researchers spotted.

The problem was that the scrying screens were *wrong*.

It was nothing obvious—the researchers themselves would have spotted it if it had been. But Vex had training on this too, and his penchant for detail and his more practical experience with dungeons helped him pick up on it quickly.

The scrying screens didn't quite line up with one another. One was slightly delayed. Which was *weird*, for a scrying spell that was supposedly happening in real time. It wasn't possible to miscalibrate a scrying spell like that.

"Uh. Kestel?" Vex tried, glancing at the head researcher and then back to the screen that he'd noticed was off. "I think you should take a look at this. This isn't created by a different scrying spell, by any chance, is it?"

"No, no, all the scrying spells we use should be functionally identical. We need consistent results. We can put the spell through different filters, but . . . Anyway. Why do you ask?" Kestel interrupted himself while speaking, like he knew he would keep going if he let himself.

"This one's slightly delayed." Vex paused. "And the spell resolution looks a bit off."

Kestel paused, frowning, and took a closer look. "Are you sure?" He asked. "I'm not sure I see it . . ."

"It's pretty subtle, and it's hard to tell since the angles don't line up between the different screens, but yes." Vex frowned. "The question is *why*. That shouldn't be possible with scrying spells, should it?"

"Definitely not," Kestel muttered. "All information is sent in real time, and there's no time compression that we've noticed . . ."

"Try switching all of them to the [**Mana Sight**] filter," Vex suggested.

"You know a lot about our operations." Kestel looked at Vex strangely for a moment, then peered a little bit closer, as if he recognized something about the lizardkin—but then, when Vex took a step back, he shook his head and looked away. He spoke again, but this time he was clearly speaking into the [**Mass Telepathy**] spell, and only verbalizing his words for the benefit of the adventurers. "Switch all screens to [**Mana Sight**]. Simultaneously, please."

It took a moment, but every scrying screen spontaneously lit up with magic. The dungeon was *filled* with it, dark, glittering stone suddenly lit up by swirls and whorls of mana. This mana didn't quite dance or move in the way that magic normally did out in the wild. It moved with purpose, marching to an unseen rhythm, touched by chaos.

Almost like a heartbeat, Vex mused. He'd seen it before, but it was always a sight to behold.

"Whoa," Misa said out loud. Vex blinked; he'd forgotten that she didn't have the ability to see magic the way he did. The way his own sight worked was still *different*, and didn't look exactly the same as it did on the scrying screens, which had only the basic [**Mana Sight**] filter. "Does it always look like that?"

"It's usually a little livelier," Vex offered with a small smile. "But yeah, more or less."

Misa watched it for a moment. "I can see why you like magic so much."

There was something noticeably wrong now, however. The researchers were still fiddling with the screen that had seemed time-delayed—mana still wasn't visible in the filter, and now the discrepancy was obvious. It flickered a few times, even, traces of mana appearing in the air, but in patterns that were obviously different from all the other screens.

"It looks confused," Derivan muttered, his voice odd. "It . . . *is* confused?"

"What do you mean?" Vex asked, his voice coming out sharper than he intended. He winced, but Derivan didn't seem to notice.

"Physical Empathy is picking up on it," Derivan said. "Whatever is causing that, it is something alive."

That was not, it turned out, something that could be said without an immediate response. Kestel didn't speak, but it was apparent that he'd barked out some kind of order by the way he tensed and the way the other researchers immediately sat upright. The delvers in the dungeon responded almost instantly as well, reaching for their weapons and standing back-to-back warily.

There was nothing apparent in the corridor. But then they glanced up and to the right, where the [**Scry**] spell was watching them. One of them—the captain—narrowed his eyes, like he'd seen something or was peering at something that was indistinct—then there was some shouting that they couldn't hear over the scrying screens, one of the delvers reached for a spear, and—

—the screen cut out.

That one did, anyway. The other scrying screens were still operational, and one of the delvers walked over to where the spear was lying with a frown. On the tip of the spear, impaled, was . . . something strangely indistinct. In the scrying screen, it looked almost like a distorted cloud of static, with mana oozing down the spear in a distinctly un-mana-like fashion.

When the [**Mana Sight**] filter was turned off, the screens showed nothing on the spear at all. Vex frowned, watching it carefully; he couldn't conduct any spell analysis at a distance like this, but had that been a monster that was made of mana?

Like the Mana Abomination they had fought. But nothing nearly so visible, because it was a small distortion rather than a large one; it wasn't created of so much compressed energy that it could be seen by the naked eye.

"Good catch," Kestel said to them, a little bit late and a little bit distracted—but there was a manic sort of gleam in his eye, and a small grin was spreading over his snout. "Looks like we've discovered something new! I've never heard of a dungeon monster like this before, have you?"

"No," Vex said cautiously, glancing at Kestel and then back to the screens. "It looks like some sort of creature made out of mana. Given what it was doing to the [**Scry**] spell . . . some sort of spell parasite, maybe? It took over part of the spell and tried to mimic it?"

"That's our main theory!" Kestel beamed. "It's even *named* Mana Feeder in the kill notification, so we're thinking that's exactly what that is. You're good at this. Have you ever considered joining one of Elyra's dungeon-research teams? I could put in a good word for you."

"Ah. No." Vex flinched a little bit at that, but he relaxed slightly when he felt a metal hand on his shoulder. "I'd prefer not to. But thank you."

"Pity, pity," Kestel said, though he seemed too distracted to press Vex about it. The head researcher glanced through the screens again. "It looks like the rest of the spells are fine . . . I wonder what would have happened if it kept going. How does it feed, anyway? It was feeding the spell output back to us, but at a slight efficiency loss . . ."

Kestel continued muttering to himself, wandering away from them and over to the other thing that sat on the stone platform—a rather large stone tablet, with an illusion spell overlaid on top of it that seemed to be his notes. It wasn't particularly visible to the rest of them, though. Vex saw a thin veil of white mana strung across the screen, and deduced that it was some sort of privacy function tied into the spell.

He glanced at the rest of his team. "That thing is . . . a little bit too much like the Mana Abomination we fought for me to be comfortable."

"Kestel said it's new, right?" Misa frowned, worried. "You think it's something related?"

"*New* can mean a lot of things," Vex said, hesitating. "The Adventurers' Guild doesn't really bother keeping a log of all the monsters we encounter, because we encounter them all the time—it's not uncommon to find new monsters, or new variants of a monster, every time we discover a new dungeon. Elyra *does* try to keep a log of everything, but their data comes from a more limited set of dungeons."

"So it's new to Elyra, but we don't know if it's *significant*," Sev grumbled.

"Organisms that interact with mana in some way are pretty common," Vex said. "It's an abundant resource, and it's everywhere. But not ones *made out of mana.*"

Kestel chose that moment to wander back over to them. "I made a ton of notes!" he said, in a voice that implied that he expected to hear applause—though he didn't seem particularly bothered by the fact that no one applauded. "Hopefully we find another one of those. We know to keep an eye out for them now. They're hard to spot even with [**Mana Sight**], because there's so much mana around in dungeons . . . Tricky. Bodes well for this dungeon! Who knows what else we'll discover."

"Looks like you'll be discovering something else soon," Misa said, gesturing to the screen.

The delving team had come up to a door. That door stood out, looking like an old, decrepit plank of wood pressed flush against the polished black stone of the dungeon.

"Ah! A challenge room!" Kestel grinned. "Perfect. We wanted to get to at least one of these before we pull back the delve team; they can take a break after this, and we can send you in next. What do you say?"

"I don't know—" Sev began.

"Sounds perfect!" Misa declared loudly, glaring at Sev. He smirked at her, and she grumbled. "Smartass."

"Good!" Kestel clapped his hands together, turning to the screen.

"How do you know it is a challenge room and not a bonus room?" Derivan asked curiously, glancing at Vex. "I have always just thought of them as . . . rooms."

Vex opened his mouth to answer—

"Ah! Good question!" Kestel said, immediately turning back from the screen while Vex blinked rapidly at how suddenly the head researcher had inserted himself into the conversation. "Challenge rooms force you to go through them to progress. Bonus rooms don't. Sometimes bonus rooms don't have physical entryways at all, and have entrance requirements that automatically transport you in when you fulfill them."

Kestrel glanced at the screen as if ordering the delvers to pause while he rambled. "Those ones are always strange. I love them, because I don't understand how they work, but some researchers hate them because the patterns between different rooms make no sense. I've seen it require specific combinations of spells, or spoken words . . . Sometimes you need to replicate a specific situation?"

"Ah," Derivan said, sounding a little bit stunned at the block of information Kestel had just thrown at him.

Vex chuckled a bit and patted him on the arm. "Some of Elyra's researchers are pretty enthusiastic. You get used to it."

Misa grinned at Vex. "You *do* know that's just what you sound like *all the time*, right?"

"No it isn't!" Vex said, looking offended.

"I understand it when Vex says it," Derivan said.

Misa smirked at that, shaking her head, and turned back to the screen as Kestel gave the delvers the go-ahead. The delve team opened the door into a strange, rocky cavern. All six of them streamed in, looking cautiously around the room—challenge rooms like these were never really clear about what needed to be done to complete them. Littered about the floor were what looked like mana crystals.

"Are those crystals, or flowers?" Misa asked, squinting at them through the screens.

"If it's a dungeon? Probably crystals," Vex answered. "But if it's a challenge room? Almost definitely a trap."

"Don't worry!" Kestel said cheerily. "We're prepared for all the traps a dungeon can throw at us."

Misa peered at him. "It's never a good idea to say that out loud."

"Bah! Confirmation bias!" Kestel said, clearly enjoying the opportunity to use the words *confirmation bias*. "Things will happen the way they happen regardless of whether I say they'll turn out well. I just remember all the times they *don't* turn out well, because it's usually terrifying."

"Well," Sev said, "in this case the dungeon adjusts itself to delvers, so if you've prepared for a lot of things . . ."

A strange orb formed in the center of the room, floating.

". . . you might create a problem you can't deal with," Sev said, eyeing the orb suspiciously. "Is it just me, or is that orb kind of menacing?"

Kestel paused. "Definitely not just you," he agreed.

CHAPTER 29

IT'S JUST FLOATING THERE. MENACINGLY.

Misa frowned as she looked at the screen. There was something bothering her, and it *wasn't* the strangely menacing orb floating in the middle of the room—which in and of itself was rather concerning, considering it should really have garnered all of her attention.

There was something else. She couldn't quite place her finger on what it was, though. Everything seemed fine, and none of the others seemed to have noticed anything . . .

Misa kept her mind sharp and her eyes focused. Something about this was ringing *danger* to her, and the fact that it might be triggering her [**Danger Sense**] when she wasn't even in the dungeon was worrying.

"Is anyone else's [**Danger Sense**] going off?" Misa asked quietly. Sev and Kestel both looked back at her, but they each shook their heads; they didn't sense anything.

"It's definitely some kind of trap," Vex said cautiously. "But I've never seen anything like this before. I don't know what it is."

"It's something new!" Unlike everyone else, Kestel seemed rather enthusiastic about the discovering-something-new aspect of all this. Misa suppressed the urge to glare at him. It wasn't that he wasn't concerned about the safety of the team, she told herself; he loved discovery, but that didn't mean he was disregarding safety.

At his command, the delve team approached the orb cautiously. When nothing happened, the captain carefully took off his pack, gesturing for the other delvers to stand back; they each stood a respectable distance away from him, keeping an eye out for any other dangers. He had several tools in the pack, Misa saw—what they were, she had no idea.

All in all, a well-trained team. They more than likely had their own version of [**Danger Sense**]—and there was no reason they wouldn't have said anything if they had sensed something. So was the danger not to *them*?

Or was it not [**Danger Sense**] at all that was giving her this sense of foreboding?

Misa had one more skill that she'd never quite been able to figure out—the text on it was vague, it was a passive skill, and as far as she knew, it had never been triggered.

[**Guardian's Premonition**] [**Passive Skill**] [**Grade: Maxed**]
You know when the gate might fall.

There were other strange things about that skill, too, like the fact that it was a *unique* skill for her otherwise rare class, and the fact that it had been maxed right from the get-go, no skill leveling needed. There was only one gate that she could think of that it might be related to—the gate into her village, the one that had been trampled and crushed—and, well . . .

. . . That gate had fallen a long time ago.

The point was that if it wasn't [**Danger Sense**] that was pinging her, then it was that skill, and she had no idea what that meant.

"I have another skill that's warning me something might be about to happen," Misa said out loud, just to make sure she wouldn't get anyone killed by keeping this information to herself. "Keep an eye out."

Sev, Vex, and Derivan all nodded; Kestel gave her a bit of a strange look, but seemed to take her warning seriously. "What tier is your skill?"

". . . Unique," Misa answered after a moment, and Kestel's eyes sharpened.

"I'm going to link all four of you into our [**Mass Telepathy**]," he said. "Please consent."

There was a moment of *pressure* as a new skill wrapped around her mind and asked her permission to enter. The moment she accepted, that feeling of pressure vanished, and she heard Kestel speaking clearly across the mental link.

We have a unique precognitive skill warning that there might be a problem in the near future, Kestel said without preamble. **I want you to do a full check. Run through all the surveillance skills you have.**

Something still seemed wrong. Misa leaned forward with a frown; the others were still talking, but the noise faded into the background. This wasn't even [**Guardian's Premonition**] or [**Danger Sense**], just her own instincts coming into play; one of the delvers was moving a little strangely, and something about the movement fired off an old memory—

"Skills are useful when it comes to learning," V'karro told her. "But pit two fighters against one another, and the more experienced one will still win. Skills tell you how to do something, but experience tells you how you can change them. Tweak them to suit your needs."

"Oooh. I bet I can use that!" Misa grinned up at V'karro, her eyes bright. She was eleven at the time, and had a reputation for finding small little tricks that people could perform with their skills. "That means inexperienced fighters are gonna be using the same instincts, right? So if I watch how they move—"

"That's a risky game to play," V'karro interrupted, shaking his head and hiding his small grin of amusement. Misa saw it anyway, though, because she was observant. "If possible, don't fight people at all. And if you do, don't assume they're inexperienced."

"Show me some anyway," Misa demanded, a little petulantly, and he chuckled and obliged.

It was an old, old memory.

But one of the delvers was moving in a way that was familiar to her—a subtle twitch of the fingers, shifting toward the belt, in exactly the way an inexperienced user of the skill would activate [**Stealth Bolt**]. She *knew* what V'karro had said; never assume that anyone was inexperienced, and yet . . .

Even if she was wrong, that delver was definitely activating a skill of some kind, and there was no reason for anyone to be activating a battle skill. Every other delver was looking around cautiously at the edges of the room, and they weren't looking at *themselves*, at their own team; and—

—and there had been five of them, hadn't there? Not *six*.

Fuck, she said, and then cursed again mentally when she realized she'd accidentally transmitted the word into the telepathic link. It didn't matter. *Convey information in as few words as possible,* she told herself. **Look out! Headcount!**

To their credit, the delvers immediately jolted, glancing at one another— but no one quite noticed the one among them reaching for a crossbow bolt. The captain shouted something that was indistinct through the telepathic link, that sounded like he was demanding the team take off their helmets so he could verify their identities, and then several things happened almost all at once.

The man who had been reaching for a crossbow bolt narrowed his eyes, looking not at all concerned, and moved quickly to load the bolt and aim it— not at any of the delvers, but at the orb.

The captain glanced at him and saw what was about to happen—his hand snapped out and he lunged, trying to interrupt the path of the arrow.

The other delvers nearby reacted with startled surprise, then cursed, reaching for their weapons, but by that point it was too late; her warning had helped, but only a little. Only enough that they had the time to watch it all happen, because whoever the sixth delver was—certainly not a delver at all— he was monstrously fast.

The man's finger pressed down on the crossbow's trigger mechanism, and the bolt fired from the crossbow. It glowed with raw, imbued magic.

The captain's hand brushed just the edge of that magic in his attempt to stop it. His flesh rotted down to the bone almost instantly, like his health didn't even exist. His face was still contorted with determination—he hadn't had the time to react.

And [**Guardian's Premonition**] finally, *finally* fully activated for the first time since she'd gained the skill, and she *saw* what was about to happen.

The bolt would strike the orb, charged with what seemed like necrotic energy. She didn't know what the orb was, or what it was made of, but she saw the way that silver-black mana raced across its surface like fire taking to oil—until the entire thing was enveloped in impossible magic.

Then it would destabilize. It would explode, flinging that necrotic energy all over the room in a wave so intense that there was no defending against it. The entire team would be dead, reduced to bones and a few scraps of rotting flesh, for the few that had defensive skills that would serve to protect some meager portion of them.

Misa saw this, and she spoke.

"No."

[**To Fall Yet Hold the Line**]

And there was, perhaps, some part of her that knew this was a truly ridiculous extension of the skill. That she shouldn't have *tried*. She felt the skill resist, even as she leveraged her will against it; she briefly saw the blue boxes that speared across her vision.

Nearby, Derivan started, like he'd seen something strange. He turned to her and reached out—

But the impossible happened, and she vanished from the room.

"We need to get in there! That's our friend!"

Derivan was listening to Vex yelling with a strangled sort of panic in his voice. Whatever had happened with Misa, she'd been disconnected from the telepathic network. So had the rest of the delve team, for that matter. The scrying screens had been taken over by a static interference, something that they hadn't thought was possible before they'd discovered the Mana Feeder; now no one knew what was happening inside the challenge room, or if any of them were still alive.

We can't get in even if we want to. Kestel's response was clipped and through the telepathic network—he didn't bother speaking. He paced, tense, even as he rapidly cast several diagnostic spells to try to restore the scrying magic. **You know that. You *should* know that.**

"There has to be a way," Vex argued, but from the defeated look on his face, Derivan knew that the lizardkin didn't know of one himself.

Derivan himself was distracted, because one of his stats had increased. He wouldn't have checked, if a brief error message hadn't popped up and obscured his view; it had happened right when Misa seemed to tense, staring at the screen.

And then when he'd checked his stats . . .

Shift: 2

He wondered. What was a *Shift*, exactly?

Vex had subsided, looking frustrated; he had no solutions. But Derivan's mind was racing.

Dungeons became locked off after a team entered. There were other rules, too, governing what locked off a dungeon, but this was the single one that could not be circumvented.

Except. Maybe it could be? Misa had clearly circumvented it. Whatever *means* she'd used to circumvent it—likely her skill, knowing her—had to be in some way related to the stat gain she'd triggered for him. And there was the fact that he had started this life as a monster, too, and monsters were rarely prevented *entry* into dungeons. For them, it was the reverse.

The chatter on the telepathy network became about fixing the scry interference. Derivan shook his head; this was nothing he could help with. There was only one thing he could do, as far as he was concerned.

"I am going to try to enter the dungeon," he said. Vex and Sev both looked up at him, startled. "My status might allow me access," he added, and Sev's expression cleared; Vex's expression changed, looking briefly hopeful.

"Can you bring us all through?" the lizardkin asked.

"I do not know," Derivan said. "But we can make the attempt, I think. It is better that we do. But if I cannot . . ."

He saw the worry in Vex's eyes.

"I will still need your help," he added, partially to try to ameliorate Vex's concerns; the lizardkin looked troubled, but he seemed to try to focus as Derivan spoke. "I trust your knowledge of magic. And I suspect that will be needed for what we face here. But let us try to enter the dungeon first."

"We'll need to equip you all with the scrying anchors," Kestel said out loud this time. He was staring at them in a mixture of wariness, hope, and interest. "We need to be able to see what's going on in there, and there are spatial anomalies in the dungeon. If you really can get in, then you should be able to follow that path and not have to fight a single monster."

"Hit us with it, then," Sev nodded, and Kestel cast the spell. There was a slight tingle, and that was it, but the three of them were all suddenly visible on the scrying screens.

Nothing to it. They ran for the dungeon, and when they arrived—the guard had already been informed, and stood aside for them—Derivan held on to his friends' hands, and *pushed* against the barrier.

> **<ERROR>**
> **Access deni—**

And then the notification vanished, and the three of them stepped through.

CHAPTER 30

UNSTOPPABLE FORCE, IMMOVABLE MISA

As a general rule, almost all skills had some sort of range limit, even if that range limit wasn't stated. A fireball's range depended on its strength; the farther it traveled, the more the fire or the magic that maintained it would dissipate, and the weaker the spell was. A melee skill's range depended on the size of the weapon you were using, and how much you could physically extend yourself.

More esoteric skills from rarer classes tended to bend the rules; they tried to obey the rules as they were written in the box. And while Misa had to be *aware* of an attack in order to block it, she was, in fact, aware of this attack.

But she was separated by the dimensional boundary that dungeons that were being actively delved had around them; she was aware of the attack only because of the particularly strange combination of scrying magics used to view what was happening in real time across that boundary.

As far as anyone knew, physically crossing the boundary should have been impossible. It was an uncrossable boundary, dictated by the rules of the system.

And so the question became this: What were the rules as written in this scenario?

Misa didn't know. There were strange interactions, sometimes, between skills; rarer ones especially often had unpredictable results when tested against the boundaries presented by the system.

Misa rolled the dice.

There was a bare fraction of a heartbeat's worth of time that passed where the system seemed to freeze, uncertain. There was a moment that was stretched into eternity.

And then she was in the dungeon, in front of the necrotic bolt, her mace already raised in defense. The bolt clanged uselessly against the metal, but she still felt the bite of an impossible, shearing pain as the system ripped away her health, almost as if in punishment for the abuse of her skill—

—but it wasn't done yet. Her system was going wild, notifications pouring through the air in front of her.

> <ERROR>
> Theoretical range limit for Skill exceeded! Attempting to compensate
> . . .

> <ERROR>
> Reality-displacement boundary found between user and Skill target! Unable to compensate—

> <WARNING>
> Boundary weakened by unknown effect. Proceeding with Skill . . .

> <ERROR>
> Skill conflict detected! Skill [Inexorable Bolt] conflicts with [To Fall Yet Hold the Line]. Resolving Skill differences . . .

> <ERROR>
> Multiple errors detected during Skill use. Resolution failed. Compensation failed. Local boundaries degrading. Engaging fallbacks . . .
>
> Fallback resolution determined.
>
> Skill [Inexorable Bolt] has succeeded. Skill [To Fall Yet Hold the Line] has succeeded. Averaging results along local reality axis.

What the fuck?

Misa scarcely had the time to think the question—she got her answer.

She blocked the bolt. She didn't block the bolt. The skill both failed and succeeded, and the *average* was picked between two possibilities; Misa was only half-present, one version of her blocking one version of an unerring bolt. The other version was never there, the bolt slamming into the orb, and what had happened in her vision immediately came true—necrotic energy washed into it like a black tide, turning it pitch black and exploding outward in a searing wave of energy.

In one version of events, the delve team was unharmed, and Misa was there, having blocked the [**Inexorable Bolt**]. In the other, the bolt struck, and necrotic energy ripped through the entire team, and Misa had never been there.

A ripple pulsed, bringing together both possibilities into a single result—and every member of the delve team staggered and collapsed. Their flesh faded away like it had never existed, leaving behind only bone and empty sockets.

For a single, horrifying moment, it looked to Misa like she had failed. Like the only thing she'd succeeded in doing was bringing herself into the dungeon, with no backup and a dead team to show for it.

They're skeletons, Misa thought, dazed. *I—I didn't block it? But I swear I fucking . . .*

The skeletons *moved*.

"What the fuck," one of them shouted in horror; a skeleton of a human staring at his own hand with a morbid sort of fascination. "What the *fuck*—"

"Calm *down*," the captain barked—at least, Misa thought he was the captain. All she had to go off of was the fact that he was closest to her, and to the pack on the ground. She'd seen two versions of him, both standing in slightly different places, and she still hadn't completely reconciled what had happened.

Were they all . . . *undead* now?

The sight was horrifying enough to make her feel vaguely nauseated, and the fact that any of them had the presence of mind to stay calm was frankly astonishing. "Look at your notifications," the captain added. "And more importantly—"

"Miss." The captain directed his gaze at Misa; she didn't know how to react, staring into empty eye sockets where she'd once seen life. "You're in a high-level dungeon now. No matter what happens, you need to keep your wits about you."

"I . . . Yeah. Okay. I can do that." Misa swallowed once, her eyes hardening. They were skeletons. But they were alive? She could work with that. But . . .

. . . No. There was a bigger problem. A bigger danger. She'd almost forgotten.

"He's still human," Misa hissed, pointing at the man that had fired the bolt. He was staring at the delve team in bemusement. Her senses screamed at her—this man was *dangerous*, he'd orchestrated the death of the entire team and hadn't changed in the resulting explosion, he didn't seem shocked or bewildered or even the slightest bit concerned—

"Well, of course I am. You think I'd do that if I couldn't make sure I stayed alive?" He yawned, bored. "But now you've gone and ruined my plans. I guess it wasn't a complete waste, though. This is pretty interesting."

"What the fuck," Misa said, gritting her teeth. All her worry about *danger* instantly vanished, replaced by anger. Treating lives like they were playthings? *Fuck all of that.* "Explain, or I swear to the fucking gods—"

"What, you think I'm just going to monologue at you?" The man smiled at her. "I got over that impulse two or three centuries ago. It's fun, but it's not really worth it." He sighed dramatically.

"That said, it looks like that thing is going to finish transforming any second now, so maybe it'll do my job for me, eh? I'd say good luck, but frankly, I kind of just hope you all die." The man waved, starting to step backward—

The captain *slashed* forward in an impossibly fast movement, his blade sweeping out to catch the man's neck. The strike *hit*, Misa was certain it did, and yet the blade passed through the flesh like it wasn't there at all; instead, he finished stepping backward, *through the wall*, and the captain's follow-up strike slammed into the black stone and skittered off ineffectually.

They were left with an orb of magical energy, somehow forced into a state that the system considered the "average" between its original and necrotic form. As far as Misa could tell, this meant that the necrotic energy wasn't completely taking over the orb. It was *trying*, stuttering in waves as it began to flicker over whatever the rest of it was, but then it would fail.

And cracks were forming along the orb—almost like it was starting to hatch.

The entire team was tense, staring at it as the magic gathered and became almost palpable. Misa repositioned herself—or, more accurately, she had *been* repositioned near the back of the line. The captain was grateful for what she'd done, but her level still made her a liability in the upcoming fight.

Misa didn't argue. He was right. At best, her skill allowed her to run interference. As powerful a skill as [**To Fall Yet Hold the Line**] was, it had severe limitations.

She was grateful she had it. Whatever just happened wouldn't have been possible without the skill, and though the outcome was questionable, no one on the delve team seemed to be reacting strongly.

Yet, anyway. It was possible they were saving the hysteria for when they were out of a crisis.

But the limitations of the skill were showing themselves almost immediately. The delve team didn't have a healer on hand; they were all built with self-healing, self-sustaining skills, given the penchant dungeons had for separating people. Misa was a dedicated damage-soaker without any of those skills—any damage to her, for the duration of this fight, would be permanent. She could keep charges of her skill for emergencies, but it got progressively more dangerous to use it each time, and once she was too low on health she would be nearly useless in the fight.

She had a couple of health potions, and there was [**Every Last Drop**] to soak up some mana instead of health, but even those wouldn't last forever . . .

It was too much to think about. Misa shook her head; better to focus on the fight.

The orb cracked in half.

A blinding energy that wasn't quite light erupted from within. *Mana*, Misa thought, dazed; it didn't interact with her eyes in any way, but they still watered from the sight. She saw streams of red from where the mana was so dense that it distorted light, saw the way it flowed outward in a mockery of the humanoid form in an eerie reminder of the Overseer.

Two arms, then three, then five. Three on one side and two on the other; the balance of the new creature was lopsided. Three arms were made out of red, arcane energy, the original color of the orb; two were made from the darker necrotic energy.

The torso was a thin, wispy thing that barely existed save to hold the limbs together, and the legs were barely present at all—two protrusions jutting out from below its torso, brushing against the ground. They weren't holding up any of the creature's weight, appearing to exist solely because it was mimicking some vaguely humanoid form.

"Get ready," the captain said, his voice grim.

The mana creature, or whatever it was, screeched. A system display fizzed into being, oddly reluctant, above its head.

Level 73 Aberrant—Arcane + Necrotic

A level seventy-three *typed Elite*. It was the sort of thing you heard about heroes fighting, every time there was a dungeon break of some sort and monsters flooded out; not the type of monster Misa expected she would face for many years, yet. But she was here now, surrounded by a team of soldiers much stronger than her.

Soldiers that had just been turned into skeletons through a paradoxical skill interaction. Misa grimaced slightly. There was no telling if that would affect their fighting abilities; it *shouldn't*, but then nothing about that skill interaction should have happened. She felt guilt for what she'd done to them—

She put the thought aside. She could feel guilty later, as long as everyone was alive, for now. As long as she made sure everyone stayed alive.

Breathe. Watch. React.

The Aberrant attacked.

It moved in a clumsy, shuffling way that should have been uselessly slow; indeed, for a second or two it seemed to be genuinely tripping over itself. Then that movement turned into a fall, and the fall's momentum was somehow redirected and boosted, and it shot with blinding speed toward the lizardkin captain.

The captain blocked. Arms filled with arcane energy crashed into the edge of his blades, and the monster *screeched* again, a painful surge of sound that bled into Misa's health. It didn't seem to take any damage from his blades, even though he tried to twist and slice; the blades skated off the arcane energy like it was nothing, and then the Aberrant twisted, plunging both necrotic arms straight into the center of his chest.

A pause.

The Aberrant and captain both seemed briefly confused—and then something seemed to click. He somehow grinned, though his head was nothing but skull and bone. "Necrotic damage ain't gonna do shit to us now. Didn't think of that, did ya, ya bastard?"

The Aberrant screeched again, not understanding a word and yet still managing to sound just a touch alarmed. It understood enough to know that the fact that its prey had survived a hit made it dangerous.

The captain, of course, pressed his advantage. A blade spun and twisted in his hand, even as the other kept the arcane arms occupied; the second blade slammed into the Aberrant's center mass, directly toward the cracked glass orb that still hovered in the center.

But it skittered off yet again. They were almost at an impasse, except the Elyran delvers were all still vulnerable to the blades of arcane mana that masqueraded as arms.

Misa saw three other delvers lunge at the Aberrant, trying to score hits with their own enchanted weaponry; just as before, the blades seemed to deflect off the creature's body. It saw that its opponents couldn't hurt it, and the mana in the upper portion of its torso parted in a strange crescent—

Was it *grinning?*

Fuck.

CHAPTER 31

TRIGGER

The Aberrant seemed to regain any confidence it had lost. It swept itself in a dancing circle, creating a blast of arcane energy that knocked back every one of the delvers that were lunging at it; while they staggered, off-kilter, it flung itself at one of them and slammed him into the ground. There was a shout, half-panicked and half-determined, trying to fend off the blow—but arcane energy plunged into his chest, and he *screamed*.

React, you idiot! Misa roared the words at herself. She'd been frozen, still off-balance from what had happened to the soldiers when she tried to save them. Before she could do anything, though, another one of the delvers did; he switched out his blades for a flail, and brought the weapon swinging directly into the creature's center mass.

For all that it seemed impenetrable, it was still *light*, its body mass nothing more than a collection of mana. The force of the strike sent it flying and crashing into a nearby wall. But that was hardly enough—the laws of physics seemed to bend around the creature; how did it exert so much force if it had almost no mass behind it? Even now, it was getting up like nothing had happened . . .

"We need to retreat!" the captain called. The Aberrant seemed dazed but mostly unharmed; if the blunt force had done some sort of damage to it, it wasn't obvious. "We can't damage it! Back toward the main hall, now! We need to see if we can get back in contact with the research team!"

Normally, the research team would give them an analysis of the enemy and a strategy—but they'd been cut off.

And the Aberrant did *not* want them to retreat.

Misa saw what it was planning to do a second before it acted, and this time, she *reacted*.

She'd reserve her skill for when it was necessary; along with the extra damage she'd taken from the thing's screams, she was down to about 70% of her health. She could take six more hits with [**To Fall Yet Hold the Line**], and a few more with [**Every Last Drop**] and her mana; for the most part that was better than tanking the hits herself. Any hits this monster dealt would no doubt wipe out all her remaining health, given their level difference.

But the monster was *light,* and she could use that.

She swung her mace directly into the Aberrant's leg as it sailed over her head, the monster apparently planning to collapse the exit before they could escape. Forward momentum turned into torque, and the monster was sent flipping over backward into the upper edge of the doorway.

When it wasn't actively applying force, it seemed to be vulnerable to having forces applied to it. Useful to know, but only good for keeping it knocked back, perhaps. The captain was already moving, launching himself toward the Aberrant before it could recover. "I'll keep the bastard occupied!"

Then he kicked the monster, *hard.* He'd evidently figured out the same thing.

It slammed into the opposite wall of the cavern and *screeched.*

Misa winced. The sound alone was enough to chunk her health *again,* but it didn't help that the soldiers didn't move to retreat quite as quickly as they should have.

"He's telling you to retreat, so *go!*" Misa roared, and the shout was enough to startle the other delvers into moving. They weren't completely used to their bodies yet, she could see—without flesh and muscle, their bodies were just a lot lighter than they usually were. That discrepancy kept throwing them off.

What Misa was wondering was why none of them seemed to have any *skills* for the situation. They seemed to be all physical-combat fighters, but surely that wasn't a good setup for a delve team?

There was no time for that, though. The Aberrant could see them retreating, and while the captain was slowing it down, he couldn't stop *everything* it did. It blew past him in a sudden, flickering movement, charging straight at the retreating team; two of them tried to block it, but they were tossed aside like they were made of paper, and it slammed into a third—

Nope, Misa thought. *Fuck that.*

She didn't have a lot of health left. But she didn't *need* a lot of her health. She blocked.

It screeched at her, loud and painful, and that one she *didn't* block since the damage it did was minimal; the skeletons that had been tossed to the side scrambled back to their feet. They looked like they wanted to help—

"Fucking *go*!" Misa yelled, right as the Aberrant tried to spear her with an arcane blade; she didn't *react* in time, momentarily distracted, but right before the blade would have pierced her the captain body-checked the Aberrant out of the way.

"Listen to your own advice, miss," he said, and then seemed surprised. "Huh. Well, what do ya know. I'm usually more out of breath after that."

"Are you going to be okay?" Misa asked, her voice steely. The captain chuckled, even while the Aberrant circled them from farther away, still grinning that manic grin.

"We're about to find out, I s'ppose," he said, perhaps a little more cheerily than he should have, given the circumstances.

"What's your name?" Misa asked, because it felt wrong to just run without knowing the name of this person, and she wasn't sure she wanted to run at all.

"Name's Harold," the captain said easily, but his eyes were sharp and tracing the Aberrant's movements. It was twitching sporadically, like it was about to attack.

Just as it darted forward with incredible speed, Harold reached back and pressed a hand to her shoulder—

—and suddenly she found herself in the corridor outside the room, among the other delvers; they visibly started at her appearance, bones rattling.

He'd figured her out, then. But what kind of skill was that?

"We need to get backup," one of the now-skeletons told her, and she nodded, a little hesitantly. She wasn't the only one, either; they all had some experience with dungeons, and while it was necessary to retreat sometimes, dungeons never liked it when they did.

Especially when retreating from a challenge room. There would almost certainly be a trap, in fact, but they were all on the lookout for it; as long as they were careful, they'd probably be able to work around it.

That thought was, perhaps, foolishly optimistic.

Misa only barely caught the glimmer of a trap activating in the corridor ahead of them, along with a flicker of a familiar laugh. It gave her just enough time to respond. The others were reacting too, but they didn't seem to have skills they could do it with—they just sort of gathered in front of her, as if they could protect her from the flames of concentrated night that were spewing forward from the opposing wall.

Misa did the only thing she could do—she blocked it with [**To Fall Yet Hold the Line**]. She slammed a glowing mace into the ground, and a shimmering shield appeared in front of all of them, blocking the flames.

One of the soldiers tried destroying the trap, dashing forward and slamming his flail into it, but it took barely a scratch of health as damage, and he quickly retreated back into the range of the block.

"The fire's filled the corridor ahead, too," he told them. He sounded worried. "And that fire does a *lot* of damage."

Misa wasn't paying much attention. She gritted her teeth. There was a problem here, and the problem was how the skill worked with sustained attacks. She'd tested it before, but the results had been rather useless. It was as likely to tick multiple times during a sustained attack as it was to only tick once. There was some metric by which it operated, but she hadn't figured it out.

And the secondary problem was that she couldn't move while she was doing it.

"I can't hold this for long," Misa said grimly once she saw her health tick down twice. "Run back. I dunno if you heard that laugh, but this trap should have stopped by now; it's the fucking guy with the crossbow again. Whoever that is."

The soldiers tried to help, using a variety of skills to try to smash apart the traps, but they just had so much *health*, and they kept having to run back into the range of the block to have the time to heal and recover—

33% left.

"Go *back*," she said. She knew her team—they would be on the way. Not a single one of them would give up on her if she just vanished, and they were exactly the types of fuckers that would find a way into the dungeon, rules be damned. They'd find a way to help the soldiers, too.

Her job now was to keep them alive. She'd done this same thing a very long time ago, though it was more battle-fraught than this. This was what she *did*. She protected. It didn't matter *who*.

"I'm not going to see anyone die on my watch," she said, her voice firm. "Go back. Backup will be coming."

"But you—" a delver protested, but her health hit zero, and the block flickered out—

> **Activation conditions for the bonus room <The Village's Last Defense> have been met.**
> **Transporting: Misa, level 42, [Fallen Guardian]**

There was a flash of light. Misa's vision flickered into nothing: not darkness nor blinding light, but *nothing*. A momentary emptiness.

There was a sensation of being dragged across an impossible distance.

Then her sight returned, and she was no longer in the dungeon. The sun shone above her, bright and ignorant of everything she had just been through.

Of the fact that she had almost died.

But not even that mattered to her, because her eyes focused on the box that had appeared as soon as she could see again.

> **The village of J'rokksur will soon be besieged by monsters following a dungeon break. The defenders of the village cannot stand up to such a siege by themselves. Help the villagers mount their final defense, or die trying.**

There was a long, long pause.

Misa didn't read the entire message. Her eyes focused on a name she hadn't seen for far too long.

The world had vanished from around her, between one moment and the next, and she found herself somewhere else. Somewhere that was painfully familiar.

Too familiar. She'd lost this place before, except now it was standing proud and strong.

It was the village she had failed to defend, once upon a time.

She'd almost suspected it, given what the dungeon had called this room. But it hadn't seemed possible, and the mere idea of it had seemed so cruel . . . She'd heard of it before, dungeons that replicated events from the past. Dungeons that required you to take on historical events. They were one of the few ways Platinum adventurers were able to uncover new aspects of their broken history.

But this?

What were her choices here? To fail and fall one final time? Or to succeed, and be forced to endure a vision of what had never been? When the bonus room ended—when she completed her task—all of this would be gone. No matter whether she succeeded or failed . . . again.

She stared at her old village. She could hear the sound of children laughing, could smell her favorite stew cooking in the communal pot. She heard the sound of her own mother, loudly complaining about the quality of the fish she'd been given.

The fact that she'd been so close to death her health had hit zero meant almost nothing to her. Not in front of this . . . this mockery of what she had lost.

Misa fell to her knees and wept.

—◊—

Derivan had been a fraction of a second too late. Vex and Sev were behind him, screaming something—but he didn't quite catch the words. He was too busy staring at the scene in front of him, a dim horror flickering in his soul.

Misa had been there. Not strictly visible, around the bend of the corridor, but he knew the sound of her voice, the glow of her skills. He knew what it looked like when that skill *failed*.

He'd seen the dark flames blazing in front of him and known something was *wrong*, but even pouring on all the speed he could, he just didn't have the stats. His blades slammed into the weak stone that was emitting the flames just a second too late, and whatever health they had didn't matter, because health didn't matter for him. Rock shattered, and the flames guttered out.

Vex had tried to cast a spell. Sev had just tried to *heal*. But range and line of sight were factors, and neither of them had quite been able to destroy the trap or heal their friend in time.

It took them a moment to actually read and understand the messages that appeared, announced for all of them; the horror was too great, for a moment, for them to process the boxes. Derivan was almost afraid to look, worried at what he would find.

"Please, no," Vex whispered.

Derivan looked, and he felt relief. The messages were only about the activation of the bonus room, and the transportation of Misa into what was likely an old, painful memory.

And once they saw that, a grim determination settled in their souls, wiping away the horrified fear that had been starting to grow.

"We're not letting her do that alone," Sev said.

"No," Vex said. The lizardkin clutched at his dagger, his face still pale but set with an almost uncharacteristic fierceness.

"We are not," Derivan agreed. His own sword was still clutched in his hand, fragments of broken rock from the trap he'd destroyed clinging to the metal. The glow of the system box shone off his metal, visible only to him.

Misa would not be alone if they had anything to say about it.

CHAPTER 32

ABERRANT

Derivan would have frowned, if he could have. The eye lights in his helmet dimmed to show his worry.

Helping Misa was, of course, easier said than done. None of them had any idea how they could get to where she was, and Kestel was frantic through the telepathic connection, telling them to find the delve team.

That telepathy faded into a horrified silence as the flames faded and revealed a corridor full of blackened skeletons in front of them.

Sev, Derivan, and Vex all tensed. The fact that all those skeletons were upright didn't bode particularly well for them, since it meant they were more likely to be monsters, but none of them seemed like they were about to attack—if anything, they looked . . . a little depressed. Almost enough that Derivan could read the emotion even without Physical Empathy.

"Are you . . . all right?" Derivan couldn't help but ask, though he kept his words cautious and his hand on his blade, in case anything happened.

What are you doing? You need to find the delve team, someone on the research team snapped. **Kill them and get it over with.**

Derivan ignored whoever that was, focusing instead on the skeleton that stepped forward—a lizardkin skeleton, judging by the snout and tail. The defeated slump of its shoulders turned almost *angry* when he spoke, and it snapped at him. "What do you think? If you'd been just a second faster—"

"They still *saved us*," another lizardkin skeleton pointed out, putting a hand on the first one's shoulder.

"—We could have survived if we ran back into the room! And if they'd just done it *faster*—"

"That's not how it works and you know it, Ixiss," the second skeleton said.

Ixiss? A voice came through the telepathic connection, sounding horrified. Was it Kestel speaking? The emotional balance was different, and made it harder to identify.

"Are you the backup?" a third skeleton asked.

There was a short pause as the adventurers—and the research team, really—processed that this *was* the delve team.

What . . . happened to them? That was definitely Kestel, still emotionally off balance but slightly clearer.

"We are," Derivan replied, looking down the corridor. He was worried. He could hear fighting in the distance.

"How did you get in?" the first lizardkin skeleton—Ixiss, Derivan remembered—asked suspiciously. "That shouldn't be possible. I swear, if you're another dungeon trick—"

"*Ixiss*," the skeleton that had a hand on the lizardkin's shoulder hissed again. "Give them a chance to explain before you start threatening them!"

"Uh," Vex spoke up, raising a hand. "One of us has a skill that lets us . . . get through dimensional boundaries like that. But we're still in contact with the research team, so if you need to verify anything—"

"Tell me what our delve team code is," Ixiss immediately said.

AA63, Kestel said over the telepathic link, sounding tired.

"AA63," Vex repeated dutifully. Derivan had no idea what that meant. Some kind of numbering system? Vex seemed to know, though, with the way he sagged slightly.

Ixiss . . . had eye sockets, and so couldn't narrow his eyes at them. He still managed to give off the *impression* that he was narrowing his eyes at them, stepping forward and rattling his tail in a threatening sort of way. "Fine," the lizardkin hissed at them. "But if I so much as smell a hint of betrayal—"

"You'll have to forgive him," the other lizardkin skeleton finally said, using her grip on Ixiss' shoulder to pull him back. Her posture was significantly friendlier than his, and she gave them a relaxed, evaluating sort of look. "He's a little on edge. On account of the whole . . . being turned into skeletons because a dungeon monster snuck in and posed as one of us thing."

"Is that what happened," Sev managed. Derivan glanced at him—the cleric was glancing between the skeletons, tense but taking breaths to calm himself. Vex seemed nervous, too.

"It's better than—" Ixiss started, and the other skeleton smacked him on the snout. He looked stunned.

"Shut up. They can hear us, idiot," she said. "My name's Iliss. This idiot's my brother. We're like this because someone—your friend, I assume—appeared and saved our lives, but there was some sort of skill interaction that messed with it. We have the notification boxes to prove it."

"Who *was* that, anyway?" one of the others asked. "She just . . . showed up. And then . . ."

They fell silent briefly.

"She's our friend, like you guessed," Sev said quietly. His grip on his staff was tense. "We need to get to her."

"You're going to have to deal with the challenge room first either way. I don't think we'll be replicating the activation conditions for that bonus room, so your best bet is to use one of the dungeon rewards to get there. Our captain is still fighting in the room ahead," Iliss briefed quickly. "There's a monster we can't damage. We were going to try to come back and contact the research team, get them to reapply the scrying and telepathy spells. See if they can figure out why."

What kind of monster is it? Kestel asked, and Derivan relayed the question.

"Level 73 Aberrant. Arcane and Necrotic types," Iliss said.

"What?" Vex frowned at that, and Kestel made almost the same noise over the telepathic connection. "That shouldn't be possible. Those mana types are incompatible."

"Well, we're also all skeletons now, so," Iliss said dryly, "I think *impossible* flew out the window a while ago."

"You are remarkably calm about this," Derivan observed.

"We're a delve team. We've been through some shit," Iliss said bluntly. She glanced back at one member of the skeletons, though, one that still hadn't said anything and was staring at their own hands, trembling slightly, and she sighed.

". . . Most of us, anyway," she added quietly. "Some of us are new."

Get to the challenge room. We need to see what we're dealing with, Kestel said. Derivan nodded.

"We are going to check the challenge room," he said out loud, perhaps unnecessarily. Iliss just shrugged and fell into step behind him, and the other delvers did as well; Derivan led the way, with Vex and Sev following close behind him.

The captain of the delve team—still in skeleton form, with his equipment loosely hanging off a body that it was no longer fit for—was still holding off the Aberrant. To his credit, he didn't seem to be the slightest bit exhausted. "I can do this all day, ya bastard!" he told the Aberrant, who screeched uncomprehendingly at him.

Iliss, somewhere behind Derivan, sighed. The captain seemed to notice, though he didn't look their way or give any indication that they were *there*. He spoke at the same volume, still shouting as if he was shouting at the Aberrant. "I hope ya got some kind of solution! I can keep this up for a while yet but not forever!"

Clever. He was even maneuvering the fight so that the Aberrant was focusing on him, and the rest of them wouldn't be in its field of view—though given it didn't really have eyes, it wasn't exactly clear what sort of field of view it had. It certainly didn't seem to notice or care that they were there, though.

"I hope the miss is all right! I saw some notifications but I couldn't check 'em!" he continued yelling. "And if anything happens to me, I want ya to know my team was great! Ixiss is probably the best fighter I've got—"

"Oh, by the gods," Iliss groaned. "He's gonna keep talking. Figure out how to kill that thing *quick*, please."

Vex was staring ahead, concentrating on the Aberrant. **It's weird**, he said over the telepathic connection. **The necrotic and arcane mana aren't inter-acting at all. It's just sort of . . . there. It's like there's an invisible bound-ary between the two types of mana. Some kind of metastable barrier? Reminds me of . . .**

He trailed off, not elaborating.

There shouldn't be one, Kestel frowned. **That's not how that works. Arcane-type mana attracts and transforms into most other types of mana on contact.**

Yes, well, it looks like there is. Can't tell you why. Vex's eyes glowed slightly as he focused in on his [**Mana Sight**], but it didn't seem to give him too much more information. **It has some type of mana core . . . I'm assum-ing that's its weakness. There's a crystal in the center, holding its body together. But physical attacks can't seem to get to it.**

Yes, it's an Aberrant. But physical attacks are what Aberrants are weak to, Kestel said. **It shouldn't be *immune* to them.**

Aberrants are a known type of monster? Derivan asked.

Yes. We've encountered them in a few dungeons. They always have some quirk based on their mana type and have a physical core that we need to hit for them to take health damage. They have a skill, [Ethereal Body], that makes other hits just whiff through them if you don't hit the core.

"Great," Sev said out loud. "An aberrant Aberrant. Do we need to try magic?"

Bad idea, Kestel said quickly. **Aberrants aren't exactly immune to magic, but physical damage is usually the most reliable. Magic reacts unpredictably with whatever mana type they're comprised of. Arcane-type Aberrants in particular can usually take over *any* magic you try on it, but with the mixed types on this one . . . I don't know. It could end up being worse.**

"We need to know why it's immune to physical attacks," Vex said, frowning slightly.

"Do you think it's a system glitch?" Sev asked. "The system's obviously been more unstable than usual lately. And there's whatever happened with the delvers . . ."

Vex was silent for a moment, but then his eyes sharpened a bit. "I think you're right. And if that's what it is, then . . . Derivan? We're going to need you for this."

—⁂—

It took more time than Misa wanted for her to be able to gather herself, but gather herself she did. She wasn't sure how much time had passed, really. An hour? Maybe two? Probably not nearly that much, but she had no real concept of how much time had passed; she was still trembling slightly when she got to her feet, but she took a breath and tried to let her emotions pass through her.

Meditation. Vex had taught her how to do it once before. She'd thought it was a waste of time; who knew it would be proving itself useful here?

There didn't seem to be any way out of the . . . bonus room, if it could be called that. The whole place just looked like a perfect replica of her village and the field surrounding it. Which meant that the only way to leave would be to succeed or to fail.

Illusion or not—cruel or not—Misa was *not* going to let her home be destroyed in front of her a second time.

Part of her did wonder, though, what would happen if she traveled away from the village. There were open skies above her and no walls that she could make out. She knew what direction the monsters had come from the first time around. Would it be the same this time? Could she go there and see what had happened?

Vex would know. He always knew the little intricacies of how dungeons worked. Misa abruptly realized that her team must be wondering what had happened to her, and, feeling a little frantic, tried to check the message interface through her system.

<WARNING>
Time differential is too significant for system-based messages to operate in real time.

... Huh.

There was a message waiting for her from Sev, blinking in the system; it was just four words. [*We're coming to help.*]

Her heart still stung a bit from the situation she was in, but she couldn't help but smile slightly anyway. No hint of hesitation, no hint of doubt. They didn't even know how they were going to do it, but they were going to do it anyway.

Well, if anyone would figure out how to join her, it would be them. Hopefully they'd find a way to deal with that Aberrant, too.

Feeling a little better, Misa took one last deep breath, staring fixedly in the direction of her village before finally heading toward it. She could still hear the sounds of her friends and family—all faces she hadn't seen for what felt like a lifetime. She was bracing herself for it, really. She'd long assumed that she'd never see these faces again ...

If nothing else, it would at least be an opportunity to commit them to memory, one last time. It was an opportunity she didn't think she'd ever have.

CHAPTER 33

PAST PAINS

Misa hadn't actually spawned very far away, and it took only a minute or so of walking for her to reach the walls of her village. She felt her heart tightening as she approached—there were guards stationed near the gates of the village. Those guards had been the first ones to . . .

"Name and purpose, miss?" a guard asked as she approached. Misa recognized him immediately; it was V'karro. How strange was it that she'd remembered him not too long ago, and now she was seeing him again? The old guard that had taught her about skills, once upon a time . . .

He'd probably saved the delvers' lives, even if he didn't know it. It was because of his training that she'd spotted anything at all.

For the first time in a long time, Misa reached back into her memories, trying to place what she remembered of him. He had always been kind to her. He'd always wanted a daughter, apparently, but he never really had the opportunity—and while he wasn't a replacement for her father, he'd always been like an uncle to her.

V'karro now was as kind as she remembered. Most guards were more suspicious of people they regarded as newcomers. What made her hesitate was the fact that she didn't know whether or not he would recognize her, and she didn't know which one she preferred.

She'd been so much younger when this had happened.

". . . It's me. Misa," she eventually replied, her voice rougher than she intended. Part of her wanted to pretend everything was normal—but she couldn't. She couldn't stop remembering that very same face covered in blood, stiff after death had taken him.

She tried to wipe the thought away. She wouldn't let it happen again. But

V'karro saw the change in her eyes, she was sure; the guard's eyes softened a little more as he studied her.

There was something that might have been a flicker of recognition, but it seemed to disappear almost as soon as it appeared.

". . . I'm afraid I don't know anyone by that name, miss," V'karro said apologetically.

Misa took a deep breath. She didn't know what she'd expected from the dungeon, and didn't know if it was worse or better that the orc didn't know who she was. "Sorry," she said. "I must've mistaken you for someone else. If you're not him, then you must be V'karro, right?"

"That's right," V'karro grinned at her; part of him seemed relieved that the apparent distress in her eyes had faded. "You've heard of me?"

"You could say that," Misa said with a chuckle. She didn't know how he could possibly expect anyone outside their little village to know who he was. They were in too remote a place, their adventurers barely strong enough to keep their village stable and connected to the system. But she saw the way he brightened at the thought that his antics might have spread some ways outside the village, and she didn't want to take that away from him. "That's not important, though. Can you bring me to talk to Orkas? It's important."

"The village head?" V'karro asked, raising an eyebrow, and shrugged when she gave a determined nod in response. "Well, if you're sure. He's been a bit grumpy lately, though, so you best be careful."

"I think I know how to handle him," Misa said with a light chuckle.

Her heart still ached. But a part of her was looking forward to seeing her father again.

Misa had spent so many years thinking about what she could have done differently—what *everyone* could have done differently. This was her chance to put it all into action.

The only wrench in her plans was that if the village didn't remember her, it'd be far harder to convince them to listen to her. They were all rather stubborn. So, first things first, she needed to convince the man whose word the entire village trusted.

The only problem was that Orkas had been her father, and he was . . . sort of an asshole. Sometimes. Not all the time, and mostly not to her—but to strangers?

Well.

"You're telling me that we're going to be attacked soon, and we need to prepare our entire village for it." Orkas's voice was disbelieving, and his arms were folded across his chest. He'd done much the same every time he reprimanded her. "You understand why this is hard to believe?"

"Yes," Misa admitted. "But it wouldn't hurt to prepare even if you didn't believe me."

"It might." Orkas narrowed his eyes at her. "Our village barely has any visitors. Certainly not enough for me to believe that any outsider would know enough about us to ask for me right off the bat. The Kingdoms are very vocal about their desire to track down rare classes, and though we have always turned their emissaries away, getting us to prepare for some nebulous, impending disaster would surely reveal any trump cards we have."

Misa sighed.

Her father had always been paranoid about the Kingdoms. It wasn't his fault, really—he'd lost his older brother to Anderstahl, long before he'd joined this village. From what she'd heard, the man was a powerful warrior and Guardian, not unlike the class she'd eventually achieved; Anderstahl had taken him, and her father had never heard from him again.

He refused to believe his brother might still be alive. Arval, he said, would have done everything in his power to get back to him. A long time ago, Misa took his words at face value; now, she wondered how Arval would have managed to find him in the first place, considering everything he did to keep the village hidden.

Maybe her uncle was still alive somewhere, she thought suddenly. She'd never really thought about it—the memories of her home were too painful. But if Arval was still alive . . .

He deserved to know what happened to his brother, didn't he?

"Got nothing else to say?" Orkas's eyes were still narrowed at her.

"I don't have any way to prove that an attack is coming," Misa admitted with a frustrated glare. "And you've created a situation where anything I tell you could just be another lie used to try to get you to reveal your secrets. What else am I supposed to say?"

She couldn't tell him that this was a dungeon's test, could she? She had no idea how he'd take that. She couldn't tell him that she was his daughter, or at least the daughter of another version of him. She didn't even know what was different in this village. Was Orkas still with her mother?

"Then we agree that there's nothing more for you here," Orkas said with a derisive snort. "Tell whatever Kingdom you came from—"

"I'm not *from* another Kingdom!" Misa exploded. "For fuck's sake, just *listen* to me and get everyone ready! We don't have time for this!"

"Not until you tell me the truth!" Orkas thundered at her, and Misa fumed.

"You wouldn't believe me if I told you!"

"*Try me.*"

"*Fine.*"

Fuck not talking about it. Misa had no idea if this was the right thing to do, but it was too late; the words were already spilling out of her mouth.

"All of this already happened, *three goddamn years ago*, and I couldn't do *shit* to protect it! Do you want to know how I felt when I woke up *surrounded by the corpses of everyone I ever loved?* Uncle V'karro's body was right next to me! You were dead in the fucking doorway, a pile of monster corpses in front of you! You killed every last shit that tried to get into our house and you died doing it, and it *still wasn't fucking enough because Mom was dead anyway!* And now this *stupid dungeon* is making me relive this *shitty fucking day*, and I just want to fix it, and *you won't fucking listen!*"

Misa's chest was heaving. Her eyes were wet; she couldn't see her father's expression clearly through the film of tears in her eyes. She hated the fact that she was crying again, but she didn't know what she'd expected—coming face to face again with all these long-dead souls, looking and sounding exactly like the people she'd known for most of her life . . .

There was a long silence, broken up only by the sound of Misa's shuddering breaths.

". . . I thought it was strange that your name was Misa," her father said softly, his tone suddenly quiet. The hostility was gone, replaced by a strange sort of distant pain. "That was what we wanted to name our daughter."

Misa didn't answer. She tried to get her breathing under control so she *could*, taking slow, shaky breaths. There was a dim realization that her father was saying something important, and she took it in slowly, wrestling her own emotions under control as he spoke.

"She was stillborn," Orkas continued. He didn't look at Misa. Instead, he stared into the distance, painful memories reflecting in his eyes. "Charise was never really the same after that."

Charise. Her mother. Misa was quiet for another moment as her breath steadied, and Orkas seemed willing to give her all the time she needed to calm down. When she did, she spoke with a quiet voice.

"How is she?"

"As fine as she can be." Orkas shook his head. "Some days are better than others. When you . . . when our child died, she would not stop saying that the world was wrong. That this was not supposed to happen. I thought it was mere denial; that she was speaking with the grief of a mother ... and yet now you're here, telling me a story much along those same lines.

"And today, of all days, she woke, and told me that things would be better today. That the world was right again. I did not know what she meant, and I did not want to believe, when I first heard your name ..."

Orkas's eyes hardened. "You understand, of course, that if you are lying about this, there will be consequences."

Misa nodded slowly. "... I wish I was," she said softly.

Orkas nodded. He stood abruptly, brushing his cloak to the side as he stepped around the table. "Daughter," he said, as if tasting the word. He placed a hand on Misa's shoulder. "... I wish I could be more of a father to you. But some truths are difficult for the heart to accept, and even if I completely believed you, I do not *know* you. This version of me never saw your childhood, was never able to help you grow nor make the mistakes that I am certain that I made.

"You claim this to be a simulation by a dungeon. I can only say that it does not feel that I am a mere simulation. Whatever this dungeon has done ... Perhaps it is cruel, to give us both a glimpse of what could have been. Or perhaps it believes it is being kind. I cannot say.

"But for what it is worth ..." Orkas's voice grew briefly rough, though he was facing away from Misa and would not meet her eyes. "I am looking forward to seeing who my daughter could have been."

Misa swallowed, feeling a lump in her throat. She would *not* cry a third time. Instead, she nodded, and Orkas gestured for her to follow.

"Come. I will prepare the village and set up the traps as you outlined. But you should meet your mother."

CHAPTER 34

A MOTHER'S INTUITION

As it turned out, the decision to not cry for a third time was a stupid one. Misa decided to give herself a pass. Her mother was holding her again, sobbing into her shoulder, and as much as she hated seeing her cry, she was *alive*.

Maybe only here, and maybe only for now. But she had thought she'd never be able to hold her mother again at all.

Of course, she'd never imagined her mother as being the type to cry, either.

"Mom," she said softly. "It's good to see you." *Again*, she wanted to say, but then she'd never seen this version of her mother before, had she?

"*Misa*," Charise cried, clinging tightly to Misa's larger form and refusing to let go. "I knew you were back—I knew as soon as you were here—but I thought I might have been going insane . . ."

"You weren't." Misa's tone was gentle, and her voice was steady, though her eyes were still wet. Orkas had said it was difficult for him to truly be her father, since he'd missed so much of her growth; by contrast, with her mother, it didn't seem to matter. Charise was just . . . glad to have her there.

It hurt her heart to see the way her mother trembled. Misa was used to seeing her mother as a whirlwind of energy; she was a woman who always seemed to know what she wanted and what she needed to do to get it. It had something to do with her class, from what Misa understood—she'd never been told exactly what it was, but it seemed to give her a powerful and unmatched intuition that paired perfectly with her attitude.

From the stories she'd heard, Charise had been the one to pursue Orkas, back when they first met. She'd beaten him in a duel to do it, and when asked what she wanted for a prize, she'd requested a kiss.

Apparently, no one in the village had ever seen Orkas blush before. Or since.

That was the confidence that Charise once had. Misa had never seen her mother like this, on the cusp of breaking down entirely.

"I knew something was wrong," Charise told her. "I had a skill. I saw the world split when you died . . . and something impossible happened. But I didn't understand. I still don't."

Misa hesitated. Orkas hadn't explained anything when he dropped her off, only said her name.

"It's . . . complicated," she hedged at first—but she saw the way her mother sagged. She needed answers; she'd gone twenty years without them, working only with an intuition that told her what had happened was impossible. It was a wonder that her mind had stayed intact at all.

So Misa gathered herself, and explained what had happened. Less angrily than she had with Orkas. Not with any anger at all, really. This time her words came out soft and anxious, a part of her worried that this revelation would be the final piece that broke her mother; Charise's silence as Misa spoke only made that worry grow.

When she finally spoke, though, rather than distressed, she seemed *relieved*. Her tears had abated somewhat during Misa's explanation, though she continued to hold her daughter close.

"It . . . doesn't answer all my questions, but it explains a lot," Charise said. She smiled gently, wiped her tears away, and then sat on the mossy ground; she patted the space next to her, and Misa took a seat. She didn't fail to notice the way her mother still shook slightly when she moved, but she was slowly starting to calm—to regain that inner vibrance Misa knew her for. "Is it morbid to say that I'm glad you survived? If any one of us was going to . . ."

". . . Don't say that, Mom." Misa glanced away. She didn't want to think about it. Part of her knew—she couldn't help but know; Charise had never hidden how much she loved her—but confronting that knowledge was . . . It was too much for her right now.

Charise nodded slightly, withdrawing and looking away. "Did I ever explain my skills to you?"

Misa shook her head. "You always said you would one day, but you didn't want to do it yet."

"Yes, I wouldn't have." Her mother managed a weak smile. "[**Intuitionist**] is a strange class, and talking about it will sometimes grant listeners the class directly. It's not something I wanted to inflict on you. I wanted you to be able to get a class of your own."

"There's a class you can spread just by talking about it?" Misa asked, sounding a bit alarmed. Her mother chuckled, though the sound was small.

"I know what you're thinking. It's a self-solving problem. It doesn't work if you're intentionally trying to spread it," Charise told her. "It has . . . an intuition about it, you could say."

"Mom," Misa groaned.

"It's a common class, but people don't talk about it much because it's mostly uninteresting, besides its ability to unintentionally spread. I don't know for sure, but my intuition tells me"—here Charise gave her a wry smile—"that the class is granted to you if you intuit something about it. Or if you intuit its existence, which is how I got the class, even though I didn't want it."

"It still feels like some kind of trap," Misa mumbled. "Wouldn't there be some way around it? What if you told someone to go talk about it in the middle of a village without telling them what talking about it does? What if you put up posters about it? What if—"

Charise blinked as Misa rambled, and then openly laughed.

"You always did love exploiting the system," she said with a grin. Misa smiled back at her, momentarily feeling like everything was *normal* and *right* in a way that it hadn't been for years—

—and then her mother just *paused*, as if struck. Realization hit her, and Misa stared at her, too, feeling like her heart had stopped for a split second. Her mother blinked once, twice, falling completely silent; she seemed to strain, reaching for something Misa couldn't see . . .

And then a tear fell from her eye. "Ah, shit," she said to herself, shaking her head. "I almost had it."

"Mom?" Misa asked softly.

"[**Intuitionist**] comes with a skill, [**Intuition of Truth**]. It's not a lie detector, exactly, but it gives you a gut feeling about the underlying nature of things, and I've trained mine carefully. It keeps . . . trying to give me the 'true' version of events. What really happened, not what happened here, wherever 'here' is. But it's an *intuition skill*, not a *knowledge* skill; it can't tell me everything. It can just give me . . . glimpses."

Charise blinked, then sniffled. ". . . I want to know what your childhood was like very badly, Misa. I want to know what kind of mother I was. What kind of father Orkas was. But that knowledge is so distant to me, and yet it is just out of my reach, and I feel like if I could just grasp at the truth . . ."

Her mother sighed, looking tired. "At least now I know I was right," she said softly.

Misa reached out to take one of her mother's hands into her own. She didn't say a word. This woman was her mother—she wore her face, her mannerisms, her clothing, and yet she didn't know this version of her mother at all; she didn't know what she had been through.

Charise shook her head. "Everyone told me I was lying to myself when I said that you should be alive. And the truth is that I, too, thought that that was what I was doing. It didn't make any sense. In any ordinary situation, [**Intuition of Truth**] would have forced me to confront the truth of your death. But . . . whatever the nature of the skill is, it seems that it doesn't care for simulated reality, only the true one."

"I mistook the voice of the skill for my own voice, and I didn't understand why my skill wasn't helping me confront what happened to you. It was . . . difficult to stay sane in the face of that, let me tell you." Her mother gave her a small, weak smile. "Though I'm glad I did."

"I can't imagine," Misa admitted.

There was a small silence, and then her mother spoke, her voice soft. "Once this is over . . . You don't know what will happen to this place, do you?"

"I wish I did," Misa said, tightening her fists. She'd sent a message to Vex some time before, but there was no response yet. "But I don't."

"Then I better say what I never had the chance to say in either lifetime," Charise said, slowly getting to her feet. She smiled the warmest smile she could muster through the tears glimmering in the corners of her eyes. "I am proud of the woman you became. You did everything you could then, as I know you will do everything you can now; no matter what happens now or what happened then, know that I love you, and that you will always be my daughter."

Misa swallowed the lump in her throat. Did this count as another pass to cry?

. . . *Fuck it*. She felt the tears come, and saw her mother lean down to gather her into a hug.

Just a few minutes, in the arms of someone she never thought she'd see again. She'd thought it was a cruelty, that the dungeon was doing this to her.

But perhaps it was something of a kindness, too.

"Now, before you help save us all," Charise said, smiling gently at her. Misa's heart ached at the sight—it was so familiar, but it was so much more tired than she remembered. "Do you want some fish stew?"

Misa choked back a tearful laugh. "Yeah. Sure. It's been a long time since I've had any. It was my favorite, you know."

"How could it not be?" her mother said with a chuckle. "It's mine, too."

And when she took her first sips of the stew, she had to stop briefly. The rich smell brought her back to the days of old, when everything was simple, and at the same time . . .

It made her think of her home. The new one, the one she'd found with Vex, and Derivan, and Sev.

"Hey, Mom?" she asked, her voice rough. "Can you teach me this recipe?"

Charise looked at her, surprised. "You like cooking?"

"No," Misa chuckled. "But . . . I want to share this with some friends. A little piece of home."

"Ah." Charise paused and smiled. "Of course. And I'm glad you found some friends. If you get a moment . . . Perhaps you could tell me about them?"

Misa looked to the horizon. The village would take time to prepare for everything, and if she understood the timeline right . . . they had almost a day left before they would be attacked. She had her plans, and she'd given them to Orkas; she'd had her plans for years.

So she had a little bit of time.

"I'd like that," she said quietly. "I'd like that a lot."

—m—

Everything was prepared.

Misa had told Orkas everything that she remembered of the invasion that would come. She'd explained the countermeasures she'd thought of, in the days and weeks following the attack, when she was wandering listlessly and carrying the village's store of mana crystals on her back. She'd further explained the details of the dungeon they were in, and how that might change the attack.

They'd both agreed that if they were meant to fight off Platinum monsters, they would have no chance, no matter how good their preparations were. The original horde that had attacked their village had been Iron-ranked, with the Elite monsters in the low tiers of Bronze. With their best warriors and mages only at low Bronze, they'd been very quickly overwhelmed.

This time, with Misa at a higher level and this being a dungeon . . . whatever it was, the horde might be up to Silver. That was as confident as they were about the array of traps and walls they'd made. The horde would, if everything went the same way they did the first time, abate by itself within a couple of hours. Misa still had no answers about what had triggered that attack, for there had been no indication that a dungeon break was near—nor did she know where the monsters had gone after it.

But the information they had was enough. It meant that at worst, they simply needed to endure and keep the walls of the village strong for a few hours.

The first signs of the attack would happen soon, Misa knew. It had started with a bright beam of light in the sky, accompanied by a tear in space that felt *wrong*, even as far away as their village was from that tear. Then there was a great rumble of the earth, and a darkening of the sky.

Hopefully, they were ready.

Hopefully, Sev and the others would be here soon, too.

Her grip tightened on her mace, and she watched the horizon, waiting.

CHAPTER 35

TO MAKE A DIFFERENCE

Whatever's allowing that arcane and necrotic energy to stay apart is only barely stable. I don't know exactly what it is, but I'm guessing that any amount of physical disruption will destabilize it," Vex explained. "That's why you can't damage it."

I'm not sure I follow, Kestel sent over the link. He sounded . . . slightly calmer, but also strangely out of breath, for someone on a telepathic link. **How does that link to it being *invulnerable*?**

"I think it's invulnerable because of health and [**Ethereal Body**]," Vex said. He watched the Aberrant closely as it clashed with the captain; it still hadn't noticed any of the team on their side of the corridor. "[**Ethereal Body**] prevents it from taking any damage to its health, an effect that manifests as allowing physical strikes to whiff through its body unless we directly strike the weak point. But it can't do that second part of the effect—if it did, you'd be able to destabilize it."

And that would kill it, Kestel summarized. **You think that because we can't physically strike it without destroying it, the health system is preventing us from hitting it at all?**

"Pretty much, yes," Vex nodded. "If you look carefully, nothing the captain is doing is touching its body. It's skittering off just before it touches it."

In the challenge room, the captain roared as he slammed his blades down onto the Aberrant, and the Aberrant raised all five of its arms to block; the impact forced its body partially into the ground, kicking up a cloud of dust. But Vex was right—the captain's blades were hovering a millimeter away from the Aberrant's arms, like there was some invisible barrier that couldn't be breached.

"Normally it would still take some damage to health, even if we weren't allowed to actually touch it . . . but it has [**Ethereal Body**], and that skill technically prevents damage to health." Vex paused. "Any spell I cast would have the same problem. It wouldn't hit the Aberrant at all. Mana would disrupt that system, too. It can move *itself*, because it's in full control of its own mana, but . . ."

"We could throw a rock at it," Sev suggested. Vex blinked and stared at him. "What? A rock doesn't have health, does it?"

"Well, no, but if you throw it, you're attacking it, so it becomes part of the system," Vex said.

"What about the floor? It's stepping on the floor," Sev said. "Can we make it stub its toe?"

"I don't know what that means," Vex said, raising a brow.

". . . Do you not—does toe-stubbing not exist here? Does the system prevent toe-stubbing? How have I not known this all this time— Wait. I have an idea. We throw *Derivan* at the Aberrant."

"I believe I can throw myself at it fine," Derivan said.

Iliss and Ixiss were both staring at the adventurers in abject confusion. "What are you talking about?" Ixiss said. "You're acting like you face something like this *every day*."

"I mean, not *every* day," Sev said. "But a lot of days? It just feels like this kind of stuff keeps happening recently. I'm not really surprised at this point; I'm more worried about getting to Misa. And apparently we need to deal with *this* problem first, so . . ."

"I have a skill that allows me to strike past health," Derivan added helpfully. "That is why they suggested throwing me."

"You're a shit liar," Iliss said automatically, and then she paused, frowning. "Wait, shit. Are you? Fuck. I actually can't tell."

"He's definitely lying," Ixiss said, doing the thing where he narrowed his eyes, except he had only eye sockets and was really just conveying the impression of narrowing his eyes very well. ". . . Wait. No."

"I am definitely not lying," Derivan said, with no conviction whatsoever.

"*Anyway*," Iliss said, "I'm going to ignore the question of whether or not you're lying and address the bigger problem here, which is that destabilizing it is dangerous. That's what happened the first time—there was an orb made out of arcane mana, and a monster hit it with some sort of skill infused with necrotic mana. Your friend tried to block it, and she . . . half-succeeded?" Iliss hesitated. "I'm not really sure what happened there. But I'm worried that if you mix the same two types of mana again . . ."

"It'll explode violently?" Vex guessed, and Iliss nodded. He grimaced slightly. "Yeah, it might do that. On the plus side, it's going to be mostly necrotic energy, which means your captain and you four will be immune to it, and as long as the rest of us stay out of range, we should be fine."

"Except for your friend," Iliss said, jerking her skull toward Derivan.

Vex hesitated. He'd avoided saying that Derivan would be immune to it, given he was lacking any kind of organic matter. The enchantments anchored in his armor were unlikely to be affected by anything except powerful dispel-oriented skills.

"I'll cast a spell on Derivan to protect him from necrotic energy," Vex finally said, stepping forward. He reached forward a little hesitantly, looking up as if to make sure Derivan was okay with it—and when the armor nodded at him, he placed a palm on his chest and *cast*.

It was nothing more than a basic light-and-illusion spell, causing a ripple of dark-gray light to surround Derivan before dissipating. But it was a sufficiently convincing illusion, it seemed; no one questioned it.

"There. You should be fine now," he said. "Derivan, you *should* just need to let it hit you . . . but that seems dangerous, so try to hit it first? Even better if you can hit through the joint where the arcane and necrotic mana are."

Derivan nodded. Vex looked like he wanted to say something else, but he didn't speak as the armor stepped through into the challenge room.

As Derivan stepped in, the Aberrant stopped and turned, as if it could sense him stepping into the room. It *screeched* at him, a sound that rang throughout the room and reverberated against his armor. If he'd had health, Derivan suspected it would have hurt him; as it was, all that happened was that he cocked his head slightly.

The captain looked over at him in a way that seemed distinctly worried. "Ya got a plan?"

"I need to hit it," Derivan said. It wasn't much of a plan.

"Well, ya ain't gonna have much of a choice there," the captain muttered. He was watching the Aberrant carefully as it staggered, a falling, twitching movement that seemed incredibly out of place on its frame—

—Derivan wasn't prepared for the sudden *attack* as it launched itself at him, all momentum suddenly changing into a vector pointed straight in his direction. He braced himself, knowing he didn't have time to dodge, but the captain gritted his teeth and *threw* himself into the Aberrant to knock it off course. It screeched in anger, tumbling across the ground.

"Move!" the captain shouted at him. "Yer too close to the others!"

Derivan moved, rushing in closer, angling himself so that the corridor wasn't in the Aberrant's direct line of sight. He wasn't as fast as he wanted to be, but he was still relatively fast, the enchantments that animated him firing rapidly through his armor. The captain yelled out a warning that Derivan barely managed to hear through the Aberrant's screech and threw himself to the side, *barely* avoiding the ball of coalesced energy that streaked past his helmet.

It could fire projectiles. Good to know.

It didn't seem to *like* doing it, though. The Aberrant seemed angrier than ever that even that strategy had missed, and it charged at him as though in a frenzy, a relentless flurry of strikes; the captain tried to stop it, hooking a blade between its feet to try to trip it—but the thing barely cared for gravity to begin with, and stepped nimbly over even while assaulting Derivan.

It took everything the armor had to deflect those blows. [**Barrier**] could only do so much; every time an arcane or a necrotic arm struck at him, he had to twist out of the way, using only the barest flicker of a [**Barrier**] to deflect the blow. With the arcane arms he could barely even do that, for it seemed to suck up his mana and grow a little stronger.

All he needed to do was slice through that space between necrotic arm and arcane body, and yet for all that he tried, the Aberrant twisted and danced out of the way with incredible speed. Even the captain barely seemed to be able to fight it off now; despite its singular focus on him, it knew what it needed to do to avoid being thrown, or shoved, or pinned.

It was *learning*. And it seemed it knew that, too, from the way it was grinning.

Derivan had a thought.

Health wasn't allowing other people to interact with the Aberrant meaningfully, because its skills meant it both could not take health damage and could not be disrupted without risking instant death.

He didn't have health. He could act outside that system.

He also had [**Intermediate Mana Manipulation**].

The Aberrant was made of mana.

Why did he need a sword at all?

He reached out with the skill, touching on both the arcane and necrotic mana at the same time. One felt like *change* and *volatility*, the other like *death* and *rot*, and he twisted them together with an effort of will—

There was a moment of resistance.

And then the two types of mana met.

Arcane mana decided it would have a better time being necrotic instead, and then rippled across the Aberrant's entire being; in a moment, it was made out of only necrotic energy. A flash of light flickered over its body. Health wouldn't protect it anymore—the mere act of disrupting its body wouldn't instantly kill it.

Though it was, of course, already in the process of dying, because the nature of that change was *violent*. Energy rushed across the monster's entire form in an instant, exploding outward in a brilliant display of light and dark, churning through the room in a way that sent even the captain flying back; Derivan, who had significantly more mass, was pushed back several steps before he caught himself.

Then that energy washed away, leaving Derivan feeling oddly tingly.

Your p#ar##ty has killed a level 73 Aberrant! XP awarded.

On the ground, perfectly intact, lay a single crystalline orb—the core of the Aberrant.

"Dungeon reward," the captain said softly. "Well, what do ya know. You did it."

Very carefully, Derivan picked up the orb, watching light glimmer through it as he moved it around. It looked like it was made out of glass, but it diffracted and stole the edges out of any light that went through it, giving the inside of it soft, changing hues. He walked back toward the corridor with the others as he did so, hearing the *clack* of the captain's bones against the stone floor as they walked.

You need to bring that back to us, someone said over the telepathic link, sounding excited. Kestel was oddly silent. **That's the least damaged reward we've seen. I don't know what you did back there, but—**

"Smash it," the captain said.

What?! The voice was outraged through the telepathic connection. **But—**

"I looked at my notifications. Misa's your friend, isn't she?" the captain said. "If she unlocked a bonus room, then you can use the dungeon reward to get there. Use it. Don't listen to whatever the research team is saying."

There was a frustrated silence over the telepathic link.

"And we'll help you," the captain said suddenly, projecting his voice loudly enough that his team could hear it. "Or I will. The rest of you get a choice. But you know damn well what Misa did for us." He hesitated, like he wanted to add something else, but he glanced to Derivan and refrained. "Break the orb."

Derivan did, crushing it in his fingers. A notification popped up, one in front of each of them, though the armor only saw his own.

> **You have beaten the Crystal Challenge and defeated the Aberrant it produced, despite <ERROR>. Congratulations.**
>
> **The bonus room <The Village's Last Defense> was unlocked during the battle. Entry to the bonus room has been unlocked as an additional reward category.**
>
> **Randomizing rewards . . .**
>
> **Rewards offered:**
> **[Access to <The Village's Last Defense>]**
> **[Elite-Grade Equipment]**
> **[Stat Boost]**

There was silence for a moment, as Derivan looked at the four soldiers beside the captain. They seemed to be contemplating the choice, but one of them broke the silence first.

"I'm sorry," one of the soldiers said. For all that he was a skeleton, he looked . . . tired. Maybe a little bit broken. "I can't." He gestured, helplessly, at his own body. He seemed guilty, though Derivan felt he didn't have an obligation to help. Misa's rescue had not been a transaction; he knew her well enough that he could say that on her behalf.

"I'll help," Iliss said, and Ixiss huffed beside her.

"I'm going to have to if *you* do it," he grumbled.

The last soldier—a thick, broad-shouldered orcish skeleton—grunted. "I will help."

"Come with us anyway," the captain ordered the one that had refused—and when he began to protest, he shook his head. "I won't make you fight. But whatever blew up that orb is still out there, and I'm not leaving you to go through the dungeon alone. You'll sit back and be defended like all the rest."

That quieted him. He nodded.

Derivan looked at Sev and Vex. "Shall we?" he asked.

There was no answer; there was no need for one. They each reached for the button on the notification at the same time, and a whirl of light surrounded them, blazing into a brilliant white as it transported them into the bonus room.

C H A P T E R   36

INTUITIONS

Misa watched as light cracked open the sky.

Something was wrong, she knew. It was too early. The first time this had happened, it had been in the middle of the night; it was part of the reason it had taken so long for their village to respond. It wouldn't have been enough even if they'd managed it, of course—the fact of the matter was that they simply didn't have enough people to fight off a horde—but it had contributed to how quickly they'd been run over.

Maybe that was for the best. She couldn't imagine what it would've been like if they'd been taken out *slowly*, over a long, protracted battle. Losing the people she loved one by one over a period of hours instead of minutes . . .

. . . Misa swallowed, put her mind off of the memory, and watched.

The earth shook. The air sparked. There was that long-familiar sensation of a tear in space, although this one felt different—

—the beam of light was in the wrong place.

"Stop!" Misa shouted, running toward it. The guardsmen and her father looked at her, bewildered; they were already preparing to fire in that direction. But this wasn't the dungeon break—it couldn't be. Too many things were wrong. [**Danger Sense**] wasn't even going off.

Orkas, thankfully, trusted her, and shouted for his men to hold their fire. In the distance, as the light faded, she saw eight figures slowly resolve in the distance—three of them particularly familiar to her. Her heart raced. *Relief.* They'd found their way, and they'd managed to do it *before* the break started.

Misa slowed down as she approached, and grinned at her friends, keeping the relief out of her voice. "Shit, guys. Almost thought you wouldn't make it in time."

"We were always going to," Sev smirked at her, though his smile dropped a bit when he noticed the redness in the corners of her eyes. It didn't take much to put two and two together. "Are you doing okay?"

"No," Misa answered honestly. "I want to know what the fuck this place *is*. I want to know why my village is here. I want to know why *my parents* are here and why they don't remember me—"

Her voice cracked slightly as she spoke.

Vex came up to her and gave her a hug without saying a word; she had to crouch down slightly, but Misa hugged him back, letting the rest of her words stay unsaid.

Too many questions. Not enough time.

"I cannot tell if this is a cruelty or a kindness," Derivan murmured out loud, mirroring her thoughts from before. But he looked at her, and then he added, "But we will find out, one way or another. And if there is a way to preserve what lies here . . ."

Misa's heart skipped a beat. She hadn't even *thought* about it. She'd been afraid to. But Derivan watched her, a steadiness she didn't have flickering in his eyes, and even Sev and Vex seemed ready to do whatever it took—

"Don't give me hope," Misa said, almost too soft to hear. "Not about this."

She didn't even know if they were real. She didn't want to acknowledge the fire of hope that had been burning in her heart ever since she'd seen them.

She didn't know what she'd do if she did, and that fire went out again.

"Watch out!" one of the guardsmen called at them as they returned, readying the bow. His voice was much shakier than his bow. "Skeletons! Behind you!"

"I know," Misa said, raising a brow at him. "They're on our side."

"O-our side?" The guard lowered his bow slightly, but if he had any hackles to raise, they would be raised. "They're skeletons. *Monsters*," he hissed. Misa looked back at the original delve team apologetically, but most of them seemed unbothered, except for one that shrank back into himself.

"They're allies," she said. "They got hit with a bad dungeon effect. Stop being a dick."

"Are they going to be helpful?" Orkas finally spoke, having arrived from where he'd stationed himself to command the battlefield.

"Four of them are," Misa answered, glancing back at them. "One just needs a place to shelter."

Orkas's grip on his staff tightened. "I'm not putting them with the non-combatants in the village."

"Dad, he—" Misa cut herself off, gritting her teeth and ignoring the flinch that she felt when her father's eyes tightened at the word. "*Orkas.* He's a person like anyone else."

"He's also powerful enough to slaughter everyone in the village with all of us outside," Orkas countered. "I can see his level."

"If he wanted to do that, he could do it anyway," Misa said.

"But we'd have a chance to stop him."

"*Orkas,*" a reproving voice said, and both Misa and her father jerked slightly, glancing to Charise; the woman seemed filled with life again now that she'd had an opportunity to talk to her daughter, and there was a fire back in her eyes that hadn't been nearly so strong before. Misa didn't miss the way Orkas's entire posture softened when he looked at her. "He needs food and rest."

"He's a skeleton," Orkas said, perhaps a little stubbornly. Charise rolled her eyes.

"Fine. He needs rest, then. I'm going to make sure he gets that rest."

"He might—"

"He *won't,*" Charise interrupted firmly, and then looked over at the lone skeleton, who stood awkwardly away from the others, not quite looking at them. "Will you?"

Very slowly, he shook his head.

"Good," Charise said, apparently satisfied with just that. "I'm going to bring you into the village and feed you some stew. It'll do you some good."

"He is a *skeleton,*" Orkas said, a little exasperated.

"I'm sure I'll figure something out," Charise said dismissively. She waved for the skeleton to follow her, and—perhaps a little nonplussed—he did.

Misa watched both her mother and her father. It was so . . . like them. She didn't have the words to speak, so she just watched as Charise led the skeleton deeper into the village; that left them with the captain, the two lizardkin siblings, and the orc, who seemed to be taking Orkas in slowly.

"How long before the attack?" Vex asked, his tail swishing about anxiously. She glanced over at him.

"A few more hours, the first time," she answered. "No guarantee it'll happen the exact same time now, but it's what we've got to go on. We almost thought it was happening early when you guys arrived."

"I thought the timeline might have been off, but it seems we're still on track," Orkas rumbled. He sagged slightly. "I admit a part of me hoped that you were delusional. That you are my daughter returned to me through some odd quirk of magic, and not the tale you told me. But your friends are here now, and they bring with them men or monsters that could only be the result of a dungeon . . ."

He shook his head, seeing Misa open her mouth to respond. "No. Ignore my words. Focus on the battle ahead. We must plan again now that we have more resources on hand."

"I'll . . . strategize with my team," Misa said, strangling the rest of what she wanted to say.

"Then I will speak with the allies you brought with you," Orkas said, tilting his head to indicate the captain and the three delvers with him. They nodded back at him and he led them off, presumably to discuss how their skills could contribute to the fight ahead.

The guards left with them, leaving the four adventurers alone in the field just outside her village. For a moment, they were silent, none of them quite knowing what to say.

Sev broke the silence. "That was your dad, huh?"

"And the woman was my mother," Misa said. "Or she still is. I don't . . . know. It's complicated."

"We don't have many examples of dungeons doing things like this," Vex said quietly, answering the unspoken question. "A few bonus rooms here and there, explored mostly by Platinum rankers that don't talk about their time in them very much, except to fill out the blank spots in our history books."

"Is the rest of the world still . . . here?" Misa asked. "What if we just asked everyone to leave? Get them to evacuate the village, run somewhere the horde won't find us?"

Vex winced. "Trying to do something other than what the dungeon tells you to do usually results in the dungeon dissolving the bonus room early."

Dissolving. Misa let that word sink in for a moment.

"We're supposed to get answers from this dungeon," Misa finally said. "What do you think this will tell us?"

"I don't . . . know. The answers we get might not be from this bonus room at all," Sev said. "But this is a dungeon break, right? What do we know about dungeon breaks?"

"They happen when no one delves a dungeon for too long," Derivan said, reciting the answer as if from memory. "The mana accumulates in them, and eventually they seal themselves off. It is important to delve dungeons before that happens, and it is usually lucrative enough that adventurers are eager to do so. But sometimes dungeons are less noticeable, or disguise themselves well, and a dungeon break happens before we are able to head it off."

"We didn't know about this one, or we would've delved it. Or at least moved," Misa said with a sigh.

"I guess I should've asked a different question," Sev said. "What *don't* we know about dungeon breaks?"

"We don't know why they happen," Vex said. "We know mana accumulates in the dungeon, but we don't know why the dungeon seals itself off after a while, or why it 'breaks' and sends monsters flooding out. We've never been able . . . to . . ."

Vex trailed off. Misa glanced at him, and she saw Sev and Derivan doing the same.

"We've never been able to figure out where those monsters go," Vex said softly. "It's rare that we clear out every single monster that emerges from a break. We just hold out and survive, or we evacuate. So there's always an excess of monsters after the break ends, but the monsters just . . . leave, and we don't know where they go."

"No one's tried tracking them?" Sev asked.

"We've *tried*," Vex said. "We haven't *succeeded*. Even scouting and tracking classes just lose track after a while."

"Is that what we're supposed to figure out?" Misa frowned. "The task is to defend the village. Once we complete it"—she stopped herself midsentence, frowning, and then forged on—"are we going to get a chance to follow the monsters and find out what happens once we complete it?"

"I don't know," Sev said with a sigh. "Probably not. But do we have any better ideas?"

"What happens when a dungeon breaks?" Misa asked, looking at Vex. "Physically."

Vex frowned. "A sealed dungeon starts to shrink into a ball of condensed mana," he said. "When the dungeon break happens, that ball of mana cracks, and it causes a rift in space that monsters flood out of."

"Has anyone ever gone inside that rift?" Misa asked.

"No?" Vex looked at her, blinking. "Dungeon breaks are bad enough as it is. You don't go *into* the place the monsters are flooding out of."

Misa gripped her mace, saying nothing.

"Misa," Derivan said, and there was a touch of warning in his voice; no doubt he could read her. She grinned at him, though that grin was tense.

"I'll be honest," she said. "All these plans I made, thinking that if I was just clever enough, there might have been a way for my village to survive . . . I don't think they're enough. Not when the dungeon is setting up the scenario. Not when it wants to balance it to be a *challenge*, and we have Gold-ranked delvers on our team, Silver-ranked adventurers, and Bronze- and Iron-ranked guardsmen. There's no challenge here that's balanced. There's no way everyone's going to come out alive."

"We can't leave them to fight without us," Sev said. "That'll make things worse."

"The traps will *help*," Misa said. "They'll stall them. They'll make the horde fight for every bloody step forward they need to take. We've set up enough defenses that they can hold out for a while, even without our help."

"So you want to just . . . dive into the rift that the dungeon break opens?" Vex asked, staring at her.

"I think it's our only chance," Misa said. "We're still going to be fighting the monsters. We're not *technically* going off the objective. We can reduce the numbers they have to deal with and we can figure out what's going on."

"Misa," Derivan said, sounding doubtful. "This seems . . ."

It seemed crazy, she knew. Even *she* thought it was crazy.

So why was she so sure that this was what they needed to do? Them, and only them?

In the corner of her mind, just barely beginning to stir, were the beginnings of what felt like [**Danger Sense**]. But she knew now that it wasn't.

[**Guardian's Premonition**] rang in her mind more clearly than ever.

"Trust me," she said. "Please. I don't want to abandon them either. But this feels like the only chance we'll have."

CHAPTER 37

CORE

Misa stood with her companions in the makeshift tent Orkas had constructed for himself, where plans and maps were laid out on the table and weapons were scattered to the side; this was his "command center," though they'd really just lugged a table out of the village and draped a cloth over the whole thing.

Orkas had, rather predictably, exploded when told of the plan.

"You can't go into the rift alone!" he thundered. Misa glanced at Sev and the others, standing just nearby a touch awkwardly.

"I'm not alone," she said, though she should have predicted that all that would do was turn her father's fury on the rest of her team.

"You're going to go along with this plan?" Orkas growled at them. "It's suicide. And the village still needs your help."

"Misa has a skill," Derivan answered, stepping forward. "It tells her this is the path we must take for our survival. We do not mean to abandon your village. But if this succeeds, you will not have to hold out as long against this horde."

"We have Gold rankers with us now," Orkas said. "You brought us allies. We can win this."

"A dungeon's challenges must always be difficult," Derivan said quietly. "You know this. We have brought Gold rankers in, but it will not make things easier."

"You—" Orkas started, and then stopped, letting out an explosive breath. He gritted his teeth, not saying anything for a moment; Derivan watched him almost impassively, but when he spoke, his voice had a touch of sympathy in it.

"You are worried about Misa," he said.

"I don't know her," Orkas answered. Misa frowned a bit, looking away.

"You feel like you should," Derivan said. "There is a part of her that is familiar to you."

Orkas seemed for a moment like he wanted to be angry; there was a twist to his expression as rage flashed into his eyes. But that emotion vanished just as quickly, and was replaced with simple tiredness.

"How could she not be?" he said. "I look at her, and I see traces of me. Traces of her mother. Even this skill you mention, urging her toward a path not many would walk . . . does that not sound familiar to you, Misa? Like a skill that Charise—that your mother has?"

Misa didn't answer for a moment. "Maybe?" she eventually said, hesitant. There was a definite similarity, but that similarity seemed distant to her. "But it's not like skills are inherited."

"No," Orkas said. "They're not. But *who you are* influences the skills you get, and if you were raised by someone like Charise, then you would have seen bits and pieces of her skill at work. Part of you would have learned to see things the way she does. To put things together, even when the links are not obvious. And sometimes that can turn into a skill."

"The skill's never worked properly before now," Misa said, still hesitant. "It never seemed to activate, and I wasn't sure what it did. The description isn't clear. It just says, 'You know when the gate is about to fall.'"

"Hasn't it?" Orkas asked. "Intuition skills are not always obvious. They can be, sometimes, in particularly crucial moments. But otherwise, they're nothing more than a guide. A voice in the back of your head."

Misa fell silent.

She'd wanted to stay at the crater where the dungeon would form, hadn't she? [**Danger Sense**] had been telling her to pull back, but there was another part of her that wanted to stay; a part of her that, she had reasoned, wanted to get a mana crystal of a grade that would make a difference.

She'd wanted Jerome to pay, even, until Derivan had spoken up in favor of helping him. She'd remembered, at the time, the rage she had felt shortly after she lost her village—she hadn't been *kind*. She hadn't been cruel, exactly, but there was an emptiness to her that echoed through everything she did, and it had taken time to patch over that hole in her heart. Even now, that wound ached.

It was still her choice, at the end of the day, whether she wanted to listen to that voice. For a long time, she'd ignored it. That was what led to her endless days after her village had been lost, the time almost a blur to her now. And the first time she'd chosen to listen to it, it had led her on the path that eventually resulted in her meeting Sev and Derivan.

Misa knew immediately that she couldn't prevent every one of these monsters from reaching the portal. She knew immediately, also, that coming here and stopping the horde at the source was the right decision—because she could see their levels now, and they were nothing like the ones they had fought before in the village. What had once been Iron monsters and Bronze Elites were now up by a full tier or more; the presence of combatants across the range from Iron to Gold had changed up the math significantly.

Fortunately, they were ignoring her presence for the most part. The monsters—terrible, insectoid things that stood on two legs and swung blades with four—were marching steadily toward the gate that shone in the distance. Inside, the portal was no longer some small, three-meter-tall hole punched out of space; it was a massive, horizon-spanning *thing*, shining brilliant light that cast harsh shadows behind every monster.

In the distance seemed to be the *source* of the monsters—yet another enormous gate, though that one was not nearly as bright as the one she'd just come through. If anything, it was a void, devouring any light that dared to touch it. The monsters emerged from somewhere within, the void sticking to them like clinging shadows that fell away after a moment in the light.

Derivan, Sev, and Vex landed beside her; she heard two of them take in a sharp breath at the sight. Derivan merely lowered himself into more of a fighting stance, the light of his eyes flickering into a narrowed gaze.

"They are not attacking us," he observed after a moment.

"Not yet," Misa said grimly.

Most of the monsters were ignoring them—but not *all*. A few had stopped, the ones closest to them, and had begun to circle their party; a chittering growl emerged from deep within their throats as they prepared to fight. Misa's party prepared themselves, too, shields and barriers shimmering into existence in front of Vex and Derivan respectively; Sev had retreated once more to the center of the three.

Misa gripped her mace.

"We come in peace?" Sev tried.

Misa snorted. "No, we don't."

It didn't matter, because at the sound of their voices, the monsters screeched and *attacked*.

Not intelligent, then.

That made things easier.

Her vision flickered in the dull black of [**Guard Stance**], and she readied her mace. An old, old memory came to her. She'd talked about this with

Orkas, and had demonstrated it as best she could; it was one thing that didn't change, even though their levels had increased.

Their patterns were still the same. And as long as those patterns were the same, she could fight. She could hold them off. She was stronger than she had ever been, and though her village was miles away, she could feel it like it was at her back.

A monster launched itself at her, and she twisted in position right before it would have landed a hit; she stepped forward in a shoulder check, shoving it backward, and then *stomped*. It jerked beneath her feet, chitin cracking as it let out a screech of anger, and scurried backward.

It wasn't enough to kill it. But she did far more damage than she had last time, and she had her friends by her side.

"We need to get to the source and end this," she said. "Let's go."

CHAPTER 38

STONE HEIGHTS

Vex was realizing that getting to that dark, oozing gate on the other side of the core-space was easier said than done.

That was what he'd decided to call it for now, since he had no other words for it, and there was no literature to explain what it was. Core-space—an intermediary space between the world and whatever it was that created monsters during a dungeon break.

Not that he'd had all that much time to figure out the name.

"Watch out!" Sev shouted. Light blue flared across their vision as he cast, divine magic flickering into existence in front of them; a Gold-ranked Elite insectoid slammed into them just a second after the barrier formed. Thin, needlepoint legs stabbed into the surface of the barrier, poking holes through it easily but not quite tearing the whole structure down.

Derivan sliced through the limbs that poked through the holes, eliciting an angry screech. Vex tore through it a second later with a [**Mana Blast**], concentrated into thin lasers that burned holes in its chitin. But he could already see a problem. They needed a way to clear a large number of enemies; fighting through them like this was slow, and would exhaust them long before they managed to reach the gate.

Fortunately, he'd had time to figure this space out. He'd had time to *understand*, thanks to Misa and Derivan's efforts in protecting the two more-fragile casters. This space wasn't filled with ambient mana, not in the same way the Nucleus had been.

But there was something else he could take advantage of. Something almost reminiscent of what he had done with Jerome, when he'd disabled the spatial expansion in the house they fought in.

They were in an area that was highly spatially compressed. Now that they were inside the core-space, they, too, were being spatially compressed.

So what if he *undid* that compression at the moment his [**Fireball**] landed?

That couldn't be the only thing that he did, was the problem; if all he did was increase the size of a [**Fireball**], then all he would do was agitate far more monsters than the team could handle, for a single spell would be far from enough to kill all the Gold- and Silver-ranked monsters the spell would undoubtedly hit. He needed to scale up the damage, or else modify the spell so that it took out the monsters it hit in some way.

Manaburn would be useless. These insectoids were warriors, not mages, and unlike a lot of lower-leveled creatures, they didn't rely on mana-based attacks to do damage; they had raw stats to fuel their strikes.

[**Sleep**] had no guarantee of working on monster physiology.

Which meant a different route. Something he'd seen before, even.

"Misa," he said calmly. "I'm going to make a [**Fireball**], and I'm going to need you to hit it with a [**Paralyzing Bash**]."

"What?" Misa winced as one of the insectoid creatures crashed into her right as she spoke; she swung her mace wildly, knocking it away as it tried to cut and slice into her. It was a good thing they were light. "Fine. Ready when you are."

"Almost," Vex responded, and focused on his spell. [**Fireball**] was still his favorite for modifications.

He hadn't quite understood how the Overseer had managed to absorb and reflect Derivan's [**Paralyzing Slash**] back when it had happened. But now, with the fight against the Aberrant, he thought he understood.

Arcane mana was the key.

He finished the spell. It was a [**Fireball**], but it was not. The core was pure Arcane, and the inner layer of the spell was set to invert the spatial compression set upon it; the outer layer was linked to the core, to allow Misa's [**Paralyzing Bash**] to propagate into the core—

<**ERROR**>

Unknown Skill attempted!

Parsing . . .

> **Displaying best approximation.**
>
> [**Arcane Mimicry ### Fireball**]

It was an imperfect attempt, he knew immediately. He saw in the corner of his eye Derivan cocking his head, as though curious, or like he'd noticed something strange. Perhaps his Magic stat at work? All Vex knew was that there was still a key he was missing. But the spell was cast, and hopefully it would be good enough—

"Now!" he shouted, stepping backward, and Misa kicked off the monster she was fighting in a sharp, vicious movement; in the next instant, her mace crackled with the familiar black lightning that was characteristic of any of the [**Paralyzing**] series of skills, and the blunt end of her mace smashed into the spell.

It soared into the air like a ball hit with a bat. For a long moment, everything seemed still; even the monsters paused, as if they had no idea what to make of the spell flying over their heads.

Then it struck the ground, and everything turned to chaos.

The spatial layer triggered, undoing the effect of spatial compression on the spell; just before it shattered, the spell *expanded*, growing to more than ten times its original size. Then that layer of the spell shattered completely, unleashing what had once been arcane mana in a spherical burst, except this was arcane mana that had adopted the element behind Misa's [**Paralyzing Bash**]. It wasn't fire that exploded into the air, cooking everything it touched.

It was *lightning*.

Electricity blazed outward in a display that looked bizarrely like a [**Fireball**], as if the spell was still trying to adhere to its original parameters; rather than smoke and fire, bright sparks of current scattered, branching out and then back in, trying to secure a shape that it didn't quite know how to maintain. It ripped through the monsters that it struck, not *quite* hitting them with the stun effect, and doing the damage that pure elemental lightning would do instead.

Which was a lot more damage than a [**Fireball**].

"What did you do?" Misa asked, her eyes wide.

"Piss off a lot of monsters," Vex answered grimly.

Technically, they'd managed to transform a [**Fireball**] into a lightning storm; stripped of the stunning aspect of the [**Paralyzing**] skill, the spell had turned into pure lightning instead. The mana-to-damage ratio on the spell outstripped most of what he could do, even, because lightning was a higher-tier element than fire.

So a small part of him was in awe, and was recording the details of what had happened for further investigation later.

The rest of him was far more concerned about the fact that while the lightning had brought many of the monsters *close* to death, it hadn't killed them. The [**Paralyze**] effect would have been better. This was what he had been trying to *avoid*.

"Incoming!" Sev shouted, because just as Vex had predicted, the range of the skill had been *large*, and they now had a huge portion of the horde just running at them. One of them was faster than the others; a level sixty-two Elite launching itself through the air at impossible speeds straight toward them.

Vex and Sev both tried to call up a barrier, but Derivan was suddenly *there*, and he used the sheer momentum of the monster's own body against it, bracing his sword against a trio of [**Barrier**]s and his own body against another three—

—enchanted metal pierced chitin with ease, and where the health of the system would normally have reversed the damage, the monster simply *died*. The force was still enough to shatter all six barriers, sending him stumbling backward, and it took effort for him to force the remains of the insectoid off his sword.

"We must run," Derivan said. "We are getting too distracted. They will not end until we stop the source."

Even Misa didn't protest. "We'll take out what we can on the way," she said instead.

It was Derivan that took the lead this time, functioning as a first line of both offense and defense; Misa was at the rear, positioned so she could see any attacks that were coming in from the sides and block them. Vex and Sev ran side by side between the two, trusting Misa to cover them.

Together, they formed a sort of lance, keeping the weaker members of the team protected while they cut through the monsters that tried to stand in their way—but that didn't mean it was *easy*.

More than once, Misa had to overextend, blocking two attacks at once in a way that left her panting for breath and exhausting her in a way that couldn't quite be accounted for by stats. More than once, Vex had to rely on [**Dagger Proficiency**] and his protective barriers to fend off a monster long enough for Derivan or Misa to step in, for there were so many that neither of them could completely block all attacks. Even Sev seemed taxed to his limits, though healing was normally an easy task for him; the gaps between his healing spells grew and grew.

And there was no time limit here, unlike their time in the Nucleus. There was no defensive structure they could build; the barriers they had were instantly destroyed, because *these* monsters were smart enough to break them.

They needed to make their way to the gate at the other end of the corespace, and it felt like it was farther away than ever. It didn't help that the gate was only producing more monsters, and it felt like they were struggling against an endless tide.

"This isn't working," Sev eventually said, his words grim. He was focused despite his words, though, divine magic flowing through him to keep Misa's and Vex's health topped up; at this point, it was more crucial to keep Misa's health high than Vex's, because she sometimes had to block as many as five attacks at once. "We need another plan."

"We don't have anything better," Misa growled out. The metal of her mace *clanged* against an insectoid blade, the monster letting out a frustrated chitter as it was blocked. "Derivan's lost most of his skills and I'm a defender. Vex—"

"We could do that lightning spell a few more times," Vex said. A complicated spell construct hovered between his hands; he'd switched between a few different spells now, trying to find one that worked best for the situation. "But I don't want to risk drawing another crowd this big."

If there was just a way to *get them all to the gate*. But he didn't have any teleportation spells, and they would all far exceed the amount of mana he had to him even if he had; teleports were the type of spell that required mana crystals to fuel. Prodigious as his mana stores and generation were, they weren't enough to handle teleportation.

If there was just another way . . .

Derivan's eyes narrowed as two insectoids threw themselves at Vex all at once, and the lizardkin watched in barely disguised awe as the animated armor slipped between them both; for all that they were high-leveled, the chitin they were made of was just that—ordinary chitin.

He didn't slice. He *punched*, dropping his sword so that he could drive his fist straight through the chitin; insectoid armor cracked in a spiderweb pattern before abruptly caving—

Vex averted his eyes, looking instead at the ground.

And he paused.

If he could reverse the spatial compression on a [**Fireball**] . . .

An ordinary [**Stone Wall**] wouldn't be enough to launch them. But it was a different matter entirely if the ground he was standing on was spatially compressed and he undid that spatial compression as the ground was rising—

"Actually," Vex said. "I think I have a different idea. Stand close, quick."

The other three glanced at him, looking briefly bewildered—they were having a *moment*—but didn't actually need much convincing. A [**Stone Wall**] was, thankfully, a relatively quick spell to cast, and all he needed to do was cut a few runes in the air to disable the spatial compression the same way the lightning storm earlier had.

"Derivan, grab everyone, please," he requested politely, feeling a little foolish even as he said so—but Derivan was the largest of them all, and it was better than the four of them being scattered as they were launched. He squeaked a little as he was pulled close, with Sev on the other side of him and Misa in Derivan's other arm—

"Better be quick, Vex!" Sev called, sounding vaguely panicked.

He cast.

Stone sprang into existence beneath their feet, tilted toward the gate.

Spatial compression failed as his runes countermanded it, and they were *launched*, straight toward the void gate.

"VEX GODSDAMMIT I'M AFRAID OF HEIGHTS—"

The monsters looked up, puzzled, as a screaming cleric soared through the air with three others.

It was a momentary distraction. Once the party left their sight, they returned to their original goal—the bright, shining light that called to the anger that burned within them.

CHAPTER 39

MEMORIES

Misa had thought the space with the horde was a void. It had been an inky, dark space, lit only by the light of the portals on either side. Seemed pretty void-like to her.

She had never been wherever *here* was.

The space on the other side of the gate was somehow darker than even that, to the point where Misa thought that it was perhaps only this place that could truly be called a void. Looking out into the distance left her feeling *cold*, almost, like the sight was enough to drag something vital out of her.

And yet somehow, everything here was perfectly lit; there were no shadows at all on her or any of her companions. It was . . . odd, to see them like this. Some details stood out, and others were smoothed over; Derivan's engravings and Vex's scales were nearly impossible to see without the telltale shadows and light glimmering off the edges, but the otherwise-subtle dyes on Vex's leathers were suddenly accentuated.

Vex had tried to cast [**Featherfall**] as soon as they were through the threshold of the gate; they didn't know whether or not to expect monsters on the other side, but they wanted to be prepared. But he hadn't needed to—as soon as they were through the gate, their momentum fell away, and they were left . . . not falling, exactly. But not completely still, either.

They were drifting, and here it seemed that their thoughts influenced the direction they drifted in. At first, they floundered, worried they would be attacked; Vex nearly tumbled into Derivan, and Misa almost shot off into the distance. But there was barely any indication that this space had monsters at all. There where whispers of insectoid shapes, perhaps, closer to the gate. Those shapes were near impossible to see. Misa could only *feel* them ghosting past her, like they were still immaterial.

She shuddered.

"There is something strange about this place," Derivan said quietly after they had all settled and drifted closer together. "I do not know what it is, but something feels . . . familiar. Except it is not familiar at all. I do not recognize the part of me that knows this place, and the feeling is unsettling."

The armor fell silent. Vex glanced at him, though he seemed pretty anxious about being in this space himself. "Are you okay?"

"I am fine," the armor said. "But I would like to leave this place, I think."

"We need to hurry up anyway," Misa said. She was looking ahead, toward the only thing that existed in this space.

In front of them, in the center of this strange, inky void, was a single glowing spark.

It sat atop a pedestal of crystal that might as well have been attached to nothing, for all that it was just floating there. Sharp-looking flecks of metal were embedded into the top surface of the pedestal, serving no apparent purpose.

Above that spark, a strange, wispy beam of light spiraled outward from the device, twisting up into the air, and it was only when Misa followed it with her gaze that she saw the chaos above. Pinpricks of light were scattered above, each nearly infinitesimal in size, though some were larger than others. Looking directly at any one of them granted her a scattering of impressions that she couldn't quite parse—one would be a forest, another a small city, and a third a small village set out in the middle of nowhere . . .

The last one made her wince. It was the one that the trail of light led to, and it was the smallest among the others by far.

When she looked into the sky again, there was nothing there. She had to follow that trail of light with her gaze before it reappeared, and staring at it too long gave her a headache—

"Misa," Sev said, interrupting her thoughts, and she blinked once, tearing her gaze away with a shudder of disgust.

She didn't know why, but the sight felt *wrong* to her.

But there wasn't time to worry about any of that.

"What is this?" Misa asked instead, gesturing to the shimmering blue spark sitting on the pedestal. "Is this related to the monsters somehow?"

"I haven't read anything about this," Vex said with a frown. "There are theories about dungeons having a power source . . . but it's never been located. Maybe this is what that is?"

"If it's the power source, we'd just need to remove it to get the monsters to stop," Sev said.

"Perhaps," Derivan said. He leaned in closer, then jumped backward when a system screen buzzed into existence in front of all of them.

> **X-51 ####### #####R**
> **INTEGRITY: 7%**
> **WARNING: DESTABILIZATION IN PROGRESS. EVACUATION HIGHLY RECOMMENDED.**

Buzzed. They could all see it, and unlike the usual system screens, this one was flickering strangely, like it was unable to completely form.

"Let me . . ." Vex murmured out loud—and then he visibly winced, clapping his hands over his eyes. "Ah!"

"Vex?" Derivan was immediately by the lizardkin's side, one hand on his back. "Are you all right?"

"I'm . . . fine." Vex grimaced, blinking a few times as if to get the spots out of his eyes. "I tried to analyze it like I do with some magical artifacts; I didn't see any mana around it, so I wasn't expecting it to be so *bright*. But there *is* a lot of mana around it, it's just not visible in . . . whatever this space is. I guess however the various [**Mana Sight**]s work, it doesn't work here? My analytical skills still work, but when I tried to analyze it, the skill bombarded me with so many runes I couldn't see straight."

"What does that mean for us?" Misa asked.

"I . . . Give me a moment." Vex blinked a few more times, glanced carefully at the artifact, and then quickly looked away again. "Okay. I don't have a chance of interpreting whatever is going on in the runes. But I can sort of tell how the mana is moving based on the power in those runes, and it looks like there is a *massive* amount of mana flowing into that thing."

"*Into* it?" Sev asked.

"So it's not the power source," Misa said. She narrowed her eyes. "We don't have time to waste to figure out what this does. I'm going to grab it."

"Grab it?" Sev frowned at her. "It's a glowing blue dot—"

Misa grabbed it.

The crystalline pedestal below suddenly flickered and died, the color changing to a dull gray. At the same time, the spark became inexplicably heavy, and Misa grunted and stumbled, rotating in the air as she was suddenly forced to use both her hands just to lift the thing. "Shit," she said.

Above, the wispy trail of light began to flicker and vanish. It had been dying anyway, but now it was entirely dead, and those pinpricks of light above were no longer visible to them.

"*Shit* is right," Sev swore, staring back at the gate. "We better go. The gate's closing."

"This thing was maintaining the gate?" Misa glanced at it, then cursed when she saw it was rapidly shrinking. "Shit. Okay. Let's go."

Fortunately, it wasn't all that difficult to carry the spark when she could move through space with a thought. Misa didn't have time to appreciate it, though, because another thought had dominated her mind.

If they succeeded—if unplugging whatever this was had stopped the monsters from appearing—then her time with her village was coming to an end.

Misa held the spark close. She didn't know why, but she was getting the feeling that it was going to be *important*.

Orkas could taste blood in his mouth.

It was a phantom taste, really. The blood had vanished from his mouth as soon as it appeared, and he had taken a chunk of damage to his health instead; far preferable to the injury that had actually been dealt to him. He didn't particularly fancy having a large chunk torn out of his face, or having one of his tusks broken.

So that wasn't a problem. What *was* a problem was that he was pretty sure they couldn't hold out against the horde as long as they needed to.

It had been fairly obvious from the get-go, really. As soon as the first monsters had appeared, Orkas had known there would be a problem. Everything they'd devised hoped that the horde they would face would consist largely of Bronze monsters, with Silver Elites at most; the fact that the majority of the monsters they had to face were Silver was already a problem.

They had the allies that Misa's team had brought with her, as much as he couldn't bring himself to completely trust them. They were proving extraordinarily effective, too; experienced delvers in all, they were cutting through the insectoid horde with a brutal efficiency.

But there were only four of them. Even if all five of them had been fighting, it wouldn't have been enough.

Their walls were holding for now, though, so there was that. Misa's plan had been pretty good—he'd been impressed. She'd even drawn up a blueprint for him of the way all the traps and walls should be laid out, and it had only required minor corrections on his part, because her memory of the village didn't quite match up with what they had.

A part of him wondered how much history had changed here, without Misa.

The rest of him was more concerned about the monster screeching in his face, acidic spittle flying into his eyes. Orkas grimaced and roared in pain, thrusting his spear blindly forward; he heard the *crunch* of chitin as the spear slid into its flesh—

—[**Spearing Thrust**] took over, and the shockwave from the skill tossed the monster back long enough for him to pour a bit of healing potion over his eyes. *Fuck.* That stung. They hadn't been prepared for fucking *acid spit.*

The other guardsmen were struggling with much the same near him, he knew. And he could also see that they were tiring—none of them were built for a prolonged fight like this. A lot of them were *scared,* too, because for all that they were guardsmen in the village, the village itself had been relatively peaceful; there simply hadn't been any reason to *fight,* until now.

He heard one guardsman scream as an insectoid blade cut deep into his shoulder, and he felt something in his heart harden. Anger and resolve, of a sort; anger that this had already happened once to his village, apparently, and that they were being forced to go through it again. Resolve to beat the circumstances that had been forced upon him, because he'd already failed once, and he could not and *would not* fail now that he had warning.

If the timescale Misa had given him was correct—and everything else she had given him had been correct so far—then they would have to deal with this for at least another three hours.

Orkas was confident they could survive at least one. Some barriers and walls had fallen, but they had built them in layers, and were able to retreat back to the next when the first one was broken. The support of the skeleton crew that Misa had left him kept some of those layers holding strong for longer than they'd expected. Some of the monsters were arriving *injured,* easier to kill than the others; no doubt Misa and her team were doing damage to them. It lightened his heart to see it.

But he was worried.

His resolve could only bring him so far. Their walls would fail *eventually,* and at the current rate, even with the extra barriers they had built, they'd retreat to the last layer before two hours were up. They needed to end it early. Misa had been right.

So he needed to trust the woman who called herself his daughter, and trust that she and her team would end this before things went too far—

Something in the air *changed.*

Orkas blinked rapidly. His vision had suddenly split into two, and he felt a pounding headache searing its way into his skull; when he touched his head, he saw his hand come away with blood. *How?* Injuries weren't retained; that was the entire point of the health system . . .

He stumbled. Was he missing a leg?

Part of him knew he should have been worried. He should have been terrified, even. Unexplained, impossible injuries meant another monster, one that had [**Injury**]-style debuffs and was invisible—

—but that wasn't right, either. He knew this, because these injuries were *familiar.*

He knew this because he *remembered,* and the pain of his injuries were nothing compared to the memories he now had; memories of having a daughter, of her first laugh, her first smile. He remembered the first time she'd picked up a mace he'd left lying on the ground and declared it *hers,* and then sparred him for the right to keep it.

He remembered losing on purpose, laughing as she pinned him down and declared her victory.

He remembered her fascination with classes and skills, and her complaint that it seemed unfair that some got rare classes, and others got common ones. He remembered her saying that she would find a way to use her skills well no matter the rarity, and how she worked with every member of the village to better use their skills; sometimes for absurd, useless things, but she had such a bright heart that they all went along with it.

He remembered their arguments, the times they had fought, certainly, but in the pain of having lost his daughter before she was even born, those memories faded into the background. The joy was what stood out; the joy of having his memories back, of those lonely days replaced with a happier family. His wife's laughter, her smile every time her daughter did something new or interesting. Her whispers to him about how their daughter would grow up to be someone brilliant.

He felt himself losing his grip on his weapon, but he couldn't find in him the energy to care; his head ached, and his heart pounded, and his body was fresh with all the injuries he'd sustained when he went down fighting to protect his family. He hadn't even known Misa was out there, fighting alone.

The monster he was fighting let out a victorious screech and sent a blade careening toward his chest. He was too gravely hurt to stop it, but he forced himself to try, to react. To reach for his weapon. To do *anything.*

But before he could do any of those things, Misa was suddenly there, her mace tight in her hands. She swung it hard enough into the mantis monster's face to send it flying backward, milliseconds before the blade would have pierced his chest.

Her gaze was furious.

Not at him; never at him, not truly. She was angry at the world, and if he knew her . . .

She was about to throw everything she could think of at it to fight it.

"We *won*," Misa declared to the air, glaring at something—at a very specific something, in fact. A system screen? "Like *hell* I'm letting you do this to my family. I am *not* watching them die a second time."

CHAPTER 40

COMMONALITIES

The boxes hovered in front of Misa, and she glared at it like she could make it go away through sheer spite.

> **Congratulations! You have completed the bonus room <The Village's Last Defense>. The following rewards will be granted when you leave the bonus room.**
> **Bonus Room Rewards:**
> **[Unique Quality Gear: The Blade Arcane]**
> **[Unique Skill: Heart and Home]**
> **Bonus room dissolution commencing. You will be returned to the Crystal Challenge room once dissolution is complete.**

> **<WARNING>**
> **Errors have been encountered during dissolution. You may notice strange effects.**

The notifications had appeared almost as soon as they had left and returned to the "bonus room," for all that Misa was loath to call it that. They'd raced to get back to the village, even as the timer ticked down. She'd returned only just in time to stop that attack from touching her father, and even then, it had been a close one. If it hadn't been for [**Guardian's Premonition**] guiding her eyes and telling her where to look . . .

But there was something else that chilled her and made a fire rage within her veins. It was how *familiar* all of these injuries were. She'd seen all these injuries before, on the bodies of her friends and family.

"Sev," she said, and there was a quiet steel in her voice. "Can you help with the wounded?"

He nodded once at her, and divine magic flooded to him. One small piece of it drifted off to heal her father; she watched as it stitched his wounds back together, and Orkas's health rose again . . . But it was slowly ticking down, still. Sev had to move and keep moving; the level difference helped, but there were *so many* he had to heal.

Misa would have gone to them herself—she *wanted* to. But something else was ringing in her head, for [**Guardian's Premonition**] had not gone silent, even after she rescued her father.

The gate would still fall.

She could see it now, even. Superimposed over the gate to their village was the image of a fallen, wrecked one, sliced into ribbons of wood and twisted steel. She remembered the sight well; it was what had remained after the dungeon break first destroyed their home.

Her mind raced for a solution. She didn't understand why old injuries were appearing. But some of the guardsmen were looking at her in awe, recognition sparking in their eyes, and if she read her father's expression right . . .

"I remember," he whispered to her, and she nodded. She fought back the urge to say everything she wanted to say *now*, when she still had the chance; there would be time for it later. She would make sure of that.

"I'm going to fix this," she said instead, and she saw the way Orkas looked at her.

Pride. Familiarity.

Resignation. But underneath that resignation, the smallest spark of hope.

"Vex," she said, glancing at the lizardkin. "This isn't normal, is it?"

"No," Vex said, shaking his head. He moved with a sort of horrified anxiety, his eyes darting about like he was desperate to find a way to help—but he didn't have any ideas either. "It's not supposed to be like this. The room just . . . fades away."

That had *partially* happened. The sky was nothingness now, instead of the blue of before. The monsters were fading away, though there were still skirmishes here and there, mostly between the now-skeletal delvers and the remaining monsters as they fought to protect the guardsmen.

"We cannot solve this alone," Derivan said.

"Good thing we have a whole village," Misa answered. She couldn't quite bring herself to smile, but there was a grim ferocity to her words.

They needed answers they didn't have; too much was unknown to them.

Fortunately for them—and unfortunately for the dungeon—it had given them the one person that could make a very, very good guess.

"I was hoping I'd see you," Charise said, grinning weakly at Misa.

Misa had found her mother not too long after barging her way past the gates—Charise was already on the way *there*, as if looking for her. She was limping, grimacing in pain with every step, but there was that delver that was carefully helping her every step of the way. He wouldn't meet anyone's eyes.

For all the pain that she was clearly in, though, her mother's eyes were bright and knowing.

"If things weren't so urgent . . ." Charise began. She sighed, and looked at Misa with a small, fond smile. "I can't convince you not to do this, can I?"

"No," Misa said, though the smile made her heart ache.

"Okay," her mother said once, accepting it with a nod; her face grew more serious as she leaned into her [**Intuition of Truth**]. Almost immediately, she frowned and glanced at Misa's hand. "You have something with you. Something important."

The spark she'd taken from the dungeon. She'd almost forgotten about it. The weight of it had left her mind, and as soon as it had, it weighed almost nothing; now that she was thinking about it again, she grunted, straining to lift the thing. "Do you know what it is?"

"No," Charise said, shaking her head, but she frowned at it nevertheless. "But everything . . . bends toward it. I can't even look at you without my attention being drawn there. It's linked to why everything is happening this way. [**Intuition of Truth**] isn't that detailed, but it doesn't need to be for me to see that."

Misa frowned, opening her hand to look at the spark. Even now, to her eyes, it looked tiny and unassuming; she couldn't imagine it holding the unimaginable amount of mana that Vex claimed it contained. She remembered seeing the thin wisp of light emanating from it, drifting up into an endless sky full of those tiny pinpricks of light . . . there had to be thousands.

The one it was linked to had been her village; she was sure of it. The sight would have been beautiful if it hadn't filled her with dread. Was that why? Was this thing doing this to the village?

"You need to use your intuition skill, too," Charise said, interrupting her thoughts. Her mother peered at her closely, then took one of her hands in both of her own, giving her a gentle smile. "Breathe. Let it guide you."

Misa listened. [**Guardian's Premonition**] pulsed in her mind. The gate was in the process of falling; she had to know *why*. She had to know what she could do to stop it.

She didn't know why, but it guided her into memories of her childhood. She remembered the village as it was, whole and intact, everyone hearty and whole.

> **X-51 ####### #####R synchronization has reached 50%.**

The notification startled her when it popped up; at the same time, Charise let out a gasp that was something like relief, and she stood a little taller.

Not a coincidence. Was it reacting to her memories?

> **<ERROR>**
> **Dissolution of bonus room has halted. Unable to proceed.**

> **<ERROR>**
> **Unable to resolve problem within local parameters. Calling for administrator assistance . . .**

> **<ERROR>**
> **######Y ###### is not valid loot. Please drop it and allow dissolution to proceed.**

If anything, the last message just made her clutch the spark to herself even tighter. They'd clearly gone off the rails in some way, but if that was allowing her village to stay intact . . .

> **<WARNING>**
> **Drop the ######Y ######.**

That definitely wasn't a normal system warning. Everyone else saw the messages too, considering the way they stared at the air in front of them, startled.

Administrator assistance. That would make this the second time they'd encountered an administrator? The first time—

> **Fine. You were warned.**

The sky was pitch black; it had been the first thing to disappear as the dissolution began. But now that pitch-black darkness began to *move*, the night sky undulating in a way that should have been impossible, and again—yet again—the system overlay appeared, visible to anyone that dared to look up.

Which was pretty much everyone. They all stared at the window in the sky and swallowed.

<**Overseer of Sky**>
<**Level ??? Serpent of the Night Sky**>

"Ah, shit," Misa said softly.

But it wasn't the appearance of the boss monster that worried her.

It was what she could see in the distance. It was not unlike what she had seen in the inner recesses of the dungeon; again, there were those small specks of light in the distance.

Only this time, they were growing, slowly but surely, and [**Danger Sense**] and [**Guardian's Premonition**] were both blaring at her.

"It's a [**Meteor Storm**]," Vex whispered softly, terrified. "Misa, you can't . . . we can't block that. There has to be hundreds of them. I've never seen . . ."

"How long is that going to take to hit us?" Misa asked.

"I-I don't know. A few minutes? Maybe a little less than ten?" Vex said, hesitant. The Serpent was still undulating in the air; it seemed to believe that its spell was all that was needed, and it was content to wait it out. Misa spared a moment to wonder if there was another god trapped nearby, wrapped in chains.

"I can block it if I have enough mana," Misa said. "I have 1,162 health. Ten percent of my health is 116 health. The cost markup from [**Every Last Drop**] turns that into 232 mana. I don't—" She grimaced slightly. "I don't have nearly that much mana. But we have a huge fuckin' mana battery in this thing, right?" She lifted the spark they'd stolen from the dungeon, albeit with some effort.

"It is also what sustains this place, if the system messages are correct," Derivan cautioned.

"It has enough mana," Vex said. "I . . . I think. It's hard to look at it directly. But the mana levels in it are barely dropping even now. It *should* be fine. But I don't think it's as easy as calling that mana yours, Misa."

"Quick test?" Misa offered. They tested it.

It did not, unfortunately, count. The skill drained all her mana and then part of her health, and she winced at the strange feeling that flooded through her at the mana loss.

"I might be able to connect my mana pool with it, since I have [**Expert**

Mana Manipulation], and that would make it 'my' mana. But I don't have any way to share my mana with you." Vex glanced worriedly at the sky again; the meteors were getting closer. Brighter.

Rather than look worried, Misa's face lit up, and she exchanged a glance with her mother. "Gabriel!"

"Gabriel?" Vex asked, puzzled.

"*Gabriel*," Charise said, suddenly catching on. [**Intuitionist**] filling in the pieces, perhaps

"This way. Come on; we need to find him quick," Misa said. Charise seemed to know exactly where to find him, and was veering directly toward a large, portly man. He was staring at the sky, his mouth agape, and trembling; Misa winced. She'd forgotten that not everyone was used to dealing with . . . all this. "Gabriel," she said.

"Misa." His eyes went wide as he turned to her. "I-I died. Misa, I can't— I *died*. I'm going to die again."

"You won't," Misa said softly. "But we need your help. Can you help us?"

"*I'm going to die*," he said emphatically, and curled up on himself—

Charise stepped in front of him. "No, you're not," she told him, hauling him to his feet. "You're going to help us all live; do you understand? But *we need your help*, and we don't have time for you to argue."

"I need you to do a [**Trade**]," Misa said. "You still have that skill, right? The one that lets you trade resources?"

"I— Yes?" Gabriel sounded thoroughly confused, though a part of him seemed to latch on to the conversation like it was a lifeline; he needed just *anything* that was approaching normal for him. He kept his gaze firmly on the nearby wall too, like he could avoid the sight of the meteors that way.

"Vex, connect with the . . . whatever this thing is. I need you to [**Trade**] our mana, Gabriel. Can you do that?"

A short silence, and then a hesitant voice. "[**Trade**] between Vex and Misa. Resource: Mana. Quantity: Custom."

A window popped up in front of both Vex and Misa, and Vex stared at it, surprised.

"I'll explain later," Misa said. She glanced at the meteors; she imagined she could feel the heat of them on her skin already. "Just . . . trade me that mana for now."

> [**Trade**] complete. **1,000,000 mana has been transferred to Misa Evergreen.**

"Good," Misa said.

She'd spent a long time trying to figure out skills, after all, when she was a child. She'd even told her mother about it just before this, as she reminisced over the childhood that Charise didn't remember. [**Trade**] had fallen out of use a long time back. It was far easier to just hand over what you wanted, and the basic degree of trust that people had in one another hadn't been so harmed that the skill was necessary.

But she'd made the strange discovery that mana counted as a resource. She'd tried to trade other, silly things; concepts, stats, levels, health. None of those had worked.

Mana had. There were nuances to the trade, and she'd abandoned it as useless when she found that the mana couldn't be used to cast spells or fuel skills in the traditional sense; it "belonged" to you, but it wasn't a part of you.

Except perhaps in this one very, *very* specific case, when the cost was applied to mana that belonged to her.

One more quick test, and when the damage pinged off the extra mana instead of her health, she grinned, glanced at the Serpent in the sky, and gave it the finger.

"Fuck you," she said, and activated [**To Fall Yet Hold the Line**].

CHAPTER 41

TO HOLD THE LINE

If there was one thing Misa had never really understood despite trying to, it was how [**To Fall Yet Hold the Line**] worked.

It was, by all accounts, an absurd skill—there was no reason it should be possible to block every attack. More to the point, she'd just seen the results of an impossible application. When she blocked an unblockable attack, rather than one skill trumping the other, *all of reality had sheared in half*, and then the system had chosen the "average" of those two results.

She suspected, therefore, that whatever mechanism the skill operated by would be strained by what she was doing now, attempting to block hundreds of attacks simultaneously. Every single meteor counted as a separate attack, and every single one of them was an attack she would ordinarily fail to block. Not by slight degrees like before, either. By *massive* degrees.

But she had [**To Fall Yet Hold the Line**]. So she would not fail.

There had been another instance before, when she'd attempted to block something that was outside the realm of what should have been possible for her to block—the intrusion of the system on Derivan's mind. Her memory of that moment was faint and fuzzy, like there was some specific detail about it that she couldn't quite recall in perfect clarity.

Except now. When she used the skill now, straining it to its limits, that memory slammed into sharp focus, for the system couldn't hide from her what the skill did while it was doing it.

She wielded nothing against the meteors, and she felt the skill reaching. Not a sword, for a sword could not strike down a meteor. Not a dagger. Not a staff or a wand or a focus, either, for there was no version of her—no iteration of Misa that wielded any of those weapons—that could strike a meteor down.

At lower levels, the skill forced her to move in physically impossible ways, adopting what would allow her to best block a skill. At higher levels—when no amount of physical convolution would allow her to block an attack—it began to reach for other versions of her: versions that were *similar*, but had a slightly different weapon. A sword instead of a mace, if that would be more effective. A wand or a focus instead of a sword, if she needed to counter some magic. She didn't know any magic herself, but there was some version of her out there that did.

Shields were few and far between, but even at the outer edges of her possibility of self, those failed. There were no shields she could wield that would block all of these simultaneously.

All this knowledge came flooding into her mind, because however the skill operated, it was *reaching*. It was going out to the very farthest edges of everything Misa had been and ever could be, and it was coming up empty, for there was no version of Misa that existed—or that ever would exist—that would be capable of stopping an entire meteor storm by herself. There was no weapon, in the system-limited world where the level cap was supposedly a hundred, that could stop what was essentially an apocalyptic event.

And so, out of other options, the skill reached out to her and asked: what weapon could she wield, against a power such as this?

And Misa answered.

I am more than the sum of my parts. The effect I have on the world is more than the footprints I leave behind. I have carried my village with me for years; their hopes, their dreams, and their prayers. I have met new friends, and they, too, are now part of my power. Because my power does not lie in what I do alone.

The weapon I wield is not sword nor shield, not staff nor wand. It is in the lives I have touched, with kindness instead of cruelty, compassion instead of rage. It is in the strength of community, in acting together to enact change that cannot be accomplished alone.

The skill responded.

There was no version of Misa that could stop hundreds of meteors alone; a single one was an apocalyptic event, all by itself. But she would not fail to block this attack, and she had a lot more to leverage than just herself.

Thousands—then tens of thousands of mana poured into the skill through the mana she had borrowed, stolen directly from the [####### A#####].

Ghostly versions of people manifested in the air—most of them the people of J'rokksur. Each of them carried with them something special.

Not a class. Not a unique skill. All of them had common classes, and common skills.

These were just versions of them that had had their lives touched by Misa. Variations that had learned to abuse their skills to truly absurd degrees. Not alone, perhaps, but working in concert, with maxed-out skills. These were variations of them that had lived with Misa for years, and grown up with her. They were from a village that had survived the horde and learned to fight with everything they had.

[**Classify**], from the village [**Categorist**], who very reluctantly [**Classified**] a group of meteors as a mannequin.

[**Clothe**], from the village [**Tailor**], who worked together with the [**Cobbler**] to bestow a pair of massive shoes on the lowest two meteors in that group.

[**Light Steps**], from one of the guardsmen, who had a buffing skill that could make any piece of footwear tread lightly.

[**Adjust**], from the village [**Builder**], who could move rocks slightly. "Slightly," as it turned out, was quite astronomic when dealing with the scales and distances involved for meteors. The impact would still have done damage if not for the [**Light Steps**] buff, which caused the entire set of meteors that had been [**Classified**] together to land with a move that could only be called *dainty*.

Those particular rocks rolled peacefully onto the ground, struck some invisible border where the dissolution of the bonus room had begun, and vanished.

Misa grinned at the sight. The sky began to undulate in anger, but not even a second had passed, and they were far from done.

The village pickpocket—who had received the class when he had once pickpocketed a friend as a joke and hated it, though no one judged him for it—[**Stole**] several meteors, then [**Trade**]d it with the [**Quartermaster**], who [**Store**]d it.

There was a version of Derivan here who had learned to Shift and had boosted the stat to impossible numbers. He slashed with a hand, and holes were outright torn in space; holes that sent one meteor crashing through and into another, and those fragments into another five, sending each crashing off course.

There was a version of Vex who had learned to master *magic*—not through runes, not [**Mana Manipulation**], but magic as he wished it to be. It was an art, in his mind, and this version of him had leaned entirely into it; he had discarded his dagger for a brush, and he painted strokes in the air. Each stroke of mana became a glittering panel of light, and the meteors that struck those panels flashed into a dozen shades of prismatic color before shimmering down into nothing.

There was a version of Sev who stood, silent—but behind him were figures, and one of them looked like the familiar form of Onyx. He gave Onyx a nod, and Onyx stepped *into* him, reaching out with a hand; half a dozen meteors were instantly crushed together, turning into a perfect sculpture of Velykos; the priest they'd met, back in the Guild temple.

The skeletons each—being highly leveled combat classes already—had their own attacks they could levy against the meteors. Five attacks streaked into the sky, even from the one that had refused to fight; one of them was the captain, launching his entire body at a meteor. Another one was an arrow. The third physically leapt up with a greatsword that should have been too big to carry, the fourth struck with a mace that shattered the rock, and the fifth held up a shield that somehow held up against a meteor.

There was *Jerome*, or a ghostly figure of him, who appeared in front of a meteor and seemed prepared to convert it to gold—only that meteor swerved, for some reason, and never hit him at all; it smashed into the side of the bonus room instead, and dissolved into nothing.

And with that, the sky was clear. Misa couldn't help but stare in some awe. Some of those were things that she'd assumed was possible but never tested; for obvious reasons, [**Common**] classes were rarely put into combat situations. Especially noncombat classes. Even the tests she'd done with the other villagers as a kid . . .

She glanced around. Some of the villagers looked awed, too. Vex and Derivan were staring up at the sky, watching with a glimmer of something inscrutable.

"Can I *do* that someday?" Vex whispered.

"I am sure that you can," Derivan answered, gentle.

Others just looked afraid of what would happen next, which was . . . valid. Misa grimaced. This was just the opening salvo, and the sky was *angry*, rippling in furious coils as it prepared to strike again.

And then it *did*. It was a single attack, springing its head at the village like a snake going for a bite, covering kilometers in an instant. Misa gritted her teeth and *blocked* the single attack—her weapon this time was a greatsword of strange, fractal design that seemed to suck all the kinetic force of the attack into nothing—and then she was falling.

Vex caught her with a spell. Orkas and Charise were both running up, one demanding to help and the other asking her if she was all right; she nodded tightly to the latter but didn't know how to answer the former. She didn't have any ideas. Just blocking the thing felt like it had drained her on a fundamental level, for all that she was supposedly still full on health.

At least the snake seemed stunned from having its attack stopped.

"I'm okay, Mom," she said out loud when Charise didn't stop worrying. Footsteps made her glance to the side, where she saw Sev running over.

"I think I have an idea." Sev's words were half-panted out; evidently, he'd been running around for a while. There were lines of exhaustion around his eyes. Determination still burned in them, though, strong as ever. "I'm not sure if you saw, but some of those meteors hit the edge of the bonus room and disappeared."

"And the Serpent attacks ridiculously fast once it lines up for a strike . . ." Vex thought out loud. "You want to get it to hit the side of the room?"

"Exactly." Sev managed a fierce grin despite his exhaustion.

"That might work," Misa said. She glanced up and winced. "It better work, actually. I can't keep this up forever, and that thing looks pretty fuckin' mad."

Sev looked up too and grimaced. The Serpent was glaring down at them in two glowing spots of light, looking like miniature suns narrowed into slits. If it had been stunned, it was already coiling around for another attack.

"Dad," Misa said, glancing at her father. "You need to evacuate the villagers. I don't want them anywhere near where this thing is going to hit."

"There isn't anywhere to run even if we wanted to," Orkas said, shaking his head. "But it's focused on *you*."

Ah. Because of the [####### #####**R**], still held tight in her hand. She'd almost forgotten.

"All right, then," Misa said. The Serpent was already coiling up again, preparing for another strike. "I guess I'm going to be the bait."

CHAPTER 42

THE SERPENT OF THE NIGHT SKY

Dirt and rubble exploded into the air as the Serpent struck the ground, the snakelike head snapping at them the same way a snake would. Misa hadn't blocked it this time—the villagers, while not completely clear, were far enough away that they wouldn't have been hit by the direct strike. The Serpent itself seemed smaller, too; not so small that it could be dodged easily, but enough so that the impact smashed apart a few homes, and not the entire village.

The force of that impact was still enough to flicker damage into their health, though. Vex, Sev, and Misa all grimaced; Derivan was the only one that escaped relatively unscathed. Four of the delvers were still fighting with them, though they had been farther away and thus escaped relatively unscathed.

Their arrows weren't doing much to the Serpent, though. The health bar of the Serpent had barely budged, for all the arrows they'd pumped into it, and they were running out. None of them were mages, either.

"Sorry we dragged you into this!" Sev yelled at them, maybe because he felt like he owed it to them, and one of them yelled back something about having been through worse.

Which was . . . concerning, actually. But they didn't have time to think about it much.

Derivan ran forward while the snake was recovering from the impact of its own strike. He stabbed his sword into its side, and there was a roar of anger and pain in response—the very *ground* shook, and prismatic blood gushed out of the gap he'd opened up. He had to jump back a second later as the Serpent shook itself wildly, pulling back.

The living armor was their second-best bet at ending this. His strikes didn't affect the Serpent's health, but it was still clearly *injured*. And it was certainly getting wary of him, with the way it reared back, sunlike eyes narrowing at him suspiciously.

Their best bet, of course, was still baiting the snake into smashing into the side of the bonus room. But that was easier said than done. It was far too easy for any one of them to get knocked in instead, and none of them wanted to test what would happen in that situation.

Misa stared up at the sky serpent grimly.

Though it was more wary of them now, every so often, it would turn to glare at her—and that glare would coincide with a popup of yet another blue box, demanding that she drop what she was holding. That she drop the [####### #####R]. She still didn't really understand what it *was*, but she understood that it was the only thing keeping this place together, so like hell was she letting go of it. Why let her grab it at all if it was going to be a problem?

But if the Serpent was going to glare at her every time she received a box, then maybe there was something more to it than that. A surge of anger that accompanied an order, perhaps, or perhaps it *was* the Serpent sending her those boxes . . .

It struck again before she could finish the thought, headed directly for her once more. Misa tried to throw herself out of the way—she couldn't *block* this time; she had to make it miss and strike the wall instead—but it was still fast enough that it clipped her, and the angle of attack meant that it slammed into the ground instead of into the edges of the room. Derivan attacked with a stab again, slicing into the Serpent's flesh-that-wasn't-flesh, spraying the ground in more of that strange prismatic blood.

Misa, meanwhile, was sent careening backward through the dirt. She stopped before she hit the edge of the room only because Vex and Sev both put a barrier up in her way, and she smacked into them both, groaning in pain.

[**Every Last Drop**] protected her with that borrowed mana, but only barely.

"I need to be higher up!" Misa growled out, biting the words out through the pain. The Serpent reared back into the sky, circling around again, watching them. "Anyone have any ideas?"

"Flight spells can't move you fast enough to dodge that thing once it starts attacking." Vex watched the Serpent carefully. He was obviously nervous, but his eyes were bright and alert. "We need something different."

"A well-timed block, perhaps," Derivan suggested. "If we know the moment it is to attack . . ."

The Serpent seemed to want to attack her every time she received a box. If she could use that as an early warning—

"Captain!" Misa called. "Harold, right? That's your name?"

"Yes, ma'am!" Harold called back at her. "Y'need somethin'?"

"I need you to fire an arrow into the sky, between that thing and the border. Do it when I tell you to," she said. "Then fire a second one near the ground, in any direction except the border."

Harold cocked his head, and Misa had the strange feeling that he was raising a brow at her, despite the lack of any eyebrows. "If that's what ya need," he said. "But we're on our last coupla arrows now. We gotta get this right."

"Believe me," Misa exhaled, "I know."

<WARNING>
Drop the ####### #####R.

"Now!" Misa shouted.

An arrow flew into the air, almost directly upward—boosted by a skill, clearly, because it moved far faster than it should have been able to. Misa waited a second for the arrow to reach the right height, and then *blocked* the attack, ignoring the spike of pain in her head.

Her mace struck the arrow, and it splintered.

For a split second, she hovered in the air.

In that same split second, the Serpent narrowed its eyes at her and *struck*.

She glanced down, hoping that the captain had remembered the second part of her instructions—she barely saw the flicker of the arrow crossing the ground. She blocked that attack, too, finding herself on the ground a second later, another broken arrow shattering itself on her mace—

—above her, the Serpent tried to pull back its attack, but it was too late; it had gathered too much momentum—

—the Serpent *smashed* into the border of the bonus room.

There was a loud cracking sound. Unlike everything else that had struck the border, the Serpent didn't outright *vanish*. Instead, it swerved, hissing angrily as it tried to stabilize itself.

It failed. It crashed into the ground, one burning eye staring at them. Its head was odd and misshapen for a serpent—like chunks had been carved out.

"Did it work?" Vex asked beside her.

"It doesn't look hurt," Sev said.

In Misa's hand, the fragment burned. The spark. The [####### #####R], or whatever it was. Her head throbbed with two sets of memories, one in which the Serpent was whole, and one in which it had always looked like this—chunks of flesh missing, an entire eye gone. It seemed just as angry as ever, and yet—

"I think it worked," she said quietly. She didn't know how to parse her memories yet, nor did she even have the words to explain what she thought might have happened. Vex and Sev didn't seem to remember—

"It did work," Derivan confirmed next to her. He looked just as concerned. Part of Misa felt a raw sort of relief, though, at having someone else to corroborate what she was saying.

"Understood," Sev said simply, and Vex gave a quick nod beside him.

"But I believe it is not over," Derivan added. The Serpent was on the ground, yes, but it was very much not *dead*; it was slower, and it seemed a little confused, perhaps. It wriggled awkwardly, then glared ahead, like its gaze alone would be enough—

"Magic!" Vex shouted, sounding alarmed; a crystalline barrier formed in front of them as he sliced his dagger through the air. Misa prepared to block the attack as the snake's mouth yawned open and a beam of light blazed forward; it scattered against the crystalline barrier, diffracting into a dozen weaker beams that burned the ground.

Misa lowered her mace. [**To Fall Yet Hold the Line**] wasn't needed. Part of her was relieved; that skill had drained her.

The moment the attack broke was the moment they took to attack—all four of them charged, joined quickly by the other four delvers that brandished their weapons. Vex and Sev stayed a little farther back, of course, but they still prepared to cast. Sev had light-blue divine magic playing around his fingers as beams of light shot from his staff, and Vex seemed to be concentrating on a spell of some kind; Derivan ran until he was close enough to slash into the Serpent yet again.

And then Vex cast his spell.

It looked almost directly inspired by the beam of light the Serpent had fired from them—an equally bright ray of light shone from Vex's dagger as he began cutting into the air, and it only shone brighter and brighter as he continued. The snake was flinching backward somehow, trying to get away from the light, but there was nowhere *to* go, and soon the whole place was lit up like it was daytime—

The Serpent collapsed.

It didn't appear to be dead—it was breathing, albeit in slow, ragged breaths. But its eyes were closed. Perhaps even more telling was the fact that its skin, once the color of the night sky, now shone a rippling blue. Prismatic blood still oozed from its wounds, but it was still.

"What the fuck was that?" Misa asked.

"Uh . . . That was [**Daylight**], but mana-boosted a lot," Vex answered, sounding a little embarrassed. "It's a Serpent of the Night Sky, so I figured that might do something?"

"It still has most of its health," Harold reported. He wasn't attacking it yet, apparently concerned that doing so would break it out of whatever trance it was in. "I don't think any of us can take down all its health. Maybe that friend of yours." He glanced rather significantly at Derivan.

"I am unsure I could do that," the armor replied, glancing at the monster.

Misa was angry, admittedly. But it looked in many ways broken, defeated, and it was lying down there on the ground . . . For all that it had health, they had clearly won, at least for the moment.

There were no more blue boxes warning her to drop the [####### #####**R**], at least.

"What do we do now?" she said quietly.

"I want to try something," Sev said. "Last time we fought an Overseer, it was keeping Onyx prisoner, right? Vex, you mentioned that the chains were burning with your magic—the magic that you hit the Overseer with."

"Yeah," Vex nodded. "I still don't really understand it. My best guess is that the Overseer is in some way directly linked to the chains . . ."

"I'm thinking these Overseers are prisons," Sev said, his words soft. "Living prisons. And I want to find out which god is imprisoned here, if anyone."

Vex blinked at him, surprised—but Derivan didn't seem nearly as surprised. "Misa's skill showed me part of what I can potentially do, I think," the armor said. "I may be able to . . . I feel there is something here I can breach, in much the same way I did when we stepped into the dungeon. But . . ."

"But?" Sev raised an eyebrow at him. Derivan grimaced.

"The weakest point is here," the armor said. He gestured to the wound he had cut open in the Serpent, still oozing prismatic blood. "The journey might not be pleasant."

CHAPTER 43

A PRISON OF BROKEN WEBS

There were a number of things they had to do, of course, before they could stroll into what was hypothetically the prison of yet another god.

For one thing, they had to make sure the bonus room was relatively stable. The dissolution didn't seem to be progressing, and no one was receiving any new boxes; the injuries of all the various villagers were healed, and now they were all trying to recover.

That was the good part. The bad part was that it was somewhat difficult to explain to them why they weren't trying to immediately kill the Serpent, and in particular why they wanted to go *into* it.

There was, of course, also the concern that whatever effect was keeping the bonus room up would fail the moment they entered the Serpent.

That one, at least, was a concern that was easy enough to alleviate. Charise was there, shaking her head. "It will not," she said. "This space is tied strongly to what you're holding. As long as it doesn't break, this place won't break, either."

"[**Intuitionist**] at work?" Misa asked, and her mother grinned at her. "You know it."

That was not, of course, actually enough for Misa to be satisfied. She had Derivan take her in and out of the prison a few times, quickly, checking if the dissolution had progressed while she was gone—but it had not, and it seemed that Charise was right.

So that, at least, was fine; Misa could come with them.

The second thing they needed to decide was if going into the prison was worth it at all. For that, they collectively decided that it was; they were meant to find answers here, after all, and all they had was the barest beginning of one. The pieces were all there, but they had nothing to put it together. No real idea of what it all *meant*.

. . . And, of course, if there truly *was* another god trapped in there, it seemed only right that they try to do for them what they could not do for Onyx. Perhaps it would even be Onyx again, and there would be a second chance to rescue him, though none of them really thought that would be the case.

Still, it was enough for them. They all linked hands, and Derivan found the part of himself that touched upon Shift; he brought them all up to the wound in the Serpent, where he'd already stepped through with Misa, and *pushed* at the now-familiar crack in space and time.

They found themselves in a prison of prismatic webs.

It was completely unlike the blank, empty space they'd first found Onyx in, with nothing but a long series of chains trailing up to the figure in the center. This one was lit up by a fractal brilliance that would have been beautiful if not for the way those very same webs clung to them, a sticky, off-feeling substance that couldn't be easily ignored. It took effort to step through the webs, to make their way deeper into the prison.

And it *was* a prison—that much was obvious. The farther in they got, the denser those webs became; they were forced to stop before they reached the center, for a sheer drop appeared in front of them, the ground disappearing into endless prismatic light.

In the midst of the light, far into the distance, was a single, solitary figure. It was covered in so many dense webs that it seemed nearly impossible for it to move.

It was dressed in red robes that were adorned by golden filigree, flowing around its figure. More striking, however, was the head, or lack thereof; a sphere of roughly hewn gold sat in its place, a strange, distorted hum rising up around it.

Every time that figure moved—every time it breathed—the light around it would shift and warp, every web twisting to move and hold it down.

It was also enormous, dwarfing them in size. Onyx had been human-sized, but this god—if it was a god at all—was nearly the size of a small mountain. It was only the fact that the ground they stood on was far above it that they were able to stare down and look at it in full, or else it would have towered high over them, and yet . . .

For all that they'd made it in here, they realized they didn't exactly know what they were going to *do*. This wasn't like the chains, where they could weaken them and heal the god; this wasn't like Onyx, either, who knew who Sev was and had been willing to lend them a hand. There was no guarantee this god would want to help them at all.

But there was only one way they could start, really.

"Hello?" Sev called out. His voice echoed strangely in this liminal space, the words somehow bouncing between the webs rather than being absorbed; small fragments of his own, distorted voice came back to him when he spoke, and he grimaced slightly. "We're here to help."

The figure below them shifted. It seemed to glance up at them, though it was hard to tell if it did—the golden orb it had for a head shifted slightly, but there was no face to indicate where it was looking. "Hello?" it called back.

Sev paused.

That was a *child's* voice. Distorted, yes, and difficult to make out with the way the cobwebs repeated the sound, but that was almost certainly a child. That was the last detail that made it click—the sphere of gold and the golden filigree, the state he was in, like the webs were still ripping away something vital from him.

The way the meteor had shied away from the ghost of Jerome that Misa had somehow summoned, instead of striking him.

"Aurum?" Sev said carefully. The god beneath them jerked—then winced when the webs tightened around him.

"That's me," the god said. "Can you help me? I'm—I'm stuck."

The smallest waver in the god's voice. Just the slightest hint that he was *afraid*, though he should have been bawling by now, if the age of his voice was any indication. But who knew how gods worked? Onyx had been humanlike, but he was one example out of many.

"Do you know where you are?" Sev's tone was gentle.

"No," Aurum admitted. "I dunno . . . I don't remember much, actually. I remember being scared. I'm less scared now. 'Cause I can't remember what I'm supposed to be scared of, I think? I feel like that should be scary . . . but it's not."

A short pause.

"It's nice to talk to someone again," he added. "It's been lonely here. I don't have any of my angels. They usually take care of me. I remember one of them finally came back . . . They looked so worried. I was really happy to see them. And then . . . I dunno what happened after that."

Another pause.

"Can . . . can you keep talking?" Aurum said. "I just . . . wanna know that you're there."

". . . We're here," Sev answered. He didn't trust himself to say any more; beside him, he could *feel* how tense all of his companions were. Misa let out a quiet *fuck,* and winced when the sound echoed more than she wanted it to.

"Oh, okay," Aurum said. "Thank you."

"He really was just a child?" Vex said quietly. "I thought maybe Jerome was just delusional. Or he was tricked. The way everything was coordinated . . ."

"His angels were probably just as scared as he was," Misa answered. Of the four of them, she was the most visibly angry, though she didn't seem to know where to channel that anger. There wasn't anything here to punch, or block, or . . .

There was just *this*. A lonely, scared child, wrapped up in prismatic webs that seemed to be—what, stealing his memories? But Onyx had remembered who he was; he'd remembered Sev, and he knew enough to comfort his cleric. What was different here? What made this different from what happened with Onyx?

They were in a dungeon simulation of a bonus room. Was this part of the simulation, or was this external to it?

"Can you tell us what you do remember? Anything about yourself that you remember?" Sev asked before the silence could stretch on for too long— already he could see Aurum beginning to fidget beneath the webs, as if forgetting that they were there. Every so often, he would move too much again, and the webs would tighten around him, and he would remember.

"Um . . . yeah! Yeah. I dunno. I don't remember much." Aurum seemed to try to gather himself. "My name's Aurum, but you already knew that. I'm a god, I guess? Never really felt like it. But I have a bunch of angels, and sometimes they tell me what to do, if I'm not sure. They play with me a lot when I get bored, and they teach me things. Sometimes they get a little sad, 'cause they tell me I can't grow up. They dunno why; they say it's just the way it is.

"Sometimes I get people that pray to me, and I wanna help them. But I don't know how to help them, and I think sometimes I hurt them instead . . . I try not to. The angels told me I can't just give away powers. I gotta think. There are rules. I don't remember the rules . . .

"I wanna see them again." Aurum trembled a little bit in his spot, the movement causing a dozen webs to shake along with him, scattering into fractal cracks. "I miss them. I miss the people that prayed to me, too. I like them, even if they're not all very good. But I don't remember any of their faces—"

Aurum stopped talking, and began to cry.

It was an odd sight. He drew up into himself, breaking a few of the webs as he did so, and not seeming to care as some of the other webs tightened around him, and then he just . . . shook. His shoulders heaved. But he was quiet, no sound escaping from him.

"Aurum?" Sev said, and then when the god didn't reply and just kept crying, he sighed. "Aurum, we're going to figure something out, okay? Just . . . give us some time."

He turned to Derivan and spoke quietly. "He's not pretending, is he?"

"Not to the best of my knowledge," the armor answered. "I . . . We must find a way to free him. We cannot leave him like this."

"I agree," Vex said. His voice was small, and he looked on the verge of tears himself, but damned if the lizardkin didn't also look determined.

"He's also *actually a child*," Misa muttered. "How . . . why? A child shouldn't be a fuckin' *god*."

"We're going to get him out," Sev said. "We're going to figure out what to do with him after that, but for now . . . whatever this is, I want to tear it down."

"Easier said than done," Misa said. She rammed her mace into a nearby cobweb—not difficult, considering the things were everywhere and clinging to them even now—and the weapon simply slid through, leaving the web intact behind it. "These things look fragile, but they're not."

"When you attack them," Vex pointed out. "We can move through them fine. Aurum can too, a little bit. He broke a few just now."

"So they're impervious to attacks, but not . . . movement?" Misa frowned. "That doesn't make any sense."

"They are not impervious to attacks," Derivan said. "They are impervious to *weapons*." He demonstrated by striking through one of the webs near him; it tore apart easily enough as his arm struck it, and fragments of glittering light fell to the ground.

Vex watched for a moment, then began to strike out with his dagger. A series of quick, precise strikes—not at the webs, but in the air, carving out runes—and a spell circle glowed; from that spell circle came a burst of ice that blasted forward, cutting through a number of webs . . .

. . . and leaving them intact and unharmed afterward, having gone through the webs with barely a whisper. The wizard grimaced. "I was hoping that would work," he said. Derivan patted him gently on the back.

"[**Manaburn**] worked before, didn't it?" Sev suggested.

"On the *chains*, and it spread through them all. I don't want to actually set this place on fire," Vex said with a grimace. "Aurum's still trapped in most of those webs, and I don't know if it'll hurt him."

"We can't run through every single one of these webs," Misa said. "If we go down there, we're going to be as trapped as Aurum is."

"There is what you are holding," Derivan said. "The spark that we retrieved from the dungeon. It was able to preserve the village in some way—prevent its full dissolution, yes? Perhaps it can serve another purpose here."

He paused, looking around. "Even if we are able to remove these webs . . . we do not know how to return Aurum to his plane. It is not a true solution. Nor do we know how to preserve your village, Misa, so that we can return to the dungeon without them being destroyed.

"We also don't know how to *use* this," Misa said, lifting up the spark to look at it.

She paused. The rest of them did, too, staring at what was in her hands.

It was pulsing with a golden light.

CHAPTER 44

HINTS TOWARD AN ANSWER

Misa stared at the spark for a moment, nonplussed and unsure what to do. Part of her almost instinctively searched for a system notification to explain what was happening—but there was nothing. Just the gentle pulsing of the spark in her hand. There was no hint from [**Guardian's Premonition**], either; her village felt . . . safe. At least for the time being.

"Um . . . do we know what it's doing?" Vex's tail swished nervously behind him.

"Nope," Misa said. "No notifications, either. It's just . . . glowing."

"What did you do with it before?" Sev asked.

"I just . . . remembered my village." Misa's voice went soft for a moment. "Not as they were when they . . . when the dungeon break happened. Before that. I remembered what we were. What we should have been."

The glow pulsed brighter. And there was *wind*, Misa realized suddenly; wind that hadn't been there before. Or something that seemed very much like wind, in any case. The prismatic cobwebs they were surrounded by were all swaying, like they were being pulled by some unseen force.

Misa shifted the spark experimentally, stepping to the left. The movement of the webs followed her.

"It's . . . drawing in the webs?" she said hesitantly.

<ERROR>
B-63 ####### #####R integrity failing. Conflict detected. Calling for administrator assistance . . .
<ERROR>
Unable to contact administrator. No fallback mechanisms found.

> **Unable to compensate.**
> **<WARNING>**
> **B-63 ####### #####R integrity is at 97%.**

"That's not ominous at all," Misa muttered. She glanced to her companions. "You guys can see those too, right?"

"Yup," Sev said.

"Definitely," Vex added, staring at them a little wide-eyed.

"They are rather concerning," Derivan agreed.

"Glad it's not just me," Misa muttered, and then she glanced away from the spark and back toward Aurum. "Hey, um . . . Aurum. Are you doing all right?"

There was no answer. The god curled in tighter on himself, if anything, and refused to give a response. Misa grimaced slightly—he'd wanted any form of companionship just a few moments before—but she understood. She remembered where she'd been just after she'd lost her village; this wasn't exactly the same thing, but if Aurum was as much of a child as he seemed . . .

"We have to try something," Sev said softly, and Misa nodded.

"Even if we left now," she said out loud—more to convince herself than anything, it seemed—"we'd be stuck in the bonus room. We can't keep ourselves in there forever. We came in here to get answers, and so far, all we've gotten is more questions . . ."

"We need a lead," Vex said. "And I think we might have to take a risk here. Just . . . slowly."

"If there is a problem, I can get us out of here quickly," Derivan said.

Misa finally nodded. But it was still with some trepidation that she reached out with the spark she was holding, and let the corner of the closest prismatic web touch the very edges of it—

—the pull that was drawing in all the broken fragments of color suddenly became much, much stronger.

It was strong enough that Misa felt herself getting dragged forward, even though she wasn't holding a particularly tight grip on the spark; Sev, Derivan, and Vex were all resisting a pull of some kind, too, although it seemed to be strongest on her. But she couldn't spare a thought for them, because she was suddenly filled with the impression that she couldn't stop this even if she tried; that this would have happened the moment the spark began to glow.

No. Before that. The moment she had synchronized with it and that notification had popped up. The moment she'd used it to save her family and everyone in her old town.

She didn't regret a second of it. She had no damn idea what was happening, but she still glared up into the wind-that-wasn't-wind.

"Bring it on," she whispered.

Those words, too, were lost to the wind.

X-51 ####### #####R synchronization has reached 75%!
<WARNING>
B-63 ####### #####R integrity is at 72%.
<NOTICE>
X-51 ####### #####R integrity is at 29%.

There was a rush of those webs being drawn into the [#####R] she was holding, the glow growing brighter and brighter with every web that got sucked in. She got the impression that the spark was growing *smaller*, too—not that it was getting weaker, but that it was getting more compressed. It was starting to feel heavier, with every web that was drawn in—

"Guys?" Aurum's voice suddenly cut through the wind. It didn't die down, exactly; the wind was as strong as ever, and every web was still being pulled in with tremendous force. The sticky panels of prismatic light on Aurum were pulling away, though, peeling off and starting to soar through the air toward the spark. "What's—what's happening?"

"It'll be okay!" Misa called out, gritting her teeth. "Don't worry! We're going to get you out of here!"

Aurum looked up from where he'd curled up into himself. His frame seemed terribly small, for all that he was an enormous figure in the distance, and his voice echoed with a tiny hope. "Really?"

"Of course!" Misa shouted back. It was with a confidence she didn't really feel. But Aurum seemed to be able to move more freely now, so whatever was happening . . . it seemed to be a good thing.

She *hoped* it was a good thing.

The webs kept getting pulled in, and the notifications piled up; she dismissed the ones that all functionally said the same thing. B-63's integrity was failing, whatever that meant, and X-51's integrity was going up. Whatever *that* meant. Evacuation notices came and went, but all she knew was that X-51 was the shard she was holding on to, and that perhaps its being repaired was a good thing—

<WARNING>
B-63 ####### #####R integrity is at 5%! Sapients detected within B-63 boundaries. Initiating emergency evacuation and connecting all functional nodes to nearest ######## #####R.

The pull abruptly stopped. The spark in her hand shone with a light so bright that it was nearly impossible for her to look at it—it blazed like a tiny sun in her hands, and she had to force herself to look away. She knew without looking that whatever had just happened had repaired it.

She also knew that something was happening to the very fabric of the space they were standing in.

Derivan shouted something, but she couldn't hear what he said; it was like her ears were filled with water. Vex's eyes were wide, and he was cutting runes rapidly into the air, like he was trying to protect them against something. Sev's eyes were narrowed in concentration, and a divine glow was rising up around them, like he was healing them with everything he had.

Misa tried to block. She didn't know what was happening, but if her friends were reacting this way, then there had to be something she could block, right?

But nothing happened.

She didn't know why she was having so much trouble processing everything, either. But she watched, feeling like she was moving in slow motion, as Vex cast not a shield but a *platform*, and Derivan ran down to grab just the edge of Aurum's robes; she saw Sev's magic encase all of them in separate, individual bubbles.

She saw black, all-encompassing cracks suddenly spiderweb through space, sparing only anything the four of them touched.

No reaction from [**Guardian's Premonition**], though. She only hoped it meant her village was safe.

—◆◆—

Misa was . . . somewhere.

Or perhaps she was nowhere.

Her friends were with her; she knew that much. She couldn't see them, but she felt their presence. One of them was anxiously coiled, another firm and steady, and the last one nervous but unafraid.

Someone spoke. They spoke in worried tones of gravel and granite, of roughly hewn rock shaped into perfection. "You shouldn't be here," the voice told them. "You aren't ready for this. How did you . . . Oh, no."

"Another piece has been lost," a softer, quieter voice said. This one spoke with tones of falling water and refracted light. "They cannot see yet. They aren't ready."

"Can you remember?" the first voice spoke to them. "You must try. The answers cannot be given to you, for those answers are already gone, and recently; you can only feel the shape of the holes they left behind. We had hoped things would be different in this pocket . . . that a piece of what *was* would help you find what used to be. But it does not seem to have worked."

Misa was silent. She had no answer.

Sev was less silent.

"Onyx, is that you?" the cleric's incredulous voice echoed in the not-space of wherever the fuck they were. The words were like a jolt to her psyche; she felt herself *return*, her mind pulled back from the strangely dissociated space she'd found herself in. "You know I hate it when you're cryptic. Just *tell* us."

"I—I literally cannot do that," Onyx said, and he sounded like he'd been caught off guard, along with some combination of exasperation and amusement. Maybe a touch of fondness, along with a hint of sadness. "I have tried. Three times."

"You have?" Sev asked, sounding confused. And then, perhaps a little less confused: "I thought I'd need to rescue you. Are you okay . . . here? Wherever here is?"

"I am still in need of rescue, alas," Onyx said, a touch of dryness entering his tone. "But you have time to rescue me yet. Do not worry yourself about me overmuch. I know the sight of me must have been worrying, and I apologize, for there was little I could do . . ."

"Onyx, if you apologize because someone else chained you up, I'm going to find a way to save you just so I can beat you in chess."

"You have never beaten me in chess."

"*That's* the part you find unbelievable?"

"Have you seen what you and your team have been doing lately?" Onyx's voice slid back into that amused fondness.

"Enough of this," the second voice cut in—the one that sounded like waterfalls and light. "We don't have time for this banter. They can't stay here long. They need to go back."

"Um . . . how do we do that?" Vex's voice spoke up, this time, sounding timid.

"Your friend just has to wish for it," Onyx told them.

"Me?" Misa asked hesitantly.

"No," Onyx said, and he gestured to the steady presence that was Derivan. The gesture was more of a feeling than anything physical. "You. Shift."

". . . Ah," Derivan said quietly. He sounded distracted, but his voice sharpened a moment later. "There is nothing more you can tell us?"

"Nothing more," Onyx said.

"We will come back for you," Derivan said, his voice sincere. He focused for a moment, or he gave off the impression that he was. And then there was a sharp *pulse*—

—and they were staring at the night sky. The moon hung in the air amid the void, staring at them in a way that was almost accusatory.

The dungeon was gone. The research team was in the distance, and there were sounds of shouting and panic filling the air.

In front of them, a long string of notifications piled quickly, one over the other, almost too quick to read.

More important than anything else for Misa, though, were the dozens of people just behind them. She'd scarcely had the time to notice them at all before Orkas and Charise both burst through the crowd and grabbed her in a great hug.

And for a small, infinitely valuable moment, nothing else mattered.

CHAPTER 45

AFTERMATH

For all that everything seemed to be fine for the time being, there were a *lot* of things that needed the adventurers' immediate attention.

The first were the system notifications. Several of them were just strings of errors, but a number of them were distinctly ominous.

<ERROR>
B-63 ####### #####R integrity has failed. Unable to sustain local dungeon. Examining dungeon contents . . .

Dungeon contents cannot be erased. Remaining R-fragments have been redistributed to all three Major A#####s. All system users will be notified of this change.

Local parameters that were previously reliant on B-63 R###### ###### have been attached to the closest available ######.

<WARNING>
X-51 ####### #####R has no attached processing node. It will not be able to permanently sustain B-63. Estimated degradation: 5 months, 12 days.

Additionally, several local sapients were found to have no synced backup on nearby ####### ######s. These sapients will be reverted to the nearest backup if X-51 ####### #####R completely degrades.

The last warning made Misa flinch—she didn't need to know what the missing words were to understand what that meant, though there were certainly *implications* that she'd have to discuss with the others when they had a moment to sit down and talk.

But the implication that her village was on limited time, even after what they'd gone through to save them . . . that left a cold chill in her heart. She glanced back at the rest of the villagers, seeing a number of them staring in concern at what was presumably the same warning.

Strangely, Orkas and Charise were the ones that didn't seem concerned at all. They glanced at the notification, then seemed to scoff.

"Don't worry about us," Charise said before Misa could find the words she wanted to say. She gave her daughter a smile. "A timer isn't a death sentence, and you don't need to solve every problem we run into. You've given us a chance, and I promise you we're going to use it."

"You defied the odds once," Orkas added, his voice a low rumble. Then he glanced back at the much more worried-looking villagers and raised his voice so they could all hear him—or perhaps he simply used a skill. "And now *we* will defy the odds. Misa has already shown us what we can do. It's time we figure out how the system *really* works and break the hold it has on us."

The cheer that started up was small at first. But it *grew*, and what caught Misa's attention was that it wasn't her father that they were looking at when they cheered.

They were looking at *her*.

There was a fire in their hearts that had been sparked by Orkas's words, but the fuel that kept it burning was what she'd shown them they could do.

She wasn't sure it had completely settled into her heart that her family was alive again. They'd been gone for so long, and she'd only just begun to accept she wouldn't see them again—and yet here they were, and there were still so many questions about how all of this could be *possible* . . .

"We should go check out what's going on over in the research camp," Misa finally said, though her words were still hesitant. There was nothing she wanted to do more than spend more time with her family now that the immediate crisis was over—but there were a few more notifications hovering at the edge of her vision that she hadn't focused on yet. Rewards for the bonus room, most likely. The shouting was getting intense, though, and while it wasn't necessarily their *job* to head off trouble, she still felt she owed them that much.

"Before we do that," Vex hesitated, glancing at the spark Misa was holding, "I don't think I've read any records of dungeon delves that talk about this. Elyra would love to do some research on it, but . . ."

He glanced up in the direction of the research camp, then frowned. "It's up to you," he finally said. "Elyra has a lot of resources they can pour into researching that thing, but their priority isn't saving lives. I would hide it. We can always give it to them later."

Misa glanced at Vex for a moment, then at her parents. Slowly, she nodded, and pocketed the spark. The shouting in the camp was getting louder, and there were ripples coming from it, that felt like the activation of strong skills—

"The *delvers*," Misa cursed. They weren't with them, and if they weren't with them, then they'd landed back in the middle of the research camp; the researchers themselves knew about what had happened, but the guards—

—and there was the fact that the head researcher—*Kestel?*—had stopped talking to them, and the damn telepathy had cut off—

They'd assumed it was a matter of being transported to the bonus room, but they were no longer so sure that was the cause, as more of the research camp came into view.

The research team was split into two groups. One group surrounded what looked to be Kestel, though it was difficult to be sure; there was a figure lying prone on the ground and a small group of researchers that had arrayed themselves protectively around him. They each looked nervous, and the glow of skills lit up their hands.

The second group of researchers, meanwhile, were standing safely behind the guards and exhibiting no small amount of hostility. They were practically glaring in Kestel's direction.

"Shit, this doesn't look good," Sev muttered. He raised his voice slightly, interjecting just as one of the guards looked to be about to start shouting again. "What's going on here?"

The guard that had been about to speak froze, hand twitching to his blade before recognizing who it was that had spoken. "You four," he said, narrowing his eyes slightly at them.

"...Yes?" Sev paused after the guard didn't continue, staring at him. "Congratulations on counting?"

The guard's hand tightened on the hilt of his sword, clearly not appreciating the joke. "Step away. The situation is complicated enough as it is."

"It wouldn't *be* complicated if you just let us fuckin' *explain*," the captain—Harold—snapped.

"Don't listen to him," one of the researchers standing behind the guards said. "We need to take them in for questioning."

And then they started talking over one another, raising their voices at one another until they were once again shouting. The adventurers exchanged glances—none of this was going anywhere. Vex cast a quick spell, flickering a rune over the tip of his dagger, and Misa spoke into it.

"Shut the fuck up," she said.

For all that she spoke at a normal volume, the sound echoed loud enough to make all three groups in front of them flinch and fall silent. Misa glared at them *hard*. "This isn't going anywhere," she said. "One at a damn time."

"And what gives you the right—" one of the researchers began indignantly, but stopped when Misa turned her glare on him.

"Guards first," she said. "What happened here?"

The guard that had initially told them to step back scowled but answered the question anyway, having clearly realized that their own approach wasn't going anywhere. "There was an altercation among the researchers," the guard said. "This group here said Kestel betrayed Elyra."

"He didn't betray shit!" a human woman shouted. She was one of the researchers standing next to Kestel protectively. "He just wanted to figure out what happened *before* reporting everything back to Elyra!"

"*One at a time,*" Misa repeated, though her voice softened a little when she looked over at the woman—she looked frightened but determined. The weapon she was holding was barely a weapon at all, just a dinky little knife she clearly kept more as a keepsake than for fighting. "Why would that be a betrayal?"

"Because we need to report anything that happens to *them*." It was the same researcher that was standing behind the guards that spoke—a lizardkin sporting a dangerous-looking crossbow, though he wasn't holding it correctly. He jerked his head toward the delvers, and Misa was fairly certain that if Harold had still been able to scowl, he would have. "House Varil will have our heads if we don't."

"Okay. I don't know what any of that means." Misa paused for a second, then looked at Harold. "It doesn't explain what happened to Kestel."

"He was trying to stop us from reporting it, so we had to stop him," the lizardkin sniffed. Misa narrowed her eyes dangerously, then turned to Harold.

"I take it you know why this is such a big deal?" she asked.

The skeletal figure of the delver team's captain didn't respond for a moment. He stared at the guards long enough to make the researchers there shift awkwardly, self-consciously. Ixiss was the one that responded, stepping up beside his captain to give the answer.

"House Varil is in charge of producing many of the soldiers and elite combat teams in Elyra," he answered shortly. "They produce fighters that are *obedient*. They just don't tell anyone how they do it."

"I'm not liking the sound of that," Sev muttered.

"Not many people do, so they just don't ask questions. Out of sight, out of mind," Iliss said, stepping up next to her brother. "It's usually too late for most of us once we figure out what's going on. It's not mind control or anything fancy like that; it's just . . . emotional suppression. We're not allowed to *feel*."

Iliss shook her head, shuddering slightly at an invisible memory. "Whatever you did back there broke the enchantment slightly. It's degrading now." She nodded at Misa. "'S'why we're grateful to you, even if we're stuck like . . . this."

"That and the saving-our-lives part," Ixiss added.

"We kinda helped save you guys back, though, so I figure we're even on that front," Iliss said. Misa managed a small grin at that.

"If ya report us to House Varil," Harold said—the captain was finally speaking up, stepping forward with a heavy weight to his voice. Even without eyes, his gaze was very firmly on the researchers that seemed determined to report him and his team, and the guards took a subconscious step back. "They'll come back for us. And I don't know about y'all, but I ain't going back to them."

"That's *exactly* why we need to report this," the researcher that had been arguing for this hissed back. "If you don't get punished, we will. The Houses come down hard on anything they think is a risk, and this undermines their authority. Even if we didn't say anything, they'd *know*, because they track every one of their soldiers. They'll be able to tell when you don't come back, and they'll know that *we helped you*."

"Not if you just say we're dead," the captain said, staring firmly at the researcher. "Varil doesn't need to know a damn thing. Tell 'em we all died in action. For all intents and purposes, we *did*. We ain't gonna be soldiers of Elyra anymore."

There was still tension in the air—but even the guards seemed a bit uncertain now. The activities of noble houses seemed a bit above their pay grade, but the explanation they were being given was certainly damning.

"Kestel was trying to protect you?" Sev asked, glancing at Harold. The captain shrugged.

"Honestly, knowing him, it's a mixture of wantin' to protect us and wantin' to do research on us," he answered bluntly. "He ain't a bad man, but he's very focused on the learnin'. Can't say I get it, but he tries to do right by us, and I'm a mite pissed that he got hurt in all this."

The researchers were whispering among themselves, and even the guards looked uncertain. The one lizardkin man was still arguing very much in favor of telling Elyra—and considering all it would take was a simple discreet message through the system . . .

"They're not going to be able to keep this secret forever," Vex said quietly. "But I think if we can get the Guild to take them in, they'll be okay. At the very least, House Varil will have a lot more trouble attacking adventurers."

"I think we can swing that," Sev said, glancing at the guards and researchers. The ones standing around Kestel were still looking around suspiciously, but they at least seemed a little calmer now. All of them were clearly in need of healing, though. "But also, I'm not going to wait for them to figure out what they want to do. I know where I stand here. I'm going to go make sure Kestel's okay, and then we're taking everyone back to the Guild so we can figure out what happened to the dungeon."

CHAPTER 46

HEALTH AND HEALING

For the umpteenth time, Sev glanced at the notifications hovering at the corner of his eye, even as he stormed closer toward Kestel. The researchers flinched back at his approach but calmed when they saw his robes and the focus he wore around his neck; he was clearly a cleric.

The notification was distracting and persistent, though. He'd been doing his best to ignore it, with everything else that was going on, but . . .

<WARNING>
No ######s are available for Coalesced Entity <Aurum, God of Gold> to attach to.

Potential substitute found. Allow attachment of <Aurum, God of Gold>?

ACCEPT / REJECT

Sev's memories of what happened while they were in that not-space were still fuzzy, and while they were slowly becoming clearer, there was too much happening for him to focus on. So he focused his attention on who needed him, instead, promising himself he'd look at it more closely later, when he could discuss what had happened with his team.

And as he approached Kestel and the researchers surrounding him, he realized they were more badly hurt than had been apparent. It wasn't just their health—they had status effects on them that were still ticking away, no doubt from whoever had cast the spells on them in the first place. Sev couldn't tell what those status effects *were*—not without casting diagnostic spells—but he could tell that they were *there*. His eyes narrowed.

"Hey!" he shouted, and when everyone turned their attention to him, he glared. "Turn off your damn spells. We're not fighting anymore."

"That's not for you to decide," the one lizardkin researcher muttered, his gaze still hostile—but one of the nearby guards glared at him, and he flinched. He didn't seem quite as brave without the guards on his side. A quick twist of his wrist, and the researchers Sev was near sagged with relief.

"Please," one of them said—a young man, by all accounts. He barely looked eighteen. Sev glanced at him, ready to heal, but he shook his head and pointed to Kestel instead. "Help Kestel. We don't even know if he's . . ."

Sev glanced over at Kestel and winced.

The man was dead.

Well, no. Not *completely*. But he was out of health, and the system had stopped his heart, a consequence of its nature; if health was the barrier that kept people in perfect health until their last hit point, then running out of health meant . . .

Well.

Sitting on top of Kestel's chest was a small artifact, pulsing and whirring. Two interlocking bronze and silver rings rotated gently around a grade-two mana crystal at its core, and from those rings, three slithering lines of visible mana anchored themselves to Kestel's chest. Sev recognized it; it was a [**Resuscitator**], an artifact meant to preserve the life of someone that had hit zero health, in the same way that cleric skills like [**Gentle Repose**] did. It would force Kestel's heart to keep pumping, keeping his blood circulating, but . . .

That only solved half the problem. The other half was oxygen.

And there was the fact that as long as Kestel remained "dead," in that his heart wasn't pumping of its own volition, the system wouldn't connect to him, and basic healing skills would have minimal effect. There was already the telltale blue, veinlike effect across his scales that spoke of system sickness.

Not for the first time, Sev cursed his connection to the system. If he had skills that worked the way Derivan's skills did—if he could just work *around* the health problem instead of being forced to work with it . . .

But there was no time to waste on idle thoughts.

"Vex?" Sev called, and the lizardkin scurried over. "I need a basic wind spell. Something to keep air moving in and out of his lungs."

Vex nodded. Soon enough, a light green rune glowed over Kestel's slack jaw, and air started circulating in and out of his lungs. It wasn't the most ideal way to do things, but it would have to do for now. "How long has Kestel been like this?" Sev asked.

"A little more than half an hour," one of the researchers answered him, looking anxious. "Is—is he okay?"

No he fucking isn't, Sev thought, but he kept that thought to himself; he kept his voice under control when he replied. "He will be."

Healing magic was miraculous, but it couldn't do everything. There was a reason it had taken so many priests to prevent him from dying, back when he'd collapsed in the temple—the system didn't like that people could circumvent the whole *zero health* thing. It took a lot of healing spells and powerful healing magic; he had [**Divine Inhalation**], but . . .

He glanced at the skill box again, summoning it out of the air. It wasn't a spell he liked using.

[**Divine Inhalation**] [**Active Skill**] [**Grade: Maxed**]
Granted by request. Take in injuries, absorbing them into your psyche. Inhalation limit based on available memory.

He would have called it a cruel skill, were it not for the fact that Onyx had specifically withheld it from him. "Heal anything" was an ability he wanted— of *course* it was—and this was the closest skill that came to it. The associated cost, as far as he was concerned, was nothing.

Then again, that was how he'd gotten [**Traces of the Lost**] to begin with. A class based around sacrifice shouldn't have surprised him, given what he'd been doing with it.

But if ordinary healing skills wouldn't work . . .

"[**Divine Inhalation**]," he muttered; not because he had to speak the name of the skill out loud, but because it helped prepare him for the experience.

No matter how much he prepared himself, though, he could never quite be ready.

The skill activated, and he felt what happened more than he saw it.

The first time, in the temple, when his heart had stopped—he'd been thankfully unconscious for most of that experience. Now he couldn't help but be *aware*, every facet of the experience embedding itself deep into his memory. He felt everything that Kestel would have felt had the lizardkin been awake at this exact moment, multiplied tenfold.

He felt the way his heart refused to beat on its own.

He felt magic threading itself into him like a foreign implement, forcing his heart to pulse, to send blood circulating through his body.

He felt the bitter grasp of death approach him as dark, cold magic threaded its way through his veins. There was a sense of betrayal, and a sense of . . . anger? Protectiveness. What Kestel had felt in the moments before he'd been attacked, perhaps; Sev had never exactly been clear on how this particular skill worked, especially for injuries such as these.

The skill ended, and he gasped for air, bending over—and he wasn't the only one.

For now, though, his mind was still half-focused on that experience of *death*, of being dead, and of having nothing but an artifact supporting his continued existence; it sat in his mind, refusing to dislodge itself, and *fuck* but he'd forgotten how bad this felt.

When he'd cast it on Onyx to try to heal him, while the god was still in his chains . . . he'd felt something similar. But it hadn't been anything this bad, perhaps because whatever had been done to Onyx was outside the scope of mortal experiences; whatever had happened to him, whatever he'd absorbed, he hadn't quite understood.

"W . . . what's happening?" Kestel spoke in a voice that lacked its usual exuberance; the lizardkin spoke with a slight waver in his voice and a tremble in his frame. He looked around with bleary eyes, and Sev grimaced. Never good signs after a revival like this.

"Hey. It's Sev. Take it easy. You got hit pretty hard back there." Sev kept his voice low and even, gesturing for the other researchers to give him space—they'd crowded around Kestel in relief, which was understandable but patently unhelpful. Vex had cut off the wind spell almost as soon as the other lizardkin started breathing, and he'd taken a few steps back; it wasn't the first time Sev had helped someone that had "died," though the circumstances were never really quite so . . . extreme. "Are you doing okay?"

"I . . . I don't know." Kestel shook his head, still seeming disoriented. He blinked a few times, then stared at something in the air, frowning; the blue veins were retreating, at least, so he was reconnected to the system. Probably some notifications. Sev fired off a few quick, lower-power heals at the man, bringing his health back to full anyway. Just in case. Kestel didn't react; he just continued staring at the air in front of him.

"Take your time," Sev said to him gently, then glanced around at the other researchers. "I don't want to keep him here. We should bring him back to the Guild, if possible; there are more priests there, and they'll be better at diagnosing the full suite of status effects he might have. Recovering from this kind of thing isn't easy."

"You can't heal him yourself?" one of the researchers asked, perhaps a bit timidly, and Sev hesitated.

The easy answer was no, he couldn't.

The more complicated answer was that he *could*, perhaps, but [**Divine Inhalation**] was not a skill he could use on mental status effects, and the other class skills from [**Traces of the Lost**] would demand a greater sacrifice from him. Some crucial aspect of who he was, perhaps, or yet another treasured memory.

"No," he finally said. "Status effects aren't really my specialty. Other priests will be able to do it better than I can. We'll get Kestel the help he needs; don't worry." Sev tried to offer the researcher a reassuring smile—he was the young man that had spoken earlier—but that lizardkin that was hanging around the guards spoke up again.

This time, at least, he sounded a *little* guilty. Though not very. "We should bring him back to Elyra. We have better medical facilities there."

"Elyra is *much* further away, and unless you have a teleport circle handy, it's going to take too long for us to get him there." Sev kept his temper under control, if only barely. The other thing was that Sev simply didn't trust Elyra with this—not after what he'd just heard about how House Varil handled their people. "The Guild is closer, and the temple's priests are good at what they do. We're taking him back to the Guild."

The Guild *also* had more adventurers, and they'd hopefully be willing to help with the situation. They'd need a few guards to prevent anything from blowing up . . .

"If you're going to the Guild, then *we're* going back to Elyra," the lizardkin spat at him, and Sev just stared.

"Okay," he said plainly.

That would solve a lot of problems, actually. He wouldn't have to worry about the Guild housing all of those researchers on top of the villagers, the delvers, and Kestel's little group. And there'd be less of a chance of a fight breaking out.

"Bye?" he tried adding. The lizardkin just stared at him, looking vaguely infuriated, and then stormed off back toward the camp, muttering something about packing. Sev shook his head, turning his attention back to Kestel; the lizardkin still looked a little lost and was staring listlessly into the air.

"Hey," he said gently. "Do you think you can walk?"

Mutely, Kestel shook his head.

"All right. We'll carry you." Sev glanced around—Misa and Derivan had approached and were standing by Vex, a respectful distance away; the remaining researchers on Kestel's side were watching with worry, and one or two of the guards had decided to stay instead of accompanying the rest back to Elyra.

Okay. That could work.

It was a *far* larger troupe than he was used to leading, though.

"Let's get back to the Guild," he said. He glanced at the notification that was still in the corner of his vision.

Was it just him, or was it glowing just a little more urgently?

CHAPTER 47

OF GODS AND ######S

They were leading the way back toward the Guild. They'd tried to get Kestel to tell them about whatever status effect he had, but the lizardkin seemed incredibly reluctant to talk about it, and Sev didn't push the matter. There was the small matter of the *entire village* that they'd brought with them, too, but the delvers were in on it, and the few researchers that joined them seemed too frazzled and worried about Kestel to question it too much.

Yet, anyway.

The group was much larger than they were used to, though, and Sev couldn't help but keep glancing back, worried that—today of all days—they would be attacked. Monster attacks in the wild weren't necessarily *uncommon*, but this particular route should have been cleared many times over, considering how close to the Guild it was. It wouldn't have surprised him if this was the one time they got attacked, though.

They'd be fine, he told himself. Orkas was more than capable of handling a large group through a journey, and the delvers had dispersed themselves throughout the villagers to try to help in case of an ambush. The researchers were huddled up near the front, anxiously hovering around Kestel, who was lying down in a makeshift stretcher and not really saying much of anything.

Sev had asked Misa, Derivan, and Vex to come with him off to the side— they needed to discuss everything that had happened, and now seemed as good a time as any. Maybe more, because that notification was *definitely* flashing more urgently at him. Oops.

"I've got a notification about Aurum," Sev said quickly, and Misa immediately paled.

"Oh, *shit*. I fucking forgot—there was so much happening—is he okay?" she demanded.

"I don't know. I think he's fine *for now*, but I have a notification about how he doesn't have anything to attach to." Sev nodded toward the spark Misa was keeping in her pouch. "The text doesn't appear correctly in the system, but I'm guessing he needs one of those."

"He can't attach to this one?" Misa asked worriedly.

"Doesn't seem like it. Can't say I know why." Sev frowned, glancing at the notification again, then sending a copy to his friends to look over. "It's asking me if I'll let him attach to *me* instead, and I just wanted to talk to you guys about it first. It might be dangerous, so you'd need to be ready, but . . ."

"It might also be his only option," Vex said quietly.

"It is your choice, ultimately," Derivan said, glancing over the notification. "It sounds as if it may affect you the most, if it is asking to attach to you. But I believe Vex is right—if it is his only option, then he is our responsibility."

". . . I'm leaning toward yes," Sev said. "I mean—fuck. He really did seem like a kid, and I don't know what's going on with him now, but if what happened at the end there is any indication . . ."

"Shitty fucking system," Misa muttered, then nodded to Sev. "I'm ready if anything happens. Go for it."

Sev nodded. He hit the Accept on the notification, and paused as the text flickered.

Processing . . .

". . . Okay. It says it's processing," Sev said, feeling vaguely disappointed. He'd been expecting something more dramatic to happen. Maybe it'd happen later?

"Should've expected that," Misa grumbled. "Like I said. Shitty system. While we're at it, though . . ." Misa gestured at where she was keeping the spark. "What the fuck *is* this thing? The system's not displaying the text correctly for any of you, is it?"

"It is not," Derivan said. "Though the text has been changing every so often."

"I've noticed that too," Vex said with a frown. "If something's trying to hide the words from us, it's not doing it very well. We've seen a few different letters already. First word starts with an R and ends with a Y, second word starts with an A and ends in an R."

"You were paying attention?" Misa blinked at the lizardkin. "There was . . . a lot of shit going down. I didn't really note them down."

"I like puzzles," Vex answered with a slightly embarrassed shrug and grin. "There's not a lot of words that make sense as the first one. I think **reality** makes the most sense, given what it's doing. The second . . ."

"There's a few that would work, I think," Sev said. "Uh . . . Author? Avatar?"

"Abuser," Misa suggested with a smirk. "*Reality Abuser* would fit."

"That feels a little on the nose," Vex said with a chuckle.

"Anchor, perhaps?" Derivan suggested. "[**X-51 Reality Anchor**] would make a certain amount of sense—"

Derivan paused as he spoke, feeling a strange reverberation echo through his armor as he spoke the words, like they had some sort of significance. He looked at his friends carefully, worried that yet another infolock had come into play—but they all seemed to have registered what he'd said just fine.

"[**X-51 Reality Anchor**] . . ." Vex tested out the words, frowning. "I guess that's . . . right? Based on what the system is doing to the words? But I dunno what that means. That term hasn't come up in Elyra's research into dungeons before."

"What would a reality anchor do?" Sev asked. "Theoretically."

"Anchor reality, based on the name," Vex said with a half-grin, making Sev frown at him. He chuckled, then shrugged. "I don't know, but it'd explain some of the notifications we got. And maybe what happened to the dungeon? If every dungeon has one of those . . ."

"Perhaps the dungeon collapsed because the anchor that was holding it in place was broken," Derivan suggested. "But we do not know what the anchors *do*, precisely, only that your villagers are now tied to it in some way."

Vex shook his head. "Let's go back to the beginning and go over what we know. We can throw out ideas once we're all on the same page, and we can make sure we all have the same information. What did you *see* when we first found the reality anchor?"

"It was sitting on a pedestal of crystal," Misa said. "It was glowing, and there was a stream of light going from it into one of those specks of light in the void. Uh . . . I don't know how to explain it, but it felt like the light led to J'rokksur? Or a version of it."

"There was a notification about how the reality anchor was failing," Sev offered. "Something about low integrity, and destabilization."

"The dungeon that that anchor was attached to was destabilizing, and that led to a dungeon break," Vex theorized. "Good enough for a starting theory, I think?"

"There's more," Misa said. She shook her head slightly—even now, the memories of what she'd seen were unpleasant. "You saw what happened with my family getting hurt. Those were the same injuries they had . . . the first time."

She grimaced a little, muttering to herself. "Fucking system," she said. "Or anchor. Whatever."

The others winced in sympathy. They'd seen the injuries, but they hadn't known the cause, and certainly hadn't known that the people in J'rokksur were re-experiencing the injuries that had killed them.

"You healed them later, right?" Sev asked. "I managed to keep them stable with my healing, but it wasn't what did most of the work. How did you manage to reverse the effect?"

"[**Guardian's Premonition**]," Misa answered. "It kind of . . . guided me, I guess, into using the anchor? I focused on my memories of the village when it was still alive and well . . ."

She fell silent for a moment.

"I am sorry so much of this made you relive your past," Derivan said, his voice sympathetic. Misa sighed, not replying for a moment—then forced herself to exhale in a laugh.

"I mean, it ended better than I could've fuckin' hoped," she said, forcing herself to smile. "Yeah, some of that was kinda shitty, and I'm going to have some nightmares. I don't give a shit. I'll talk to the Guild therapist if you guys make me. But I have my family back again, and that's . . ."

"Far more important?" Sev offered.

"*So* much more," Misa said, shaking her head. "Then there was a message about how I 'synchronized' with the anchor, and that seemed to sort of . . . heal people. Or reverse their injuries. I dunno."

"We might have to talk to your parents a bit more for that one," Sev said. "Find out what it felt like on their end."

"So they're [**Reality Anchor**]s and you can synchronize with them," Vex said. "Presumably, X-51 is linked to your village in some way, and synchronizing with it somehow damaged the B-63 anchor. No two coexisting anchors, or something like that?"

"Something like that," Sev agreed. "Obviously they manipulate reality in some way . . . maybe they anchor dungeons, let them have all the strange effects."

"It would not explain the people of J'rokksur," Derivan said, and they fell silent at that. Misa in particular seemed to be lost in thought for a moment, prompting Sev to look at her.

"You're going to want to spend some time with your family, right?" he asked quietly.

"I mean, of course," Misa snorted. Then she glared at him. "Don't think you fuckers have gotten rid of me, though. Just because I have 'em back doesn't mean I want to stay put with them. We gotta figure out this anchor thing, make sure we fix it in time for them, and we gotta figure out a bunch of other stuff, too. Like the guy who attacked the delvers in that dungeon."

Sev smiled a bit as she started to speak, but he frowned when she mentioned the man in the dungeon. "I almost forgot about him."

Misa snorted. "I fuckin' didn't."

"Are we sure he's still around?" Vex asked. "I mean, if the dungeon got destroyed . . ."

"But it didn't," Misa pointed out. "The notification said the dungeon's been *redistributed*, whatever the fuck that means."

"To the Major Anchors," Derivan said, reflecting on the then-censored word in the notification; *Anchor* fit perfectly.

"Major Anchors . . ." Vex mused out loud. ". . . That's got to be the Kingdom dungeons, right?"

Sev paused. "Now that you mention it," he said. "They're the biggest dungeons we know of, and there are three of them."

"The dungeons on the Outskirts are bigger," Misa pointed out.

"But those ones are *broken*," Sev said, shaking his head. "If we're right about reality anchors, then dungeon breaks happen when those anchors start to fail. Those dungeons wouldn't have working anchors anymore. The largest functioning anchors would have to be the ones in each of the Prime Kingdoms."

"We did not get a dungeon break here, though," Derivan said.

"The anchor was broken suddenly," Sev said. "With the J'rokksur dungeon, the anchor was failing, but it wasn't broken, and the dungeon break was already happening. So maybe it's just a process that starts when the anchor starts to break . . ."

"We're speculating too much," Vex said with a shake of his head. "We've got some answers but not all of them. The notification said system users would be alerted, so I think we'll know if the Kingdom dungeons are the ones that this dungeon was 'redistributed' to."

"And whoever that was, it's probably best to assume he's not dead," Misa added grimly. "If he was telling the truth, he's been alive for hundreds of years. A small snap in reality probably won't kill him."

"He might even know what's going on," Vex said quietly. He sighed. "We're going to have to get authorization to explore every one of those dungeons, aren't we."

Vex looked, perhaps unsurprisingly, quite reluctant. He hadn't exactly hidden his distaste for Elyra, and the worry he had about it was clear. "And it's probably going to have to be Elyra first, considering everything that happened."

"... Probably," Sev said with a slight wince. "Are you okay with that?"

"If you are not," Derivan said, "we will figure out another solution."

Sev glared at Derivan a little over Vex's head—there *wasn't* another solution, not really. Making promises they couldn't keep wasn't something they were in the habit of doing. Vex seemed vaguely comforted by the words, anyway, and leaned into Derivan as he considered it for a while. The armor didn't seem to mind.

"... I'll have to face it sooner or later, right?" Vex eventually said, his voice quiet. "It's not going to go away. And I'm on a deadline as far as going back to Elyra goes, anyway."

"Do I need to punch someone?" Misa asked. "Because if you need me to punch someone, I am *there*."

Vex laughed slightly at that, unable to help the slight smile that crossed his face. "Yeah, I'm aware," he said, shaking his head. "I don't think punching anyone is going to help in this case.

"Uh ... We might need to kidnap someone, though."

"*Kidnap?*" Misa narrowed her eyes, considering this for a moment, then nodded. "I mean, if you say we need to do it, I'm ready to do crimes."

"We should really be asking more questions," Sev said dryly, but he was notably also not protesting.

"If Vex believes we must do crime, then I am inclined to believe we must do crime," Derivan said without a trace of irony.

Vex couldn't help but laugh outright, the little bit of melancholy he had turning into mirth; what tension he had dissolved out of him.

"You guys have a knack for making me feel like everything's going to be okay," he finally said, smiling a small smile. "Just ... thanks."

CHAPTER 48

REWARDS, PART 1

"Though you wouldn't *actually* kidnap someone without hearing my explanation first, right?" Vex asked, just to be sure.

"Well, no, of course not," Misa said, looking suspiciously willing to do exactly that. She glanced surreptitiously at Sev and Derivan, then leaned into Vex, mock-whispering. "I mean, those two won't, but you just tell me who we need to kidnap—"

"*Misa*," Vex said, laughing as he pushed her away. She grinned at him, sticking her tongue out, and he shook his head with a fond sort of exasperation. "It's a *last resort*, guys; I'm not actually that serious about it. I'm hoping we won't have to, but . . ."

A small shadow crossed his expression, and he shook his head, changing the subject. "Let's figure out everything we can about the reality anchor first, and then when we've gotten the chance to rest a bit, I'll tell you what I can. I . . . need a bit of time to get ready to talk about it, anyway."

"Take your time," Sev said seriously. "We've got plenty of time before we reach Elyra, if we go there by conventional means. And we're going to have to convince the Guildmaster to take care of all the extra people, too . . ."

"J'rokksur can take care of itself," Misa interjected.

"Yes, but they still need the space to do that," Sev said dryly. "I guess they could try to go back to where J'rokksur originally was, to rebuild, but . . ."

". . . Yeah, it's pretty far from here," Misa acknowledged with a slight frown, shaking her head.

"It's not practical for a whole village to travel far, and even if we secure the teleportation magic to get them there, they'd need a protective escort the whole time while they're rebuilding," Sev agreed.

"It's up to Dad, but I don't think he'll spring for that when he could just rebuild nearby," Misa admitted.

Sev nodded. "What I'm saying is we have some time before we actually reach Elyra," he said, glancing back to Vex. "Don't worry too much about telling us everything as soon as possible. Tell us when you're ready."

"Thanks," Vex said. "I'll, uh. Try to be ready before we actually reach Elyra."

"That would be ideal, yes," Sev said with a chuckle. "As for the reality anchors . . . I feel like we've gone through just about everything we know. Presumably they're related to why dungeons are able to do everything they do, and there's clearly a link to the gods in some way . . ."

"We still don't know *how* they do all that," Misa said with a frown. "It's some fucked-up shit. And what did it mean when it said *backups*?"

"Perhaps reality anchors keep a record of some sort," Derivan suggested. "It would explain . . ."

He trailed off before he finished speaking. It would explain how the dungeon was able to revive J'rokksur wholesale—but it brought up other questions as well. Misa seemed to understand, given the way her eyes darkened slightly, but she didn't say anything.

"What I don't understand is *why*," Vex said, changing the subject. "Reality anchors are obviously a system construction, but why have them at all? Why have dungeons? Elyra doesn't do a lot of research on this—they're more interested in the *how* of dungeons, or how to best take advantage of the effects—but there's obviously a purpose to it, looking at what we know is happening to the gods."

"A lot of people say that it's the system's way of giving us a challenge," Sev said. "But that's . . ."

"It seems a poor way of challenging a populace, if the consequence for failure is death," Derivan observed quietly.

"I don't think 'challenge' fits," Vex agreed. "And there are too many things about the system that just . . . It's *bad*. I'd argue it hurts more than it helps. The idea that the system exists to challenge and empower people is a popular line of thought everywhere, even in Elyra, but too many things don't make sense."

"We should think about the relationship between anchors, gods, and overseers." Sev hesitated as he spoke, glancing at the box that still claimed it was "processing." "They might not all be linked, but they're presumably all core to the system in some way."

"The fuck was the system doing to Aurum, anyway?" Misa asked. There was a touch of aggression in her voice, but it was soft, too—genuinely concerned. "Kid was having trouble with his memories? Is that what happened with Onyx?"

"I . . . don't know," Sev hedged, hesitating. "I wasn't *there* with Onyx when the system was trying to erase him. I could feel the link between us weakening, though, and I tried to heal him through that. But if erasing a god looked like anything . . . I imagine it would look something like that."

There was a small silence at this.

"It was like he was being digested," Misa said softly. She frowned. "But that wasn't happening with Onyx . . ."

"It might be different for different gods," Sev said.

"I can't imagine," Vex said softly. "He was just having his memories slowly stripped from him, and he even *realized* it, but it took away his ability to care about it. If that can happen to a god . . ."

"We're going to need to be especially careful moving forward," Sev said with a sigh. "If we can't find something to protect our memories specifically, we need to know if we've lost something. We seem to be somewhat protected under at least one infolock, but . . ."

"There might be more out there," Vex agreed. "I'll . . . have to try to research memory-preservation magic. Or at least something that can alert us if something's altered . . ."

"I may be able to help," Derivan finally spoke up, a contemplative slant to the glow in his eyes. "Though I am unsure. I have . . . suspicions about what has changed regarding my status."

"I'm worried something's already changed and we don't know it," Sev muttered, and to that, the others had no response. They were each silent for a moment, contemplating the idea.

". . . It's a beautiful day out," Vex finally said after a moment, glancing up at the sky. The sun was shining brightly overhead, the sky a brilliant blue—a strong contrast with the darkness of the dungeon and the chaos of the bonus rooms. They were walking along a path that had been roughly cleared in the grass using some basic [**Pathmaker**] skills, presumably.

It was all very plain—there was nothing but grass and the occasional flower littering the field—but it *was* beautiful, and it was a breath of fresh air after all the destruction they'd seen in the dungeon break, and even in the research camp after they'd returned.

"It is," Sev agreed. "That's something positive we can focus on, at least."

"Speaking of," Misa said, "we should probably go over our rewards while we can? See what the bonus room gave us, preferably *before* a fight breaks out. And maybe see if there's another hint about whatever the fuck is going on."

"Right, right. I've been too distracted by the thing with Aurum to check mine," Sev said with a grimace.

"I got . . . an item and a skill." Vex's eyes flicked over an invisible notification, but his tail betrayed his anxiety; it coiled around nervously. "I haven't accepted them yet. I just . . . I don't know; I have a lot of doubts about what the system is doing now, I guess. I don't know if there's a *price* to all of this that we're not seeing."

"Like the possibility that it's being powered by forgotten gods," Sev muttered with a sigh. He looked conflicted. "Onyx seemed like he was doing . . . I mean, not all right. But he was *alive*, and I don't know what that place was, but he was stable enough there . . . He's obviously still working to help us out. I think he would've said something if he thought we shouldn't accept system rewards."

"The system's fucked, but we still have to work within its bounds," Misa said. She furrowed her brows slightly, glancing surreptitiously toward her pocket, where she kept the reality anchor. "For now, anyway."

"Coming from anyone else, that would be incredibly ominous," Sev said dryly, and Misa just shot him a half-grin.

"My reward notification is . . . strange." Derivan peered closely at the screen in front of him, then shook his head. "Mostly errors. Perhaps I cannot receive rewards from the system?"

Misa frowned. "We can just work on getting more stats for you, I think. Or we can try to figure out what your existing stats do, and find new ways to leverage them. Magic has a lot of potential. Geas . . . Uh, we probably don't want to touch that. Slime is weird. You're already using Physical Empathy. Shift?"

"Shift had a lot of potential, if your skill was any indication," Vex said thoughtfully. "Do you know what it does, exactly? It looks like you have more of a handle on it now."

"Watching . . . myself . . . gave me an idea of what Shift might be," Derivan said with a nod, though he glanced at Misa as he did so. "Though I feel we should perhaps also discuss exactly what that was."

"I have no fucking idea," Misa said flatly, then frowned, more at herself than at her companions. "Or I mean . . . that's not strictly true, I guess. I kind of know, but it's hard to explain. [**To Fall Yet Hold the Line**] seems to work by trying to grab a version of me that wields a weapon capable of blocking the attack. There wasn't a version of me that could block an entire meteor storm on my own."

"A *version* of you?" Sev asked with a frown. "What does that mean?"

"A version of me that made different choices, I guess?" Misa shifted uncomfortably. "Lived a different life. Wielded different weapons. Apparently

I've been switching weapons this whole time when blocking, and the skill just kind of masked it from me . . ."

Misa paused, her voice trailing off, and frowned at a notification that appeared in front of her.

> **<NOTICE>**
> **Your understanding of [To Fall Yet Hold the Line] has increased. Skill evolution to Elite is now available.**

"Guess I've got a skill evolution now," Misa said, staring at the notification a little suspiciously. "On top of the other rewards. I should feel happy, but . . . I think I'm with Vex on this. I don't think we should turn this down *now*, but we should be careful."

"We should find out what the delve team received, if they are willing to share," Derivan said. "I believe that will alleviate some of our concerns."

"Yeah, that's probably for the best," Sev muttered. "Uh . . . right. We were talking about our rewards. I think I have an item and a skill too, but the box is grayed out until Aurum is done . . . attaching, I guess. Whatever that means."

"And I have the same," Misa said. "An item called [**The Blade Arcane**] and a skill called [**Heart and Home**]."

"I have an item called the [**Accedere Root**]," Vex said, furrowing his brows slightly as he looked over the name. "And a skill called [**Delineate**]. Uh . . . not sure how useful that one is."

"I'll let you know once mine's done graying out," Sev said with a wince. "Derivan? I know you said yours was errored out, but is there any indication of what might happen if you accept it?"

"I . . . do not think I have a choice," Derivan said with a frown, poking around at the air. "It seems it will not allow me to access other aspects of my status until I accept this reward. But there is nothing specific in the notification about what I might gain, and there is no option to refuse." He waved a copy of the screen out to his friends—his system still allowed him to do that, at least.

> **<NOTICE>**
> **Congratulations on completing <The Village's Last Defense>! Here are your rewards, should you choose to accept them: <ERROR>**
>
> **ACCEPT / <ERROR>**

"... So we have no idea what's going to happen if you accept it," Misa said, peering at the text.

"I suppose not," Derivan said. "But I do not believe it wise to wait, since I may have gained other stats. I did not particularly have the time to check mid-battle."

Misa grimaced. "You're probably right. Uh . . . I'll catch you if anything happens, I guess. I haven't accepted the skill evolution yet, so I can block anything hostile if that happens. You ready?"

"As much as I can be," Derivan agreed. He glanced at the others—neither of them stopped him, though Sev looked pensive and Vex looked outright worried.

Well, no need to delay any further.

He reached out and hit Accept.

CHAPTER 49

REWARDS, PART 2

The first problem appeared almost immediately—Derivan found that he couldn't move.

He wasn't as worried about it as he thought he should have been, though he stopped mid-walk and that caused his friends to look at him with concern and alarm.

The second problem took a moment to appear, and it was in the spate of notifications that immediately appeared to him.

<ERROR>
Unable to find item <ERROR>.

<ERROR>
Unable to find Skill <ERROR>.

Rerolling rewards . . .

<WARNING>
Item and Skill tables are larger than expected. Results may be undefined. Contact an administrator if you have any concerns.

<WARNING>
Insufficient energy available to generate your rewards. You may be incapacitated while rewards are generated.

Generating rewards . . .

Part of the problem here was that Derivan didn't really have a way to communicate that he was *okay*. He saw his friends panicking slightly, glancing back toward the main group of people that were moving—the delvers were looking over in concern, given the party had stopped in place.

"I can't get a foothold on anything to block," Misa said, frustrated. "It's not an attack."

"He doesn't have health, but I don't sense anything wrong with him that I can heal, either." Sev's voice was worried.

"His mana circulation . . ." Vex paused, sounding thoughtful, and peered a little closer at Derivan. His eyes glowed a bit as he poured more mana into the skill. "It's being pulled somewhere. It's pulling mana away from the runes that enchant his armor; that's why he can't move. I don't know if I can just stop it. It might hurt him."

"Where's the mana going?" Misa asked.

"I'm trying to trace it now," Vex said. "It doesn't look like it *goes* anywhere; it just drains off into nothing . . . which doesn't make any sense."

Derivan paused at that. *Was* it going off into nothing?

The Shift stat was still relatively new, but his understanding of it had grown tremendously. He was, if anything, a little bit concerned about what it did—it seemed to weaken space around him, allowing him to *shift* between places. Unsurprising, he supposed, considering he'd obtained it when Histre performed a planeshift.

He'd used it subconsciously a couple of times, even. The first activation had been when Misa had blocked the attack that was headed for the delvers, essentially teleporting through the dungeon barrier; the second had been when he'd pushed through the dungeon barrier himself, together with Sev and Vex; and the third time he had simply eased the transition slightly when he'd been brought into the bonus room.

Now he used it in a slightly different way—he simply felt at the space around him. There was definitely something strange about it that he hadn't noticed until he'd directed his attention right at it. He felt the way the system was pulling at his mana, and the way that mana sank into . . .

. . . a hole in space. A weakening in space?

It took a small application of Shift to bring that part of space back into alignment with the rest of reality.

"Oh!" Vex said, sounding surprised, then glanced contemplatively at Derivan. "I think he's all right. He did something . . . I can see where the mana's going, now. Uh . . . it's going to your pocket."

Misa blinked. "My pocke— *Oh.*" She made the connection about the same time the others did, her eyes widening slightly.

The rewards chose that moment to finish processing.

**Congratulations on completing <The Village's Last Defense>!
Here are your rewards:**
   Item: [Flame of the #######]
   Skill: [###### Night]

Derivan jerked forward as his ability to move was suddenly returned to him, startling Vex, who was closest to him and let out a little yelp as he flinched backward. The armor reached out to catch his friend before he could fall, chuckling lightly.

"Thank you for keeping an eye on me," he said sincerely. He glanced back at his notifications. The skill settled neatly into his status as he focused on it, and the item . . .

Out of the system box, a warm, amber-colored crystal appeared, landing in an outstretched hand. Where the light glanced off of it, the light moved, shifting and flickering like it belonged to a living flame; when he rotated it in his hand, it almost seemed to flare, like a fire that had been fed with oxygen. Just as quickly, though, the illusion faded.

Derivan didn't know what to make of it. They'd have to get it properly appraised; his attempts to pull up a box on the item just gave him more errors. And the skill . . .

[###### Night] [Active Skill] [Grade: 1]
<ERROR>

. . . didn't have a particularly helpful description.

He shared them both anyway, causing all of them to raise skeptical eyebrows at the box.

"Do you want to try using the skill?" Misa asked with a frown. Derivan shook his head.

"Maybe later. Away from others, except perhaps those that might be able to mitigate the effects of the skill, should something go wrong." The armor looked briefly uncomfortable. "I would like to ask the Guildmaster for assistance in this, if possible. Perhaps she would have a means of identifying what the skill does."

"That might be for the best," Sev agreed.

"What about . . ." Misa gestured a little bit to her pocket, referencing the way mana had been flowing between Derivan and the reality anchor. "Is there a link there?"

"There was a notification about insufficient energy," Derivan offered.

"So the anchors power the system in some way?" Vex said with a frown. "Maybe?"

"That's the best we've got for now," Sev frowned. "A lot of implications with that, but maybe we'll bring it to the Guildmaster and see if she can make sense of it. Or to Kestel, if he's . . . okay."

The four of them fell silent for a moment. Sev glanced worriedly over at where Kestel was being kept—the researchers were still tending to him, and there was always one of the delvers hovering nearby at any given time. Everyone was worried, and no one had been able to get Kestel to talk about what was on his status screen yet; no one knew what status effect he might have.

"Perhaps Vex can receive his rewards next?" Derivan suggested after a moment of silence. Better to have a distraction, he thought. He glanced to Misa, who looked only briefly put out before she was once again excited by the prospect of new skills to abuse.

"Yeah, go ahead, Vex. I wanna see what you get," she said with a grin. Vex nodded, reaching out to the notification—

Derivan had briefly prepared for the lizardkin to drop, in case the same thing happened to him, but thankfully that didn't happen. Vex instead received his rewards immediately: a strange, gnarled root appeared in his hand, and at the same time, he glanced into the air as his status updated. He sent a copy of the new skill he had out to the three of them a moment later.

[Delineate] [Active Skill] [Grade: 1]
Designate a desired location for use.

"It's not very specific," Vex said with a frown. "Same category of skills as [**Classify**], I think, but hard to say until I test it out. I'm guessing the rarity means it's more useful than it appears."

"[**Classify**] is as well," Misa said. Her eyes were practically gleaming. "We can definitely find some uses for this."

"You're next, Misa," Sev said.

"I know," Misa said, grinning, and then reached out to tap her own notification. She shared the resulting box almost immediately, wanting to read the skill at the same time as the others—in fact, she nearly dropped the sword that appeared in her hand as she gestured, having forgotten that [**The Blade Arcane**] was supposed to be part of her rewards. "Whoa!"

"Is that sword . . . made of arcane mana?" Vex peered at it, vaguely concerned.

"The blade is, anyway," Misa said, waving it around. The hilt was a complicated thing of silver metal, twisting in on itself before coiling outward to form the edges of the hilt; it was very prettily designed, though it didn't particularly look easy to craft. There were gaps in the metal that made it look like a single piece of silver had been bent and coiled into itself rather than molded into the shape.

The blade itself was made of dense arcane mana, just as the name suggested. It was a light-red energy that shimmered in the air as she waved it around. "This thing isn't going to explode if it's hit by certain types of mana, is it?" Misa frowned. "Like what happened in the room?"

"And with the Aberrant," Sev added, glancing to Vex.

"It . . . shouldn't?" Vex frowned, looking carefully over the sword. "I'm pretty sure it won't. Enchanted items have to be *useful*, and this thing would be useless if it exploded at the touch of the slightest bit of mana. I mean, except in very limited ways."

"Perhaps we should test it with a less-harmful type of mana," Derivan suggested. "Just in case."

"We *can*," Vex said, considering. "It doesn't react with ambient mana, which tracks with how arcane mana tends to work; there's a triggering threshold it needs to cross to trigger. So if I just generate a mass of light mana . . ."

The wizard stepped forward, holding a ball of light in his hands; Misa held the blade out to him and gently touched the ball against the tip of the sword.

Nothing happened.

Nothing obvious, anyway. Misa's mouth formed an O, and she blinked twice. "It's prompting me to see if I want to change the blade type," she finally said. She gestured slightly, pushing the blade forward, and the orb of light vanished from Vex's hand; at the same time, the blade of arcane mana shifted into a light-yellow hue, with shimmers of arcane red in the mix.

"And I can turn it off whenever I want . . ." Misa grinned. "This'll be *useful*. We should still get it fully appraised, though, in case we're missing anything. As for the skill . . ."

Misa glanced at the notification box and frowned. "It's processing that one," she reported. "You guys see that too?"

"Yup," Sev agreed. Vex and Derivan both nodded.

"Is the system just having a slow day or something?" Misa said a little skeptically, staring at the box.

"If the system is tied to the anchors," Vex said thoughtfully, "then ... *maybe*? We've just kicked out whatever anchor it usually relies on and replaced it with this one, which the first anchor created in the first place."

"That's going to get confusing to think about," Misa muttered. "That anchor *made* this anchor, and then this anchor siphoned back from that one ..."

As she was speaking, the skill finished processing, and all copies of the box updated at the same time.

<WARNING>
Due to actions taken before receiving the Skill [Heart and Home], the original version of the Skill is corrupted and cannot be received.
However, a synergy has been detected between [Heart and Home] and item [X-51 RE##### AN####].
Synergy has been processed, and a new Unique Skill has been awarded.

[An Anchor of Heart and Home] [Passive and Active Skill] [Grade: Max]
Cost: 10 units of <ERROR>
Home is where the heart is, and for you, the line has been blurred between these two things. You carry a piece of your home with you, just as your home will always carry a piece of you.
The passive effect of this Skill is retroactive and permanent.

CHAPTER 50

THE ONLY ADVENTURERS WITH A NEGATIVE KILLCOUNT

Misa stared at the wording of the skill, briefly speechless. The others went silent as well. It took a moment for them to process what it all *meant*—the wording of the skill was vague to begin with, and there were a lot of things it could mean, but the fact that it had merged with an artifact that was responsible for apparently *shaping reality*?

That was a little outside the scope of what they'd expected.

Misa was the first one to speak.

"Is this the reason I didn't die?" Misa said. Her words were soft, and she reached out to brush the edge of the box with a finger; the corners fizzled as she touched it. "When my village was attacked?"

"Perhaps it is the reason you were able to stabilize your village," Derivan offered quietly. "I do not know if it is the reason you were able to survive. The way you describe it . . ."

Derivan trailed off, like he was concerned his words would affect her. Misa shook her head. "Tell me," she said, softly but firmly.

Derivan nodded. "The way you described it before . . . your village was razed to the ground. Pieces of it survived, certainly, and perhaps because of this you did as well. Perhaps so long as any part of your home remains intact, you cannot die.

"But that skill is vague, and that seems to me a dangerous thing to assume. And if it *does* work that way, it may mean that any damage you sustain will propagate back to your village . . ."

Hardly a free pass to take damage or allow herself to be hurt, in other words. Misa grimaced a little as he spoke. She wasn't sure that this skill was *helpful*. Her bread-and-butter blocking skill required her to sacrifice part of her health, and if that damage propagated back to the village . . .

"You might be right," Misa said with a frustrated half-growl. "It's hard to say for sure unless we actually test out the skill, and it's taking a damn risk just to test it. And the description says there's an active component to it, but we have no way of knowing what that active component does, and the cost is another error message."

"Until we test it properly, yeah," Sev sighed. "We'll have to test a *lot* of things when we get back to the Guild, I think."

"At least we won't be doing it alone?" Vex piped up softly. Sev snorted and grinned at the lizard, ruffling his nonexistent hair, to Vex's yelps and protests. "You're just rubbing my head! It's weird!"

"Do you want me to stop?"

". . . No. It's kind of nice."

Which was, obviously, a cue for Derivan and Misa to join in.

—ᨆ—

There was predictably quite a bit of chaos when they arrived back at the Guild.

Sev and his team had decided to go on ahead—they could move faster as a small group than the larger travel team that was lagging behind—and they decided to bring Kestel along with them, in case he needed the medical attention quickly. The lizardkin didn't say much when they explained the situation to him; he simply nodded, allowing Derivan to pick him up. The four adventurers glanced at each other, worried but not willing to voice that worry in front of him.

So of course, the first thing the Guildmaster saw when they returned was Derivan standing with an incapacitated head researcher in his arms. She froze.

"Please tell me that's not who I think it is," she said. "Max is out right now. She used her skill again and vanished. So I'm assuming this isn't what it looks like, or she would *definitely* be here."

"It's the head researcher," Sev confirmed. "But uh . . . we didn't do this to him, if that helps?"

"That part I assumed," the Guildmaster said dryly. "All right. We're bringing him to the temple. I'm coming with you." She walked briskly down the stairs to join them. "I'm assuming you came here to find me?"

"We came here to let you know there's a large group headed this way," Sev said, a little awkwardly. "The population of . . . an entire village. Also some of the research team."

"What." The Guildmaster froze for a moment, then let out a muttered curse, bringing up her system interface so she could start typing out commands rapidly. "What happened? Quick explanation, please. You can tell me in detail later."

"I resurrected my home village and they all need a place to stay," Misa volunteered.

The Guildmaster stopped walking.

"You did what." Her words were flat.

"I . . . resurrected my home village and they all need a place to stay?" Misa repeated, this time with a questioning sort of lilt at the end of the statement. She hadn't completely processed how ludicrous everything that had happened was yet, and . . .

. . . well, thinking about it, she really just wanted to go and talk to her parents. Stay with them for a day or two. She wasn't about to leave the team, but she missed them, she realized.

The Guildmaster still hadn't said anything, and it took her a moment before Misa realized it—she'd been too busy reminiscing. "Um. Guildmaster?"

"Explain," the Guildmaster said with a long-suffering note of pain in her voice. "I know I said 'quick explanation,' but you've apparently broken *all the rules we know of,* so I'm going to need to know how you did this. Especially if it can be replicated. And how much Elyra knows about it. I'm shielding Kestel from hearing the details, although I'm not sure he can process much of it right now."

"Uh . . ." Misa exchanged glances with the rest of the team—who looked a little less surprised than she *felt,* so she was assuming she'd been the only one that hadn't particularly considered the potential political fallout.

Fuck that, though. It was her home. Why would she?

She explained what had happened in a little more detail to the Guildmaster as they continued to the temple, leaving out the details of the reality anchor for now, though she made it clear that she was skipping something. The general gist of the tale she told was that the dungeon had generated her old village from scratch, right down to every person that lived in her village. As far as she could tell, they were nearly the same as the real thing, with one difference.

Even the Guildmaster grimaced as she explained the details of how she'd been cut out of the lives of the villagers. It hadn't been done properly—it had left a hole. And though many of the villagers couldn't tell, Charise had the skills to feel the hole her daughter had left, every moment of every day.

"I couldn't just let the dungeon take them away from me again," Misa said quietly. "So I stopped it. The specifics are a little complicated, and I think it's probably best if we explained that when we have some privacy, but that's the gist of it."

"You just . . . stopped it." The Guildmaster rubbed the bridge of her nose slowly, which was rather monumental because Misa had the feeling that the only reason they'd seen her do that was because she'd *allowed* them to see her do it. That or she was stumped enough to have forgotten to use whatever skill she kept using. "You realize that's not something people can do."

"I did it," Misa said, a little lamely. The Guildmaster snorted.

"You also know you're the only team to ever come back with a negative on the killcount," the Guildmaster said.

"I do now?"

"And does Elyra know about this?"

Misa hesitated.

". . . I think it's best to assume that they do," she eventually said. "We didn't formally introduce the villagers to anyone who went back to Elyra or anything—the ones we did introduce them to are all coming here. But that doesn't mean that they don't know. The villagers are a pretty big group, and they're a pretty big group that came out of nowhere. Even if they don't know that they're necessarily *resurrections . . .*"

"They know to keep it quiet, I believe," Derivan added helpfully. "But many of them are frightened, and several of them are children. I concur with Misa; it is best to assume that Elyra knows."

"Fuck," the Guildmaster grumbled. "It'd be better for us if they don't. I'm *hoping* they don't. It'll be a lot harder to keep up security if Elyra's trying to get past our defenses all the time."

"You're going to help house them?" Misa asked, her voice hopeful.

"Of course we are," the Guildmaster said dismissively. "We have people that can build a village quick, no problem. It might not be in the best shape to start with, but we can always improve it over time. Besides . . ."

The Guildmaster paused here, and her voice turned soft, regretful.

". . . The fact of the matter is that the Guild failed your village," she said. "We cannot help every village out there, but we try to remember all the ones we fail. J'rokksur is on that list, and it is not a failure I have forgotten."

Misa was silent for a moment, staring at the Guildmaster. She'd never met the woman, she was pretty sure. But there was a nagging feeling at the back of her mind that maybe she *had . . .*

It was difficult to say, considering the kind of skills the Guildmaster had. But she thought maybe she could remember someone indiscernible that she'd met two years back, when she'd been at the peak of her self-destructive phase. She'd been consumed by the loss of her home, and a stranger had given her a purpose.

A small one. A relatively useless one, even. Who the fuck asked people to clear out basement rats? But then she'd actually gone into the damn basement, because what else was she supposed to do, and the rats had been . . . well, enormous.

Adrenaline was the feeling she'd felt back then, and it hadn't been exactly what she'd needed. It was what came *afterward*—when the owner of that house thanked her, thinking she was from the Adventurers' Guild and paying her, and reminding her remarkably of her mom—

"Did you set me up?" Misa demanded. "All those years ago. To join the Adventurers' Guild."

"I did not," the Guildmaster replied dryly, glancing at Misa. "But if I did, I wouldn't tell you."

. . . Well, she was honest, at least.

"What's more important is what we're going to do about J'rokksur," the Guildmaster said. "Even if we can hide them for now, it's not going to last forever—an entire village appearing is something that's going to show up on the Kingdom's radars. It doesn't sound like what you did can be replicated—gods know the dungeons are hard enough to understand as it is—but that doesn't mean people won't want to try."

"Elyra will want to try the most, I think," Vex said quietly. "Anderstahl is less interested in dungeons."

"That is likely," the Guildmaster agreed. "I'm anticipating the most trouble from Elyra, and Elyra has its own problems right now."

"The food thing," Misa said with a frown. "Is it that bad?"

"It's getting worse," the Guildmaster said with a sigh. "Food production in Elyra barely keeps even with its population to begin with. They had a stockpile they managed to build up, especially with people that had the relevant skills, but now even that stockpile is starting to decay—the [**Preservation**] spells they're using are failing, and they don't know why."

"Is *magic* just failing there?" Sev wondered aloud, and Vex paled at the thought.

"A lot of things in Elyra are run by magic," he said, sounding worried. But he shook his head a second later. "I don't know. If all magic was affected . . . a lot more systems would be collapsing. A lot more than just the food, at any rate."

"We're headed to Elyra next anyway, right?" Misa said. "We can investigate it then."

"I'm not sure that it's exactly our *job*," Sev grumbled.

"Oh, I can make it your job," the Guildmaster said brightly.

"What." Sev's voice was almost as flat as the Guildmaster's had been when she'd been told about the entire village being brought back.

"How would you like to be the Guild's official delegation?" The Guildmaster grinned. "We need to send people to Elyra to help out with the food crisis anyway, and the kind of status we can give you here would help you a lot in gaining access to their systems. Like their dungeon, for instance."

". . . We do need to access the dungeon there," Sev said, though he looked incredibly put out at the idea of being a political delegation. Misa didn't blame him—she didn't feel entirely comfortable with it either. Vex mostly just looked a paler green than usual, and Derivan was about as stoic as ever.

"There you go," the Guildmaster said. "That's settled, then! You're going to be our new Elyran delegates, which means I can tell Jerome that he's *not* cleared to go to Elyra, no matter how much he says that he's much better now."

Sev blinked. ". . . Is he . . . doing okay?"

"He won't stop flirting with Max," the Guildmaster said. "The two women he has with him don't seem very happy about it, but he's sort of oblivious."

Misa groaned. "Dammit, Jerome."

CHAPTER 51

A STAFF IN THE MOUTH IS WORTH TWO IN THE . . . WAIT, NO, WHAT?

The temple's activity stopped almost instantly the moment Derivan walked in with Kestel in his arms. Many priests had a basic [**Triage**] skill running at all times, and the fact that Kestel had immediately caught their attention was just as immediately alarming; Sev winced slightly as he watched a few clerics practically pull the silent scientist out of Derivan's arms, bringing him over to the corner of the temple they usually kept for the sick and infirm.

It was a small corner of the temple, admittedly, compared to the large marketplace they kept for potions and other healing products. The problem lay in the fact that it was rare for them to really have to keep patients for long; illnesses outside the scope of standard healing spells and the buffer of health were uncommon. Status effects that could not be instantly cleared were even more uncommon.

So that corner of the temple was a makeshift area, set up for those with no health left and were being kept on what was effectively life support, or those with cursed status effects like [**Petrification**] or [**Inward Petrification**]. The second one was strange and poorly understood; planeshifters had explained it once as an illness in which muscle turned to bone, and magical attempts to reverse it had only created ill-defined, loose pieces of muscle that were attached to nothing and caused more harm than benefit.

All of which Sev thought about in an attempt to distract himself from the possibility that Kestel was hurt in a way that he couldn't heal, or in a way that he could only heal at great personal cost. The rest of the temple's infirmary was effectively empty; there were mattresses and vaguely crumpled, messy sheets, along with some healing artifacts that had collected dust.

"He has several concurrent status effects on him," one of the priests finally said as he walked over to them—Sev recognized him, actually. He'd been the somewhat obnoxious fellow that had kept preaching to him when he'd been at the temple not too long before. The priest clearly recognized *him*, too, but was staying professional. "What happened to him, if I may ask?"

"We don't know the exact details," Sev said, glancing awkwardly at the rest of the team—they should've brought one of the researchers with them. They'd at least be able to recount the story. "There was a fight of some kind and he lost all his health. He was kept alive with a [**Resuscitator**] for about half an hour before I was able to heal him."

"That explains some of those status effects," the priest muttered with a sigh. "Some of them will wear off with time—effects like [**Dazed**] and [**Non-responsive**]—but others are going to take more work, and more mana crystals besides. Status effects are expensive to remove, and several of them are in later stages. We don't have the mana crystals we need to heal him completely."

"Shit," Sev muttered. The Guild was short on mana crystals as it was—and, glancing at the Guildmaster, she seemed to feel the same way. She was frowning to herself, gesturing with her fingers like she was doing some mental math. "Will he be okay in the meantime? It'll take us a while to get . . . How much do you need?"

"A grade four, at least," the priest answered, and Sev grimaced. So did the Guildmaster.

"And the price of the actual treatment?" he probed.

"We don't charge," the priest said, shaking his head. "We get most of our gold from potion sales anyway, and we don't actually need a lot of gold. Plus, there's been a paladin that's been throwing around his gold a lot lately."

"Actual gold, or currency gold?" Sev asked warily.

"Both," the priest said, his tone a touch exasperated. He'd clearly tried to explain the difference before. "We just pile up the non-currency gold in the corner."

"Someone needs to explain gold to him," Sev muttered.

"Not it," Misa said immediately.

"I don't think that's our job?" Vex said, though he phrased it like it was a question.

"We're getting there," the Guildmaster said wearily. "He'd been a bit pampered in Anderstahl, up until he got kicked out, so."

"How much time will Kestel take to recover, once we provide the mana crystal he needs?" Derivan asked, bringing the topic back to the matter at hand. The priest frowned, considering.

"We can prevent the status effects from getting *worse*," he eventually said. "Until we get the mana crystal, that's the best we can do. Even without it, he *might* be able to make a recovery on his own, but . . . it's going to take a long time, if it happens at all. Right now, he'll barely be able to walk."

Sev sighed, glancing over at Kestel. The man was lying somewhat listlessly in the bed, staring up at the ceiling; it was a bed that had been modified for lizardkin, with a slit down the center of the mattress for the tail to slip comfortably into. It was a testament to how out of it he was, then, that he just lay awkwardly with his tail crumpled beneath him, until a younger priest reached over and carefully nudged him into a position that wouldn't hurt his back.

"I . . . will try to make room in the Guild's budget," the Guildmaster said eventually, softly. She was staring at Kestel too, Sev realized, and there was a note of familiarity in her eyes; no doubt this was something she'd seen before. "But we have other adventurers in similar conditions, in other branches . . ."

"The mana crystal thing is really a problem, isn't it," Misa said, glancing sympathetically to the Guildmaster.

"You have no idea," the Guildmaster said with a sigh. "But we should get going, if we're going to prepare for that many people arriving. The priests will take care of your friend, and I think I might post a guard here too, just in case . . ."

The Guildmaster frowned for a moment, lost in thought. Sev picked up on the thread of conversation, turning a weak smile to the priest that had helped them. Velykos was nowhere to be found, and he wondered if he'd find the stone elemental again before they had to leave for Elyra; he hoped so. He wanted to make sure the guy was doing alright.

"Thanks for all the help, uh . . ." Sev trailed off, somewhat embarrassed, as he realized that he hadn't ever actually asked for the man's name. He'd probably introduced himself at some point—presumably at the start of all the preaching—but he hadn't really bothered to memorize it.

"Ixome," the priest said, which was a strange name for a human, but Sev didn't question it.

"Thanks, Ixome," Sev said. "And uh . . . sorry about last time. With the staff."

"Believe it or not," Ixome said—and this time there was a touch of dry humor in his voice—"I've been informed by my colleagues that preaching at someone is not a good way to get them to repent. And I've had a number of informative dreams with my goddess since then."

"Informative dreams?" Sev raised an eyebrow.

"They involved a number of staffs," Ixome said, his words still as dry as the desert. "I took them as the lecture that I imagine they were intended to be."

"I . . . see," Sev said, blinking once. Ixome didn't seem like he was inclined to elaborate, so he decided not to ask.

"Regardless," Ixome said, changing the subject, "I do apologize for my behavior back then."

Sev nodded. "Water under the bridge," he offered, though Ixome gave him a strange look at the idiom. "Meaning don't worry about it. Do you know if Velykos is around?"

"He makes it a habit to pray around this time," Ixome said. He started to head back toward Kestel. "My mana's back, so I'm going to go help stabilize those status effects. If you're looking for Velykos, you'll find him in the back gardens."

"I'll find him later," Sev decided, glancing back at the Guildmaster. "There's still a lot we need to figure out before we get to have some downtime."

"That's an understatement," the Guildmaster said. She glanced back at them. "You want to talk to Kestel before you leave?"

Sev hesitated, glancing at the others. Misa frowned, and Vex looked down slightly, like he didn't know what to say. Derivan simply bowed his head.

"I think it's best we let the priests work for now," Sev said quietly. "He's going to be crowded enough as it is when the researchers come to see him . . . I'll slip a message to him through the system that he can read when he's awake enough, so he knows we all wish him well."

And he did. All four of them did, actually, adding their own little notes to Sev's message of well-being; it was marked as unread when they sent it, and when they looked over, they could see that Kestel was sleeping. Probably for the best that they hadn't gone to speak to him, then.

The Guildmaster led the way out of the temple, back toward the Guild. "I'm not sure we can spare the mana crystal Kestel needs," she said without preamble. "There's been a spike in dungeon activity, everywhere that we know of. Elyra and Anderstahl have both sent correspondence to us about a strange notification from the system, about *something* being added to their dungeons, coinciding with the time dungeon activity increased. We've gotten reports from adventurers from Bronze to Platinum about it."

Sev grimaced, and the Guildmaster leveled a glare at him, though there was no real heat to it. "This is your fault somehow, isn't it."

"In our defense," Misa said. She stopped.

"In your defense?" the Guildmaster quirked a brow at the half-orc.

"Yeah, I got nothing," Misa said with a shrug. "We'll do what we can to take pressure off the Guild. It's the least we can do."

"I should hope so," the Guildmaster said with a sigh, but she didn't really seem frustrated. If anything, she was contemplative. "It's strange that all of this is happening now. Why now, of all times?"

"I think it's . . ." Sev started, and then he fell silent, shaking his head. "Sorry. Can't say. It's probably under the infolock. We can try again, since this is *new* information, but . . . Derivan?"

Derivan glanced at him. He gave the Guildmaster a moment to use whatever skills she needed—she already seemed prepared for a headache—and then began to speak. "Sev suspects that it is because the gods appear to have plans for this as well," the armor said out loud. Onyx had nearly said as much to them, along with the other individual, back in the space they'd fallen into before they'd returned to reality. He didn't know who the other one was— another god, most likely, perhaps one of falling water. "If what Aurum did is any indication, then the gods must be aware that they are being targeted, though they do not seem to know why."

"*Targeted*," the Guildmaster repeated in disbelief. "Max briefed me a little on what happened with Jerome, but she couldn't tell me the specifics. If you're saying gods themselves can be targeted . . ."

She shook her head and sighed. "And yet," she said. "Somehow, the part that I'm most worried about is the fact that you can tell me all this *now*, when you couldn't before. Something changed, and until we know what . . . be careful."

CHAPTER 52

DISCUSSIONS

They stepped through the doorway into the Guild, and the Guildmaster paused as she was speaking; she glanced expectantly to the desk where Max usually sat as the receptionist, and frowned slightly when she saw the desk was still empty. "I hope Max is all right," she muttered.

"Is there any reason she wouldn't be?" Sev asked, a note of worry entering his voice. The Guildmaster shrugged, gesturing into the air as she seemed to check through her messages; seeing nothing, she shook her head and dismissed it.

"[**Right Place, Right Time**] is a gamble," the Guildmaster answered. "She never knows for sure that it'll take her where she wants to be; it'll only take her where she needs to be. The nature of the skill should mean that she's never put into a situation she can't get herself out of, but it doesn't guarantee safety."

"Do you at least have a way to keep an eye on her?" Sev asked.

"It's called trust," the Guildmaster said dryly. "I'm pretty sure you know it already."

"I mean, you keep an eye on *us*," Sev muttered. "And if you know she has a skill that might land her anywhere . . ."

"We have some measures of last resort if we need to track her down, but we only use those after a certain amount of time has passed without a message from her, and that hasn't happened yet," the Guildmaster admitted as she climbed up the stairs. "She'll be fine, Sev. We have more important things to worry about right now."

Sev agreed, conceding the point. Still—as they strode up the stairs and back toward their room—he couldn't help but glance to the empty receptionist's desk with a bit of worry.

Hopefully, Max was okay. If she wasn't . . . well, there wasn't much they could do for her right now. He'd have to trust that the Guildmaster and her people knew what they were doing.

"I've already sent out orders to ask anyone with building skills to help build an extension to this town," the Guildmaster said with a sigh, once they were settled back in Sev's room. Sev barely realized how much of a meeting room his room had become; he was starting to wonder if he should ask for a big table of some sort to be put in.

As it was, they just sat in their assortment of chairs in a circle around the room, privacy wards activated. "Luckily this isn't really a full village; more just a number of people who decided to live around this Guild branch because of the relative safety it offers . . . so we should be able to build an extension without any complaints. Most of them will probably even be glad for it. But I take it there's more to your story than you've explained."

"Quite a lot," Sev said with a sigh. He glanced at Misa. "Uh . . . Misa, you want to take this one?"

"Might as well," Misa said with a slight grimace. "I already explained half the story. Not really one for telling stories, but . . ."

She explained everything they'd been through, starting from the moment she'd reality-fucked her way into the dungeon. That was the exact term she used, even, which—to her amusement—made Vex cover his face in embarrassment and Sev grumble at her.

"I don't think I was supposed to be able to just teleport into the dungeon like that," Misa said with a slight frown. "It's the only time I felt the skill resist me. But something helped me through."

Derivan nodded. "Shift activated," he said. "I did not realize it until later. But if Shift allows the weakening of boundaries in space, then I believe I subconsciously assisted your . . . teleportation."

That made sense. Misa continued on to explain what had happened when she tried to block the attack from an unknown assailant, all the way down to the consequences and the way the perpetrator had vanished afterward; the Guildmaster frowned at that, and took a moment to send out several messages. Most of them, she explained, were along the lines of *Please don't attack any skeletons you see escorting a village*, and two of them were warnings to both Elyra and Anderstahl about a potential intelligent monster appearing in their dungeons.

The rest of the explanation faced less interruptions, though the revelations were nevertheless severe, and the Guildmaster's expression was grim. Vex watched carefully the whole time, looking for the fluctuation in magic he'd learned to associate with the infolock activating—but there was nothing. They were able to talk about everything down to the reality anchor and the way it had seemingly altered reality, to the way they'd found Aurum trapped within yet another Overseer, to the way they'd managed to rescue him.

The last part, Misa admitted, was more a stroke of pure luck than anything else—and she wasn't completely sure that what they'd done there was a good thing. She was glad they'd saved Aurum, whatever that meant with the god of gold now in the process of being anchored to Sev—but she was also worried about what breaking the new dungeon's reality anchor might have done.

Last, but not least, they explained what had happened . . . after. No one had any idea what to call that, or how to explain what existing there had been like. There were similarities to the space they'd first found the reality anchor in, but it was so much *less*.

The conversation died there, the five of them lapsing into silence once they'd explained what they'd heard from the two presumed gods they'd spoken with. It was hard to tell exactly what was going on with them—were they *hurt*? They didn't seem to be. Were they putting on some sort of front? That seemed more likely. Or was it something else entirely, and their guesses were way off the mark?

"It's interesting that the infolock didn't seem to engage at all," the Guildmaster said with a frown. "I'm actually a little worried. I was expecting you to be able to tell me almost nothing, and now I'm concerned that something else happened and we just don't understand it yet."

"Not much we can do about that, though," Sev said, and the Guildmaster acknowledged that with a tilt of her head.

"As far as the matter at hand goes, I'm almost tempted to say that this is an issue you should bring to the priests at the temple instead." Her brows furrowed slightly as she spoke, as if she was genuinely considering the idea. "They're better equipped to deal with matters of the gods. Except . . . if all the gods are desperate, they may not be the best source of help."

"They also tend to see the gods as perfect and flawless," Sev pointed out. "If we brought this to them, it might cause a bit of a panic. I'm not saying we shouldn't tell them at all—that seems like a good way to accidentally create a rift between the Guild and the temple—but I think we should be careful about who we tell. It shouldn't be a public announcement."

"Gods forbid we make public an announcement like *The gods are being targeted and stolen away*," the Guildmaster said, grimacing at the very thought.

"Yeah. On that, I think, we agree. And as much as this feels like it's over our heads, I don't think we can afford to ignore this."

She sighed. "I'll leverage what Guild resources I can to look at this problem, but . . . you four are pretty much one of our stronger assets at this point, and you seem to be at the center of this one way or another." She grimaced slightly. "There's no way those fights didn't get you guys some levels, right?"

Misa frowned, hesitating. "It actually didn't," she said. "We checked. It's not that we didn't level at all, but the levels we got out of it are pretty much just enough for a couple of stat points."

"Except for me!" Vex piped up, eliciting an amused smile from Misa. Once upon a time she might've been jealous, but that was a time that felt far away, now. "It pushed me over the edge into Silver. I got a new skill for it, too. [**Splash of Mana**]. I haven't experimented with it much, but it's some kind of skill that allows me to manipulate the texture and behavior of mana." The lizardkin's eyes gleamed with excitement, and Derivan couldn't help chuckling lightly.

"He is looking forward to experimenting with it," the armor said fondly.

"And no one can stop me!" Vex proclaimed.

"We wouldn't dare try," Misa said with a faint grin. The Guildmaster only watched, though a slight smile slipped into her expression; it vanished just as quickly when she focused her attention back on the subject at hand.

"I want you to train on the way to Elyra," the Guildmaster said. "Like I said, one way or another, you four are at the center of this—and the matter appears to be somewhat urgent but not so much that you can't afford some time to train."

"We're running on *some* timers," Misa said with a slight frown. She explained the degrading anchor quickly, though she added that she wasn't quite sure if anything had changed with the way the anchor had merged with her skill.

When she was done, the Guildmaster looked . . . sympathetic, but her face was still hard.

"Be that as it may," she said, and then she sighed. "I've seen this with adventurers before. They get caught up in something big happening, and it always seems like there's something urgent right around the corner, and they just don't have the time to stop and relax, or to train and prepare. You *cannot function* if you don't do both of those things.

"If you don't take some time for yourselves, you're liable to make a mistake and get yourselves killed, and whatever benefit your gods are trying to pull to get out of this situation will end there. If you don't take the time to train, you may not be strong enough to face whatever challenges come next—worse, you may not understand your skills and resources well enough to leverage them in the coming fights. This has been your greatest strength as a team so far. I underestimated you when I said you're the kind of team that can fight a tier above your rank. Level almost doesn't matter for you four.

"But that's only if you polish the advantage you have. It's important to focus on your goals, don't get me wrong, but it's just as important to strike a balance between all these things, and not allow yourselves to be consumed one way or another." The Guildmaster's eyes were serious. She spoke almost like she was looking through them, like this was something she'd seen again and again—

...it probably *was* something she'd seen before, wasn't it.

Slowly, Misa nodded, though her hand instinctively went to the pocket where she kept the reality anchor. She couldn't help but worry, for all that her family had said they'd also work on the problem, for all that her skill claimed there was now some permanent connection between her and her home.

Her pocket was empty.

Misa froze for a moment in panic. "The anchor," she said out loud, and all four of the others looked at her sharply.

"Did you lose it?" the Guildmaster asked, her voice urgent.

"I— It shouldn't have been *stolen*," Misa said. She tried her best to keep the defensiveness out of her voice. "I haven't been close enough to anyone for it to be pickpocketed."

"Let's think through this," Sev said. "I doubt something like that would get stolen so easily. When was the last time you checked it?"

"Right before I accepted the bonus room rewards," Misa said with a frown, and paused. The box had *said* there was a synergy between her skill and the item. She hadn't heard of item-skill synergies before, but ...

Sure enough, Vex spoke up, a slight frown on his snout. "Item-skill synergies don't *usually* consume the item," he said. "It's been reported maybe once or twice that I've seen, and in those cases, it's usually possible to check the item box by concentrating on the skill box."

Misa frowned. "You could've told me that before," she grumbled.

"I forgot," Vex said, embarrassed. "I don't remember everything all the time, you know."

"I know, I know," Misa said. "I didn't mean it. Just stressed. Okay, let me see ..."

CHAPTER 53

SPLITTING THE PARTY
FOR FUN AND PROFIT

The half-orc pulled up the box for [**An Anchor of Heart and Home**] and exerted an effort of will. The system didn't exactly come with *instructions*, though it was rather intuitively built and would respond intelligently to most thoughts directed at it. The problem was that one needed to know that a command existed to be able to perform it.

The other problem was that intuitiveness of use aside, the whole system was clearly starting to fall apart. But that was neither here nor there. Sure enough, it took only a slight twist of perspective for the skill to suddenly flicker, changing form.

> [**X-51 R###### A####R**] [**Grade: Unknown**]
> *<ERROR>*
> *Item description missing.*
>
> *<WARNING>*
> *Integrity at 89.7%. Degradation rate is currently: MEDIUM. Time before a##### falls below critical stability threshold: 5 months and 12 days.*
>
> *<WARNING>*
> *#####r boundaries are currently in flux. Stable point identified using Skill: [**An Anchor of Heart and Home**].*

She flicked copies of that box over to the other four without saying a word.

". . . So, the anchor's merged with you in some way?" the Guildmaster frowned at the box for a moment, then glanced at Vex. "Do you know if it's possible to separate the item and the skill after something like this happens?"

"You haven't seen something like this before?" Vex asked, surprised.

"Believe it or not," the Guildmaster said dryly, "I don't actually have access to the endless resources and records that Elyra does, and things like this are actually *rare*. How frequently do you think adventurers get rare items and rare skills?"

". . . Semi-frequently?" Vex ventured. The Guildmaster stared at him flatly, and he deflated.

"You four are a terrible example of what's common," she said, though her tone implied she was vaguely amused. "Can they be separated or not?"

"I don't know," Vex answered. "Not that I know of."

"Isn't this a good thing?" Misa asked, sounding a little protective. "The skill's . . . It might help me protect my home, even when I'm away from it."

"Depending on what it does, it might also make you a target, and if it's that important, I was going to ask you to give it to us for safekeeping," the Guildmaster said with a sigh. "But this might be the second-best thing, as long as you don't go around telling people you have it."

"This is going to make training even more important, isn't it," Sev said with a slight grimace. The Guildmaster shrugged, and favored him with a faint smile.

"It's always going to look like a bad time to take a break," she said. "There's always the next milestone to look at. The next hill to climb. If something's sufficiently urgent, then yes, by all means, run for that goal as fast as you can and don't stop until you've done what you need to do.

"Right now, you have time. Not a lot of it—not an infinite amount of it—but you *have* it, so make use of it as much as you can so that when you do need to run, you have everything you need to do it.

"There are a couple of quests that need to be completed that are between this branch town and Elyra. I'm sending you there anyway, so do me a favor and try to complete them. I'm sure you're not opposed to helping a couple of villages on the way?"

"I mean," Sev hedged, but she'd gotten him with the allure of *helping people*. "Um. Yeah, I guess we can do that. Anyone opposed?"

"If we haven't found a way to stop or slow the anchor degrading in three months," Misa said, "I'd like us to focus on that. But we'll be in Elyra by then. I don't think the trip will take more than a week. Maybe three, if we're completing quests on the way."

"We will keep an eye out on the way," Derivan said. "There is no guarantee that Elyra will contain the solution we need. Perhaps we will find a solution sooner than we expect."

"That's a good point," Misa said. ". . . Yeah. I feel a little better about that now."

"I need to go have a meeting about all of this," the Guildmaster said with a sigh. "Before I go. What happened to Kestel?"

"Oh." Misa grimaced a bit. They'd forgotten, in the midst of everything else. She quickly explained what had happened, going over how Kestel had apparently tried to protect the delve team from being reported.

The Guildmaster rubbed her temples like she was getting a headache. "Those skeletons you mentioned will be joining the Guild, right?"

"We were hoping they could. They're strong. They'd be an asset," Sev said.

"And they need Guild protection so Elyra doesn't just steal them away," the Guildmaster muttered. "I'll get something made for them. Disguise enchantments, maybe. Oh! Speaking of."

The Guildmaster reached into her pocket and tossed an amulet at Derivan, who caught it. "The amulet I promised," she said. "It'll stop people from being able to notice that you're not quite what they expect."

"Thank you," Derivan said, bowing his head. "I will use it wisely."

The Guildmaster snorted. "You're too polite," she said as she headed out the door. "Use it however you like. Knowing you four, I expect yet another fundamental rule broken by next week."

"I can't tell if she's overestimating us or underestimating us," Misa commented once the Guildmaster left.

"I give it two days tops," Sev said with a grin.

"I'm not sure we should make this a competition . . ." Vex ventured.

"Perhaps one day, if you will help me test my Magic stat," Derivan said.

Vex immediately nodded in agreement. "Okay!"

Misa snorted, and Sev just laughed. Then they settled down to discuss their plans for the next few days.

It'd be another day or two before the Guildmaster could arrange for a caravan to take them to Elyra—which, they decided, gave the four of them just enough time to split up and focus on themselves for a bit. Sev's status was still stuck behind the *Processing* notification, the task of anchoring Aurum to him apparently a costly one; he told the others he'd update them as soon as anything changed regarding his status, and that he'd try to stay relatively close to someone that could help.

Vex and Derivan, as before, decided they'd stick together to experiment and explore what they could do with their skills. Derivan's Magic stat was vague enough that they figured there might be more to it, and keeping them together would help Derivan train up the Slime stat, too, though the benefit of that particular stat versus the cost was growing untenable.

Misa wanted to visit the village as they went to rebuild. It wouldn't be the same as J'rokksur, but it would have all the same *people*, and that was what mattered. She made the other three promise that they'd join her tonight for dinner before they all split up; she'd be cooking them something from her home, she said. None of them questioned where she would find the ingredients.

"All right, let's get some sleep," Misa said, glancing outside the window and grimacing. The sun was close to setting—she didn't think the village would be arriving by tonight. By the morning, maybe, if they got some rest. "I want to greet Mom and Dad properly when they get back. It's been . . . it's been too long."

"We're looking forward to being properly introduced to them," Sev said with a smile.

Misa laughed. "Yeah, you say that now. Wait till Dad gets a chance to interrogate you three. Remember, come find us at eight for dinner. Sev, *do not* show up at eight in the morning."

Sev held up his hands. "I wasn't planning to!"

Misa narrowed her eyes at him. "Suuure."

—⁂—

At exactly eight o'clock the next morning, Sev found himself standing outside Jerome's room.

He wasn't *actually* going to intrude on Misa's reunion with her family. For one thing, she was still asleep, and he wasn't going to introduce himself to them without her *or* try to wake her up. For another, she just . . . seemed like she needed some time to catch up with them. He thought instead about what he wanted to do, and two things jumped out at him.

One, he wanted to visit Jerome and make sure the guy was doing okay. He wasn't exactly sure how much the paladin knew about what happened with Aurum, or what the state of his divine connection was. If nothing else, he felt the paladin might want to know what was happening with his chosen god.

Two, he wanted to visit Velykos. The stone elemental had been pleasant company, and while he wasn't sure what he wanted to do, with the infolock apparently not working . . . he wanted to see if he could give something back to him. He'd make sure there were priests around, of course. Just in case.

So he'd found the replacement clerk and asked where to find Jerome, and he'd been led to this door. Jerome's party members—the two elves—were apparently out at the moment, the clerk had told him.

"Do you know what's happening with Max?" Sev asked, vaguely worried.

"I'm not informed on that kind of thing, no," the clerk said with a shake of his head.

"And your nametag says that your name is . . . *also* Max?"

"Max" let out a long-suffering sigh. "Yes, I've been asked this question before."

"Just so we're clear," he said. "You're not actually the same Max."

"No, sir," the clerk sighed. "We just happen to have the same name. I dislike subbing in for her for exactly this reason, you know."

"Aha! You called me *sir*." Sev pointed triumphantly at . . . well, not at the clerk. That would have been rude. He pointed instead at the wall *next* to Max, his hand jerking to the left at the last minute, leaving this other Max to stare at him rather unimpressed. "The *real* Max would never call me *sir*. You're definitely not her."

"Sir," the clerk said, sounding vaguely exasperated. "You can only delay entering the room for so long. Jerome is expecting you."

"Just as insightful as Max, though," Sev muttered with a sigh, and eyed the door critically for a moment before giving it a knock.

He didn't know why he was so nervous. It shouldn't have mattered. He was visiting someone that was under heavy supervision; there was a reason this clerk was here in the first place, though he wouldn't be listening in. He'd just be on the lookout for skill activations.

The door opened, startling Sev. Jerome stared out at him, looking surprisingly . . . normal.

The man wasn't wearing any extravagant armor or anything of the like. He was dressed in casual clothes—*planeshifter* casual clothes. A cotton T-shirt and loose-fitting pants. Sev was almost jealous, looking at him; they seemed comfortable.

"Uh, hi," Sev said awkwardly. "I'm here to visit. Give you some news about Aurum."

"Oh!" Jerome's face brightened somewhat. "Man, I've been kinda worried about the guy. Haven't heard anything at all over the connection. You know if he's okay?"

"I think he is," Sev said with a slight grimace. "The system's being a bit weird about it. It says he's attaching to me, so . . . I'll let you know if he's okay once that's done. Whatever that is, it's taking a long time."

"The fuck does that mean?" Jerome frowned at him. Then he winced slightly and caught himself. "Uh. I mean . . . Do you know what that means?"

"You know about as much as I do," Sev said with a shrug. "Therapy's doing a number on you, huh?"

"Listen, man," Jerome groaned. "They keep giving me *lectures*. I didn't come to another world for this shit! And they won't stop until I actually understand them! It's not fair!"

"Are you sure that's the therapy?" Sev raised an eyebrow. "That doesn't sound like therapy. That sounds like the introductory classes the Guild conducts for new adventurers."

Jerome's face was blank. "What's the difference?"

Sev sighed, changing the subject. "Never mind," he said. "Look, I'm glad you're doing well. I gotta get going. I'll keep you updated on Aurum?"

"Obviously," Jerome said, and then paused. "Uh, I mean . . . please."

Sev stared at him for a moment, then laughed. "You know what, I'll give you credit for trying."

CHAPTER 54

SCULPTING STONE

Sev found Velykos in the gardens behind the temple again, rather than inside the temple proper. It was quite the sight, really. As old as Velykos was, he was still *large*, and he towered over the majority of the trees and flowers and herbs that filled the temple garden.

The garden itself was beautiful. Part of it was set out to harvest potion ingredients, that much was clear—there were rows and rows of identical plants, each in various stages of growth and carefully marked accordingly. But the rest of it? The rest of it was beautifully laid out, more haphazard art than anything orderly; clusters of bright, five-petaled flowers grew in broken zig-zags around twisting vines, and a variety of trees brightened the atmosphere with various colors.

Really, Sev was never going to get over the fact that this world had trees that came in bright blue.

"Hey, Velykos," Sev called, and the stone elemental turned to him in surprise. He seemed pleased to see Sev, though, and gestured for the cleric to join him, though he also put a stone finger to his not-quite-lips.

"There is a bird here," Velykos said, his voice surprisingly quiet. It sounded like the gentle drift of sand down a dune instead of the usual gravel and rock. "It injured itself. I have been taking care of it."

"It doesn't have health, huh?" Sev said, peering at the bird that Velykos was talking about. It was sleeping, the little thing, a tiny chest rising and falling with every breath.

. . . He had no idea what kind of bird it was, though. It had an incredibly long beak, and its feathers were almost prismatic, shimmering in a number of different colors every time the light glanced off it from a different angle.

"It is too insignificant," Velykos answered. "Though perhaps significance is not the marker by which the system identifies an object . . . It is good to see you again. Your name was Sev, yes?"

"Yeah," Sev said. "I wanted to check in. Make sure everything was going okay after what happened. I'm sorry about that—I didn't know what would happen."

"It is fine," Velykos said with a hum. "Nillea forgives all. Though . . . do you come here to speak of your god again? The one whose name cannot be spoken?"

"Recent events have led me to believe that I can talk about it now," Sev said. "But it's not something I'm *sure* about. I made sure to tell some of the priests before I came here, so they're keeping an eye on us, but . . ."

"Why do you wish to tell me of your god?" Velykos asked calmly. Very, very gently, he placed the bird he was holding back into its nest, the stone he was made of displaying an astonishing flexibility. "Not to preach, I assume."

"Definitely not," Sev said, letting out a slightly uncomfortable laugh. He knew what *that* felt like. But how was he supposed to explain that he thought Velykos had lost a piece of himself? That he'd been forced to choose a different god, and to forget about the old one?

Though, in all fairness, there was a lot about the relationship mortals and gods had that made Sev uncomfortable.

"Can you tell me a little more about your mentor?" Sev asked, deciding to switch tacks. "The daemon you said became a friend?"

Velykos nodded. Slowly, he rose to his feet, Sev feeling once again a little overwhelmed by the way the stone elemental just towered over everything around him; it was a wonder that he didn't trample the grass beneath his feet every time he took a step. "Walk with me," the stone elemental said. "I want to tend to the garden."

"Of course," Sev said, surprised.

"His name was Ramos," Velykos explained after a short pause. He was inspecting some strange-looking flowers that grew out of the trunk of a tree rather than out of the ground; each petal shimmered strangely, like they were barely real. "Though he did not tell me his name until I had known him for many years. Their names are important to them, you see."

"Magically?" Sev asked.

"Culturally," Velykos said, glancing at Sev. The human blinked once, feeling a little bit embarrassed. "Their names hold no power over them, no matter what the planeshifted rumors say. But their true names are an intimate thing, given only to people that they trust beyond measure; people they consider family."

"Is it . . . okay that you're telling me his name, then?"

"He is long gone," Velykos said mildly. "And it is equally important to them that their true name is used when they are dead. They believe an element of themselves lives in their name; if it is used when they are alive, then their selves are diluted. But if they are gone, it is the only way they live on."

"Ramos, then," Sev said, and Velykos nodded approvingly at the way he said it; quiet and respectful, like a prayer for the lost.

"He was a kind man," the stone elemental said. "Dedicated to the god he chose to worship. Daemons do not ordinarily have a good relationship with gods; they live a life of rejection. By the system, by the gods, and by the world itself."

"But Nillea chose to accept him," Sev said. He was stepping in territory he thought might have be within the realm of the original infolock. If he was *right* about who Ramos and Velykos had worshipped—if it had been Onyx instead of Nillea . . .

"Yes," Velykos said, though he took a moment to pause as he more carefully inspected yet another flower. Sev saw a brief flash of divine mana before a gentle mist of water settled over the plant. "It is strange, if I reflect on it. Though Nillea is a goddess of the Earth, she is not known for her kindness toward daemons. I suppose she saw in him someone that was trying to do better and wanted to give him the opportunity . . ."

Velykos stopped, and this time not to examine any plant or flower. He stopped like he'd been struck by a thought, and he turned a grave look toward Sev. "This is why you come to speak to me, is it not?" the stone elemental said. "I hear the stories. I know a little of what you and yours have been involved with. Gods and angels."

"How much did you hear?" Sev asked with a small frown. As far as he understood, most of that information wouldn't have been able to propagate—even the Guildmaster had said Max hadn't been able to explain much of what happened with Jerome and what Aurum had been doing. "And how?"

"I hear through Nillea," Velykos said. "Through dreams, occasionally, though sleep for a stone elemental is sporadic. Sometimes through skills. [**The Walls Have Ears**]."

"That . . ." Sev paused. Creepy name for a skill. "I'm not sure how to feel about that."

"It is a bypass," Velykos said. "I should have tried it earlier. The skill is less literal and weaker than it sounds; I do not truly understand what I hear. I gain a half-formed instinct about what may have transpired, instead."

"Somehow that doesn't make me feel better about it," Sev said a little dryly, and Velykos tipped his head in acknowledgement.

"I do not use it often," the stone elemental said. "Only when I suspect that my perception is being messed with. Which is more often than I had expected when I first moved here."

"Ah, right. Because of the Guildmaster." Sev gathered his thoughts. "That's how you found out how the skill works?"

"It is, yes," Velykos acknowledged. "I have informed her of the skill and what it does, out of courtesy. She does not contest my use of it."

"That was kind of you," Sev said, blinking once. "Kind of her, too, I guess. I'm surprised she let you use it."

"She said it keeps her honest," Velykos said, shrugging his massive shoulders with a rumble. "I am given to understand that her colleagues do something similar so that she does not simply run unchecked with her abilities."

"I didn't realize that was something she was worried about at all," Sev said. "Huh. Good for her, I guess."

"We were discussing the gods," Velykos reminded him. "You came to speak to me of your god, I believe."

"Yeah," Sev said. He hesitated, still, an unnatural trepidation rising up in him. He remembered the last time he'd done this, when he'd woken up on the floor and been told he almost died. He remembered what he'd done for Kestel, and the memories he'd taken on in return—the very sensations he'd been lucky enough to skip the first time around. The thought of his heart seizing and stopping, his blood flow suddenly not enough to keep the rest of his body running—

"—You are panicking," Velykos said gently, over the ringing in his ears, the stone elemental raising a stone chair through the earth. He nudged Sev backward to get him to sit, and conjured a droplet of water for him to sip from—an *actual* droplet of water, a tiny sphere of magically animated liquid that stayed solid in his hands.

Sev stared at the droplet for a moment, mesmerized, and then took a small sip from it.

". . . Sorry about that," Sev said after a moment. He took a deep breath. "I wanted to tell you about what I think really happened," he added softly. "I don't know if I'm right. But you told me that Ramos liked to sculpt things out of stone . . ."

"He wanted to leave behind a mark on the world," Velykos agreed. "He acknowledged that even stone would wear down eventually. But he wanted to leave the world more beautiful than when he found it."

"Does that sound like a follower of Nillea to you?" Sev asked. His tone wasn't accusatory—it was genuinely curious. He didn't know much about Nillea beyond that she was a goddess of the Earth. "What does Nillea represent?"

Velykos took a moment to consider the question. "She represents a respect for the Earth and the bounties that come from it," the stone elemental eventually answered. There was a slight frown in his voice. "An appreciation for the natural beauty of the land."

Ah. *There* was the contradiction he'd failed to spot the first time. Not in the events of the story itself, necessarily, but in the domain of the gods.

. . . Maybe he needed to pay a little more attention when it came to the gods, Sev thought to himself with a grimace. He *was* the cleric of the party, and the one that would be expected to know more about the gods . . .

Sev glanced up at Velykos to see how he was doing. The stone elemental was frowning to himself, little pebbles rolling around in agitation along his form. Subconscious elemental manipulation, maybe?

"It is strange that he was a follower of Nillea, now that my attention has been called to that fact," Velykos said at last. "You believe this has something to do with your own god?"

Sev nodded. "Onyx was a god of change," he said quietly. "Well. A minor god of change, anyway. He was a god of sculpting, of leaving a mark on the land that's all your own.

"It just . . . It seems to fit a little too well, you know?"

CHAPTER 55

MEMORIES

Velykos was silent for a moment, processing Sev's words. He seemed to use gardening as a distraction as he thought, bending down to pluck weeds from the dirt with a delicate precision that Sev would not have expected from him. Every weed he plucked disintegrated as he clenched his fists, which . . .

. . . was mildly worrying, Sev had to admit. He was relatively certain Velykos hadn't been disintegrating plants before. A larger part of him, though, was more relieved that there had been no apparent adverse reaction—no visible twitch from Velykos as he failed to process what Sev said, and certainly no unnatural drop in his own health.

"It does fit well," Velykos eventually said, his voice soft. It wasn't *angry*, exactly, which made Sev exhale a sigh of relief. "I am unsure how to feel about it. I have followed Nillea for such a long time, and you tell me now that I may have chosen to follow the wrong god . . ."

"Nillea may have done good for you regardless," Sev said. "I mean, I don't know her, obviously. But you're not powerless; you've got a skill that helps you remember things *around* infolocks . . . maybe she wanted you to know."

"If that is true . . ." Velykos's words trailed off as he thought on the matter, and then he nodded to himself, as if satisfied with whatever conclusion he'd reached. "Then I am grateful, I think. But I do not understand. You said he *was* those things; is he not any longer? And are you not a cleric yourself? If he is your bonded divinity, and you maintain your ability to use and cast skills . . ."

"I don't know all the answers," Sev said with a slight grimace, looking down. "I still have all my skills and I don't know why; yeah, you're right about that. I know Onyx isn't *gone*, and maybe that's why. Or maybe it's because the circumstances with my class are kind of fucked up to begin with."

"But there is more you wish to share," Velykos said, and Sev nodded with a sigh.

He'd pointed out to the Guildmaster that informing the entire temple about what was happening would have been a bad idea—but informing Velykos? He didn't know the stone elemental very well, it was true, but he almost felt like he owed it to him. Velykos's god, if he was right, had already *been* erased; the connection he had now was a fake, a remnant forged from the connection he'd once had.

"He *was* a god, yes," Sev said quietly. "Whether he is now . . . I don't know. I don't fully understand what happened to him. But this is something you need to know, and something you need to tell only people you trust, because I don't know what kind of panic this might cause if it gets out."

"You have my word," Velykos said solemnly.

"The gods are dying," Sev said bluntly. "Maybe not directly, and maybe not in a way we understand. But every so often, the system picks a god and begins to scrub it from existence. It erases that god's understanding of themselves, and it erases everything that god's followers remember of them. All paladins, clerics, anyone who follows that god and relies on them for power— they're prompted to choose a different god. And when they do, they forget everything about the one they followed before."

There was a long silence after Sev spoke. Velykos continued silently in the garden, his footsteps barely so much as bending even a blade of grass—but the rocks on his body were agitated now, the pebbles trembling against him in barely suppressed fury.

"This would explain a lot," Velykos said. "Though you understand that this is difficult to believe without proof."

"And proof is hard to provide for something like this," Sev said with a sigh. "Look, I understand if you don't believe me—"

"The strange thing is that I do," Velykos interrupted. "I know that I should be skeptical, and yet . . . a part of me insists that I accept your words no matter how little sense they make. [**The Walls Have Ears**] kicking in, no doubt. And so, I must believe that you are in fact telling me the truth. That the god Ramos originally worshipped was not Nillea but this Onyx that you speak of. That the god I followed in turn was originally Onyx, until that was taken away from me, and replaced with a different god . . ."

Velykos's voice trailed off and then became firm. "Yes. The more I speak of it, the more certain I am. I have lost something crucial to me in the exchange, I think."

"What makes you say that?" Sev asked tentatively.

"Because I remember a moment in which I changed," Velykos said bluntly. "My memories still say that I follow Nillea, and that I have always followed Nillea. But there is a marked change in my behavior—a marked change in the carvings on my body, if you follow them."

Sev paid attention for the first time. Stone elementals aged by carving and eroding away at their own bodies, the designs slowly becoming more intricate with time—he'd already seen that the first time, but until Velykos had pointed it out, he hadn't noticed the way the engravings *changed.*

Initially, they were artistic sworls and patterns, landscapes painted in impressionistic, abstract ways. Sometimes, they were clearer and cleaner, but Velykos's markings there were filled in like it was at the whim of an artist; it changed with his mood and with the day.

And then after a certain point—new carvings were all in the same style. It was never the exact same image twice, but there was no variation, no change of mood; a lined capture of different natural landscapes, from cliffs and canyons to sunsets and forests.

"I recall being more adventurous in my youth," Velykos mused out loud. "At a certain point, I wanted to be an adventurer rather than work in this temple. There was no real appeal to me when it came to plants and gardening . . . That all came after a certain point."

"After you lost Onyx, you think?" Sev asked quietly.

"That is what I suspect now, yes," Velykos said. "What would you say Onyx was like?"

Sev squirmed a little. "He was just . . . a guy," he said. "He tried to encourage his followers into doing whatever they wanted to do, within reason. Told them they could sculpt the shape of their own lives. He was a big proponent of that sort of thing."

"Nillea is a goddess of slow change and eventual growth," Velykos supplied. "They are perhaps not too different in that regard, and yet . . . I remember a time when I wanted with far more passion than I have now. There was a time I wanted to explore the world, as Ramos had done, to find my own inspirations and make my own sculptures . . ."

"Do you still make them?" Sev asked.

"I do not," Velykos said with a regretful shake of his head. "Most of my efforts are focused now on potion-making, so that the adventurers who come to the temple have something that will keep them alive. And I have found that many of the other priests do not have the . . . delicate touch that is occasionally required for potion-making, shall we say. They require my assistance."

"You sort of fell into this life, huh?" Sev glanced around at the garden contemplatively. "Are you the one that takes care of this garden?"

"I am," Velykos confirmed. "It is the source of many of our ingredients, though not all of them. Some plants cannot be sustained here and must be grown in the wild; for those, we set quests out for adventurers to harvest them."

"I wonder if this isn't a small part of your self trying to express itself," Sev muttered to himself. The garden did strike him as that, in a way—one half strict, labeled, orderly rows, and the other wild and unkempt and beautiful. But that seemed like a bit of a stretch.

Velykos smiled at him anyway, like he knew what he was thinking. "The garden is something I am very proud of," the stone elemental said. "But perhaps it is time that I consider taking up the adventurer's mantle again. If I am to seek answers about the god that Ramos worshipped, and the god that I may have worshipped once upon a time."

"You could just ask me, you know," Sev said, though he felt a little embarrassed saying the words. Velykos chuckled.

"I am aware," the stone elemental said. "And as I mentioned, I believe that you are correct in that I once worshipped a different god. I do not know if that god is Onyx, and if it is, I would like to search for a way to recover those memories."

"I guess," Sev said, though he frowned slightly. All this time, and he hadn't considered looking into a way to help people recover their memories of their lost god . . .

Well, that wasn't true. He *had*. But the fact was that he had very little to go on, and at the time he had been practically falling apart from the side effects of trying to heal Onyx as he was being forgotten.

"I will have to make sure that the plants are well taken care of," Velykos said, this time speaking more to himself than to Sev. "I believe there are a number of priests that show potential in that regard . . . I do not suppose you would be willing to care for these plants in my stead?"

"What?" Sev blinked. "I have to leave too. My team's headed over to Elyra in a day or two . . ."

Sev's voice trailed off slightly as he took in Velykos's expression. The stone elemental was, in his best approximation of the word, *grinning* at him— though it was difficult to define what he was doing as grinning. More like an amused roll of his shoulders, a slight quirk in the rocks that represented his facial expression.

"Oh. You were joking," Sev said lamely.

"I was indeed," Velykos rumbled, amused. "Though it seems my sense of humor is something I need to work on. I appreciate your candor in informing me of all this, however. There is something to be said for knowing the truth behind the matter... and I feel a drive that I have not felt in years. I will let you know of anything I find, and perhaps I can find a way to cure the affliction that has struck so many, while you search for a way to stop more gods from being consumed by this process."

"Of course," Sev said. He'd been intending to do that anyway. But his voice came out a little weak; he was distracted by a flashing notice that had appeared in front of him.

<NOTICE>
Attachment of coalesced entity <Aurum, God of Gold> complete.
Finalizing...

CHAPTER 56

MANIFESTATION

A lot of things happened all at once.

First was the sudden influx of an absolutely monumental amount of divine mana—the kind that would escape the notice of most people's [**Mana Sight**], but not the notice of the [**Divine Sense**] that many clerics had. Several priests over in the nearby temple jerked their heads over, their eyes growing wide; Velykos, in contrast, narrowed his eye-equivalents and stepped back somewhat cautiously. A spell began to form in his hands, though there was too much of a storm of divine mana for Sev to be able to tell what kind of spell it was.

But the caution was warranted, in Sev's opinion. The magic was terrifying. It acted like no form of divine magic he'd ever seen before. Layers of divine mana twisted themselves over him, then attached to his body—to his *soul*, if he was understanding what he was seeing correctly—like golden, divine strings. Those strings led a short distance away and then abruptly vanished.

Just as quickly as it began, it was over. The notification box vanished, and the storm of divine mana abruptly calmed, although it didn't disappear; instead, it started to slowly dissipate, spreading out from where it had coalesced.

For a moment, Sev was confused. Hadn't the box said that it was *manifesting*? What, exactly, had manifested, except the strings that now seemed attached to the stuff of his soul?

"What was that?" Velykos asked him, and Sev realized with a start that the stone elemental had been gathering healing magic into his hands. Now that the immediate danger seemed to be over, he let the magic flow away, joining the rest of the ambient divine mana in dispersing.

"It was . . ." Sev hesitated, then sighed; there wasn't much use in keeping it hidden, he thought. Velykos knew most of the story, anyway. "I told you that the system is erasing gods. My team was able to rescue one that we think was in the process of being erased. We don't fully understand the mechanics of what happened there, but apparently the god needs something to anchor to, and I was the only available option."

"Anchor . . ." Velykos repeated the word with a slight frown. He shook his head after a moment, not getting whatever he needed to get out of the word. "It reminds me of the connection that we share with our gods, perhaps," the stone elemental said. "Though I am certain it is not the same thing."

"The notification text implied that all gods need to be attached to an anchor," Sev said. "On top of all the people that worship them. I'm not sure exactly what relationship that implies, but . . . we'll find out, I guess."

The strings were still there, attached to him. There were no notifications that he could see about new skills, or new abilities—though his status was still fuzzy and grayed out, like something about it was still updating. Experimentally, he tugged on the strings of divine mana he could now feel.

This time, there was a response.

H-hello?

That was Aurum's voice, echoing back down through the connection; Sev metaphorically jerked back from his grip on the thread, startled. He didn't quite know how to process that. Aurum's voice was gone almost as soon as he released his grip on it, so he reached out again, feeling for the connection and this time connecting as gently as he could.

Aurum? he asked, trying to send his thoughts along the connection—the same way he'd done with Onyx, before his god had been forgotten. The sensation wasn't exactly the same; the nature of the connection was different. *Can you hear me?*

Yes! Aurum's mental voice was suddenly enthusiastic. **I'm back now! The angels were all so worried about me . . . Histre is here, too. They didn't think I would come back, but I did! Did you guys do that?**

I think so, Sev answered. *The system says you're connected to me now. Do you know what's up with that?*

I dunno, Aurum said. **Um . . . Lemme ask!**

A short pause.

All of us have to be connected, the angels say, Aurum reported back after a moment, sounding more confused than anything else. **They don't really know why. But they say it's a price we have to pay. Um . . . They say that it's also the source of our powers? It's how I can send down angels and stuff! If I pull from the connection.**

Please do not do that, Sev said with a slight wince. *You're connected to me, not to an anchor. If you try to pull anything like what you did before, with the angels, uh . . . I don't really know what will happen to me.*

I don't think I can even if I wanted to, Aurum said. **Your connection feels . . . um . . . weaker? I dunno. There's not much I can pull from it even if I want to. If anything it feels like it's almost the opposite.**

The opposite? Sev frowned. *You mean I can pull from you instead? Why would the connection be inverted like that?*

I dunno! Aurum said again. Sev sighed, and changed tacks.

Do you remember anything about what happened? he asked, keeping his mental voice gentle. He wanted to know where Aurum had *been,* before the god had been anchored to him. *After we freed you?*

Um . . . Aurum seemed to give this some serious thought, but then Sev felt the mental sensation of the god shaking his head. **Kinda. But I can't remember clearly yet. The angels say ice cream will help.**

Excuse me? Sev blinked.

You gotta eat some ice cream, Aurum told him. **I can taste it through the connection. And then I can remember things! Maybe.**

Sev paused for a moment, then let out a sigh. *You just want ice cream, don't you?*

The angels tell me to tell you that I won't speak without my lawyer, Aurum supplied helpfully. Sev groaned.

Where did you even hear that, the cleric muttered, and then looked up at Velykos, who was blinking at him curiously. He hadn't stopped tending to the flowers even then.

"Do you happen to know a place I can get ice cream?" Sev said out loud, a little awkwardly. He didn't have much hope for that; he'd never seen it in town. But if Aurum was giving him an excuse to try to find a treat for himself . . .

"There is none nearby," Velykos said, his tone implying that he'd been thrown off by the question but was going along with the flow anyway. "But I know how to make some, if you wish."

"You do?" Sev blinked up at him, surprised.

"I did not always live here," Velykos said. "And I have encountered the children of the planeshifted before. Ice cream is a common demand."

"Is it?" Sev sounded bewildered. "Are you telling me I could have had ice cream this whole time and all I needed to do was come to the temple and *ask?*"

"Well, that was not my intention," Velykos said, his tone an amused rumble. "But I would have made you some had you asked, yes. In all fairness, I doubt you could have reasonably expected to find ice cream within a temple."

"I mean I definitely didn't, but I kind of regret not talking to you guys more," Sev muttered. Then he thought about what he'd said, and amended his statement. "I regret not talking to *you* more. Maybe Ixome, since all he needed was a little bit of a wakeup call. Jury's still out on the rest of the priests."

"Do you have something against us?" Velykos asked, sounding amused. He was leading the way back to the temple, though he stopped as he passed by some plants—very carefully, Velykos reached out to the bean pods on those plants. He didn't pluck them off, instead using a tiny knife he manifested on the tip of a finger to split open a pod. He scraped out the insides with a blade of divine magic, and held it there carefully as he pressed the pod shut again.

Healing magic gently suffused the plant, and the pod seemed to heal completely. Sev blinked.

"Does that plant have health?" he asked, slightly thrown off. "Wait, no. To answer your question, I don't have anything against priests; it's just that a lot of them preach at me a lot, and . . . I care about my friendship with Onyx, you know?"

"You have a closer and more casual relationship with your god than most," Velykos acknowledged with a nod. "Many in the temple would call it blasphemous. And no, that plant does not have health; healing magic is more effective on it because it is able to absorb that mana independent of the system and heal itself."

Sev blinked, glancing back at the plant. "Huh," he said thoughtfully. That was a line of research to follow, if he could get Vex to research it. If he could heal people that were disconnected from the system . . . it'd be easier to heal people like Kestel. Healing magic was too ineffective otherwise without health to help it along.

"Will you be telling anyone what happened?" Velykos asked him curiously, and Sev blinked up at him. "It was rather obvious, and many of the priests seem eager to ask."

"Oh." Sev had almost forgotten. "Uh . . . no, I don't think so. That's something that I want to keep private. I'll say I got a divine message from my god, or something, and it's not meant for them."

"Did you?"

"I mean, *technically*, that happened," Sev said. "It's just that the god just wants to taste ice cream."

"Ah! Thus the current quest." Velykos seemed inordinately amused by the prospect. He continued leading the way into the temple—several priests immediately began to approach them, but Velykos waved at them, and they backed off, seeming to get the message.

"Wow," Sev said. "Maybe I should get you as an escort more whenever I need to visit the temple."

"Remember," Velykos said with a chuckle, "I am planning to return to adventuring, to uncover what may have happened to Ramos. You may not find it quite that easy to find me."

"Well, I'll be in Elyra, anyway," Sev said with a shrug. "Are you planning on heading in that direction?"

Velykos nodded. "It has been a long time, and all traces of him may be gone," the stone elemental said. "But that is where I last saw Ramos, and I believe I will try to track down where he went and what happened to him. There were dungeons near that area that I will have to check."

"Can you do it alone?" Sev asked.

"I hear there are teams of adventurers that are recruiting now," Velykos said with a shrug. "A paladin of gold? His party is down to three members, and they may be in need of a mage."

Sev winced slightly. "Uh . . . good luck with him," he said. He couldn't imagine what Jerome's team would look like with Velykos there, actually. "If you do join his team."

"It is just a thought," Velykos said with a chuckle.

They arrived at a small room at the back of the temple—all of the priests had their own little bedrooms, each separated by a thin cloth barrier, although Velykos's was larger than most due to the simple nature of his size. In the corner of his section was a small chest; the telltale mist of frost magic spilled out when he opened the chest.

Velykos retrieved a small bottle of milk, some sugar from the nearby drawers, and the various other ingredients he needed, including the small pods from the plant that he'd retrieved. Sev simply sat back and watched. It was nice, in a way, that so many planeshifted recipes had spread as they had.

Soon enough, he had a small bowl of ice cream, and a *very* pleased god humming along to the taste in his head.

Sev couldn't deny that he was enjoying it too.

I'm gonna try to remember, Aurum told him, while enjoying the taste of the vanilla-flavored ice cream alongside him. **The angels think I should, too. But gimme a few hours.**

Sev just nodded. Aurum had only just returned. He'd figured it might take a while. He could wait.

Hopefully Aurum didn't barge in with a world-changing revelation during dinner with Misa's family, though. That would just be awkward.

CHAPTER 57

UNDERSTANDING NEW SKILLS

Derivan had suggested they go back to the forest to test any new ideas they had about magic, and so they had. They'd informed the Guildmaster beforehand, just in case anything went wrong with the skills they wanted to test and the magic they wanted to cast—she'd assured them she would ensure there were people that would keep an eye on them while giving them privacy, through an assortment of [**Danger Sense**]–adjacent skills—so they were free to practice as much as they wanted within the forest.

For now, though, Vex was just charging up Derivan with more mana, trying to push Slime into the next stage. The amount of mana he absorbed passively had slowly increased as the stat went up; it was at a whole twenty-five now, giving the armor 2,500 mana to play with.

"I'm almost jealous," Vex admitted with a shy smile, not looking remotely jealous. If anything, he seemed admiring. "I had to go through . . . a lot more, to get as much mana as I have now. And you've already almost caught up."

"It will get much harder now, I think," Derivan said. He watched the forest with [**Mana Sight**] turned on, enjoying the playful dance of mana over the trees—it hadn't noticed them yet, and wouldn't until they began to cast. He'd try to disturb it as little as possible, but something about the dance sparked something in him, and he wanted to test that.

"It's still incredible," Vex said. "If my family knew this . . ."

He fell silent, then, and Derivan glanced at him with concern. The lizardkin didn't seem like he was willing to elaborate too heavily on the topic yet, and so Derivan changed the subject.

"You still know far more about magic than I could hope to, I believe," Derivan said with a small smile. "Do you want to try your new skill first? [**Splash of Mana**], yes?"

"Oh! Yes," Vex said, brightening considerably. "The skill doesn't actually tell me a lot about what it'll do, so I'm thinking I can use [**Delineate**] to limit the effects first. And once we've got a better idea of what it does, we can figure out what to do with it."

"Indeed," Derivan said, though he was paying attention more to the lizard's smile than the words. Misa was rather more practiced at exploiting skills than he was, though he'd had his moments.

Vex stood back for a moment, preparing the skills he wanted to cast—first, [**Delineate**], which didn't cost any mana at all and didn't seem to be a spell. The air seemed to twist and turn in the region he had marked, and now there was a barely-visible boundary sitting in the air, an almost-sphere.

"Huh," Vex said. Then he reached out and cast [**Splash of Mana**]. It was an ambiguous cast, formed with no real intent behind the spell, and so the mana that emerged wasn't typed in any particular way; instead, raw mana spilled out of him, bright and colorful to Derivan's eyes.

It splashed into the area marked by [**Delineate**], like it had struck a barrier, and then settled into a pool at the bottom of the sphere. It hovered there, invisible to the naked eye but a gentle glowing green to his [**Mana Sight**].

"It acts like a liquid," Vex said after a moment, carefully looking over the spell. The mana didn't seem to be dissipating like it normally did—whether that was due to [**Delineate**] specifically or due to the effects of [**Splash of Mana**], he wasn't sure. "That'll let me create spells that cling to people, I think, if it works that way? If I make the liquid more viscous . . ."

"Can you do that?" Derivan asked curiously, and Vex nodded.

"I didn't show you the skill box, did I?" the lizardkin said. He gestured, and the box popped up in front of Derivan; he glanced at it.

[**Splash of Mana**] [**Active Skill**] [**Grade: 1**]
Cost: Variable mana
Your mana takes on a form akin to paint, allowing you to color surfaces with it. This Skill has secrets and will grow as your understanding of mana grows.

"That's . . . an unusual description," Derivan commented after reading it through twice. He glanced at Vex with a metaphorical eyebrow raised, one glowing eye lifted over the other. "Are skills usually this direct about their growth?"

"They're not," Vex said, shaking his head. "I've never seen one be this direct, actually. Most skills *do* have secrets to them, and understanding them enough always unlocks some sort of skill growth—Misa's [**To Fall Yet Hold**

the Line] is one of them, even if she hasn't chosen to evolve the skill yet. So there's no reason for this skill to outright state it the way it does."

"And yet," Derivan mused.

"And yet," Vex agreed. He glanced at the bit of liquid mana still hovering in [**Delineate**]d space and made a gesture; the [**Delineate**] skill cut out, and the liquid mana within splashed down onto the grass.

There were two immediate effects that Derivan could observe—one was that the ambient mana nearby shied away, though not nearly as dramatically as it presumably did when a full spell was cast. The second was that the mana began to dissipate noticeably.

"It's still not dissipating as quickly as when a normal spell is cast," Vex murmured to himself, glancing over the puddle of mana and making a note in one of his journals. "So the liquid state is definitely a factor when it comes to mana dissipation rate. It's like evaporation, then?"

"If it is like paint," Derivan said, "would it not dry rather than dissipate?"

Vex paused and frowned. "That's a good point," the lizardkin admitted. "I'm not actually sure. There's a few different forms of paint I was thinking of when I used the skill, so if it doesn't anchor to any one of them, the mana might just evaporate. Or maybe it'll require me to dismiss the skill?"

They stared at the patch of mana for a moment. It was still dissipating, but the process was slow; Vex was right in that it wasn't nearly as fast as when a normal spell was cast.

"We're not actually going to watch paint dry, are we?" Vex asked after a moment of staring.

"It seems to me that we may be watching grass grow," Derivan said dryly. Vex giggled. Planeshifted humor. They weren't exactly familiar with all of the cultural norms, but they'd heard enough of Sev's sayings over the months. Sev didn't even realize they were planeshifted sayings, usually, when he said them; it was a consequence of his memory.

"Well, while we're waiting for this, do you want to try anything?" Vex asked. Derivan nodded.

"I would like to try out that skill, I think," Derivan said, then paused to consider his words. "Later. First, I wish to test my ideas of magic. You mentioned the mana would shy away once I cast a spell, did you not?"

"Yeah," Vex said. "It doesn't like it for some reason. I'm not sure why."

"Perhaps because of the way we cast spells," Derivan mused. He cast a [**Barrier**] spell once, watching as the ambient mana immediately shot away from the manifestation of . . . what he would call *dead mana*, he thought. The word wasn't exactly accurate—the mana wasn't dead by any means—but it was . . . docile. It didn't seem to have the same joy that the ambient mana here did.

So what if he changed the way he cast the spell?

He was leaning more on the Magic stat now, he realized. He tried to remember the way the spell had cast when he'd been relying on the system—he didn't have a hope of understanding the complicated runic constructs that had instantaneously formed and dissipated, guiding the mana into forming a barrier. But he could remember the way the mana flowed and *changed*, switching from an ethereal presence into something solid . . .

Instead of using his own mana to fuel the spell, he used [**Mana Manipulation**]. Instead of forcing the mana into his own shape, he asked it to move as he wanted, to change as he wanted. If his ideas were correct, if the mana was *alive* . . .

The mana responded.

It was slow and hesitant—far different from anything he was used to when he cast spells. Those formed instantly. Now, though, the mana had to understand what he was asking for, and he could almost sense that it didn't trust him. There was the way that it hesitated, the way it shied away from the grip of [**Mana Manipulation**] . . .

But he kept at it. Vex was watching him carefully, his eyes slightly wide, but he didn't say a word. The mana gathered into his hands, and then slowly shifted—not through any particular twist of his skills but simply because he'd asked.

Just above his hand was a small but gleaming . . . No. It wasn't a [**Barrier**]. It was a barrier.

The mana that was swirling farther away from them came back closer. Vex was staring at it in a curious sort of wonder. "May I?" he asked.

"Of course," Derivan said.

The lizardkin came close and poked at the barrier once, his eyes gleaming with his particular version of [**Mana Sight**]. "It doesn't *look* different to me," Vex said softly. "But it *feels* different. Stronger. You didn't get a notification about a new version of the [**Barrier**] spell, did you?"

"I did not," Derivan said, shaking his head.

"May I try a spell on it?" Vex asked.

"I would like to test its efficacy," Derivan agreed, nodding. "It is more difficult to cast than the standard [**Barrier**]."

Vex paused for a moment, as if considering what spell he wanted to use—and then he reached out with a hand. Electricity played across his scales. "[**Shocking Grasp**]," he explained when Derivan looked over at him. His fingers brushed against the barrier—

"—Ow." Vex winced, pulling his hand back sharply. Derivan had been watching as the lizardkin reached out, and he saw the spell pop and fizzle strangely against the barrier. At the same time, he felt the mana within the barrier twist, like it no longer wanted to stay in that position, and so he let go of whatever tenuous grasp he held on it; the barrier unraveled in his hands, and Vex looked at it, surprised. "Did I break it?"

"I dismissed it," Derivan said.

"Ah." Vex winced a little as he looked down at his hand. "I've never felt anything like that before. It was almost like the mana rejected me."

"A path worth exploring, then?" Derivan asked, and Vex nodded vigorously.

"Yes. I mean, teach *me* how to do that. I want to learn."

"Of course," Derivan said, feeling strangely pleased that he could do something in return for the lizardkin. He had no doubt that Vex would pick up on anything he could teach remarkably quickly, but the lizardkin seemed *excited* in a way that he rarely was unless they discovered something new.

"It might be something you can only do with the Magic stat, but I want to try anyway," Vex said. "And if it works together with [**Splash of Mana**], I have some ideas. But let's try and see what—uh, I don't know how to say the skill name out loud. The skill you have with an error in the name. You wanted to test it out, right?"

"I did," Derivan said. "You are sure? I do not mind guiding you through what I just did, first."

"Nah," Vex said. "Let's see what that skill does. We can play with magic after. I want to spend as much time on that as possible." He grinned at Derivan, and Derivan felt an urge to smile back, though all he could do was the usual faint eye-curve. He compensated by patting Vex on the head, making the lizard yelp.

Not in protest, though, so he figured he'd won there.

That done, Derivan reached into where he felt the skill, and activated [###### **Night**].

CHAPTER 58

NIGHT

A dark, glittering fog coalesced in the middle of the clearing.

Derivan heard Vex breathe in, a sharp intake of air—the lizardkin's eyes were wide with wonder, and Derivan couldn't blame him. The fog was a deep, dark shade of blue, verging on being the same shade as the night sky itself; it might very well have been, if not for the fact that it was *fog*, and so didn't do quite that good a job filtering out all that ambient light.

Perhaps rather conveniently, though, a cloud passed in front of the sun—and with that bit of extra shade, the spell suddenly turned stronger. The fog thickened, spilling into the outer layers of the clearing and slowly beginning to spread; struck by the thought that the skill might have a larger range than he'd intended, Derivan quickly turned to Vex.

"Can you [**Delineate**] a space for it?" he said. His words were oddly quiet, like part of him was worried that speaking loudly would break the transient beauty that was forming in front of them. Vex seemed to feel the same way, because he didn't respond verbally; instead he nodded and gestured, and a shimmering barrier seemed to form around the edges of the clearing.

Just replicating what seemed to be the very essence of the night would be one thing—something about this was deeply reminiscent of the Serpent of the Night Sky, and for good reason—but within the spell were what seemed like full [**Fireball**] spells. Balls of flame the size of Vex's head swirled in abstract spirals, the light they emitted shining briefly before being once more subsumed by the fog. Each one grew and shrank with every passing moment, the movement unpredictable.

"It's beautiful," Vex said softly after a moment. The lizardkin still hadn't looked away from it, but he seemed to be trying to pull himself together. "Um— is it a damaging spell, do you think? Do you have much control over it?"

"I have some," Derivan said, his own reply quiet. He could feel them now, like knobs that he'd been given control over. The problem was that the knobs were *unlabeled*, and he didn't know what each of them did.

So he turned them carefully, and slowly.

As he turned one of them, the color of the fireballs seemed to shift—from a gleaming yellow to a deeper orange, and then to the dark red of firewood. In the other direction, it shifted from yellows to the green of Vex's scales, then to the blue of the sky, then all the way down into the purples and pinks that he'd rarely ever seen outside of portraits and paintings. And his own armor, as far as purples went.

Vex breathed out slowly and stepped in closer toward the boundary of the spell—Derivan reached out to pull him back, just in case. Vex didn't resist, at least, so presumably it wasn't a hypnotic sort of spell, not that he was sure something like that existed. Vex just leaned into him, instead, staring at the shifting lights.

Derivan reached for the next knob.

This one seemed to change the size of the fireballs—they grew larger as he turned this one, though at the same time, he could feel another mental knob moving on its own. The more he turned this one, the more the fireball in the center grew and the more the other one twisted backward; he saw, at the same time, that the fireballs were growing fewer in number. At its largest setting, there almost seemed to be a blazing sun sitting in the middle of the night sky, though *sun* didn't quite fit as a word to describe what it was.

It didn't hurt to stare at, for one thing. It wasn't quite a single ball of flame, for another. The odd nature of the light was far clearer when it was so large; it moved slowly, like strips of paint crawling over a painter's canvas.

He reached for the one that had moved on its own next—and sure enough, this one seemed to multiply the number of fireballs, though their individual sizes shrank. The fourth knob made them zip around inside the fog like fireflies, leaving glittering trails wherever they went.

"That is all I can change, I think," Derivan said, and Vex nodded. He hesitated slightly, as if reluctant to call on Derivan to end the spell.

". . . We should test if this spell damages things," Vex eventually said. "Maybe drop the spell for now?"

Derivan glanced at Vex and chuckled. "If you wish to watch it for a while," he said, "we can do that instead."

Vex didn't reply for a moment—but then he nodded, maybe a little shyly. "I see mana act on its own a lot," he confided after a moment. "But I never see it act like this. Spells are always function over form, so you rarely see spells focusing on the *aesthetic* of it all . . . There are a few magi that try to focus on it. But the system isn't very good at art."

"It appears to leave that in the hands of its users," Derivan offered. "I have seen your sketches. You are quite good at that yourself."

Vex colored. "I had to learn how to draw diagrams," he said by way of explanation.

"You learned it well, then," Derivan chuckled. "I only wish you would share your sketches more, and with the rest of the team."

"I . . . Maybe." Vex looked down for a moment, then back to the spell. He took a few minutes to take it in, like he was trying to memorize it for later—Derivan adjusted the colors back to the original shades of yellow for him, and watched as the shifting shades of yellow and blue bounced off his scales.

They spent a moment more watching the spell, and then Vex nodded to himself. "Let's test it," he said. "See if the skill does any damage. Can you cancel it?"

"Yes," Derivan said. In his mind, it felt more like a switch he had to press—and as soon as he did, the fog collapsed, dissipating into nothing along with the fireballs it contained. Vex dismissed the [**Delineate**] boundary a moment after the spell vanished, then watched the clearing with slightly narrowed eyes.

"There's frost and burns on the grass," he said softly. "I think it's safe to say that spell does damage. Fire and ice elemental damage, it looks like?"

"We do not know how much, though," Derivan pointed out.

"It's hard to get exact damage numbers, anyway, unless we're sparring," Vex said with a slight wince. "Or if we find some monsters with known health values . . . There aren't really any monsters here, and it's dangerous to spar directly without Sev around."

"I was not going to suggest sparring, regardless," Derivan said with a chuckle. "Perhaps we can focus on your spells now?"

"Your skill gave me some ideas," Vex said thoughtfully. "Fire and ice together, too . . . That's not a normal presentation of a spell. It's rare for opposing elements to work together like that. Did it draw any mana from you, or is it more of a system skill?"

Derivan blinked, the lights in his helmet flickering, and checked his status. ". . . It drew some mana from me," he said, surprised. "A few hundred. I did not notice."

"You didn't feel the mana moving?" Vex asked, surprised. "I mean, that doesn't mean it's definitively a spell and not a skill, but all spells use mana . . ."

"I did not feel my mana move, no." Derivan paused for a moment, contemplating his status screen. "A side effect of the skill description being errored out, perhaps?"

"I'd still expect you to be able to sense it using your version of [**Mana Manipulation**]," Vex said with a frown. "But I think this is fine. You'll just need to keep an eye on your mana if you're casting that spell."

Derivan nodded. "I will also make a deliberate attempt to feel how my mana is moving, I think," he said. "I did not think to do so before."

Vex grinned at him. "'S'why I'm here," he said cheerfully. "To help with magic! But also, I wanna try to do some magic now, so . . ."

He paused with consideration, and began using a combination of [**Splash of Mana**] and [**Delineate**]. He was careful with how he did it, too, and with his color choices—each use of [**Delineate**] marked out a region in the frost-burned grass, and each shade of color he used for [**Splash of Mana**] came out identical to one of the shades they'd seen just before, when Derivan had used [###### **Night**].

The end result was . . . less than perfect. [**Delineate**] was a poor substitute for using an actual paintbrush, and it showed; perhaps with more practice, Vex would be able to imitate the product more closely. Derivan was still impressed, however, and Vex still seemed happy with the end result.

"Is that fire magic?" Derivan asked curiously, gesturing to an impression of the ball of fire.

"It isn't," Vex said, shaking his head. "I want to see if mana aspect matters, and [**Splash of Mana**] lets me tune the color of mana, which . . . it really shouldn't be able to do. That's not how mana works. But the system breaks the rules all the time, anyway." He pondered his painting for a moment, fidgeting with the dagger in his hand. "I'm not sure if anything is supposed to happen . . . I'm going to give it a moment. Maybe when it dries?"

"Or the different mana aspects are required," Derivan supplied. Nothing happened, still, even as the paint began to dry, and Derivan saw Vex begin to sag; the lizardkin had been hoping something would happen.

An idea struck him.

"Perhaps if we do what I did with [**Barrier**] earlier," Derivan said softly. "I used [**Mana Manipulation**] to ask the ambient mana to fuel the skill rather than fueling it with my own mana. But I did not force the mana into doing as I wished—merely guided it."

Vex frowned slightly, but he seemed willing to try anything. He reached out with his own version of [**Mana Manipulation**] and began to try to guide the ambient mana—but his version was too *strong*, and Derivan could almost feel the ambient mana shying away from his grip. Without thinking about it, he knelt by Vex, a hand on the lizardkin's shoulder, and reached out with his own version of the skill.

"Like this," he said. Vex's eyes widened, though he didn't say anything. Derivan guided him slowly—not grabbing the mana and moving it, but guiding it, pushing it toward the painting on the grass.

Derivan's skill with [**Mana Sight**] wasn't quite at the level of Vex's, but even he saw the way the mana acted—it was far different from any spell either of them had seen before. The ambient mana that surrounded them had shied away once he'd started casting his new spell. It drew closer as the painting was completed, and when it was done . . .

The mana dove *into* the painting, and brought it to life.

Neutral mana turned into fire and ice, this time with far more vibrancy and life than even [###### **Night**] had offered. Balls of fire flickered in the air like floating bonfires, emanating a heat that hadn't been felt earlier through Derivan's use of the skill; the fog that drew around them was *cold*, grass freezing into shards of ice at its touch. Vex's use of [**Delineate**] didn't seem to protect them from the effect, either.

Still—for all that the effect was powerful and threatened to burn and freeze them all at once—it never got close enough to them to actually harm them. Unlike Derivan's skill, it stayed in place, hovering just above where the painting had been. In a few short minutes, it began to dissipate, aspected mana turning back into a lifeless neutral, and that neutral mana collapsed back onto the ground like liquid.

Vex swallowed once, and slowly dismissed the skill.

"That was . . . something," he said softly. Derivan glanced at him.

"It was," he agreed.

CHAPTER 59

A PROPER REUNION

For all that she'd been looking forward to this moment—for all that she'd had trouble even sleeping in her anticipation, checking both her system messages and the view outside the window in case she could spot the villagers arriving—Misa found that she was still undeniably *nervous*.

It hadn't taken her particularly long to find the villagers when she'd woken up. Her inability to sleep had cost her; she'd fallen asleep late in the night, or in the early hours of the morning, depending on how one looked at it. By the time she'd woken up, blinking the sunlight out of her eyes, it was a solid hour past noon.

Meaning she'd missed not only her village arriving but also the time they spent setting up a temporary camp. The Guildmaster had been kind enough to leave her a message; apparently, her parents and the other villagers were having trouble with the system and couldn't send her any messages personally. But they wanted her to know that they loved her, and that they were looking forward to seeing her when she had the time.

Misa could read between the lines there, of course. She could practically hear her mother saying *Get down here as soon as possible, young woman.*

She couldn't help the stupid little grin that overcame her.

But now, standing outside the tent that her parents were in . . . she found herself strangely nervous. Anxious. She found herself pacing in front of the tent, her mind inundated with inane questions she hadn't cared about before. When she'd met them in the dungeon, there was this idea in her mind that it would be her last time seeing them—that the dungeon had given her a gift and a curse all at once by offering her that last opportunity.

Now . . . well, she had her parents back. She'd dreamed about that, once upon a time. She had her whole *village* back, and even at the worst of the denial stages of her grief she hadn't dared to hope that that might happen.

Misa found she didn't really know what to *do* with that.

The threat of the system should have been the first thing on her mind; the idea of the anchor degrading and taking her village with it. But the threat seemed so far away at the moment, and her parents were right in front of her—well, behind the flap of the tent . . .

Charise poked her head out of the door and scowled at her. There was no heat in the scowl at all. "Get in here already. I can feel you pacing from in here."

And just like that, the tension broke.

Misa grinned back at her mother. "Mother's intuition or [**Mother's Intuition**]?"

"That joke would work better if I actually had that skill," her mother said, smiling at her. She stepped fully through the folds of the tent and embraced her daughter in a hug.

For a moment, Misa felt like a child again. It was a little strange—her mother was shorter than she was now, and she couldn't bury her face in the folds of her clothes like she had once upon a time. But Charise was somehow just as strong as she remembered, and the hug was . . .

. . . well, the hug was everything she'd wished for, when she'd first lost her. It felt like a lifetime ago, now.

"Hi, Mom," she said softly, and though she couldn't see Charise smile, she could somehow feel it.

"It's good to see you again, Misa," her mother said warmly, and then took her by a hand, gently leading her into the tent. "Let's go see your father, shall we? He's waiting for you too. He's just too stubborn to come outside, the old fool."

Misa choked back a laugh, following her mother into the tent. "Sounds like him," she agreed.

She fell silent as the folds of the tent parted, and she saw what had been constructed inside.

The tent was nothing like their old home, of course. It was far too small, as large as they'd tried to make it for Orkas and Charise, and the walls were made of fabric instead of brick. And yet for all that it was different, there was an aching sense of familiarity within it.

Orkas and Charise had made all the furniture in their house by hand. It was an orcish tradition that a marriage would be consummated by the new couple building their new home together, to symbolize their entrance into a new life. System skills from the village builders had helped construct the walls and floors, but every piece of furniture had been lovingly crafted without the help of skills.

Here, there obviously hadn't been the time for that. And yet . . .

The table was just like their old table, down to all the little imperfections from inexperienced hands. Even the grain of the wood was the same; beautiful swirls coalescing in the center of the table. One of the chairs had a slightly crooked back, just like she remembered. In every chair there was a little carving of two birds, the symbol that her parents had chosen to symbolize their marriage.

"How?" Misa asked softly, her voice thick with emotion.

It was Orkas that answered. "Your Guildmaster, believe it or not," the orc said. He smiled at her, a kind smile that she barely remembered anymore, and stepped forward to pull her into a hug; she felt herself melt into the embrace just as much as she'd melted into her mother's.

"She did all this?" Misa asked, her voice muffled.

"No," Orkas said with a deep belly-laugh. "She'd be a terrifying woman if she could do all *this* on top of what she can already do. No, she pulled some strings and asked one of her adventurers to do it. A bard, I believe."

"A *bard* did all this?" Misa couldn't keep the astonishment out of her voice, and Orkas grinned at her, pulling back from the hug.

"Knew that would catch your attention. It's a common skill, too; can you believe it?" he said.

"There's no way this is a common skill," Misa protested.

"Well, he wasn't the only one that helped," Orkas said with a grin—he was clearly enjoying himself, and by the way her mother was smirking slightly, she was enjoying it too. "I'll be honest: I didn't pay attention to what other skills he used. He had a friend with him, too."

"*Dad*," Misa groaned. Her father had done this to her all too many times before, knowing her old fixation with figuring out the limits of every skill.

"The skill he used was [**Song of Memory**]," Orkas said. He busied himself by going over to a sort of makeshift kitchen and starting to prepare tea. "Makes an illusion of a chosen memory, as long as the recipient is willing to share it. Played some very pretty music, too."

It was almost strange, to interact with her father like this again. When he was in charge of the village—when he didn't have his memories of her, and she'd been a stranger . . . he'd been so much rougher. She wasn't sure how much of that was simply because she'd been a stranger, and how much of that was because he'd lived a different life.

"I'm glad you're back," she said more quietly.

Orkas paused. When he spoke again, his voice was a little rougher. "Glad I got to see you grow up, kid," he said. "Not that you weren't grown up already."

"Sit down," her mother suggested, patting the seat beside her at the table. Misa sat herself down, feeling oddly self-conscious. She had so many questions she wanted to ask—but she also had so many things she wanted to *share*, so many pieces of her life she could show them that she never thought she'd be able to . . .

"You have plenty of time," her mother told her, smiling at her like she knew exactly what she'd been thinking—and she probably did.

So she took her time. She thought about where she wanted to start. She'd already spoken to one version of her mother about many of the things she'd wanted to share, but she hadn't yet told Orkas about them, not about how she'd met her current team, about the trust they'd built together.

And that was where she started.

There was a lot to tell from the time before that, too—the time she'd lost herself in her grief, and her anger was the only thing that drove her. But that was something she could save for another time. It didn't feel right, somehow, to talk about this now. This was supposed to be a celebration.

Eventually, while she was reminiscing, talking about all the times she and her friends had saved one another, about how one of them had been rather terrible at hiding who he was and another struggled not to sass everything in sight—her mother had interrupted her there, questioning if it wasn't *her* that sassed everything in sight—her father joined them both at the table. He gave them both glasses of hot tea, and they spoke in warm tones, Misa's parents commenting on all her adventures and *mis*adventures . . .

Before she knew it, an hour had passed, and then two. The conversation trickled to a slow, more comfortable rhythm, and then Misa remembered to bring up her new skill before she forgot.

"[**An Anchor of Heart and Home**], huh?" Charise said, frowning slightly. "[**Intuition of Truth**] isn't telling me much about it. I get the impression that you're right and that's what saved you when we were first . . ."

Charise grimaced slightly at the memory, and Orkas put a hand on her shoulder, though he too looked grim. "It is something that bears testing," he said seriously. "But give us some time to make sure that the village is prepared, and to speak with your Guildmaster for any insight she may have on a way to safely test the passive part of the skill."

"Tomorrow, then?" Misa asked.

"What? No. We will test it as soon as possible," Orkas said with a snort. "Who's to know what may happen if we wait. I will contact the Guildmaster to send someone suitable for supervising a spar, and a healer—perhaps your own, if he is available. And in the meantime, perhaps we can test the active portion of your skill."

"I have a skill evolution available, too, for [**To Fall Yet Hold the Line**]," Misa said with a frown. "I haven't accepted that yet. The skill itself is so useful that I'm worried the evolution will take something away from it."

"It won't," Charise spoke with confidence, and Misa blinked at her mother. "Are you . . . sure?"

"Completely, yes," Charise said.

Slowly, Misa nodded. Intuition was a *weird* skill.

"Don't accept it yet, still," Orkas said. "In case there's yet another system glitch, or it modifies the behavior of [**An Anchor of Heart and Home**]. One thing at a time. Can you try to activate the active side of the skill?"

"Sure," Misa said, and almost immediately frowned.

The skill wouldn't budge when she tried to use it the way she used all her other skills. There was a sense she was getting from it, like she was in the wrong . . . place?

"I don't think I can use it while I'm in the village?" she said with some uncertainty.

"Then let's go outside," Orkas said. He checked his system messages and made a grunt of satisfaction. "The Guildmaster is sending an agent so we can test the passive part right afterward."

"That was quick," Misa blinked.

"She's efficient," Charise said cheerfully. "C'mon. Let's see what this skill of yours does."

CHAPTER 60

TAKING FROM A DISTANT FUTURE

[**An Anchor of Heart and Home**] had a cost to it, presumably. The system said it cost ten units of *something*, but whatever it was, the system hadn't been able to parse it. This was worrying for a number of reasons, not the least of which was that the system was evidently capable of parsing some very esoteric costs—Misa remembered Max's skill costing "an opportunity," whatever that meant.

"Ten units," in this case, was vague and worrying. But not knowing what the skill did was potentially even worse, and so once Misa was properly outside the village (or the assortment of tents that currently passed as "the village"), she hesitated only one final time. A small nod from her mother was all the reassurance she needed.

She activated the skill.

There was a noticeable *twist* in her stomach.

Misa couldn't explain the sensation of exactly what was wrenched out of her as she activated the skill—it felt like *potential*. Like possibility. But that potential wasn't drawn out of her and lost to the ether; no, it was instead *offered* to her, like clay for her to mold. It took her a moment to get over the nausea the skill induced, and another moment to understand exactly what the skill was offering to her.

It would take from her a fragment of raw possibility—a potential future. Someone she could become, given enough time. Ten units meant it would be ten steps harder to achieve, though it was unclear whether that would be ten times harder or if the growth was linear.

But in return? It gave her the ability to take that raw potential and shape it into someone else. Someone that she considered part of her "home," to be specific, and right now it meant anyone from her village. What she created would be closer to a reality fragment than a full person, connected to the *real* version of that individual back in her village.

It was all very convoluted. Misa wasn't surprised that the system had given up and simply said *Error*. Simply put, the active version of the skill was something like a summoning skill that she could use to summon . . . copies of the members of her village, for lack of a better term. They would be able to control those copies at a distance, giving them the ability to act on her behalf, if they so chose.

Right now, the skill hovered at half-spent, still pulling that fragment of potential out of her—and as she considered the possibilities, Misa frowned, and slowly canceled the skill.

She felt the potential rubber-band back into her, the feeling of relief nearly overwhelming. Misa grinned.

It was a *good* skill. But it was good to know that it was something she could cancel, that she didn't *have* to spend something that felt like it had such a high cost, if she began to cast it and it became unnecessary.

And she needed to ask before she started summoning clones of people, obviously.

"Misa?" Charise ventured when nothing seemed to happen, and Misa looked up, startled. Her mother stared at her with an eyebrow raised. "I don't know if you realize this, but from the outside it looked like you just started grinning for no reason."

"To be fair," Orkas added, sounding amused, "you did this a lot when you were young, too."

"Oh, fuck off," Misa grumbled good-naturedly, and her father only grinned wider at her. "The good news is that I didn't need to complete using the skill to figure out how it works, and I don't want to pay the cost right now. I know what it'll *do*, though. Roughly. I wanted to talk to you guys first, make sure that you know to be ready."

"It involves us, huh?" Charise said with a raise of her brow, and Misa nodded. She explained the active effect of her skill as best as she understood it, using whatever instinctual understanding had been granted to her, and her mother's brow furrowed in response. "You should try it now. At least once. So that we know what it's like, and if dismissing the summon restores the cost."

"Yeah, that was the plan," Misa agreed. "Uh . . . which one of you do I . . . copy?"

Which was easily one of the strangest questions Misa had ever had to ask. Maybe third strangest.

"Make a copy of me," Charise suggested. There was a flash of the smallest hint of a smirk . . . Misa narrowed her eyes at her mother suspiciously.

"Okaaay," she said, drawing out the word slightly. But she activated the skill nevertheless, and now that she was slightly more braced for the gut-wrenching sensation of having her own *future* torn out of her, it took her much less time to recover. It took her a moment to figure out how to shape it, but the system seemed to take over as soon as she thought of her mother. It told her how that future potential needed to be molded, nudged it into a perfect recreation—

—there was a flash of light, mana gathering into a sensation that made her skin prickle and her hair stand on end. There was a corresponding gasp from her mother, though no impression of pain. Surprise, maybe? The skill seemed to halt for a moment, as if waiting for something, and then all of a sudden she felt the skill resolve; it finished pulling from her, and then in front of her formed an exact copy of her mother.

Misa wasn't sure what she'd expected.

Charise, on the other hand, seemed delighted. She looked down at herself in her new body, patting it down quickly as if to make sure everything was still in place. For a moment, both versions of her mother were oddly mirrored— everything one version of her did, the other copied in perfect sync.

But then one version of her mother—the original—strode forward with a confident grin.

Directly toward Orkas, who suddenly looked a lot less sure of what was going on.

"Uh," he said. "Hi?"

"You know, honey," Charise began with a grin, in a very specific tone of voice.

Misa made a face and stared at her mom. "Mom. Really?"

"Hey, it's *my* extra body, isn't it?"

"You're not—" Misa sighed. "You know what? I'm not going to question it."

"You should see if you can dismiss the skill," Charise suggested. "Don't dismiss it if you can't get back whatever you spent on it, though."

Misa frowned. There *was* an option for her to disable the skill—she could feel it in the so-called mental interface of the system, allowing her to choose to pull the skill back. It'd dissolve her mother's extra body, for lack of a better term, though Misa also immediately resolved to find a better term.

But for now, she reached out to the skill, pulling on the metaphorical lever to disable the effect.

What was interesting was the fact that her mother was *right*—Misa hadn't expected to be able to gain back whatever she lost to the "cost" of the skill, but either [**An Anchor of Heart and Home**] was an exception or there was more to the cost that she hadn't thought about. A brief thought about it affecting the integrity of the anchor had her heart suddenly racing, but a quick check showed no apparent decrease in integrity.

And as the skill began to unravel, *potential* flooded back into her. But there was something interesting about it.

It wasn't the same as what had left.

The potential future that had been taken from her was still gone—Misa had no specific idea of what it had been, but she had general impressions. That was a version of her that would focus hard on using [**The Blade Arcane**], becoming more of a warrior than a tank; she didn't see herself going down that path and so had no problem sacrificing it. What returned now was a blank, undifferentiated potential; the future in which all her focus was poured into mastering the sword was still gone, but now she could . . . what, use it for something else?

"This skill's fucking weird," Misa muttered, and her mother gave her a look. "What? It is!"

"Why exactly is it . . . weird, as you call it?" Orkas finally asked, walking over to Charise's copy. She winked at him, and Misa groaned. She hadn't canceled the skill yet, but she pulled on that string now, unraveling the copy right in front of Orkas's eyes—

She realized, perhaps a hair too late, that she didn't know exactly how the effect would manifest. Orkas's face went slightly pale as the copy faded in the worst way possible, skin vanishing before everything else; even Charise winced. Her father's eyes shot to the real version of her mother as though for reassurance . . .

"Sorry about that," Misa said quietly, and her father didn't respond immediately. He just walked over to Charise and slowly pulled her into a hug. He said nothing else, but Charise seemed to immediately realize what he needed.

They were silent for a moment, the three of them—and then Orkas let out a sigh.

"Better we find out now, I suppose," he muttered.

"That felt strange," Charise said, trying to change the subject.

"It did," Misa agreed, though it had been strange in a different way for her. There was a lump of undifferentiated potential now that she could still feel in her near future, almost like a lump in her throat. It was distinctly uncomfortable. It would shape itself as she acted, she instinctively realized, but for now it was a raw nothing that could be fed back into the skill if she wanted.

And then she realized she hadn't answered her mother's question. It was hard to explain, though . . . Misa tried to draw on her thoughts of how *Vex* would have explained it. "Uh. But to answer your question, I dunno, it's some weird shit."

She paused. *Not* how Vex would have explained it. "It feels like it takes . . . a path I could have tread—a future that could have been—and it turns it into something real."

"Is that safe?" Charise immediately asked. Misa shrugged.

"I give up *something*. But I don't think it makes it impossible for me to become that person. It just makes it harder. Moves the goal further away by ten steps, so to speak."

Orkas grunted. "I don't like it," he said, wearing a heavy frown.

"It might be useful," Misa said, but she didn't disagree. It felt . . . risky. Strange. "What did it feel like, Mom?"

"Weird, like you said," Charise admitted. "It was like I had two bodies at once. It was hard to adapt to—I could only focus on one of them at a time. I could still use my skills through them, though, so . . ."

Misa whistled. "That could be *very* useful, then."

"If you can use it on more than one of us," Orkas said. "Can you?"

"I . . . think so." Misa hesitated. "I think I'd have to practice with the skill a bit, but for obvious reasons, it's going to be a hard skill to practice. The skill says its grade is maxed, but it feels . . . I don't know. It feels complicated to use."

"Some skills are like that," Orkas acknowledged. "My brother"—he winced slightly as he mentioned the words—"mentioned, back when he got his unique skill, that it felt like it had a thousand different things he could do with it. But he never felt like he understood more than a tiny portion."

"What was the skill?" Misa asked. Her father almost never willingly talked about his brother.

"[**A Thousand Hands**]," Orkas answered, and then managed a laugh at Misa's flat look, though there was a touch of bitterness in the laugh. "Look, I don't know how he got the skill either. He was an [**Alchemist**]. It let him transmute things."

"Huh," Misa said. She opened her mouth to say something else—

—And then Max was suddenly in front of her. She blinked once, and Max blinked as well, as though surprised she was there. And then she grinned.

"Hello!" the [**Adventuring Clerk**] said. "I hear you need an adventurer's help?"

"We sent in for some assistance with sparring," Orkas said, seeming grateful for the change in subject. "The Guildmaster said she would send someone. Are you that someone?"

"Probably!" Max said cheerfully. "Sometimes, I go missing because of my skills, and a great way to get me to appear again is to schedule something for me. So if you say the Guildmaster wanted me here, she probably wanted me here."

Orkas blinked at her. "I am sorry?"

"Just go with it," Charise whispered.

"I need you to hit me," Misa said.

"Say no more," Max said. She wound up for a punch, and Misa's eyes widened—

"Wait wait wait," Misa managed. Max grinned at her, and Misa groaned. "Dammit, Max," she said. "You're supposed to ask questions!"

"That's exactly why I don't ask questions," Max said knowingly. "It's a lot more fun that way."

Misa sighed.

CHAPTER 61

TWO PARTS OF A WHOLE

"You're sure everything's fine?" Misa asked again, and Max scowled at her.

"*Yes*," Max emphasized. "You're putting this off. I'll tell you about what happened *later*."

She was, technically. Misa stood in the field across from Max, far enough away that it would take a good few seconds of running for either of them to strike the other, though Max likely had significantly more speed. It wasn't that she was *nervous* about sparring—she enjoyed it.

The problem was more that Misa didn't know what her new skill would do about it, and she wasn't sure she wanted to find out.

She'd been reassured as much as possible, though. [**Right Place, Right Time**] wouldn't have brought Max here at all if the ensuing spar had a disastrous outcome. Her own mother's [**Intuition of Truth**] spoke nothing of anything bad happening.

"We were worried about you," Misa grumbled, still stalling slightly, and Max laughed.

"Are you ready yet?" she said in lieu of a response. Max bounced on her feet, and Misa sighed, lowering herself into a [**Guard Stance**].

She didn't *need* to guard. But she was more comfortable with it; this was how she fought. Standing still and letting Max punch her in the face felt odd.

"Fine," Misa said, and no sooner had she said it than Max flashed forward, as if unwilling to let her change her mind again. Her fist drew back, a strange purple gathering around it, likely the application of some kind of skill—

Misa realized with a start that she could react to the attack, if she wanted.

She hadn't gained that many levels from the fight against the Serpent of the Night Sky—whether that had something to do with the reality anchor, or if the fight simply hadn't counted for whatever reason, she wasn't sure. But whatever few levels she'd gained and the points she'd put into dexterity still seemed to matter. She wouldn't have imagined being able to match up against a Platinum ranker at any stage, and yet . . .

This was an attack she could dodge.

Technically, the point of this exercise was to see what would happen when Misa took damage—to make sure that the skill wouldn't simply distribute the damage to her entire village, or if it *did*, then to see how that could be best mitigated. But Misa couldn't help herself. She saw a punch she could dodge. She *liked* sparring.

She dodged.

Not by a lot. Her perception being faster didn't mean her body could move to match, and the two things didn't seem to scale evenly. But moving even a little was enough for the punch to ghost past her nose, the flickers of purple flame brushing past her instead of blazing *into* her. She saw Max's eyes narrow slightly with surprise, and then a delighted grin crossed the [**Adventuring Clerk**]'s expression; she twisted on the spot, instantaneously converting all her forward momentum into a *twisting* momentum as she brought the back of her heel up and toward Misa's head—

This time, Misa didn't dodge at all. She brought her arm up in a block, feeling the magic of [**Guard Stance**] guiding her movements. It wouldn't deny the damage entirely, but it would *mitigate* the damage. The purple flame, whatever it was, still charred her forearms black, and the force of the blow knocked her back several feet; as soon as it appeared, the charring was gone, restored by the effect of health.

Misa paused and glanced at her parents. "Anything?" she called out.

"Hold on!" Charise shouted back, and Max grinned at her, still bouncing in place.

"Nice moves," the clerk said.

Misa snorted. "I dodged one and blocked the other," she said. "Could've done a better job with the block. Didn't need to let myself get pushed back."

"Well, sure, but they were still nice moves." Max grinned at her, and Misa smirked back.

"If you say so."

"How much damage were you expecting to do with that attack?" Orkas frowned as he approached, glancing through the air; looking through the messages and reports he was receiving from within the makeshift village, presumably.

"Enough to take out about half of Misa's health," Max answered. She glanced back toward the camp, though it was impossible to really make out if anything had happened to it. They hadn't gone *far*, exactly, but the camp was large and chaotic. "Did something happen?"

"One of the tents in the village caught fire," Orkas reported. He was still frowning slightly. "But it may be a coincidence. The damage was not bad, and no one was hurt. The fire was put out before it could damage anything."

"How much health damage did you take?" Max asked, and Misa frowned at her health bar.

"About half my health," she said, a little disgruntled. "That doesn't seem right. Was the fire just a coincidence?"

"It was not a magical fire," Orkas said. "Someone knocked over a candle, and the flame spread. But the timing seemed too perfect for it to be a coincidence."

"Let's try again," Misa suggested. She had a health potion on hand, since she'd expected that Sev wouldn't be available for the test—it took her only a moment to down it, and only a moment more for Max to flick yet more fire into her face. Misa didn't bother dodging this time, though it felt *strange* to let someone hit her.

Just as before, the strike did about half her health in damage—and just as before, a tent seemed to catch fire.

"Same tent," Orkas reported. "Same candle, too."

"That's odd," Misa said. "Did they just light the candle again?"

"They did not," Orkas said, shaking his head. "So this is almost certainly caused by your skill. But it is a strange one. I cannot see any direct benefit. If anything, you will have to be even more careful."

"Which is hard, considering I'm the tank. I'm supposed to take hits," Misa said with a slight frown. If taking hits caused problems in the village, no matter how small those problems were, then the skill seemed to be more of a liability than a benefit—especially since there was no clear reduction in the damage she was taking.

"You can't control the passive skill at all?" Max suggested. "Sometimes you can influence how skills like those turn out."

"For passive skills?" Misa asked, surprised. She supposed she shouldn't have been, though; with all the adventurers Max worked with, she *would* know something like that. But nothing had stood out to her as something she could actively control the same way she could when she used an active skill under the system . . .

Now that she was *looking* for it, though, she realized there was something there. She couldn't manipulate it quite the same way she could manipulate an active skill, but there was a sort of dial she could adjust, and that dial was turned almost all the way to its lowest setting.

She turned that dial up, of course.

"I think you're right," Misa said, and then indicated to Max that she should try again.

Max did.

This time, there was a shout from the village as Max's fist contacted with Misa's face—though Orkas quickly reported that no one was hurt. He'd looked anxious for the first few seconds, checking through his messages frantically, but the villagers had learned quickly to avoid that particular tent.

Which, well, fair enough. Misa figured she couldn't blame them for that.

More importantly, she had taken *significantly* less damage from the hit—only about a quarter of her health. "Shit," she whistled. "That worked pretty well. Uh, sorry, Dad. I probably won't actually use this skill very often. Keep the dial turned down and all."

"You should use it if you need to," Orkas said, frowning severely at her. "Do not limit yourself because of us. Though I ask you to try not to inconvenience us for your own sake, either."

"It seems like a good opportunity to make sure the new village is as strong as possible, though!" Charise spoke cheerfully, placing one hand on Orkas's arm. "I imagine that would give you a little more durability in turn."

"I think so," Misa agreed with a nod. Charise beamed.

"We can't test anything else, I think," Max said thoughtfully. "Probably not a good idea to see what happens if you lose all your health . . . What about if something happens to the village?"

Orkas grimaced. "I can order someone to set a tent on fire," he said, sounding very reluctant to do so. But he did it anyway, as was evidenced by the column of smoke that rose up from the makeshift camp a second later.

Misa winced. "Ow," she said. The sensation manifested as a persistent heat across her right collarbone, like a burn that wouldn't go away—which was *uncomfortable.* System health usually took away pain almost as soon as it appeared, but this pain *lingered.*

And then she noticed something on her status that made her pause. "It doesn't damage me," she said in wonder. "It lowers my max health."

Charise blinked. "So, if we build up the village . . ."

"It's not a *guarantee,*" Misa said. "But I bet it'd give me more health."

"*I* bet it'd give you more health too," Max said with a grin. "How much are we putting in the betting pool?"

Misa shot Max a look. "It's a turn of phrase," she said.

"Five gold," Max responded immediately.

Misa pinched the bridge of her nose and sighed.

"One last thing," she said. "I need to accept the skill evolution for [**To Fall Yet Hold the Line**]. Any of you see anything going wrong with that?" Misa glanced between Max and her mother, but both of them shook their heads, and she nodded, satisfied.

She pulled up the skill prompt, and—as the message about a skill evolution being available flashed in front of her eyes—she accepted it.

The box flashed orange.

<NOTICE>
Sufficient understanding has been achieved to unlock evolution of [To Fall Yet Hold the Line]. Evolving Skill . . .
New Skill granted.

[**Misa's Endless Echoes**] [**Active Skill**] [**Grade: 1**]
No longer a mere guard, you have become a true Guardian—you and all your other selves.
If you would fail to block an attack, you do not. In addition, you may call upon an echo to understand more about the world around you.

Misa paused and stared at the skill.

It . . . made sense, in a way. Her echoes, or reflections, or whatever those were—were different versions of who she was. It stood to reason that they were more than just tools to wield power. They would have their own experiences she could draw from.

In theory. In practice, she wasn't so sure. There were still too many questions about her echoes—if they were variations on her that had made different decisions, did they all live in the same world? Or were those worlds slightly different, filled with other people that had made different decisions?

"Didja get something good?" Max asked, raising an eyebrow at her. Misa blinked.

"I think so," Misa said, then grinned. "It'll need some testing, and I'm always down for testing. But we don't need to fight to test this one. Hey, Mom? Want some help getting dinner ready?"

"I'm never going to say no to some help," Charise said. "Especially from my favorite daughter."

"I'm your only daughter."

"Touché."

CHAPTER 62

SKILLS, DINNER, AND INTRODUCTIONS

Over the course of cooking an entire three-course meal with her mother, Misa managed to learn a few crucial things about [Endless Echoes]. She refused to call it [**Misa's Endless Echoes**], for all that that was the "proper name" given by the system. Something about that struck her as too . . . egotistical.

Though she was relatively certain the others would tease her about it a bit. Vex, perhaps, might be more interested in how she'd had a skill named after her at all—she'd only seen that sort of thing happen with spells, though she didn't know the exact mechanics behind how the system named skills. Something to ask him about later.

Back to what she'd learned, though.

[Endless Echoes], as she understood it, was a skill that allowed her to . . . not *summon* a copy of herself, exactly. It allowed her to communicate across her selves in a limited fashion by giving her control over the variations of herself she wanted to manifest.

In the context of cooking, for example, she'd accidentally added bloodberries into the hauvre instead of the more traditional five-point fruit; a quick use of [Endless Echoes] as she tasted the result told her that the bloodberry variant was much, much tastier. The five-point fruit was just a little too sour, having gotten overly ripe since Charise had picked it on the way here.

Her mother had insisted that that shouldn't have been possible, despite her intuition skill telling her otherwise, and had continued insisting it all the way until she'd tasted the five-point fruit and spat it out, making a face.

Misa laughed at her, of course, and her mother grinned back at her. She didn't miss the way her mother's eyes twinkled, or the way her father guffawed in his corner of the tent, where he was chopping up the meats; she didn't miss the way the tension in her father's shoulders flowed out, either.

Misa was learning that her mother was *much* better at using that intuition skill than she'd ever let on.

Bloodberries, on the other hand, tasted like chocolate with just a hint of sweetness. It was the perfect complement to the rest of the hauvre, which was a cheesy, savory dessert.

Further testing had shown Misa that she could pick out variants of herself that made decisions at different times, too. There was a limit to how far she could stretch the skill out when she did this; she couldn't, for example, try to reach a version of herself that had finished cooking everything a day before, and learn from all the mistakes that version of herself had made.

She *could* pick a version of herself that had started on everything an hour earlier, which was how she knew not to mix the bloodberry juice with cymmanom. *That* surprised her mother, who stared at her keenly; apparently, she'd been expecting her to do exactly that.

So it was good to know that her skill seemed to have some precedence over other information-gathering skills. Cymmanom and bloodberry juice resulted in a violent but ultimately harmless reaction, something to do with the mana aspects naturally present in both ingredients. *That* she knew because her mother had explained it to that other version of her, and Charise's face when she repeated that information to her had been priceless.

Cooking, it turned out, had been a great way to practice using the skill on the fly.

Max was a guest in their home—or tent, Misa supposed—and so hadn't been required to cook, as much as she insisted on helping. Misa had eventually sent her running around for various ingredients that they'd forgotten, sometimes before even Charise realized that they'd forgotten them at all.

"Whatever your new skill is, it's cheating," Charise informed her at one point, and Misa had laughed in return, seeing the proud twinkle in her mother's eyes.

"It was already cheating," Misa replied with a smirk. "It's just *more* cheating now."

With all the help, it hadn't been long before dinner was finished. There would be a celebration later in the night, Charise told her, in part to celebrate the village's return and in part simply because the villagers needed it after the stress of everything that had happened. She'd seen more than a couple of people shaking slightly when they thought no one was looking. An attack like that—the *memories* of being killed that they still had—that wasn't something that would fade easily.

So . . . a celebration. Something to distract them while they tried to come to terms with their new lives.

The dinner was to introduce her parents to all her friends first, of course. Max had been invited, too, but she'd politely excused herself—she was only there to help Misa with sparring, and she'd spent her break helping them cook. Misa felt a little guilty for that and offered her a small portion of food, which Max had happily taken with her.

They'd timed it well—it was almost eight by the time they were done cooking, and the rest of her team began arriving. Derivan, for instance, poked his head into the tent as Misa put the finishing touches on a dish of cooked wyrm meat.

"You're early!" Misa waved him over. "Mom, dad, this is Derivan."

Derivan pushed his way into the tent as he was prompted, revealing that he was carrying Vex, who had his face buried in his hands.

"Misa," Vex said. "Help. He won't put me down."

"You said you were tired," Derivan said sternly.

"I didn't mean I wanted you to carry me *into the tent*," Vex moaned, his voice still muffled by his hands. "We're meeting her parents! I mean, we've seen them before, but we're doing it properly! You were supposed to put me down!"

"We're right here, by the way," Charise said, sounding amused, and Vex let out what sounded very much like a squeak.

"And that's Vex, our wizard," Misa said with a grin, very pointedly *not* telling Derivan to put Vex down. It took a moment before the armor did it anyway, seeming rather satisfied with himself, and Vex did his best to gather himself into a more presentable state.

"Wizard?" Charise asked curiously, and Vex took the opportunity to sweep himself forward in a bow.

"I dress as a rogue to throw people off, but I *am* a wizard," he said proudly.

"Has that ever come in useful?" Orkas spoke, amused, and Vex paused awkwardly.

". . . Mostly when I was solo," he admitted. "People don't mess with rogues as much as they do wizards. They know wizards need cast time and all. It's harder to surprise a rogue. And I did train myself in some basic knife skills, so I can defend myself in close combat."

"Good," Orkas said approvingly.

Their introductions sorted, Vex and Derivan quickly found themselves seats, though Vex needed to [**Enlarge**] Derivan's. The stools they had in the tent didn't quite fit the armor, and even standing up, his head threatened to brush against the ceiling. He was *tall*.

Sev was the last to arrive—he brushed open the flaps of the tent with his staff and then paused awkwardly, like he was trying to figure out how to knock on fabric. A muffled voice came through a moment later. "Um. Hello? Can I come in? I didn't want to be rude."

"Come in, you doofus," Misa called out with a laugh, and Sev sheepishly walked in through the tent.

"You're the priest that healed me," Orkas observed.

"Cleric," Sev corrected. He offered a smile. "It's good to see you doing well."

"Do you not like being called a priest?" Orkas raised an eyebrow at him.

"It's a bit too religious for me?" Sev phrased his answer like a question, his brows furrowing. "I have a strange relationship with my god. Don't worry about it."

Orkas blinked once at him and then looked at Misa, who immediately gestured that *no*, it was *not* what he was thinking. Orkas nodded back at her, in a way that was far too suggestive to make her think he understood what she meant, and she immediately glared at him.

Sev just stared at the both of them in bemusement.

"Just . . . get a seat, Sev," Misa grumbled with a sigh, giving up at convincing her father of anything. He'd either made up his mind or was just teasing her, and from the way her mother was smirking, she was suspecting it was the latter.

It wasn't long before all six of them were seated around the table. It was cramped, of course; a tent was not, by nature, intended for a large dinner party by any means. It was awkward, because half the people in the tent didn't quite know how to react to the other half, and one of them couldn't eat any food to begin with. It was quiet, because none of them knew what to talk about, or even what was appropriate.

And yet, as cramped and awkward and quiet as it was, it was perfect.

Misa felt an odd lump in her throat, looking at them all.

It wasn't a stretch to say that Sev, Derivan, and Vex had become something like family to her. They never replaced what she'd lost, of course—they couldn't. But they'd brought color back into her life in the way that friends often did, and she'd never imagined that they'd get the chance to meet her parents.

Sometimes she dreamed about it. She dreamed about telling her parents all about how she'd become a real adventurer, just like she wanted. She dreamed about telling her mother about how Vex liked presenting himself as a roguish rogue, but was in actuality a scholar that could ramble for hours on the smallest of minutiae. She dreamed about telling her mother about Sev's strange approach to clerics and priesthood, about his uncanny ability to heal nearly anything and the scathing wit he sometimes wielded. She dreamed about . . .

Well, when it came to Derivan, she mostly dreamed about telling her mother how *cool* he was. That was before she'd known he was a literal set of animated armor, of course, which only increased the coolness level in her estimation.

But that was just in her dreams. Derivan was kind, and determined, and protective of his friends, and perhaps most strikingly he was endlessly *curious* in a way that wasn't dissimilar to Vex. He'd been afraid to show it before, but now he was expressing it a little more, asking questions, learning about the world he now lived in.

The point was that seeing all of them *together*, in a way that she'd thought was impossible . . .

It felt like home.

So Misa smiled, and broke the silence. "Let's eat already. I'm fucking starving."

And, almost as one, everyone began to *talk*—like that was all that was really needed. Even Derivan, who wasn't eating at all and instead watched the rest of them in fascination. Her mother drew him into conversation several times, asking him about this and that, about what drew his curiosity the most; he spoke of magic, and of a developing interest in *culture*, in seeing how the different kingdoms handled their people. Orkas drew Sev into a conversation about his god, apparently trying to pry out details about Onyx, and when that failed he turned his attention to Vex and tried to ask the lizard-kin about whether *he* had any romantic interests (at which point Vex sputtered and began aggressively stuffing dessert into his mouth, much to Misa's amusement).

It was an almost-perfect night. The only reason it wasn't *perfect* was because it hadn't ended yet.

There was still the celebration, after all.

CHAPTER 63

REVELATION IN THE NIGHT

It was a small celebration, really. Sev heard Orkas say that he would have preferred it to be bigger, but there hadn't been time to gather everything they needed—part of why they had taken so long to reach the Guild to begin with was because they'd sent out several of their hunters and gatherers to try to collect food, both to lessen the burden they would place on the Guild and to gather enough for a small feast.

But it really was a *small* feast, and Sev felt a little guilty that he was part of the celebration at all. Misa wanted him there, he knew, and yet the food was so scarce; what was placed out on the tables barely seemed enough to feed all the villagers, let alone two extra mouths . . .

Then again, Misa had scoffed and told him to ignore it when he'd brought up the problem.

It turned out that every villager had already had dinner—the feast that was laid out here wasn't meant to be a replacement for a meal. It was meant to be a small celebration of the village, with all the popular dishes that were often shared by the best cooks they had.

Or the worst, in a few cases. It was a celebration of the little bit of culture they'd developed together as a village. That didn't mean that all of it was *good*.

"You should try the bloodberry pie!" Charise beamed at him. "Adremel made it. He's our resident blacksmith. Very quiet, keeps to himself, basically just bakes this every time we have a village gathering."

Behind her mother, Misa rapidly shook her head. Sev blinked at her once, then at the slice of pie that Charise was offering him. It steamed and . . . bubbled?

Why was the pie bubbling?

He couldn't exactly . . . refuse? Because he could *see* Adremel staring at him with a look that he absolutely could not read. The lizardkin stood in the corner of the gathering with his arms crossed, rebuffing most attempts to speak to him with a short glare—except for Vex, who was rambling animatedly about enchanting onto metal. Adremel didn't seem to mind him.

Sev swallowed, looking at the pie Charise was offering him, and—with far more drama than was probably necessary—he took the plate, carefully sliced into the pie with his fork, and took a bite.

It was *delicious*. Flaky pastry, some sort of chocolate-strawberry taste that sparked over his tongue. Sev paused, taking a moment to savor the flavor.

Then he glared at Misa. "You made me think this was bad!"

"It's tradition," Misa said with a grin. "We make everyone think Addy's pies are bad when they first try them. All the kids think he can't cook because he's a blacksmith."

"Turns out blacksmiths are really good at controlling fire," Charise said cheerfully, and Adremel grunted in the background, as if in agreement.

"Bloodberries require a lot of fine temperature control," the blacksmith explained after a moment, when the conversation between him and Vex paused. "Too hot and they taste burnt. Too cold and you can't really bring out the flavor, and they taste like overprocessed chocolate."

"The fire mana does something to the flavor, I think," Vex added.

"Now it's your turn!" Charise swung yet another slice of the pie, this time toward Derivan, who took the plate and stared at it awkwardly.

"I am . . . unable to taste?" he said.

"Don't worry about it," Charise said with a grin. "I got our skeleton friend to taste some stew; I can help you too. We just need our resident [**Taste Tester**]. Michael!"

A short, brown-haired kid popped up. "Wha?"

"We need your [**Remote Tasting**] skills again," Charise said cheerfully. Michael brightened.

"I get to have more pie?"

"Not too much," Charise warned, but he was already reaching greedily for the plate; Sev grinned a little as the kid nearly gobbled down the pie. A faint glow was the only hint that he'd used [**Remote Tasting**] at all.

Poor Derivan seemed mostly overwhelmed.

"This is what taste is like?" he asked. He moved his head experimentally around, as if trying to work at the phantom taste he was experiencing, though Sev had no idea what it felt like to him. "I am . . . unsure what to think."

"I was hoping he'd be more wowed," Vex stage-whispered to him. He was watching the display with wide eyes, though, clearly interested in Derivan's experience of a new sensation.

"Eh, cut him a break. It's his first time experiencing any kind of taste. For all he knows it's fucked," Misa said dryly, then glanced at Adremel. "Uh, no offense."

"None taken," the blacksmith said, his voice a low rumble.

As Michael calmed down a little in his wolfing down of the pie, though, he began to take slower bites—actually savoring the food he was eating rather than just swallowing it. And that seemed to give Derivan the time he needed to actually process what he was feeling, too. Vex leaned forward, his eyes glowing in the usual telltale sign of him focusing on his [**Mana Sight**], and Sev watched them both with interest.

"It is . . . pleasant," Derivan said after a moment. "Strange, to be tasting without doing anything in particular. But I appreciate the new experience."

"You're welcome!" Charise said cheerfully.

"I can kind of see what the skill is doing," Vex murmured. "Not exactly. That's not a spell, and the way it's influencing the mana around Derivan is weird . . . but I can see how it's adjusting the enchantments, kind of. I wonder . . ."

"Going to figure out how to let Deri join us in meals?" Misa grinned, popping up behind Vex so suddenly the lizardkin let out a startled yelp. He almost fell forward, and it was only Misa reaching out and grabbing his shoulder that stopped him.

"I mean, y—kind of!" Vex defended himself. Sev wasn't sure why. He didn't really *need* to. "He should get to join us. And I want to know how to help him experience more things."

"He sure seems to be enjoying himself now," Misa said, amused, and Vex looked over to see that Derivan was indeed doing exactly that—he'd found a stump of a tree to sit on and was leaning forward with his eyes closed, as though to savor the bloodberry pie.

As with all good things, though, the pie had to come to an end. Derivan made a sound that was vaguely disappointed as Michael polished off the last few crumbs, gave them a thumbs-up, and vanished back into the crowd.

"Please tell him thank you for me," Derivan said to Charise, and then nodded an additional thanks to Adremel, who nodded back at him. He walked forward to join the other three around the campfire they'd chosen, even as Charise left to find Orkas and pull him into a dance; there was music that was playing, too, fast and rhythmic and delightful. But the adventurers were tired and just wanted to talk over a fire.

Well, mostly. Vex vaguely seemed like he wanted to dance, in Sev's estimation, but he also seemed too embarrassed to ask. Before he could prompt the lizardkin, though, Misa interrupted his thoughts.

"Oh yeah," the half-orc said, glancing at Sev. "How's the thing with Aurum going? Is he attached yet? What about your rewards?"

"Oh, shit, I forgot," Sev swore. "Uh, yeah. The attachment completed earlier today, and it . . . I don't really know the details, but I can talk to Aurum the way I could talk to Onyx before. There's some kind of connection linking the two of us. Aurum said he was going to try to remember what happened while he was gone . . ."

Sev paused, listening for the connection between him and Aurum—but it was still silent. Whatever the god was doing, it didn't echo back down the connection. The most he could feel from it was a silent sort of pulse, like Aurum was *alive* and focusing on something; every so often, he could feel a faint reverberation, like a realization or a memory was beginning to touch on the god, but then it faded again.

"Whatever it is, he's not done yet," Sev said with a shrug. "Maybe he will be soon. Although now would maybe be . . . not the best time?" He glanced around at the still-ongoing celebration.

Part of him had been worried that all of this would be happening too soon for the villagers to be able to relax, but it seemed like Orkas and Charise knew what they were doing. They were practically dragging even the most reluctant villagers into the party, except for those that really seemed like they needed time to themselves, and while it wasn't a perfect solution—

—for the most part, people were smiling. That was a far cry from the worried glances he'd seen when they were traveling back toward the Guild.

"What about your rewards?" Misa asked eagerly, and Sev blinked.

"Oh, right," he said. "Give me a second."

He'd dismissed the notification a while before, and now he brought it back, blinking at the message.

Congratulations on completing <The Village's Last Defense>! Here are your rewards:
Item: [Bottle of Something Old]
Skill: [Look Up]

"What?" Sev muttered, staring at his rewards. He reached out to accept them, feeling vaguely pensive—the red lettering stood out to him. He only remembered seeing red before in once instance, when the dungeon had been supposed to spit out the name of his bonus room and had given him instead what seemed to be a message . . .

He didn't know who that message was *from*, still, now that he thought about it. It might have been Onyx, but he'd never confirmed. Maybe there was someone else he needed to look for.

Was this a message, too?

A potion bottle manifested in his hands as the notification pinged; a bright, shimmering light shone within it, spinning and turning and *singing*, though the sound was muffled by the glass.

The skill box appeared in front of him a second later, the skill name glaring that strange, off-putting red instead of any known rarity.

[Look Up] [Active Skill] [Grade: Maxed]
Look up and remember. —Onyx

Sev glanced upward. It *was* a message, then, in the form of a skill? There was nothing unusual, as far as he could tell. The sky was dark, since it was in the middle of the night, and the moon shone down on them all.

Through his connection with Aurum, Sev felt a *shock* of recognition. The shock reverberated, and the connection between them suddenly expanded, divine mana pouring in waves into that connection—he felt pressure pushing against him, asking him for *permission*, and he felt an instinctive urge to deny—

—not his own, he realized. An instinct. He was anchoring Aurum, and anchors had to reject requests like these—

—*Fuck that.*

He accepted.

Divine mana burst out of him, coalescing into robes, into an orb of gold, into *Aurum*—an avatar of him, anyway, composed purely out of golden mana. The god was far smaller than he had been in the Serpent, the approximate size of a human child, which was likely for the best; this event would have gotten people's attention as it was . . .

. . . except it hadn't. Everyone else was frozen in time, save for him and his team. Aurum bent over and *retched*, and his chest heaved in panicked, frightened breaths.

"They're gone," he said, his voice trembling. "I remember now— It's hard to remember. But you have to remember. Please. I can't say it. It doesn't let me."

"What the fuck," Misa said, her eyes wide; an instant later, they narrowed. "I tried [Endless Echoes]. There's something censored from us. I can't pull information from half the echoes."

"My status is flickering," Derivan reported. "The new stats are all going red and white."

"Mana is going wild, especially around that bottle of yours," Vex said. "I can . . . It's trying to tell me something, too. I've never seen mana behave like this."

Sev tried to use [**Look Up**], but the skill seemed to do nothing. Vex's gaze flickered over to him again when he did.

"Do that again," Vex said, and when he did, Vex frowned. "Your mana's reaching out to Misa . . . I can't see where it goes."

"I can Shift that mana to be visible," Derivan offered, and when Vex nodded at him, he reached out. There was no apparent visible change for Sev— but Vex evidently could see *something*. The lizardkin reached out.

"It's trying to touch the anchor, but the anchor is rejecting it," Vex said softly. "If I can just . . ."

He reached out with his [**Mana Manipulation**], like he was forcing a key into a lock.

Something clicked.

Sev remembered now. He remembered looking at the sky above the anchor, at the pinpricks of light, remembered staring at the Serpent of the Night Sky and its endless sea of gleaming points.

Vex and Derivan remembered the skill he'd used, the dark fog that looked just like the dark sky above them, and the fireballs that hung in the air.

Misa remembered the five-point fruit, too, the one she'd used in an echo.

There was one word that could have been used to describe all those things—one word that had been eroded into conceptual nothingness.

"It's the ~~stars~~," Sev said, though they all seemed to realize it at the same time. It was important anyway, and so he said it out loud, and ignored the way the word seemed to catch on the wind and get whisked away. He tried again, pushing on the skill, and Vex and Misa and Derivan all helped, shattering whatever remnants of the infolock remained, if it had ever been an infolock at all.

Sev looked up at the blank expanse of the night sky, and felt a cold dread creep into him.

"The stars are gone."

ACKNOWLEDGMENTS

I'd like to take a moment to thank the authors who have worked closely with me, keeping me motivated and inspired throughout my journey as a writer, as well as the ones who inspired me to write in the first place.

Argus's *The Daily Grind* was the story that introduced me to web serials on Royal Road, and is an excellently written novel that dives into weird, conceptual organisms and urban dungeons. Their other story, *Kitty Cat Kill Sat,* is a beautiful tale about humanity (for all that the protagonist is, in fact, a cat).

Aaron Shih began their journey with web serials almost at the same time I did, and I'm super proud of them for their breakout success, *Dungeon Tour Guide.* It's an excellent novel about a healer bound to a dungeon who does his best to guide and strengthen adventurers, though he gets caught up in bigger events before long.

The Council of the Eternal Hiatus has a great deal of authors who have both helped me grow as an author and kept supporting me as I wrote Edge Cases. It's only because of them that I'm this close to completing the series. We're in the process of building a community of like-minded authors and readers who want to focus on creating better fiction—if that sounds like your jam, come join us in our Discord!

Additional thanks to the LitRPG Books and GameLit Society Facebook groups.